M000218149

PRIDE

ONCE UPON A VILLAIN

BIANCA COLE

CONTENTS

Pride Copyright © 2023 Bianca Cole

All Rights Reserved.
No part of this publication may be reproduced, stored, or
transmitted in any form or by any means, electronic, mechanical,
photocopying, recording, scanning, or otherwise without written
permission from the publisher. It is illegal to copy this book, post it
to a website, or distribute it by any other means without permission.

This novel is entirely a work of fiction. The names, characters and
incidents portrayed in it are the work of the author's imagination.
Any resemblance to actual persons, living or dead, events or
localities is entirely coincidental.

Warning: the unauthorized reproduction or distribution of this
copyrighted work is illegal. Criminal copyright infringement,
including infringement without monetary gain, is investigated by the
FBI and is punishable by up to 5 years in prison and a fine of
$250,000.

Book cover design by Deliciously Dark Designs

Photography by Wander Aguiar

AUTHOR'S NOTE

Hello reader,

This is a warning to let you know that this is a **DARK** mafia romance much like many of my other books, which means there are some very sensitive subject matters addressed and dark, triggering content. If you have any triggers, it would be a good idea to proceed with caution and read the warning below.

As well as a possessive and dominant anti-hero who doesn't take **no** for an answer and a lot of spicy scenes, this book addresses some sensitive subjects. A list of these can be found on my website: www. biancacoleauthor.com

If you have any triggers, then it's best to read the warnings and not proceed. However, if none of these are an issue for you, read on and enjoy this dark romance.

ISIAH

Fifteen years ago...

The wind howls around me and my gloves feel like shards of glass as I clench the shovel, thrusting it into the frozen ground with every ounce of strength I have. The ice-cold air cuts like a knife through my flesh and straight to my bones, but despite this, my body feels numb and my mind detached from reality.

My dad watches me dig the grave with an expression so cold it sends a chill through my bones. Hatred rises within me, boiling hot and bitter, as he's the one who brought our family into this conflict with the Benedetto's and in turn that had cost Aiden his life.

Pain claws at me as my eyes shift to the body bag where my twin rests as cold as ice next to the hole I'm digging. It's almost impossible to believe he's gone.

The shock of it overrides every other feeling. And to top it all off, dear old dad is making me dig his grave.

My stomach twists as flash backs of merely four hours ago while we sat together on the sofa eating takeout pizza and playing video games flood my mind. Neither of us were aware of the horror that would befall us later on. Most of my father's men are either dead or have switched loyalties.

I wish I could rewind the hours and be the one in the bullet's path. At least then I wouldn't be in this terrible feeling of limbo, trying to block the pain that I know would tear me apart if I let it.

How can he no longer exist in this world?

My best friend is gone forever and I can never speak to him again. My muscles ache as I pour my heartache and anger into the ground as I dig. The lump in my throat warns me I'm barely holding it together, but I know my father would never forgive me if I cried right now, even though my twin is lying life-less a few feet away.

"You need to put more effort in, Joseph Isiah Dalton." He glances at his flashy Rolex, sighing. "Do you want us to get caught and end up buried in the ground with your brother?"

I glare at him, the hatred deepening, because right now that's all I want, to join my brother and end the impossible pain of his loss that I can't escape.

"Why don't you help so we can get the hell out of here?"

I've always known that our life was fraught with

danger, as my dad is the leader of the Irish mafia in Washington, but it wasn't until today that I understood it. When I tried to call the cops to report Aiden's murder, he hung the phone up and told me we had to cover it up and that the cops wouldn't help us. It's because he's wanted by them.

"Because I'm wearing a two-thousand dollar suit and I don't intend to get mud on it."

I clench my jaw, my dad disgusts me.

How can he even give a shit about some expensive suit when one of his sons is lying in a body bag?

The Benedetto family have been trying to take over Washington for a while now, encroaching on our family's territory. However, my father didn't take their threat seriously. Somehow Giovanni Benedetto has more politicians and cops in his pocket than my father, and he's managed to bring murder charges against him, meaning the police are searching the city for him as we speak.

We have no choice but to flee the only home I've known, leaving Aiden here in an unmarked grave. Sickness coils through my gut and I feel like I want to puke, but I've already thrown up so many times that there's nothing left in my stomach.

I look at the black body bag again, a deep pain spreads through every inch of my flesh at the idea of leaving him here, even if he is six feet under. We've never been apart in our fourteen years of life.

If it isn't bad enough that my father is the reason

my twin brother is dead, he's ripping me away from my life, my friends.

"Why do we have to leave the states?" I ask, trying to hold it together as I dig deeper.

His eyes narrow. "This is a hard lesson you have to learn. When things go wrong in our line of work, you have to be prepared to drop everything and start over again."

It's hard to believe he can be so cold in a situation like this. I get why we need to leave washington, but not the states. Clenching my jaw, I can't help but wish that he was the one that was dead right now. My brother didn't deserve this just because my father was too power hungry.

"And what about James?" I ask.

My dad's eyes narrow. "What of him?"

"He's like a son to you. Are you just going to leave him behind?"

He waves his hand in dismissal. "He's most likely dead with the majority of my other men."

Unbelievable. I'm certain in that moment, that he has no heart. The Benedetto family hasn't only killed Aiden, they've dethroned my father and gone behind his back, making a deal with some of his men. If he'd had more control and been smarter, he would have seen it coming. Their plan was carefully orchestrated, and the treachery ran deep, but it's because he has lost touch with everyone around him, too blinded by greed and a sense of superiority.

I finally snap. "You're the reason Aiden's dead, so

rebuilding what he lost here in Washington and, to my disgust, he succeeded under our new name, Darcy. I changed my first name to Isiah, an alternate spelling of my middle name, Isaiah. My father said it would be best to drop all ties to our past, but I wished to keep that name since it was one I shared with Aiden. We both had the same middle name, Isaiah, after our grandfather, who we never met.

He forgot about Aiden and scolded me if I ever brought up his name in conversation, so I suppressed those emotions, but not any longer. All the years he insisted we could never again step foot on American soil, let alone return to my brother's resting place, felt like a lifetime, but I waited patiently.

My father died two weeks ago. I can't say that I grieved at all. The relief I felt when I got the news that he'd been shot dead in the street by a rival was unprecedented. Even so, I had to avenge him to show strength, and I murdered the man who killed him, even though I felt like I should have been paying him a fucking reward.

Father was a monster with no soul and I'm happy he's gone. It means I can finally fulfill my sole purpose in this world, destroy the people who tore Aiden away from me.

As the sole heir of the Darcy empire, I've become quite the eligible bachelor and the youngest unmarried leader of any organization on either side of the pond. However, people perceive my age as a weakness, which is foolish.

The family responsible for my brother's death have unwittingly invited me to a party to meet their unmarried daughter, Bella. A perfect chance to exact my revenge and wreak havoc on the bastards that stole him from me.

"I'll do right by you, Aiden. If it's the last thing I do." I place the single white rose on the unmarked grave, knowing Aiden deserved so much better. "You deserved to be treated with more respect."

My father ingrained in me so deeply the notion that men in our family don't cry. I literally can't cry. No matter how much something hurts, no tears come. The monster has created a beast in his image, only I'm going to tear apart the family that tore me apart. An eye for an eye.

"I'm here to seek revenge on the people who did this to you." I lay my hand over the ground, wishing he could talk back to me. "I'll visit you more often now I'm back." The pain sears my lungs and makes it difficult to breathe. The tears won't come.

I stand and turn away, feeling the pain of his loss as if it were only yesterday. Each step I take away hurts, but I know I need to get to work. I have a family to ruin, the way they ruined us.

I will not rest until I've brought utter devastation to every member of the Benedetto family. The way they forced devastation on me.

3

BELLA

"*B*ella," my dad's voice calls from the study, making me freeze. "Come and join me."

My stomach churns, as he rarely wants to talk to me alone. Normally, it's my brother he asks to join him in his study for after-dinner drinks.

Nina looks as concerned as me as I exchange glances with her.

I stand and flatten out my dress, clearing my throat in an attempt to stall.

"Someone's in trouble," Luciana teases.

I glare at my youngest sister. "I'm never in trouble."

Cain gives me a chilling look. "That's what you think."

I try to ignore the two of them, knowing they're probably messing around. However, I can't shake the feeling that they know something I don't.

"Bella, don't make me wait," he calls.

I walk out of the dining room and into the adjoining study, my heart racing. My father is sitting on the sofa with a glass of scotch in his hand and the *Washington Post* spread across his lap.

"What do you want?" I ask.

His jaw clenches at the tone of my voice. "Take a seat." He signals to the spot next to him.

There's another tumbler of scotch on the table, which he reaches for and passes to me. "Join me for a drink."

Something is off as he doesn't usually give me drinks. I take the glass, but I can't help but feel paranoid about his intentions. Narrowing my eyes, I take a sip. "What's this about?"

He clears his throat and is about to speak when my mother's shrill voice cuts him off.

"Where is Giovanni? Giovanni Benedetto, answer me."

He sighs heavily. "I'd hoped to avoid having your mother here for this conversation." He gives her a pointed look as she walks into the study. "I told you not to interupt us, dear."

I can feel irritation growing, as he's being cryptic. "And what conversation is that?"

"We need you to do your duty for this family."

"Duty?" I question, feeling a little queasy.

He nods. "Yes, I want you to select a husband from a few eligible men from powerful families that we've vetted." The cold look in my dad's eyes makes me shudder. I know that this means he won't back down on this. He wants me to select a criminal heir to be forcefully married off to, trying to make me think I have any choice in the matter.

"Why me?" After all, Nina is their eldest daughter. "What about Nina?"

"Don't be so ridiculous, Bella," my mom says.

Dad holds a hand up to my mom to shut her up. "Darling, please stay out of this." And then he looks at me. "You know your sister is in no mental state to be married to anyone."

My sister struggles with depression and has tried to take her life more than once, but she's been doing better lately. It's not a surprise she is the way she is. My parents weren't exactly careful to shield her from the horrors of my dad's work. "No, but I'm not marrying some thug from another mob." I cross my arms over my chest. "Forget it."

My mom practically turns beet red. "Isabella, you'll listen to your father and marry whichever man he tells you to." It makes me more agitated that she's sticking her nose in. Dad's right, it would have been a better conversation without her involved.

I glare at Mom, wishing she wasn't like this. Even though my dad can be cold and violent and ruthless, at least he has more compassion than her. She's narcissistic and self-centered and only cares about the family's image and wealth. "I'd like to see you make me do anything."

She charges toward me. "How dare you speak to

me like that!" Her hand raises and I know what's coming next, but then Dad is there before she can strike, grabbing her wrist and yanking her away.

Mom glares at him. "Giovanni, talk some sense into your daughter," she cries.

His reaction is swift as he yanks her toward the door of his office. "I told you I didn't want you present for this discussion." He squares his shoulders and looms over her, asserting his dominance as the head of the family. "Leave us, so that I can discuss this business with Bella, alone."

Mom shoots me a disgusted look before returning her attention to Dad. "Fine, but don't let her give you any trouble, Gio. I won't stand for it."

"Out," he barks, glaring at her.

My entire family knows better than to cross my dad when he's in one of these moods. I can only imagine what awaits me if I don't comply with his wishes. However, the idea of settling down with a thug like him repulses me.

My mom releases a deep sigh, her gaze turning toward the door. She shoots me a stern glance as she leaves.

Dad returns to his seat and leans back into his high-backed leather chair, his glasses resting on the bridge of his nose while he peers at me. "Now, where were we?" He runs a hand through his peppered gray hair. "As I was saying, it's time for you to step up for this family. You must have known this was coming sooner rather than later, Bella." His voice is firm and unyielding. "You're twenty-one now. It's the perfect time for you to marry into a family that can bring us stability."

"You mean another Italian crime family that can bring you wealth." I ball my hands into fists. "Don't you already have enough?"

He tilts his head to the side. "I never mentioned an Italian family. There are plenty of eligible bachelors from the British and Irish families."

I grit my teeth, as if that makes it any better. "Oh great, so you want me to jump into bed with our enemies?"

He growls. "The men I've selected are not enemies, they're neutral parties. Many of them don't even live on this continent, but a transatlantic partnership could bring us everything we need."

I cross my arms over my chest. "I don't want to marry anyone."

My dad's hand comes down in a firm slam against the table, making me jump. "You'll do what is right for our family, Isabella."

He rarely calls me Isabella, except for when he's very angry with me. "When exactly am I meeting these so-called bachelors?"

His eyes narrow. "I'm hosting a party tomorrow evening and anyone I want you to consider will be there."

I grind my teeth together, knowing that I have no choice but to go along with it, even if I have no intention of getting married. "Do I get to choose who I marry?"

He steeples his fingers on the desk. "Within reason. There are families within my selection we'd prefer an alliance with."

I roll my eyes. "You mean richer families, no doubt."

He stands up and looms over the desk, glaring at me. "I didn't teach you to be a smartass, did I?"

I swallow hard. "No."

"Then why are you talking back and making smart remarks?"

It's impressive how easily my dad can intimidate. All it takes is for him to stand up and assert his dominance, and I know I've got no chance of getting out of this without doing what he says. "Sorry," I mutter.

"You will make your selection wisely, listening to our recommendations concerning whoever is interested. Do you understand?"

I shake my head. "I don't really understand why you asked me in here to discuss it. It appears it's already decided, so what was the point?"

"You're impossible, Bella," he says, sounding exasperated. "I don't want any hard feelings over this. All I want is for you to understand your role as part of this family and what it entails."

"My role?" I laugh, as it's amusing that he believes what he's describing is a role. "You mean to be sold off to the highest bidder, like cattle to the slaughter?"

I shake my head. "Is that really a role? And is this really a family?"

I know I've pushed too hard when his dark brown eyes flash with untamable rage, but he knows I'm not a push over. "Leave now." His voice is lethally calm, and that's always a warning. And then he stands, fists clenched as his rage builds.

I'm not stupid enough to linger any longer as I jump to my feet and walk hastily out of the room, shutting the door and resting my back against it. I draw in a deep breath, trying to calm my nerves and my racing pulse.

And once I feel like myself again, I walk down the corridor and back into the sitting room where my four siblings congregate.

Nina takes one look at my expression and stands. "I'm going to bed." She nods toward the door before any of my other siblings notice me, and I rush through. Thankful that she provided a distraction, as I don't want to deal with them right now.

Luciana glances at her watch. "It's nine o'clock." She laughs. "You really are pathetic, Nina."

She glares at her. "Shut up, Luciana." And then she walks out of the room to join me in the corridor. "Are you okay?" she asks the moment we're out of earshot of our siblings. "I heard Mom screeching like a banshee, and that's never a good sign."

I swallow hard, hoping to dispel the lump in my throat. "We'll talk in the bedroom," I manage to say.

Nina links arms with me and nods. We make our

way to the bedroom we share, despite living in a mansion. Ever since Nina's last attempt to take her life, we've shared a room for her safety. And to be honest, we both prefer it this way, as we are sisters second and best friends first.

Once we're in our room, I shut the door and lean against it. "They're marrying me off!" I blurt out.

Nina's eyes widen. "Who the hell to?"

I shrug. "It's not decided yet. Dad's throwing a party tomorrow evening so I can meet all the eligible bachelors. In other words, thugs and criminals like Dad." I mime puking. "Kill me now."

Her expression turns grave as she grabs my hand. "You can't leave me here all alone, Bella." Tears gather in her eyes. "What would I do without you?"

"Don't worry, I've got no intention of marrying any of them, no matter what they say."

"I'd like to know how you intend to pull that off. Mom and Dad won't accept you refusing. They'll probably force you down the aisle."

"Probably," I admit, swallowing hard. It will be difficult, but I'm just not willing to accept that this is what my life will be. A life beholden to a man I don't even fucking know. "I'll fight it as hard as I can is all I'm saying."

Nina releases my hand and rushes to her bed, flopping down on it and dramatically holding her wrist against her forehead. "What the hell will I do without you?"

The honest truth is, I don't know how Nina would

cope here without me. She doesn't have anyone else in this family that gives a damn about her. Our two younger sisters are self-centered and immature, our brother is compassionless, and my parents don't have time to pay attention to each other, let alone us. Uniquely, their marriage was one of romance rather than arrangement.

"You'll be fine." I swallow hard. "The question is whether I will be. God knows what monsters Mom and Dad have got lined up for me to meet."

Nina nods. "True."

I glare at her.

"What?" she asks.

"You're supposed to lie and tell me my future husband will be lovely."

"You know me." Nina shrugs. "I don't lie."

We both laugh. Nina is the only person who has been there for me since we were little, through thick and thin, and vice versa. We stick together no matter what, and the idea that our parents intend to rip us apart doesn't sit well with me.

"Perhaps my husband will let you live with us," I suggest.

Nina gives me a look that says it's wishful thinking. "I highly doubt it. The men that father has lined up are more ruthless than he is."

My brow furrows. "Are you saying you know who he's inviting?"

Nina nods. "I didn't know what it was, but I saw a list of names on his desk earlier this evening." She purses her lips. "It must be the guest list for the party."

"Oh great. Who was on there?"

Nina looks worried about answering. "A lot of old, ruthless men."

I stick my fingers into my throat and pretend to gag. "I'm not marrying a man as old as Dad."

She shrugs. "There were some young suitors on there. And a few I've only heard of, like Isiah Darcy."

"British?" I confirm, as I've heard of the infamous Isiah from across the pond. He's vicious and the son of a man who was shot dead two weeks ago, hence why his name is fresh in my mind.

"Yeah, he's in his late twenties, I think."

I twirl a strand of my hair around my finger, wondering what he's like. British men can be so stuck up, but then he's probably better than any of the other old balding perverts that my dad has picked out.

"It's weird," Nina says, shaking her head. "There are no pictures of him on the internet at all. He leads a very secretive life."

I swallow hard, wondering what exactly that means. "Maybe you'll find a guy you like at this thing," I say.

Nina laughs. "I'm not into old men either, Bella."

I shove her in the shoulder. "They can't all be old." I pause. "At least I hope they aren't."

"I thought you said you aren't marrying any of them, so why does it matter?"

I give her a pointed look. "We both know it's wishful thinking that I have any say in the matter."

Nina sighs heavily and we both fall into solemn silence. The threat of our world being turned upside down looms over us like a dark rain cloud ready to drown us.

/

4

ISIAH

$\mathcal{T}$he cold air wraps around me like it did that fateful night and it feels like a stark warning, as if Aiden is communicating with me to be careful from beyond the grave.

I pace down the sidewalk toward the underground club. Parties have never been something I enjoy, particularly not ones thrown by my sworn enemy, and yet here I am.

The streets where I grew up haven't changed, but I can sense the danger of being back here. I may be fifteen years older, but it's possible someone might recognize me. The name change and British accent should help with my disguise, but I fear that anyone I knew well back then will know who I am.

Tonight, the Benedetto family has unwittingly invited a viper into their lives. They may not be aware of what they did to me or who I am, but I know. I know everything they tore from me and my family. The hatred builds within me every day that passes, and it's been many days since they killed Aiden.

The thudding bass of music echoes down the street as I turn the corner, coming across two muscle-bound bouncers standing out front of the building where I'm headed.

Arrogance is a flaw when it comes to the Benedetto family, as they've invited countless individuals they've never even met out of pure vanity, assuming one of them would wish to marry their daughter, rather than get revenge for something they did fifteen years ago. Bella Benedetto is the woman on offer tonight and I view her as nothing more than my chance to wreak havoc on her family.

It will be sweet when they select me, and they will. As rumor has it, Giovanni Benedetto is getting greedy and wants a slice of the pie from the other side of the Atlantic, making me the perfect candidate since our hold on London territory is extensive.

I'll wipe their kind from the face of this earth. Every Benedetto will die at my hand if it's the last thing I do.

The guards outside straighten when I get to the door of the club, and I can tell by the look in their eyes they believe I'm too young to be here.

"Invite only," the one on the left says.

I run a hand through my hair and tilt my head. "Are you suggesting I'm an imposter?"

The guard on the right clears his throat. "He's

saying it's invite only, so if you don't have one, move along."

These two chumps have a real nerve. I slide my hand into my inside jacket pocket, which makes both of them tense, while the guy on the left places a hand on his gun.

I'd like to see him try to pull it faster than I'd pull mine. When he sees the invitation, he relaxes instantly. I pass it to him and he reads my name, eyes widening slightly.

"Apologies, Mr. Darcy. You looked a lot younger than most of the others, so I assumed—"

"You assumed that I was some miscreant that was attempting to break into a party hardly worth breaking into."

He swallows hard and nods. "Again, I apologize."

The other guard nods. "We meant no offense."

I give him a glare. "I'm sure Mr. Benedetto will be disappointed to hear you're discriminating against his guests." I step past the two men who have both turned pale. It's amusing to scare them, as I've no intention of telling Giovanni.

The bass from the music is coming from down a flight of steep steps. I make it down to the bottom, which brings me to a set of double doors, I stop and reflect.

Fifteen long years I've waited for this moment, a chance to get revenge for Aiden's death. I never expected the opportunity to fall into my lap so easily, but perhaps that's fate. Father's quick thinking and

fleeing the states to live in Britain, taking on new iden-
tities and building up his business again over there is
the reason I've been invited here, unbeknownst to the
Benedetto family that I'm originally from Washington
and was the son of their biggest rival.

It feels like I've been waiting for this moment for
far too long. Drawing in a long calming breath, I try
to focus my mind and keep in check the rage that lives
deep within me.

I push open the door and step into the fray. It's
busy with people dancing, drinking, and chatting.
There's a suave air that I expected from these people.
Everything is about extravagance and impression.
The chandeliers hanging from the ceiling are almost
so big they look tacky.

I sweep the room with one glance, ascertaining
there are approximately one-hundred and fifty people
in attendance, more than seventy percent are men.
Which makes sense, considering the Benedetto family
is searching for a husband for their virgin princess.
They don't need too much competition in attendance.

Giovanni Benedetto catches my eye almost immediately, standing near the bar he is greeting guests as
they approach. The mere thought of shaking his hand
makes my skin crawl and my stomach churn. I know I
have no choice but to play the part I'm expected to
play, as my plan requires patience and ensuring
Isabella Benedetto's parents want me as their son-in-
law. No matter how much I despise them, politeness
is key.

Walking around the outer edge of the club, I head toward the bar. Best to get it over and done with. When I approach the bar, Giovanni notices me and his eyes narrow slightly, probably because he has no idea who I am. I've ensured that no one takes my photo and kept a low profile in London to minimize the risk of someone from my past recognizing me.

He takes a sip of his drink and moves toward me. "I don't think we've been introduced before. Giovanni Benedetto." He holds a hand out to me.

"Isiah Darcy," I say, taking his hand and shaking firmly. "It's good to meet you in person."

His expression softens the moment I mention who I am. "Mr. Darcy, it's an honor to meet the man I've heard so many impressive rumors about." He tilts his head. "I must admit, I expected you to be older."

It's clear that my ridiculous wealth—wealth my father built in London in less than fifteen years—has made me an obvious target. Dad was resilient if nothing else.

"Please call me Isiah," I say, releasing his hand as my skin feels like it's burning. "Is it a good thing or a bad thing that I'm younger?" Over the years, I've managed to eradicate my American accent.

He smiles. "I'm yet to figure that out."

"I appreciate the invite, either way, Mr. Benedetto."

He shakes his head, placing a hand on my shoulder. "Let me introduce you to my daughter."

I clench my fists gently by my sides as I try to get

hold of the murderous rage clawing at my insides and trying to break free.

"Of course, lead the way."

Giovanni turns and leads me across the room. I notice a girl standing in the direction we're heading, but she has her back to us. It doesn't matter what she looks like, but it's hard not to admire her beautiful form. If that is Bella, then she's athletic and toned, but has a womanly figure with wide hips and a curvy ass that I must admit is rather tempting.

Attraction won't harm my plan if it's there, it will make my job easier.

"Bella," her father calls her name.

She spins around to face us, and my heart skips a beat as our eyes lock for a second. I'm forced to look away because of the intensity of her glare and the brightness of her blue eyes. A feature that strikes me instantly and I feel something off the moment our eyes lock. I don't like it.

She's gorgeous, to say the least, with thick, pouty lips, a slender and elegant nose, and those eyes. And to compliment it all, she has sun kissed brown hair that cascades in waves to her ribcage.

"What?" she asks, eyeing me warily.

Giovanni clears his throat. "I've got someone here I'd like you to meet."

He gestures for me to step closer. "This is Isiah Darcy." His eyes meet mine. "Isiah, this is Bella, my daughter."

I give her an indifferent look, as I don't want her

to think I'm overly interested. Women don't like men that are easy pickings.

Her eyes meet mine again and it's impossible to stave off the flash of desire that pulses through my body. And I note it's not one-sided as her eyes light up for a moment before she schools her features to appear uninterested. "Nice to meet you." She's aloof and yet polite at the same time.

"It's nice to meet you too," I say, maintaining my disinterest.

Giovanni looks pleased at the pleasant greeting. "Why don't the two of you dance?"

I clear my throat. "I'm afraid I don't dance."

Bella arches a brow. "You don't dance or can't dance?"

I smile. "The former." I can dance, however, whenever I can get away with it, I prefer not to.

She nods. "Luckily for you, I don't want to dance either." Her eyes scan the room and land on someone on the far side. "If you'd excuse me."

Her father makes a tutting sound as she walks away. "You'll have to forgive my daughter. She's a little nervous."

There are many words I would use to describe Bella Benedetto after my first time meeting her, and nervous isn't one of them. I sense she's independent and strong willed and won't be easy to tame if my plan goes as I expect.

"How about we get a drink?"

It's clear that with Giovanni dedicating so much

time to me, he has a preference for Bella to marry into the Darcy fortune.

"Sure," I say, tension coiling through my muscles at the prolonged closeness with the man responsible for my brother's death. I certainly need a stiff drink to take the edge off.

"What's your poison?" he asks.

"Whiskey on the rocks."

He tilts his head. "Scotch or American?"

"Scotch, of course."

Mr. Benedetto appears pleased with my answer as he catches the attention of a pretty bartender. "Two scotch on the rocks, please, Alice."

She nods. "Coming right up, sir."

Giovanni places a hand on my shoulder. "Tell me, Isiah, how long are you in town for?"

"That all depends on how well this goes tonight," I say.

He smiles widely. "So, it's open to discussion?"

"Of course."

"Perfect." He looks pleased by the news as Alice appears with our drinks. "I'll allow you to mingle and enjoy the rest of the evening in peace. Perhaps you can come by our home tomorrow evening at seven o'clock for dinner?"

I nod in response. "Sure, I'll look forward to it." Two nights in a row suffering this man's company sounds like hell, but I always knew it wouldn't be easy being close to my brother's murder.

"Great, enjoy the rest of your evening." He leaves

me and I'm thankful for it as I find a seat nearby and drop into it, sipping the scotch.

I notice a man sitting in a nearby seat staring at me with a strange expression on his face. He looks familiar but I can't work out why, so I break eye contact with him. Washington is, after all, the city I was born in. A city I left suddenly fifteen years ago. And while I look very different now, it's possible someone from my past could recognize me.

When I glance back up, the man in question is standing before me. "Joe?"

I swallow hard the moment he speaks because I know who it is. My best friend from before Aiden's murder. "I think you've mistaken me for someone else. My name is Isiah."

His brow furrows, no doubt thrown by my accent. "Oh, I honestly thought you were a friend I knew many years ago. Apologies." He clears his throat. "May I sit?"

Cathal was like a brother to me and Aiden before Dad tore me away from my home. I haven't seen him since, but I heard his father stepped into Dad's place once he was gone, making a name for himself from the ashes left behind after the Benedetto family did their worst.

"Go ahead." I nod at the empty chair.

He holds a hand out to me. "I'm Cathal Bingley."

I take it and shake. "Good to meet you. Isiah Darcy."

His eyes widen. "So, you're the infamous Mr. Darcy."

I swirl the contents of my whiskey in the glass before taking a sip. "Infamous, hey?"

He smirks. "Yeah, I've heard of you and you live thousands of miles away." His eyes scan the room. "Have you met the girl on offer?"

"Bella?" I confirm.

He nods. "Yeah, what do you think of her?"

Honestly, I think she's beautiful if not a bit impolite. "She's okay."

"Yeah, she's beautiful, but her sister is more my type."

"Sister?" I ask.

He nods toward a girl who's standing with Bella. She has lighter, almost blonde hair that is naturally wavy and similarly beautiful features, but to me, she's not a patch on Isabella. "Do you intend to go after her sister, then?"

Cathal shakes his head. "Rumor is she's a bit of a handful. However, I'll determine that for myself before I make any decisions." The sister's eyes move to us and she blushes instantly when she sees Cathal staring. "If you'd excuse me, I've got a girl to speak to."

I nod in response and don't say another word as he rises from his seat and walks over to talk to Nina Benedetto. The girl is a train wreck that I'd stay far away from if I were Cathal, but it would be pretty odd for me to warn against him approaching her when we hardly know each other.

Instead, I sit back and watch as he makes his way toward the two girls. Bella is my target, but I intend to remain impartial for now. It won't do being overly forceful when it's clear she's not interested in getting married at all.

Her mother is obnoxiously loud and drunk as she laughs with one of the men intended, I assume, as a suitor for Bella. As I expected, her family is the worst sort of people. Despite harboring this hatred for them all these years, I've never met them.

Her brother, Cain, is gambling at a table near the back with a hooker on his lap. And her two younger sisters, Luciana and Maria, are both making fools of themselves, flirting with men when they're both underage. My initial impression of them is that they're immature, especially since they're the heirs to the Benedetto family fortune.

One of the female servers approaches with a tray of canapes. "Would you like one?" she asks, leaning over and batting her eyelashes.

I smile. "I'd love one, thank you."

"What are you doing over here on your own?"

I shrug. "Unfortunately, it appears the majority of attendees are male."

"Perhaps I can keep you company."

I arch a brow. "Are you allowed to, or will you get in trouble?"

"I won't tell anyone if you don't."

I glance over at Bella, who is looking right at me as I flirt with the server. It makes sense to play on this and get her jealous. If she thinks I'm not that interested, it will only pique her interest more.

"Why the hell not?"

She sits down on the arm of my chair and places a hand on my shoulder. "I like your accent. Are you British?"

Bella's expression turns furious as she tears her eyes off of me. I sense from our first encounter that she's not going to be the kind of girl who falls at my feet easily. It makes the challenge all the more exciting.

The Benedetto family consists of the worst kind of people imaginable, and that has only been reaffirmed by this party and the way they act. Her mother is a drunk. Her father is a bore. And Three of her siblings are immature and stupid.

Isabella and Nina, I'm not sure what to make of yet. Other than Nina's relatively secret troubles with depression, I wouldn't know that she was anything but a normal twenty-three-year-old.

And Bella appears to have more sense than the rest of her family, but it changes nothing. Before long, I'll ensure that she wants me so badly that she'll be begging for me. And then, I'll crush her along with the rest of her pathetic excuse of a family.

5

BELLA

*I*siah Darcy.

He's far more handsome than I ever could have imagined any of the suitors would be. The man is supposed to be here as a potential suitor, but he doesn't want to pay any attention to me. Not that I want his attention. Actually, that's a lie. I wouldn't mind it. He's by far the most attractive man in this room, and he's talking to the second most attractive.

"It looks like someone has the hots for a certain British man," Nina says, teasing me.

I narrow my eyes and force them away from him. "I don't have the hots for him. But he refused to dance with me."

"Why?"

I sigh heavily. "He said he doesn't dance."

Nina's attention moves over there and I notice the man Isiah was talking to is staring over here, right at her. "Who is that guy?" she asks.

I shake my head. "No idea. It seems Dad only bothered to introduce me to a couple of the men he's invited."

"He's attractive. Maybe you should speak to him since he's looking over here."

I laugh. "Do you realize he's staring at *you*, not me?"

Her cheeks redden and she looks at me. "There's no way he's looking at me."

"Believe me, he is." The man in question is attractive, but in an entirely different way to Isiah. He has tattoos over every visible inch of his muscular body and has dark messy hair and a beard. Instead of wearing a suit, he has a shirt on done up only halfway and a pair of casual black pants. He's the typical guy that Nina goes for.

Isiah, on the other hand, has clean cut stubble and not a hair out of place. His suit looks like it was tailored to fit him like a glove, and he has that typical male model look about him. There's no denying he's the single most attractive man I've ever seen in person before.

"He's coming over," I say.

"To speak to you," Nina rebuts.

I laugh, as she's so clueless at times. "No."

Her eyes widen "I don't know what to say to him." I can see the panic mounting behind them. "He's too attractive to be interested in me."

"Just play it cool."

He clears his throat and I smile at him. "How can we help you?"

"I don't think we've been introduced." His eyes linger on Nina. "I'm Cathal Bingley." He holds a hand out to me first.

I take it and we shake. "Bella Benedetto, and this is my sister, Nina."

He smiles at her. "It's a pleasure to meet you both."

Nina swallows hard as his attention remains on her.

"Great party your father has arranged."

Nina is perpetually shy, so I get the ball rolling.

"It's okay, but it would be better if it weren't catered around finding someone for me to marry."

Cathal laughs, still unable to take his eyes off of Nina. "Oh yes, I almost forgot. That's why I'm here."

I can't help myself but glance toward Isiah, to find him flirting shamelessly with one of the female staff. She's sitting on the armrest of his chair and leaning over him.

Rage coils through me as this man has some nerve. He's here because he's supposed to be a possible match for me and he can't even be bothered to speak to me.

"I need to find a drink. Excuse me."

Nina gives me a look that says don't leave me with him, but she needs to stop being so self-conscious. The girl is beautiful. She could have any man she wants.

As I make a beeline for the bar, a young man steps into my path. "I don't believe your father has gotten around to introducing us. My name is James Wick." He holds a hand out to me.

I shake it. "Bella."

He's attractive with pale green eyes and dark brown hair that reaches the top of his shoulders. Not as devastatingly handsome as Mr. Darcy, but he's still gorgeous in his own right.

"I have to admit parties like this aren't really my thing."

"No?" I ask.

He shakes his head. "I was only invited, not as a possible suitor unfortunately, but because I'm Cathal's right-hand man." He nods at the man chatting away with my sister.

I smile. "Oh, that's a shame, as you're probably the only man worth talking to here."

He shakes his head. "Did you decide that in the minute since we met?" His eyes flash playfully.

I shrug. "The fact you aren't here as a suitor makes you better than any guy here."

He chuckles. "Cathal is a great guy."

"Oh, I have no doubt, but he has eyes for my sister."

"I was surprised to hear that it was you they were going to find a husband for, and not Nina."

I swallow hard because he's the first person to bring it up. "It's how it worked out." The last thing I want to mention is Nina's illness, especially considering his boss seems interested in her.

He bows his head. "Fair enough. I understand when secrets must be kept."

"I said nothing of secrets, Mr. Wick."

He laughs. "Call me James. I hate how formal these gatherings can be."

I must admit that this man is both attractive and likeable. "This may seem a little forward, but would you like to dance?"

"I'd love to." He holds out his hand and whisks me onto the dance floor.

I laugh as he twirls me around, clearly pretty good at dancing.

"So, Bella. Who's winning the race for your hand in marriage?"

"No one that's here for it," I say suggestively.

My father wouldn't hear of me marrying James as he's not an heir to a multi-million or billion-dollar criminal empire. He's just the right-hand man to one. Isiah Darcy is by far the richest man in this room, richer even than my dad.

He gives me a sad smile. "It's a shame I wasn't born rich, hey?"

I nod in response as we continue to dance. The sparks between us are impossible to ignore. And then I notice Isiah Darcy watching us from the edge of the dance floor with a look of rage in his crystal blue eyes.

It serves him right for refusing to dance with me.

James' hand slips lower, so it's almost on my ass. The moment that happens, Isiah starts forward as if he's ready to defend my honor, but then I see him decide against it, stopping himself from making a move.

"You dance very well," I say, breaking eye contact with Isiah and focusing on the man before me.

He smiles. "You aren't half bad yourself." He twirls me around as the music ends. "It's a shame that this can't continue."

"Why not?"

He nods toward my dad, who's glaring at the both of us. No doubt angry that the one man I've decided to dance with isn't even one of the men he picked out.

"Ah yes, Dad can be rather difficult." I sigh heavily and smile. "I guess it's time to go back to being bored as hell."

He squeezes my hip gently. "I'm glad I got to meet you, Bella."

Heat spreads through me at the way he's looking at me. "I'm glad I got to meet you, too."

"Maybe I'll see you around some time." He releases me and steps away.

"I hope so," I reply, walking off the dance floor in the opposite direction. It's the first time I've gotten away with flirting with a guy before and I must admit I like him based on the first encounter. He seems genuine and down to earth.

Dad's glaring at me as he talks to some balding, middle-aged man. I can tell he wants to have a word with me, so I move in the opposite direction at speed.

Isiah appears out of nowhere, forcing me to an abrupt halt to avoid slamming into him. "I'd be careful around that man if I were you."

I narrow my eyes. "I think I can make a perfectly fine judgement on who to be careful around." I try to sidestep around him, but he blocks my path.

His jaw works. "Wick isn't suitable for you. He's not here as a bachelor."

I smirk as it seems Mr. Darcy doesn't like me getting close to another man, which is amusing considering he was fawning over another woman no more than ten minutes ago.

"Perhaps in the future, if you don't want me to dance with another man, you should bend your rules and dance with me first." I hold his gaze. "Now, is there anything I can help you with, or are you going to move out of my way?"

When he doesn't respond, I try to move past him, only for him to grab my wrist forcefully.

"Hey—"

"Listen to me, Bella," he says, his voice low and dangerous. "Your father likes me the most and therefore you'll accept me as your husband. I'm coming to dinner at your home tomorrow evening and I intend to have the deal sealed before you can say the word no."

I draw in a deep breath. "I'm not marrying you."

He smirks, and it's a wicked smile that makes me feel sick to the stomach. Something tells me that this suave and sophisticated exterior is a disguise for a man who is rotten to the core. If his arrogance isn't off putting enough, then that alone is enough to warn me to stay clear of him. "We both know that you don't actually get a say in it."

I glare at him. "Do we?

"And I'd say your father is set on me as your husband to be." He leans toward me and his lips brush the edge of my ear. "And what is it you're set on?"

I swallow hard as a flush of heat rushes through my body.

I'm about to answer when he says, "And don't say James Wick or I'll ensure he doesn't leave this club alive tonight. That'll be the perfect way to remove him from the equation."

He talks of killing a man as if it's nothing more than ordering a drink at the bar, with far too much ease.

"I'm set on not marrying anyone." I don't let him scare me despite the fact I'm pretty certain he means it. He would murder James if he thought that somehow I'd end up with him instead.

He shifts back enough to look into my eyes, and I wish his weren't so alluring. "And you honestly believe that's an option?"

"I think that in this day and age, a woman should have the freedom to decide if she wants to marry or not."

Isiah nods. "You would think so, but that's not how it works, Miss Benedetto."

"The world has to find a way to discriminate against women in some way."

The edge of his lips quirk into a slight smile at that comment. "A feminist then?"

"Perhaps, but it's difficult to be a feminist in my circumstances."

He invades my personal space again, his lips brushing against my cheek. "You are too young, Miss Benedetto, to understand sexuality and femininity. Wait until you've been dominated by a real man in bed and see if you are still a feminist, love."

I yank away from him with a gasp. "Don't be such a pig." I turn around and walk away from him, despite my entire body being on fire. No one has ever spoken to me in that way before.

"I'll see you tomorrow evening, Bella," he calls after me, but I can't look back. If I do, he'll know how much his dirty words affected me. And I don't want that cocky asshole to have that power over me.

6

ISIAH

I stand before the pretentious home that the Benedetto family calls their mansion. It's exactly the kind of place I'd expect people like them to live in. Extravagant and over the top, much like the people who inhabit it.

Granted, I didn't get to know the family members alone last night. However, if first impressions are anything to go on, I'd say I will enjoy destroying each one of those morons.

I smooth down the front of my suit jacket and press the doorbell, tapping my foot on the stone steps as I wait for someone to answer. A maid comes to the door. "You must be Mr. Darcy."

"Yes."

She opens the door wider. "Come on in. Mr. Benedetto is waiting for you in his study."

I step over the threshold into the hall in which

everything is adorned in gilt. It's rather jarring on the eyes.

"May I take your coat?" the maid asks.

I shrug out of it and pass it to her. "Thanks."

She puts it on a coat rack by the door and then nods. "Follow me."

I wanted to murder James when I saw him alive. It all makes sense now. He betrayed my father to the Benedetto mob and that's how he's still breathing. In an indirect way, he's a part of the reason why Aiden is buried in the park. We'd assumed James had died in the fire at the warehouse. He had always been like a son to my father. When James was only six years old, his father was murdered in a raid, and that's when Dad took him under his wing and brought him into our home. Why he took such a shine to him, I'll never understand.

When I saw him dance with Bella, I wanted to strangle him. And yet, if I recognize him, is it possible he could recognize me?

A chilling thought that could blow apart my plans, but when Cathal almost recognized me, I thought it was all over. And yet the accent threw him off, which hopefully is a good sign.

The maid opens the door to Giovanni's study and announces my arrival. When I walk in, I tense at the sight of Cathal and James sitting in his study. And Cain is also sitting there, Giovanni's only son.

I clear my throat. "I was not aware that we would

be joined by others this evening." I give Mr. Benedetto a stern glare.

He stands. "Isiah, I'm glad you are here. Don't worry, these men are not your competition. Cathal wanted to get to know Nina better, my eldest daughter." He glances at James. "And this is his man, you see."

"James," he says, standing and walking toward me. "It's good to meet you." He holds a hand out.

I take it and squeeze firmly, making him wince. "Good to meet you, too."

There's no light of recognition in his eyes. I guess fifteen years and working hard on losing my accent has made it difficult for others to recognize me.

"Come and join us for a glass of whiskey and a cigar," Giovanni says.

"I'll take the whiskey, but I don't smoke."

Cathal arches a brow. "They're Cuban."

"Doesn't change the fact I don't smoke."

He laughs. "Fair enough. Suit yourself."

Giovanni hands me a tumbler with a large amount of scotch in it and then gestures for me to sit.

I sit down next to James, as it's the only free spot. Even though I want to claw his eyes out instead of sitting here and acting politely toward him.

"So, gentlemen. Tell me how business is going."

Cathal smiles. "You know how well our business is going, Giovanni. We are, after all, rivals, let's not pretend that we don't keep tabs on each other."

Giovanni raises his glass. "Smart answer." His

attention moves to me. "However, that's not the case when it comes to Isiah. You are an enigma for want of a better word."

"Exactly how I like it," I respond.

"Your control in London, however, is impressive."

I sip some of my scotch.

"Your father must have been a great man to build the empire he did. I'm sorry for your loss."

My loss.

He will be sorry, but not for my dad's death. For Aiden's death when I bring him to his knees and delight in watching the life drain from his eyes.

I nod. "It is a risk we must all live with in our line of work."

Giovanni nods. "Indeed, I heard you made the man responsible pay, though." There's a glint in his eye.

"Of course."

Cathal sits up straighter. "Tell us how you dealt with him."

I shake my head. "I'd rather not."

His eyes narrow. "Worried we haven't got the stomach for it?"

"I heard you butchered the guy and sent pieces of him to his family," Cain says.

He's right. I sent the Russian bastard to his family in pieces because that's what is expected of me as the king of the underworld in London. My first move after taking over from my father had to be one of strength and brutality to ensure I cemented my position.

The Belyaev Bratva had become increasingly aggressive in recent years, and despite my insisting that we should deal with them swiftly, my father disagreed. It came back to bite him in the ass. Now, my firm's retaliation has sent the Russians back to whatever hellhole they crawled out of. Henry, my second in command, is looking after things while I'm here in Washington and he's the only person I trust on this planet, other than myself.

"Perhaps," I say simply, swirling the content of my glass around.

Cathal looks unconvinced. "You look like too much of a pretty boy to get your hands dirty like that."

I glare at my former best friend, wondering why he doesn't recognize me. "It's a bad idea to judge a book by its cover. Haven't you heard the saying?"

He clears his throat. "Yes, but the way a man looks and holds himself can give good insight into his character."

Cathal always was a little simple minded in that regard. He's got tattoos over every inch of his body and thinks that makes him look hard, and yet I don't find him intimidating in the slightest. For me, it looks like he's trying too much to look like a bad guy.

I tilt my head. "Do you want to test that theory in a fight?" I ask. Even when we were kids, Cathal could never best me.

Gio intercepts the conversation before it takes a turn. "Enough talk of appearances and fights. Shall we go and join the ladies for dinner?"

A smirk spreads onto Cathal's lips. "I'd love to." I can see by the glint in his eyes that he's hooked on the eldest Benedetto daughter.

Shame that she'll be a victim of my revenge against them. I don't care that she wasn't actively involved in Aiden's death. She's guilty by association.

We stand and Giovanni leads the way down the corridor toward the dining room, where Bella, her three sisters, and her mom are all sitting.

Mrs. Benedetto stands and shoots her daughters a sharp look to do the same. They all rise, the two youngest reluctantly.

She smiles, and it's the fakest smile I've ever seen. "Welcome to our home, gentleman. It's so lovely to have you here, isn't it, girls?"

Bella glares at me and doesn't say a word.

Nina, who stands beside her, nods in agreement with her mom, while the two younger girls whisper something to each other and then giggle.

I don't miss the subtle predatory flash in James' eye when they land on Luciana, the youngest of the Benedetto girls, at only fifteen. The man has always been a disgusting excuse of a human being since he was a child and I sense that's carried on into adulthood. That at least explains why my father liked him so much, as he no doubt saw himself in James.

"Nina, you come and sit next to Cathal,"

Giovanni instructs. And then his attention lands on me. "And Isiah, please take Nina's seat. You are here to get to know each other, so no use having you seated apart."

Bella looks horrified as I take the seat next to her.

No doubt my comment about her needing to be dominated in bed is still fresh in her mind. "It's good to see you again, Bella."

Her jaw clenches. "Can't say the feeling is mutual."

I chuckle and move my lips close to her ear. "I bet you haven't been able to stop imagining me dominating you in bed since I mentioned it."

She moves away from me and gives me a glare that could ward off most people, but I'm not most people. "Are you serious?"

I tilt my head. "Deadly."

"If you'd excuse me, I need to use the restroom." She stands and walks away from the table before anyone can respond.

I watch her. "I assume you have more than one?" I glance at Giovanni. "I also need to use the restroom."

Gio nods. "Of course, down the hall and the first left."

I stand and walk out of the dining room with every intention of tracking down Bella. She thinks she can just walk away from me, but I'll make her realize there is no escape. She will be mine in every sense of the word.

I wait down the corridor for Bella, as I don't need to use the restroom. Instead, I intend to ambush her on the way back. And then I hear voices coming from a room further down, one of them Bella's.

I walk toward it and open the door to find Bella talking in Italian to one of the members of the staff. "Would you give us a minute?"

Bella turns rigid at the sound of my voice. The woman she was talking to looks just as shocked as she glances at Bella and then rushes out of the door, leaving us alone.

"What do you want?" she asks.

I shut the door and turn back to face her. "I wanted to speak with you alone."

Her cheeks flush as I get closer and I notice she nervously fiddles with her hair.

"Do I make you nervous?"

Her nostrils flare as she drops the strand of hair in her hand. "No, you make me angry."

I walk toward her. "Are you sure that's all, love?" I ask as I notice the way her breathing labors with each step I take.

Her throat bobs as she swallows. "Certain. Now, if you don't mind, I need to get back to dinner."

I slide a hand in front of her as she moves forward. "Not so fast." I feel a shot of electricity pulse through my veins the moment my hand connects with her stomach.

Her nostrils flare as she glances at my hand. "Get out of my way, Isiah."

The way she says my name is sinful. "Or what?"

"I don't think my father would be very impressed to hear that you're harassing me."

I arch a brow. "Is that a threat?"

"Yes," she says, holding her head up high. I'll give it to her, she's got gall. Not many people are so cocky around me because of my reputation. It's amusing, though, that she thinks she can threaten me.

I grab her arm and yank her toward me. "Listen to me, Bella," I say, staring into those beautiful bright blue eyes. "You will be my wife and when you are, you will do what a wife is supposed to do."

Her eyes narrow. "And what is it you believe a wife should do?"

I smirk. "Lay on her back and spread her legs to be bred."

She gasps and I don't see it coming quickly enough as her free hand slices through the air and slams into my cheek.

I growl and grab her other wrist so I have both of them trapped. "Careful, Bella. I will break you if you push me."

She tries to yank her arms free, but I am too strong for her. "You are a misogynistic pig. I'd rather marry any other man on this planet than you."

I chuckle. "There are far worse men than me, love." I move my lips toward her ear and let them brush lightly over her earlobe, noticing the way she shudders. "Your father is pretty convinced I'd be the right man to be your husband. I'd be a little nicer to the man who holds your future in his hands. Don't you agree?"

She pulls away a bit. "I don't agree with anything you say."

I can't help but smile as I find her resistance adorable, even if it is futile. In the end, she will break exactly the same way I intend to crush her family. They will pay for what they did to my brother.

"We'll soon see. I'm going to push for our wedding to be as soon as possible." I yank her closer so my lips are against her ear again. "And then we'll see if you can resist my cock once you've had a taste."

Bella yanks away from me. "You are a pig." She spins around and walks out of the room. Her hips sway from side to side as if tempting me to follow, but I don't. First, I need to recollect myself. My cock is hard and throbbing after that brief encounter.

I didn't expect to be so sexually attracted to the woman I intend to destroy, but it will just make my revenge that much sweeter. "Try not to dream of my cock tonight, love."

I hear her raspy gasp as she saunters into the hall-way. No matter how much she tries to convince herself she's not affected by me, I see it in her eyes and hear it in her voice.

I wait for a couple of minutes so it's not suspicious that I'm returning at the same time as her, and then I walk back in and sit next to her as if nothing happened. As I take my seat, I can feel her eyes on me.

I'm too tempted not to touch her as I slip my hand high on her thigh and squeeze, making her draw in a deep inhale of breath, the sound of which I feel in my balls. I'd imagine it's the sound she'd make as I slide my tongue through her virgin pussy.

"So, Isiah," Luciana, the youngest and yet most outspoken daughter, says. "What do you think of Bella?"

It's an odd question to ask, especially with her present. "I don't know her very well."

Bella huffs. "Maybe it would help if you'd actually danced with me last night."

I chuckle. "Why do you make a habit of talking while you dance? I hardly see how that would help us get to know each other."

Her jaw clenches. "It would make me less hostile toward you."

"Bella!" her mom says. "Don't be so rude to Mr. Darcy."

I glance at her. "Please call me Isiah, Mrs. Benedetto."

She smiles. "Of course, and you must call me Viola. I do apologize about my daughter."

"Apologize for what?" She hisses like a feral cat. "For being fucking honest?"

Viola gasps. "Language, Bella!"

I can't deny that I find it amusing that she would

take objection to a mere swear word when they earn their living from organized crime.

"There's no need for apologies. Let her speak her mind."

Bella's eyes widen slightly in surprise. "Thank you."

I nod in response. "Of course."

Maria straightens. "What's London like?"

It's out of the blue, but it's good to change the subject. "It is an exciting city. Different to Washington. Perhaps you can visit someday."

Maria and Luciana, who obviously take that as an invitation for both of them, jump about in their seats. "Oh my God, yes, we'd love to," Luciana says.

Cain huffs. "You two are fucking annoying."

"Cain," Viola says in warning.

It's just as I expected it to be tonight, carnage. Everyone talks over each other as the evening proceeds. Bella's mother and siblings, except Nina, make fools of themselves. It's hard to believe that one day Cain Benedetto will take Gio's place as head of the family, however I intend to wipe out the family entirely. And Bella and I continue to butt heads the entire night.

As the evening is winding down, Gio clears his throat. "I have a deal to conduct tomorrow afternoon with one of the senators. Would you like to accompany me, Isiah?"

I straighten at the request. "You want me to attend a business meeting?"

Gio nods.

Bella stiffens at his request, as she knows it means her father holds me in high regard. It's as if my plan is going exactly as I expected. When I got on my jet from London to Washington, I wasn't certain how it was going to go.

"Sure. Send me the details and I'll be there."

Gio smiles, and it just inflames that deep hatred I hold for him inside. "Perfect, thank you. I need someone like you by my side. You have impressive credentials."

I notice Cathal stiffens a little since it's a snub at him, but he doesn't exactly look like the kind of guy you'd take to meet a member of the senate.

"No problem. I'm happy to help."

He smiles and then glances at Bella. "I hope that soon I'll be able to call you my son-in-law."

Bella frowns. "I hope not."

"Bella," Gio booms, eyes full of fiery rage. "You will do as you are told. If we pick Isiah and he agrees, you will be married."

I smirk as silence falls over the table. And then I slip my hand back onto her thigh and move to whisper in her ear. "Sounds like you will be taking my cock sooner rather than later, love."

She slaps my hand off her thigh and glares at me in the most alluring way. It makes her look even more beautiful. And I know without a doubt that breaking this virgin will only add to the fun of finally getting revenge for Aiden.

7

BELLA

"*A*re you sure about this?" I ask.

Nina nods. "Yes. Cathal will protect us."

I sigh as we stand outside of an underground club where an illegal boxing match is going to take place. Cathal invited Nina to this during dinner the other night, and I can't deny that it doesn't seem very romantic. "And there's no way Isiah will be here?"

Nina looks a little guilty as she shrugs. "Honestly, I have no idea."

I glare at her. "You assured me he wouldn't be."

Nina sighs heavily. "How would I know where he's going to be?"

"I assumed you'd asked Cathal if he'd invited him. They did seem quite friendly at dinner the other night."

"Stop being a wuss. Dad could have picked way worse men than Isiah for you to marry. At least he's hot."

I shake my head. "That's not the point. He may be attractive, but he's arrogant and disrespectful."

Nina grabs my hand and drags me down the stairs into the underground club, which is definitely not our usual place to go out for the night. It's dirty and smells distinctly of sweat and whiskey.

"This place is gross."

Nina shrugs. "What do you expect from a place that holds a boxing match?"

Thankfully, there's no sign of Isiah. Cathal approaches and nods toward the VIP seats at the front. "I've saved us the best seats in the house. Do you enjoy MMA?"

"I thought it was a boxing match, not MMA?" I ask.

Nina frowns. "Isn't it that same thing?"

For God's sake. While I love Nina more than anything in this world, she can be a bit simple at times.

Cathal shakes his head. "Definitely not. MMA is bloody and hardly has any rules."

"I'm not sure I would have agreed to come if I'd known." I shoot Nina a glare. "However, I was told it was boxing."

"Give it a chance," Cathal says. "You might enjoy it."

"Indeed, you might," James adds, appearing in front of me. "Hey boss," he acknowledges Cathal.

Cathal gives him a nod. "Have a seat, James."

James' brow rises. "Are you sure? I have seats in the back."

"I won't hear of my second-in-command back there with the scum. I didn't know you were coming. Sit next to Bella."

James sits next to me and instantly I feel thankful that he's here and Darcy isn't. "It's good to see you again," he says, flashing me a winning smile.

I smile back. "It's good to see you, too. Do you like MMA?"

There's a flash of something undetectable in his eyes as he clears his throat. "It may be brutal, but I enjoy it, yes. Don't be so quick to judge something you've yet to experience."

"Talking of judging. What do you think of Isiah?"

He narrows his eyes. "Honestly?"

I nod.

"I think he's rotten to the core. If I were you, I'd stay far away from that man."

I laugh because it seems ironic that James is warning me away from Isiah. When Isiah warned me away from James. Perhaps the two are jealous of each other.

"What's so amusing?"

"It's just that's exactly what he said about you."

James frowns. "I'm not sure what he'd have against me."

"Wouldn't you like to know?" That deep and seductive voice speaks from behind me, forcing both of us to glance back in surprise. "Hello, Bella." He adjusts his watch on his wrist. "I'm surprised to see you here. Does your father know where you are?"

I swallow hard as I look into those piercing, light blue eyes. Eyes that have haunted my dreams ever since the night of the party four nights ago. It's as if he's under my skin. They're like pure ice as he stares at me with that arrogant smirk on his face.

"It's none of your business whether my father knows or not."

"I didn't think so," he says, standing and coming around to my side, where unfortunately there's an empty seat. He sinks into it. "I better tell dear old dad what you are up to." He pulls his cell phone out of his pocket.

I grab his wrist and look into those piercing eyes. "Don't."

He tilts his head. "Hmm. Maybe if you beg me, I'll consider keeping this a secret."

Disgust coils through me and James leans over to interject. "Stop being an asshole, Darcy, and leave her alone."

He bares his teeth at James. "I'd keep your nose out of it if I were you."

"Are you threatening me now?" James asks.

Isiah adjusts the collar of his shirt. "Perhaps."

"You know, you remind me very much of some-one," James says, staring at Isiah intently. "Have you ever heard of the Daltons?"

Isiah turns rigid by my side. "No." The look in his eyes is one I can't really place as he glares at James.

"Who are the Daltons?" I ask.

James smirks as he glances between Isiah and me. "Oh, just a crime family that used to run the Irish territory before Cathal took over."

"What was that?" Cathal asks.

Isiah shakes his head. "You need to keep your dog on a leash, Bingley."

Cathal's brow furrows. "I didn't know you'd be here, Isiah."

"I heard about it earlier and had nothing better to do tonight."

He claps his hands. "Perfect, I like you. Come sit by me," he says, nodding at the chair next to him.

Thank God.

Isiah glances at me and then at James again. "I'm alright here."

Cathal shakes his head. "Unfortunately, I haven't booked that seat and its occupant is on his way over right now."

Cathal signals to a huge beefy man who looks about double the width of Isiah and, although Isiah is about six foot four, he has to be a good three or four inches taller.

"Who is that?" I ask.

"Damien Petrov. Russian bastard always books a seat next to my lot."

Isiah doesn't look intimidated in the slightest. "Well, he can sit in the seat next to you instead."

Cathal laughs. "Good luck with that."

I notice the determination in Isiah's eyes at what I

assume he takes as a challenge. The hulking man approaches Isiah and glares at him. "That's my seat."

Isiah holds eye contact. "It may well be, but you know that seat over there." He nods toward the seat next to Cathal. "It's a lot better than this one."

Damien tilts his head. "Who the fuck are you, anyway?" His attention moves to Cathal. "One of your fucking henchmen, no doubt?"

Isiah stands and squares up to the man who's far bigger than him. "Who do you think you're calling a henchman?" His fists clench by his sides as if he's ready for a fight. A fight I certainly don't want to see.

"You," he says, poking him in the shoulder.

Isiah moves fast, grabbing his finger before the guy can even interpret the move and he snaps it. The crack of bone makes my insides chill and my stomach churn. "I'm Isiah Darcy and if you have a fucking problem, I'll break more of your bones, got it?"

The Russian looks furious and swings at him with a heavy fist, but the move is slow and laborious. Isiah ducks in plenty of time and grabs his arm, twisting it at an unnatural angle until the man is screaming.

"Now are you going to go and sit down in the other seat or are you going to make me break your arm?" Isiah asks, the calmness of his voice concerning.

Damien spits on the floor. "Fine, you win."

Isiah releases his arm, and he glares at him before moving to sit next to Cathal, who's watching in shock. I must admit I never expected to see a man like that back down for Isiah, but then I must admit Isiah has this dangerous air that he exudes twenty-four seven. He's not like other men I've met in my dad's line of work. There's something different about him that I can't quite put my finger on.

His ice-blue eyes find mine and a cruel smile twists onto his lips. "Impressed, love?"

"Hardly," I reply, shaking my head. "I don't find violence impressive."

"And yet here you are, ready to watch an illegal, bloody fight."

I tilt my head. "Not by choice."

"You don't strike me as the kind of woman that's easily persuaded to do something she doesn't want to do." His eyes sparkle with what I can only describe as playfulness.

"If that's the case, you might as well fly on back to London tonight."

He smirks. "And why is that, love?"

"Because I don't want to marry you, so it would be best to quit now and save yourself the effort."

He casually slides his hand to the back of my neck as if he has the right to touch me and squeezes. "Listen to me carefully, Bella. When it comes to who you marry, you know that you don't get a say in the matter, and therefore it doesn't really matter what you want, does it?"

Frustration wells within me. I need to find a way out of this situation. I don't know Isiah well, but I do know men like him don't like to take no for an answer.

I don't want to be married to someone like him. He's violent, controlling, and God only knows what else he's capable of in that sick and twisted mind of his.

Isiah releases the back of my neck and relaxes into his seat, placing his hands behind his head. "Now, tell me honestly, love. Why the fuck wouldn't you want to marry me?" he asks, oozing arrogance that only angers me more.

I look into his eyes, which gleam with irritating amusement. "There's only one reason why a woman would want to marry a man like you, and that's because she's a gold digger. Your money is the only positive quality you hold."

Isiah's expression darkens, and he sits up straighter, glaring at me. "I'd watch your mouth if I were you, Bella," he says coolly. "You're on very thin ice. Believe me when I say I can make your life very difficult." There's a threat in his voice as he leans in close, speaking in a hushed voice, although no one can hear us. "Especially with your dad already being wrapped around my finger. I'm going to be your husband sooner rather than later, whether you want it or not." He grabs my throat and squeezes, making my heart pound as fear engulfs me. "I intend to use you in every way possible once we're married. You'll be mine in every sense of the word," he murmurs, desire clear in his eyes.

James notices that Isiah has me by the throat and leans over, slamming his fist into his chest. "Let go of her."

66

His voice is as firm as stone, yet there's a hint of a warning in it, too.

Isiah glares at him for a few beats before releasing me and leaning back, as if he has all the time in the world. "We were just discussing our future," he says to James, a cruel smirk playing on his lips.

"And I suggest that you discuss things a little more civilly," James growls.

Cathal leans over and shouts, "What the fuck are you two arguing about over there?"

James stiffens at the sound of his boss's voice. "Nothing."

"Your dog was sticking his nose in my business," Isiah replies.

My hatred toward this man only seems to grow with each moment that passes. "Why don't you go and sit somewhere else?"

Isiah sits back, folding his arms across his chest. "Why would I do that? You are, after all, my fiancée." He places a hand on my thigh and my skin crawls. However, there's this deep ache that his touch ignites, and it's sickening.

"Did I miss something? My dad hasn't agreed to us marrying."

Isiah grins, "Your dad is a smart man. He knows what's best. It's a matter of time until he agrees, then I'll never let you go." He squeezes my thigh even harder, making heat spread over every inch of my skin.

I shove him away. "Don't touch me like that," I snarl.

Isiah's eyes darken and he stands up, fury in his expression. "You're already mine. Don't forget that, love, or you'll wish you were never born," he says in a menacing tone, before giving James a stern glare. "I've got business to attend to."

A shudder runs from the top of my head to my toes as he walks off casually, as if he didn't just threaten me and James.

James clears his throat. "The guy is a fucking asshole."

"Tell me about it," I say, releasing a shaky breath as I slump in my seat, trying to compose myself. "That man is going to be the death of me."

James shakes his head. "You strike me as strong and independent, Bella Benedetto. Find a way to beat him."

"Beat Isiah Darcy?" I get the sense that he never loses.

"There's always time for firsts."

I arch a brow. "And you think I'm going to be the first to best Isiah Darcy?"

"He's a man, not a God. Anyone can best him." His jaw clenches. "I think you need to find any way to avoid marrying him."

"And who do you think I should marry, then?"

He smirks, and I know he's flirting. "A better man."

I wish that I could marry a man like James Wick.

He's kind, but strong and compassionate. The kind of man that my father would hate.

But Isiah is powerful, and if I can't find a way to deter him, I'm doomed to marry him and be under that monster's influence forever.

A wave of sadness washes through me. "That's not going to happen..." I mutter under my breath.

James leans close, wrapping a powerful arm around me. His touch gives me goosebumps. "It may be hard, but there's always hope if you're determined enough to chase after it."

I look up at him, pondering his words and whether they could be true.

Could I really beat Isiah Darcy and marry a man like James?

It seems impossible, but his encouragement ignites a tiny spark of hope that refuses to be put out.

I smile softly at him. "You're right. I'm going to do my best to get out of this mess and marry a man of my choice. I'm not going to let Isiah Darcy win that easily."

Even as I say it, a part of me doesn't believe it. Girls like me don't get to win. I have known most of my life I'll be forced into a marriage with a man I don't want. And it's a fantasy to believe that somehow, I can change that. Even so, I don't mind believing in a fantasy for a little while.

8

ISIAH

*a*s I sit in the hotel bar, waiting with Gio for the senator to turn up, I know that he's well and truly hooked by my guise. He's practically already calling me his son.

The only one who's not convinced of this match is Bella, and I sense that her opinion doesn't really matter. Her family, like most families, takes matters into their own hands when it comes to picking a husband for their daughter.

"This member of the senate is our key to the police being on our side. If we secure him, then the sky's the limit for the Benedetto family."

The announcement makes my stomach churn, but it's only a matter of time until there won't be a Benedetto family at all. I despise having to play this part, as if I'm a friend of this narcissistic piece of shit. Once I've married Bella, then I will deconstruct their entire world as they know it from within the family until there's not a Benedetto left standing.

"And what are you intending to give him in exchange for his loyalty?"

A sinister smirk tugs on the man's lips. "Let's just say this one has a taste for very young blood, and I can provide him with just that."

I feel like I'm about to puke, as he is saying the guy is a fucking pedo. "Right."

He must sense my disgust. "I hope my words don't corrode your sense of morality. I thought being such a well-known criminal mastermind, you'd be used to such practices."

I shake my head. "I don't stoop to that level."

Gio narrows his eyes. "What level is that?"

I realize I've offended him with my words, but I can't condone pedophilia. It's disgusting. No matter what other crimes I may commit, I have to draw a line somewhere. "The lowest scum on this earth prey on defenseless children."

"I agree it's unsavory, but business is business and we need this guy on our side."

Our side.

It's not the first time he's referred to things as ours, which shows how he's thinking. I'm part of the family already. Proving just how much of a gullible son of a bitch he is to open his arms to a man he barely knows based solely on his reputation.

It means crushing this family is going to be ten times easier. Even so, he is brushing a man taking advantage of children on his watch under the carpet. I hate that I have to turn a blind eye to it in order to get my revenge, but perhaps I don't. Perhaps I can use this information to my advantage to bring all the bastards that prey on children to their knees, along with Gio Benedetto.

"And you want me to be civil to a man like him?"

Gio's nostrils flare. "You must be. There's no other choice." He hisses as the man approaches.

"Gio," he says, holding out a hand. "It's so good to see you again."

Gio plasters on a fake smile. "It's great to see you too, Alastair. I have someone I'd like you to meet. This is Isiah Darcy. He's visiting from London."

"Darcy, huh?" Alastair asks, smirking. "I've heard you caused quite a stir over the other side of the pond."

"A stir?" I ask, feeling my blood boiling just talking to a low life like him.

"Yes, I hear you ousted your competition rather impressively after he murdered your father."

The guy mentions the murder of my father rather flippantly, with a smirk on his face. If I actually gave a shit about my dad and his death, then it would be offensive.

I crack my neck. "Who exactly are you?"

"Alastair Jameson," he says, holding a hand out to me.

I eye it warily, but notice the look of encouragement Gio gives me. Clenching my jaw and shoving my warped moral compass into the back of my mind, I take his hand and we shake. Some people would question how I can murder people without a second thought one second and then draw the line at shaking a pedo's hand. The fact is, we all have lines we won't cross.

"Have a seat, gentlemen," Alastair says, gesturing toward a booth in the corner. "I hear you have some fresh meat for me, Gio."

Gio's eyes dart between me and him two times before he nods. "Yes, I will send you the details tomorrow."

Alastair looks a little frustrated before glancing at me. "So, Isiah, how long are you in town?"

I narrow my eyes, tension swirling through the air as my rage takes on a mind of its own. "It's not decided," I say, unable to keep the animosity out of my tone.

Gio clears his throat and I can see him shooting me a warning look out of the corner of my eye. If it weren't for the fact that my entire plan hinges on this man accepting me into his family so that I can bring him to his knees, I'd shoot both of them in the face right here in public.

Alastair's eyes linger on me for a few moments before he finally looks away and turns his attention back to Gio. "Well then, let's get down to business," he says briskly.

Gio nods, reaching inside his coat pocket to retrieve an envelope.

He slides it across the table toward Alastair. Alastair pulls the envelope closer but doesn't acknowledge it.

"So, what is it I can do for you today?" Alastair asks, eyebrow raised slightly.

"I have a proposition." Gio glances at me, smiling widely. I still don't know why I'm here. "Isiah is hopefully going to be my son-in-law, and you mentioned how interested you are in British politics."

No fucking way.

I'm not making any deal with this pedo, not while there's breath in my body.

Alastair smiles, rubbing his hands together as if he could visualize the money rolling in. British politics is as corrupt as American politics, and clearly this son of a bitch wants a slice of each.

"That's very interesting indeed," Alastair says, his voice making my skin crawl.

I rub a hand across the back of my neck, struggling to focus on the conversation as Gio begins making proposals on my behalf. The guy has some nerve thinking that because I want to marry his daughter that he can treat me like this and push me into a deal I don't want.

Rage prickles at the back of my neck as I try to keep it in check, since I just need to bide my time and pretend I'm interested. Once I'm married to Bella, Gio will trust me wholeheartedly, and that's when the fun begins. I'll break any bullshit deal I make with this man—hell, I'll make sure he's buried six feet under along with Gio Benedetto and the rest of his family.

I'm silent during their conversation, as the whole situation makes me sick to my stomach; here is this man with no morals or integrity, making deals with criminals and exploiting children, all while seemingly getting away with it scot-free. A fucking senator. I'm reminded why I hate the Benedettos all the more when Gio participates in something so perverse. It only cements my desire for revenge on his family even more deeply.

My thoughts are jarred away when Gio's phone begins to ring, and he excuses himself to the restroom to answer it. My eyes stray toward Alastair, whose attention is directed solely on me.

His gaze feels like daggers as he takes in every inch of me, and I notice he has a strange tattoo on the back of his hand. I haven't seen one like it before and I wonder what it means.

"So, Isiah, I've heard a lot about you. It's an honor to meet you."

"Really?" I ask, raising an eyebrow. "And what have you heard?" It's definitely not an honor to meet him.

"That you're a ruthless, cold-hearted bastard, with a vicious temper, who's never one to turn his back on a challenge."

I shrug. "So, you have heard of me."

"Yes, and Gio makes a great point. We would be good business partners, don't you think?"

I clench my jaw as I know that if I don't go along with this, Gio will be pissed. Right now, I'm having to entertain listening to an offer from a man who thinks it's fine to prey on children.

"Perhaps. What's your offer?"

"I want to get into politics and you are well connected. Word is there's a lot of money to be made if you know how." He tilts his head. "And something tells me you know all there is to know."

"And why would I help you?"

His eyes narrow. "Because I can open doors for you here in the States."

"I've no interest in your money or your country."

"Then what is your interest?" he asks, his eyes raking over me. "I find it hard to believe you're simply here because you want to marry the Benedetto girl."

I grit my teeth and I can feel my muscles tensing as he's questioning me. "That's none of your business," I hiss.

"Gio isn't the best judge of character," he says, pausing to chuckle to himself. "If you've no interest in money or the States, what does Bella bring you?"

I narrow my eyes. "Stability."

"And you couldn't find that in Britain?"

I tap my fingers on the table in front of me. "Get to the point."

"The point is, I heard about your family back home and how they came to power. I can guarantee that you're here with an agenda."

"And what agenda would that be?"

He hesitates because he has no idea. No one knows the truth. The bastard was taking a stab in the dark and now he's flailing around.

"Maybe you're here to overthrow the Benedettos," he says, hitting the nail on the head somehow. "Maybe you're here to seize power. Maybe you're here simply to strengthen your claim on power in London."

Am I really that easy to read? It doesn't seem like Gio believes that because he's convinced I'm the man to marry his daughter. This low life somehow has worked me out in three seconds flat.

"As I told you, I'm here for Bella and that's all," I retort.

He leans over the table and lowers his voice. "I have no qualms with a bit of competition, but I can't have threats to the way things work for me. If you're here for revenge, then I need to protect myself and my business interests."

"There's no agenda." My eyes darken. "And you don't know a thing about me."

He holds up his hands. "I know that you're dangerous."

"Then stop provoking me."

"Is that a threat?"

Gio returns and sits in his seat. He instantly senses the tension in the air. "What happened while I was away?" He gives me an accusing look, but the fact is I wasn't the one to cause the tension.

Alastair shrugs. "Just discussing business."

As if by the flick of a switch, he's gone from hostile to friendly in a matter of minutes.

"A potential alliance?" Gio asks.

Alastair shrugs. "It remains to be seen, but I want a way into London." His eyes narrow as he glares at me. "I believe he's the only man to give it to me."

Over my dead body.

Gio glances at me, eyes narrowing. "Are you open to this?"

I clench my fist under the table as I'm not open to it, but I have to pretend that I am. "I'll give it consideration," I say, even though it doesn't matter how badly I want my revenge on Gio and his family, one thing I will not do is make a deal with a fucking pedophile.

Alastair nods in response. "That's all I ask."

Gio takes a drink. "I'll drink to that."

There's a murderous rage coursing through my veins as I sit here with these men. After a few moments of awkward silence, Gio speaks.

"So." He runs a hand across the back of his neck. "As I said, I have some fresh meat for you, but I need this brushed under the carpet." He nods at the envelope on the table.

Alastair grabs it and slides it into his pocket without even questioning what it is. "Consider it done. When can I expect delivery of said meat?"

Gio's eyes dart to my fists, which are both clenched on the table. "As I said earlier, I'll be in touch with all the details tomorrow."

Alastair's eyes narrow. "I'd hoped I'd have delivery tonight. Do you know how long it's been? Two months since the last one."

I shudder at the way he says that and can hardly believe that I'm still sitting in my own chair. Every instinct in my body wants to act and tear this man apart, limb from limb.

"I appreciate that, but one more evening won't kill you, will it?" Gio says.

If he's not careful, I'll be killing him before he can make it out of this fucking building. There's a dark and dangerous rage trying to come to the surface.

All I want is to pull out my gun and shoot him right in the face. I know that intervening, particularly after this conversation, would be dangerous. Gio would know that I'm involved. And I need Gio to believe that I'm on his side until the time is right.

Until it's time to bring him and his family down once and for all.

"No, I guess it won't kill me." He sighs heavily. "But I expect delivery tomorrow." He tilts his head. "How many?"

"I've got two for you this time."

"One of each?" he confirms.

I'm just about ready to explode and literally shoot him dead right here in the middle of the hotel bar, when Gio clears his throat. "We'll discuss this tomorrow. Now, if you'd excuse us, we have some other business we need to attend to." Gio stands and grabs the lapel of my jacket, yanking me to my feet.

I don't doubt that my intent was written all over my face.

Alastair nods. "Of course, I will await your call." The smug smirk on his face makes me sick to my stomach as Gio nods toward the exit.

I walk away reluctantly.

"You need to keep yourself together, Isiah. It looked like you wanted to murder him right there in the middle of the bar."

"I did," I admit.

He shakes his head. "Are you telling me you've never had to deal with men with his proclivity in the past?"

"Any I have come across, I've ousted from this Goddamn planet. It's what they deserve."

Gio's jaw works. "It's business."

I shrug. "As I said, I don't stoop to that level in my business."

He nods. "Another admirable quality I'd like in a son-in-law, even if I do find you a bit judgmental."

"Judgmental? You are aiding and abetting pedophiles."

"One. And I would stop pushing the matter, unless you want to fall into my bad books," he snaps.

A warning when I need it, as that's the last thing I want. Gio must remain in favor of me if I'm going to take him down. Forcing my rage and morals into a cage deep in my soul, I shake my head. "Of course, I apologize."

"Now, let's go and get a real drink together and discuss your intentions toward my daughter."

Intentions.

He's the one that invited me here as a potential husband for Bella. All of my intentions are dishonorable. I intend to break his beautiful little daughter in every way imaginable before I crush him and his pathetic excuse of a family once and for all.

9

BELLA

"*D*o we have to go to this ball tonight?" I ask.

Nina sighs. "I asked Dad the same thing, and he practically snapped my head off over it." She shakes her head. "We've got no choice."

"Will Cathal be there?"

Her cheeks redden. "I don't think so. I'm not sure Dad approves of him."

I sigh heavily. "Figures he wouldn't even approve of a bachelor he invited as a potential suitor if his daughter likes him."

"Cathal is determined, though." Her brow furrows. "I've never met a man so assertive as him."

"Let's not forget Isiah." I roll my eyes. "It's like Dad is determined to marry me off against my will."

"I know," she says, giving me a sad smile. "Unfortunately, in this criminal underworld, we have no say in the matter," Nina says.

"But I can't stand Isiah. He's not the right person for me. He's only interested in power and money and is down right abusive."

"And what about James?" Nina asks.

I pause. "I would like to get to know him better, but you know he's not suitable because he's not rich and powerful."

Nina grabs my hand and squeezes. "If you really like him, you need to fight."

I laugh humorlessly. "What use is fighting when there's no chance of winning?"

"You are giving up too easily." She releases my hand. "Enough talk of marriage. How do I look?" Nina asks, twirling around.

"You look beautiful." I narrow my eyes. "But if Cathal isn't going, why do you care?"

She smirks. "Just in case he does make an appearance. I've got to be prepared."

I shake my head. "I don't care what I look like, particularly because Isiah will be there."

"If we have to go. We should make the best of it, I suppose." Nina gives me a small smile. "You look absolutely beautiful, for what it's worth."

I sigh and twirl to look at myself in the mirror. "That's not a good thing. I don't want Isiah to find me desirable," I say, even as butterflies flutter to life in my stomach at the sight of my dress.

The sweetheart neckline fits snugly across my chest and the skirt flares delicately from my waist in an array of shimmering sapphire blue tulle. Silver beading adorns each delicate layer of the skirt, giving it an ethereal air, as if I were passing through a cloud every time I take a step.

The back dips into a deep V with thin spaghetti straps that runs down my back before gathering into a bow at the base of my spine. Tiny little pearls adorn the bodice, adding an extra sparkle to the dress like a starlit night sky on a clear evening.

My hair is twisted up elegantly in a French twist, leaving strands at either side of my face that curl. And instantly I regret every choice I made while getting ready.

I do look beautiful, and that's not the intention. James most likely won't be at this ball, meaning I won't have anyone to protect me from the villainous Isiah Darcy.

"Come on, we're going to be late," Nina says, hooking her arm with mine and leading me out of our shared bedroom.

We descend the stairs into the main hall of the house, where Luciana, Maria and Cain are waiting already. However, there's no sign of Mom or Dad.

Luciana's eyes widen as she notices us. "You both look like you are trying to win over a hottie," Luciana says, smirking. "No doubt Bella can't wait to get Isiah into bed." She winks.

I clench my fists by my sides. "Don't be an ass, Luciana."

Maria chuckles, only encouraging her. "We've all seen the way you look at him, Bella."

"What, like I want to kill him?"

"Fuck him more like," Cain sneers.

Nina growls. "You're a fucking dickhead, Cain."

Cain raises an amused brow, simply throwing a ball up in the air and catching it again. "You two are so easy to wind up."

"And you would be easy to murder," I say.

"Please, you don't have it in you to murder a fucking fly, Bella Benedetto."

My mom appears then. "Please stop squabbling. You'd think you were all toddlers again."

Dad follows behind her. "Indeed, I don't want any arguments tonight. You all need to be on your best behavior. This ball is being thrown by one of my most important business partners."

All of us grumble in response and fall silent.

"Let's go before we're late," Dad says, leading the way out of the house and into the driveway, where a limousine is waiting to take us to the event.

"Great," Nina whispers. "I'd hoped there would be two cars so we could escape our rotten siblings."

"Me too," I reply.

All seven of us climb into the limousine and an awkward silence falls over us. It's hard to believe that we're a family at all, as there's nothing natural about us spending time together.

The limousine pulls to a stop outside of the luxurious hotel where the charity ball is being held. It's the kind of place only celebrities stay. We walk through the grand entranceway under giant crystal chandeliers that cast prisms of light onto the sparkling Amalfi marble floors, creating a surreal magical setting, even if tonight will be anything but magical.

The walls are hung with ornately framed paintings depicting different scenes from classical literature and history.

As we move from the entrance of the hotel and into the events hall, the sound of pretentious classical music swells. Everyone in the room is dressed in their finest attire, a lot of the clothes probably worth more than what most normal people make in a year for nothing more than fabric.

"Shall we find our table?" I whisper to Nina, wanting to get away from our family, who will no doubt want to mingle.

Nina nods eagerly as we slip away from our flesh and blood, finding the table with our name cards on it. Instantly, I notice the name card next to mine and want to run the other way.

Isiah Darcy.

"Goddamn it," I say.

"What's wrong?" Nina asks.

I hold up the card so she can read it.

"Oh, must be Dad."

I sigh heavily. "I hope he's late."

"You hope who is late?" That dark, sinful voice asks from behind me.

I hate how every time I hear him speak, goosebumps prickle over my skin. I can't help but shiver, my body betraying me with a thrill of excitement.

It's an irritating and yet unavoidable part of speaking with him. Turning around, I plaster a fake smile on my face and put his name card back where it was. "No one."

He shakes his head. "You hoped I'd be late, but the thing is, love." He pauses and looks me dead in the eye. "I'm never late." He sits down next to me and has the audacity to slide his hand onto my thigh and squeeze.

The move is improper and downright misogynistic, but my entire body heats, anyway. It's infuriating the way I react to him.

"Get your hand off of me."

He chuckles. "So uptight tonight, Bella. What's got your knickers in a twist?"

I narrow my eyes at him. "You."

Nina clears her throat. "You should do as she says. It's bad manners to touch someone when you have no right."

I love Nina, but she's the worst when it comes to a fight. She's too timid and shy, even if she does try her best.

Isiah opens his mouth to speak, but he's interrupted by my father's arrival.

"Isiah!" He claps him on the shoulder. "I'm glad you could make it."

He smirks at me as his hand slides off my thigh. "Wouldn't miss it."

"I'm glad to see you and Bella are getting on."

Nina scoffs. "They're not getting on!"

Luciana clears her throat. "It's great to see you again, Isiah," she says, twirling a strand of hair around her finger. "How have you been?"

I glare at my youngest sister, who isn't even sixteen and is quite shamelessly flirting with a man double her age.

"Fine thanks, Luciana," he says, his reply short and dismissive.

I notice the way her nose wrinkles in irritation at his lack of reciprocation.

Maria sits down on the other side of me. "Don't tell me we're in for another sparring match."

"Sparring match?" Cain asks.

She nods toward me. "Between these two know-it alls."

"Maria!" my mom shouts, shaking her head. "Don't be so rude to our guest."

Isiah's lips curl up at the corners in a smirk, but I can see something else hidden in his gaze other than amusement. There's something hidden beneath the surface, a darkness that I can feel emanating from him. Is he keeping something from us? What dark secrets is he hiding? I can't help but shiver at the thought. Isiah just looks amused, but there's something else in his eyes that I can't quite put a finger on. It's something dark and illicit, as if he harbors a secret from all of us.

"How have you been enjoying your time in Washington so far, Isiah?" Cain asks.

He straightens and that glint in his eyes is erased

almost instantly. "It's a nice city, not London, but it's fine."

"Fine?" Luciana says. "That's a rather dismissive word."

Isiah's brow raises. "I wouldn't call it dismissive, just honest." He takes a sip of the amber colored liquid in his glass, which looks like whiskey. "Would you rather I lie?"

"Certainly not," Gio says, shaking his head. "Honesty is an important characteristic." He meets my gaze. "Especially in a husband."

I roll my eyes. "Quit it with the husband lark."

I can't shake the feeling that this man isn't being totally honest with us. It feels like he's hiding something.

Isiah turns to me. "What is it you want to do if you don't want to marry?"

I gape at him. "Are you suggesting that I couldn't possibly do anything but be a wife?"

"Oh, here we go!" Maria whines.

Cain just chuckles and Luciana looks amused, but Nina shakes her head. "Can we get through this evening without an argument?"

"It is a woman's role, isn't it?"

Rage coils through me as I glare at him. "What exactly do you believe a woman's role entails?" I ask, anger already spiking through my blood at his blatant sexist remark.

Isiah smirks, undeterred by my hostility. "I believe that a woman's role is at home, tending to her family and looking after the children. She should obey any commands from her husband or father and remain in their shadow, doing only what is asked of her." He leans toward me. "And she should willingly open her legs at any given moment to give unfettered access to her sopping wet cunt and her tight little asshole," he whispers, so only I can hear.

I clench my fists by my sides, trying not to let my traitorous, hormonal body react to his vile words. "That's an archaic way of thinking! A woman deserves to be an equal partner in a relationship and have a say in decisions that affect her life. She shouldn't be told what to do by any man just because he's older or of a wealthier rank than her—it is unjust! A woman has as much right as a man to make decisions."

Isiah rolls his eyes and shakes his head. "Real men, like myself and your father"— he nods at my dad— "don't need a woman's input in any matters other than how to look after children. Allowing women control in our world would only bring chaos."

My dad, like the asshole he is, laughs and nods. "Quite right, Isiah."

My mom glares at him. "Giovanni!"

My fury boils over and I can no longer contain it. There's so much wrong with his mindset I hardly know where to begin. "Do you not realize how back-ward and offensive your views are? Women are as capable of understanding complex topics as well as men, if not better!" I shake my head. "There are women leaders of the cartel and they're often better than the men. To think that men possess some kind of higher intelligence or penchant for violence is ridiculous. Some women are better at it than men, even if men would never admit it."

Isiah tilts his head. "Do you believe you are one of those women?"

I give him my most intimidating stare. "Yes."

It doesn't seem to faze him though, and the honest truth is, I'm not one of those women. I don't have a penchant for violence or for running things. All my life, I've been trained for the exact fucking role he just described, and that's what makes it worse.

"Excuse me," I say, standing. "I need to use the restroom." I walk away before anyone can respond, because right now, all I need is to be on my own.

I've always understood the injustice of my position, but it makes it all the more absolute when I hear that jackass spell it out in black and white.

I go into the bathroom, which is empty, standing over the sink as I try to gather my thoughts. In the silence of this safe space, I can feel all my anger and sadness weighing heavily on me. The unfairness of what my life must become is something I can no longer brush under the carpet.

Suddenly, the door opens and Isiah walks in. He seems to take up all the space in the room with his presence and it makes my stomach flip with nerves. We are alone now, like two combatants ready to enter battle. His eyes search mine as if he can see right to my core and all the vulnerability I harbor behind the walls I so carefully erect.

"You can't run away from the truth, love," he says, breaking the palpable, charged silence. "I'm going to be your husband, whether you like it or not." He turns to the door and pushes the lock across, locking us inside.

"Bullshit," I say, clenching my hands by my sides as I stand as tall as physically possible. Inside, I'm panicking, as this predator has locked me in here with him and is blocking the exit. "If that's true, why has my dad invited two other men to the house tomorrow evening?"

It appears that's news to him as his eyes narrow. "You're lying."

"What good would it be for me to lie about that?"

He looms closer, a triumphant glint in his eye. "Let me show you why I'm the man you want to marry."

Every step brings his magnetic pull closer, as if I'm sucked in by his very presence. I hate how drawn to him I am, despite everything.

"No." My voice wavers and there's no hint of strength behind it.

His throaty chuckle sends chills down my spine. "Let me make you wish we were already married."

I take a quick sidestep in an attempt to break away, and reach the door, but he's too fast. An iron arm wraps around my waist and pulls me roughly against him. His long fingers slide beneath the hem of my dress, and suddenly I'm engulfed in flames.

I gasp in shock as Isiah boldly pushes the elastic of my panties aside and inserts a finger into my passage.

"Isiah!" I whimper in a barely audible protest, but he has me pinned in his unyielding grip.

"What's wrong, darling?" he mocks in a silky voice, his fingers working my core with precision and skill. "Can't handle the pleasure I'm giving you?"

The heat of my arousal becomes unbearable, making me clench my teeth together to resist the waves of pleasure threatening to crash over me. But to no avail. Isiah's rough treatment has me excited beyond belief, and his chiseled features make him look like a Norse God—an evil one who is determined to bring me to the heights of pleasure tonight.

His lips travel across the front of my neck, and I cling to him, my mind in overdrive.

His warm breath ghosts over my skin. "Tell me how it feels, Bella," he murmurs, his baritone voice pure velvet.

His touch sends lightning through my veins. "Tell me how it feels to be touched by a real man."

My mouth dries, as the thrill his touch elicits is purely because he's the only man who has ever laid a finger on me. Isiah is the first man to touch me like this. The first man to kiss me like this.

His lips drift lower until they are between my cleavage, awakening a fire within me that I never knew existed. "What is it that you feel, love?" His thick accent swirls around me, luring me in with its raw masculinity and a hint of arrogance.

"It feels terrible," I gasp, still trying to keep up the pretense. "Get off of me."

His laugh is pure evil in response. "You are a terrible liar. You are dripping all over me, Bella. So fucking wet it's unbelievable." He nibbles on my earlobe. "Your pussy is practically begging to be filled with my cock."

As he brushes the pad of his thumb over my throbbing clit, I bite the inside of my cheek to stop myself from crying out in pleasure. It's torturous trying to remain silent when he's making me feel like this. The wickedness of his touch ignites fire on my skin, setting me ablaze. His skillful fingers coax me closer, pushing me higher and higher until I'm trembling hard and gasping for air. I can feel the pleasure rising from the depths of my stomach, a pressure that I've never known before.

Finally, I can't take it anymore and his touch sends me over the edge. A wave of pleasure crashes over me as every part of my body screams with delight.

"Fuck, Isiah!"

My voice is a ragged cry as I reach out for him, clawing my nails into his muscular forearm.

His deep chuckle is a vibration against my ear as he teases me through it, driving me deeper into bliss. "That's right, love, scream my name."

His fingers slip away, leaving me feeling hollow

and empty. But the pleasure still lingers on my skin like a lingering kiss.

Slowly, he lifts his fingers to his lips and sucks my arousal off of them, forcing me to clench my thighs.

Humiliation hits me as the pleasure wears off and Isiah puts enough distance between us for me to look into his eyes. All I see is triumph, and it's sickening.

"I told you that you'd wish we were married, but unfortunately until we're married, I'm not going to fuck that eager little cunt."

Clenching my fists by my sides, I hold my head up high. "I'd rather die than marry you."

He tilts his head. "Don't be so dramatic, love. Your pussy tells another story. You will marry me."

"Marriage shouldn't be an obligation. It should be based on love and respect between two people who want to share their lives together! It should never be arranged."

"Too bad you're a Benedetto. An arranged marriage was always on the cards for you."

"I'd rather marry any other man at that party than be stuck with you!"

Isiah's face darkens with anger and he closes the gap between us again— close enough for me to feel his hot breath on my skin again. "Love? Respect?" he scoffs harshly before continuing in a low whisper that only I can hear: "That's not what marriage is really about— it's about power and the man putting a woman in her place."

That last comment hits me like a ton of bricks and

I snap, bringing my fist toward his face with all the strength I can muster.

He catches it in his own palm and shakes his head. "I don't think so." He bites my bottom lip hard enough to break the skin. "Something for you to remember this encounter by. And if anyone asks what happened, you say you chewed your own lip." He gives me a warning glare. "I've noticed you like to chew on your lip when you are nervous." With that, he turns and unlocks the bathroom door, walking out without a glance backward.

I slump against the wall behind me, my mind racing in chaotic circles. Isiah Darcy is a bastard, and he seems determined to prove a point. He's found my deep-seated longing for submission and mercilessly exposed it with every breath he drew. His dominance makes me shudder with both revulsion and pleasure all at the same time.

10

ISIAH

*M*y phone rings as I'm about to get into my town car and I pick it up. "Hello?"

"How's it going, boss?" Henry asks on the other end.

"I told you not to ring me!" I hiss.

He clears his throat. "We've been having trouble with the Belyaev Bratva."

I grit my teeth in frustration. "What kind of trouble?"

"They've been trying to muscle their way into our territory," Henry explains. "We can't let them think they can overstep because you aren't in town."

"Motherfuckers," I growl in annoyance. "What do you suggest we do about it?"

Henry sighs heavily into the phone. "Unfortunately, I think you have to make an appearance in London and take care of this. We need to make sure that they realize that fucking with us results in consequences."

I scowl at his suggestion, my fist tightening angrily around my phone as I imagine myself leaving Washington right when everything is going so well. "I thought I made that clear when I sent Dmitry Belyaev to them in pieces."

"Me too, boss, but they're pushing back." I can hear him rummaging around on the other end. "If you want me to handle it, I will. Just say the word."

I shake my head. As much as I despise the idea of leaving Bella here for any amount of time, while there are other men vying to become her fiancé, I won't let things go to shit in London. "No." I check the time on my watch, noticing it is midday. "I'll be there first thing tomorrow morning once I've tied a few things up."

"Sure thing. See you tomorrow." He ends the call.

It appears the moment I step out of London for more than a fucking week, everything goes to shit. Henry knows how important this trip is. He's the only person on this earth who knows the truth and the reason why I'm trying to win Bella as my wife. He's the only person who knows about Aiden.

I dial Gio's number.

"Isiah," he answers after the second dial tone. "I was just talking about you with my wife. We are really looking—"

"I'm going to have to stop you there, Gio. Unfortunately, something has come up in London that I need to go and deal with. I'm leaving this afternoon, but I'll be back as soon as it's sorted. So, I won't be at dinner this evening."

"Oh, that's a shame. We were hoping to close the deal tonight."

"Close the deal?" I ask.

"Yes, we really want you to marry Bella."

I'm thankful to hear him say those words, but it makes leaving all that more difficult. "I'm glad to hear you say that, as I want to marry your daughter." So that I can destroy your family from the inside out, just like you destroyed mine. I clear my throat. "Your daughter tried to convince me you had other suitors coming to dinner this evening."

There're a few moments of silence. "We do, but that was only in case you weren't interested after meeting my fiery daughter."

I laugh. "Believe me, I'm not easily dissuaded."

"But the question is, do I announce it?" Gio asks, sounding uncertain. "You're disappearing at a crucial time."

"I assure you that I've every intention of marrying your daughter. I'll be back within a few days at the most." To ensure Gio understands why I'm returning. "Two weeks away from London has made some of my rivals gutsy and they need to be put back in their place."

"Ah, I see." He chuckles. "I sense we're both very alike, you and I."

I fucking hope not.

This man is the reason my twin is dead and buried in a park on the outskirts of Washington.

"Well, have a good trip to London and we'll see you when you're back." He ends the call.

I dial the number of the private airstrip where my jet is being kept and ask them to fuel it, ready to leave this afternoon. And then I turn to my driver. "Take me to Dumbarton Oaks."

He bows his head. "Of course, sir."

The man I hired to drive me while I'm in Washington knows nothing about me or my past. I feel uneasy having someone I don't really know driving me around town, but I had no choice.

Kevin gets into the driver's seat and I get into the back, drumming my fingers on my knee.

I haven't returned to Aiden's resting place since the day I arrived two weeks ago. That's all it's taken for everything at home to go to shit.

Kevin pulls up at the entrance of the park.

"I won't be long. Wait out here for me."

"Certainly, sir," he replies.

I get out and walk through the gates into the park. The moment I step inside, I see that oak tree. Aiden may not have a headstone, but that oak tree can be seen for miles and it's the marker of his grave to me.

Leisurely, I walk through the trees toward it, almost procrastinating, as I hadn't intended to visit again until I'd crushed the people who ended his life. However, I can't leave this city without visiting.

Once I get to the oak, I look down at the spot where his remains lie.

"Hey, Aiden," I murmur, drawing in a deep breath to gather my thoughts. "I've got to go away for a few days to sort things out in London. I'll be back as soon as possible and then no one that did this to you will be safe. I'm not going to rest until justice is served."

I clench my fists by my sides, an ache igniting in my chest as the tears refuse to come. "I promised you, brother. And I won't break that promise."

As I stand there, it's almost as if I expect him to respond. Taking a deep breath, I feel the weight of his death on me heavier than ever. "I will always love you, brother."

Suddenly, a gust of wind hits the trees and rustles its leaves. If I were a sentimental man, I'd think it was a sign from him, but I know better than that. Aiden is gone. He's been gone for fifteen years, and nothing can change that. I have felt that hole in my soul that his death tore in it ever since that fated night.

Turning away slowly, I walk back to Kevin's car, which is waiting outside the gates of Dumbarton Oaks Park; ready to be taken to my jet and on to London.

11

BELLA

*M*y brow furrows as I walk into the dining room to find no one other than my family and Cathal Bingley.

"Where is everyone?"

Dad stands. "I didn't bother to invite the other suitors. As we've made a decision as to who you will marry."

I glance at Cathal, wondering if my engagement is going to take an odd turn. "What?"

"Oh no, you aren't marrying Cathal!" He laughs. "Isiah had to go back to London for a few days, but we've agreed you'll marry him."

"Like hell I will!"

"Isabella Benedetto, you'll do as your father tells you." My mom's voice is stern, and I know there's no getting out of this, but I want to marry anyone but him.

"I hate the man," I say, slumping down in my usual chair at the dining table.

"Hate is a strong word," Cathal interjects.

I give him a quick glance. "Maybe so, but it's how I feel."

"Hatred will get you nowhere," my father says. "Isiah is wealthy, powerful and, in my eyes, has only been a gentleman to you. He'll make you a perfect husband."

I scoff and cross my arms. "He's arrogant and controlling, not to mention a complete and utter pig. He doesn't listen to anything I have to say and objectifies me."

Mom shows no understanding. "Isabella, we've talked about this before. You're unlikely to like the man you marry, regardless."

I let out a frustrated sigh, knowing they're not going to budge on their decision, but I'm determined to make them see that Isiah isn't the right choice for me.

"You know he has said and done some disgusting things," I say, meeting my dad's gaze.

"Such as?" Dad asks.

I swallow hard. "I wouldn't dare repeat what he's said, but he cornered me in the ladies' bathroom at the charity event and touched me inappropriately."

Cain laughs. "Are you saying he fingered you?"

My mom gasps. "Cain, don't be so disgusting."

Luciana and Maria giggle. "I wouldn't be complaining if he fingered me," Luciana says.

"Stop it!" my mom shouts.

Dad looks completely disinterested by the topic of conversation. "It's normal that a man would want to touch the woman he intends to make his wife before the fact."

"Are you fucking serious?" I ask, balling my hands into fists. "I told him no, and he still touched me."

"It's pretty standard practice," he says.

"You're a fucking psychopath if you think that's fine!"

My father's face turns red with anger as he slams his hand against the tabletop. "Isabella Benedetto, enough! You'll marry Isiah and that's final. I don't want to hear another word on the subject."

An awkward silence falls over the table as I fiddle with the hem of my dress, wishing I could sink into the floor right now.

I always knew fighting their choice was futile, but I never thought my father would be fine with a man touching me without consent. Clearly, his regard for me is much lower than I ever believed possible.

"Nice wine," Cain says, swishing the contents of his glass around. "What is it?"

Trust that asshole to break the ice with such a mundane question.

"It's a pinot noir," Mom replies, still looking flushed from the topic of conversation before.

Nina leans toward me. "Are you okay?"

I swallow hard and give her a short smile. "Not doing great."

She shakes her head. "Maybe we can excuse ourselves early."

Cathal is here to see her, and she knows it. "Why would you do that when you have a very attractive Irishman here to see you?"

Cathal, obviously overhearing, joins in. "Indeed, why would you do that, Nina?"

Her cheeks flush a deep red as she shakes her head. "I don't know."

He smiles. "I'm here to see you, and you alone."

I turn my attention back to the rest of the family, who are squabbling over what meat is better: beef or lamb.

Everything seems so mundane in comparison to what my future holds. Isiah Darcy is the last man on this earth that I want to marry, and yet I'm being forced down the aisle by my own parents. The two people who should care about my welfare more than any other.

Maria clears her throat. "When will the wedding be? I need to go shopping for a new dress!"

I glare at my sister. "The thirteenth of never, I hope."

Dad shrugs. "I've yet to work out the details with Isiah. As soon as he's back, we will."

"Where is James tonight, Cathal?" I ask, ignoring my family.

He shakes his head. "Believe it or not, he doesn't go everywhere with me."

My dad interjects. "I don't like him. And I don't like how much interest you have in him, Bella."

I narrow my eyes at him. "So now I'm not even allowed to have friends?"

"We both know that man isn't interested in you for friendship."

Cathal straightens. "Are you suggesting my man is dishonorable?"

Dad looks taken aback by the question. "Of course not, it's just a matter of fact. A man like him and my daughter are unlikely to be friends."

"I agree," Cathal says. "They'd be unlikely friends, but that doesn't mean they can't be."

I give Cathal a small smile. I like him. I have done since we first met him at the party. He's not like the other suitors, although I don't like him romantically like my sister does. I'm sure he would make a wonderful husband.

"James and I get on well, so I have every intention of remaining friends with him." I hold my chin up high.

Dad looks like he wants to object, but he eyes Cathal warily. Obviously, he doesn't want to fuck up his possible match with Nina.

Nina thought perhaps Dad didn't like him, but I think he would do anything to get Nina out of this house and off his hands, whether it's the right thing for her or not.

"So, Cathal, are you going to the senate's charity event at the end of the month?" I ask.

Cathal purses his lips. "I don't usually waste my time at those obnoxious events." He places a hand on Nina's and she blushes. "But if you're going, I may make an exception."

Nina turns even more shy at his attention. "I'll be there."

"That's settled then." He claps his hands. "So will I."

The two kitchen staff that my parents hired enter with trays of food. The smell is mouth-watering, and I'd be lying if I said I wasn't hungry.

Kala puts a large roast beef joint in the center of the table surrounded on the platter by mounds of roasted potatoes.

Leo sets down a platter of steamed vegetables and a boat of gravy.

"This seems like a lot of food for the number of people eating dinner," I say.

Dad straightens. "That's because the staff expected more people."

It's not just tonight, though. Our family is wasteful, and it's something I've always hated. Especially when there are so many people on this planet literally starving.

"Dig in, everyone," Dad announces.

I don't wait, because I'm hungry, piling my plate high with food. After all, I've got something to celebrate tonight. It's a night free from that stuck up British asshole who has been harassing me for weeks. Dad can't leave the guy alone, practically having him live here. I'm surprised he hasn't already suggested it and that Isiah is still staying at the Waldorf.

Nina clears her throat. "Are you okay?" she asks, only loud enough for me to hear.

I shake my head. "Not exactly. I can't marry that man."

She gives me an odd look.

"What?"

"It's just you could have had it much worse than him. At least he's not old and creepy."

I frown. "You did just hear what I said about him, right?"

She nods. "Yeah, and unfortunately, Dad is right. It's just how things are done in our world, Bella."

"Well, it's disgusting." I cross my arms over my chest, hardly able to believe that Nina is practically siding with them. "Are you saying that I should be grateful that I'm being married off to a man I despise?"

"Of course not," she hisses, getting a little irritated. "I'm just saying that it's not the end of the world. When you first met him, you thought he was arrogant but very attractive, didn't you?"

"That was before he opened his mouth."

Nina giggles. "Right, I admit he's arrogant and stuck up and looks down on people."

"To name a few flaws," I add.

She sighs. "It's just we both knew we'd never get to choose who we end up with."

I arch a brow. "You seem to be getting a choice," I

say, nodding toward Cathal, who's in deep conversation with Dad.

Her cheeks flush a deep red. "Dad hasn't agreed yet, and it's not like Cathal has proposed."

"But you want him to propose, don't you?"

"I can't believe I'm saying it, but yes." She shakes her head. "There's no way I ever thought I'd find a man I could be happy with."

I smile as I'm ecstatic for her. She deserves to find her happiness, as she's had too many struggles already in her life and I'm sure once she's with someone who truly cares for and loves her, she'll be able to overcome her depression. Our parents have never exactly given her the support she needed. All they do is cover up her condition because appearance is more important to them than the mental health of their eldest child.

"Maybe we will both be getting married at the same time," I say, smiling at her. "At least then we don't have to worry about each other."

She sighs heavily. "But I'd have to worry about you, because you won't be happy."

"What are you two twittering about?" Mom snaps, glaring at the both of us.

"Nothing," we both say in unison.

Cathal meets Nina's gaze. "Would you like to take a little stroll outside?" he suggests.

Nina turns a deep red. "I'd like that."

Dad's eyes narrow. "It's a bit cold for a stroll, isn't it?"

Cathal shakes his head. "I always find the winter air so refreshing. We have coats."

Maria stands. "Can I come, too?"

My mom interjects. "No." She grabs her hand and forces her back into her seat. "Let them have some time alone together."

Nina turns redder at that, leaning toward me. "See you later," she whispers.

I nod, and then she stands, allowing Cathal to guide her out of the room.

"Are you seriously considering letting Nina marry that guy?" Cain asks once they're gone.

Dad straightens. "Why not?"

"He's Irish and our competition, for one thing. Secondly, Nina wouldn't make a suitable wife for any man, and once he realized we'd stuck him with a loon, he'd soon get pissed."

"Shut the fuck up, Cain," I hiss, glaring at him. "Nina's not a loon, she's sensitive. And you're a fucking asshole."

Cain bares his teeth at me. "Don't get me started on you!"

"Enough," Dad booms. "Cathal is our competition at the moment, but an alliance through marriage would bring our two organizations together, strengthening our hold over our territory. And, in regard to Nina's mental health, she hasn't had any breakdowns lately."

Luciana giggles, as if this is a funny matter. "Until

something sets her off, and she tries to bleed herself out again."

"Unbelievable. How is that amusing?" I ask, unable to believe that these people are even my family. They're a disgrace. "Nina was suffering with depression at the time and all of you are laughing about it or calling her loon. You're all sick in the head." I stand and storm out of the dining room, ignoring the shouts of both my mom and my dad to return at once.

Sometimes I wonder how me and Nina are even related to the five people sitting in that room. All of them make me sick to my stomach. Maybe it's best if I'm married off. At least I won't have to put up with their shit anymore.

12

ISIAH

I've delayed telling Gio I'm back in town as he demands all of my time.

Learning about Alastair and Gio's side business, I need to get more intel so that I can make my move to shut him down in that respect first. There's no world in which I sit back and bide my time while he preys on children for money and power. So, I stand behind the desk of an illegal hacker called Jane as she types frantically at her keyboard.

"Can you hack into his system?" I ask, feeling my patience wearing thin.

Apparently, she's the best on this side of the pond, and I need information if I'm going to expand my plot to bring down Gio Benedetto.

"Of course, I can hack into any system." She says it as if I'm stupid, making me clench my fist. I'm not used to people speaking to me like that, not since my dad died. It makes me angry just thinking about him and the way he controlled every aspect of my life for so long.

"How long and how much will it cost?"

She taps her bottom lip and then looks up at me through her thick-rimmed glasses. "Four days and five thousand dollars."

I narrow my eyes, sensing that she knows I've got money, and that's the reason why she's exploiting me, but I don't care what it costs. "Deal."

She grins at me. "Great, I'll get all the information I can from his personal network."

"I need names and places where he runs his sick and twisted ploy to lure children."

Jane pales. "Children?" she confirms.

I nod. "Yeah, the guy is sick in the head. He gives pedophiles children in order to advance his career." Amongst other terrible things, including murdering my twin brother.

She sighs heavily. "In that case, I'll half the fee. I can't overcharge you for doing what is right."

I smile. "I thought you might have been over-charging me, but it's for a good cause." I wink. "I'll pay you five thousand dollars if you get those names in two days."

"Done," she says, holding out her hand.

I take it and shake. "Perfect. And I doubt I need to say it, but discretion is key."

"Of course, as with all my clients." She frowns at me. "What do you plan to do with the names and locations?"

This girl is too nosy for her own good. "Wouldn't you like to know?"

"Seriously, are you going to bring the bastard down, or what?"

"If you do well on this job, I'll include you in my plans for him if you like?"

"Now that's what I like to hear. I'm looking forward to it." She cracks her knuckles. "Men like him need to be put down. And of course, I'll do well. There's no one better at what I do in the States."

"Tomorrow at four o'clock, I'll be back with the money for the names and addresses."

"You've got it, boss." She salutes. "I'll see you tomorrow."

I turn around. "I'll see myself out."

She doesn't respond as she begins typing frantically on her computer. Jane is no doubt going to be the perfect assistant here in Washington for all my tech needs. Slowly, I intend to build a small yet capable team here in Washington to help me take down the Benedetto family.

I have the people I use regularly in London for hacking, but I need someone local. Someone who knows the way networks are set up over here. And someone who couldn't be traced back to London and, in turn, me.

As I step out of her flat, I'm careful to check the corridor is empty. The last thing I need is anyone following me.

James Wick knows my true identity, and that's

dangerous. He could rat me out to Gio or Cathal, but I sense that showing his hand may reveal some of his own secrets too, secrets he doesn't want unveiled. Otherwise, I'm sure he would have outed me by now.

My phone rings and it's an unknown number.

"Hello?"

"Isiah, it's Cathal."

My heart plummets as I wonder whether I was wrong. Has James told him the truth?

"How did you get my number?"

He chuckles. "Don't worry, Gio gave it to me."

I relax a little at the lightness in his tone. "I see. How can I help?"

"I'm thinking about proposing to Nina Benedetto."

It's not a surprise, but I think it's a bad idea. She's not mentally stable. "And?"

"Can you meet me for a drink this evening to mull over it? As you are the only one, other than James, who has spent a lot of time with her."

I swallow hard, unsure about meeting my former best friend for a drink. Anytime I'm around him, I'm on edge, waiting for him to suddenly recognize me. "Sure, just text me a place and time."

"Thanks, I appreciate it." He ends the call.

I've got to make sure that Cathal never learns the truth, as it could scupper my plans entirely. So tonight, I'll be careful. The last thing I need is my former friend ruining everything I've worked for.

Feeling on edge, I step into the dimly lit bar of the Waldorf. Cathal is sitting at the end, nursing a glass of clear liquid.

I've got to admit, it took me by surprise when he called earlier.

He requested this meeting to discuss the possibility of him proposing to Nina Benedetto. Since I'm so close to the family, he wants my insight, which is ironic.

And if I'm honest, I'm going to tell him not to do it.

Nina Benedetto is more complicated than it's worth. And I've seen them together. It's clear he's more eager for the match than she is, and that can never go well. I instantly register the irony as Bella couldn't be less interested in marrying me, but I'm not considering her as a wife for any other reason than to exact my revenge.

"Thanks for meeting me." He stands and claps me on the shoulder.

I reply with a barely perceptible nod.

His gaze lingers on me a little too long, making me wonder if he's about to have an epiphany and remember me as I slide onto the bar stool next to him.

"What will you have?" Cathal asks, as he motions for the bartender's attention.

"Whiskey, neat."

Cathal orders the whiskey and we wait in palpable silence.

After she delivers my drink, his expression hardens as his eyes settle directly upon mine.

"So...what do you think?" he asks, narrowing his gaze slightly.

I tilt my head. "About?"

"Nina, of course."

I tap my fingers on the bar top. "Do you want my honest opinion?" I'll give him it because if he doesn't marry her it benefits me. I don't want to have to make an enemy out of Cathal for bringing her family down.

"Of course, no bullshit. Tell it to me straight."

"She's a train wreck waiting to happen."

His brow furrows. "What do you mean?"

"Did you know that she's attempted to take her life multiple times?"

He swallows hard and shakes her head. "No, first I'm hearing of it. How did you find that out?"

"It took some digging, but I did extensive research on Bella's family before accepting the invite to visit as a potential suitor."

He runs a hand through his messy hair. "Fuck."

"I'm just saying she'd be a complicated wife."

Cathal draws in a deep breath. "I really like her, though."

I hold my hands up. "Don't take my word for it. I'm merely giving you my opinion. She's not quite right mentally."

He shakes his head. "I'm not sure I can be dealing

with that shit along with everything else that I've got going on. My brother's death being one thing."

I arch a brow, as I'm pretty certain that Cathal was behind his death. It's the rumor that Cathal killed his brother to take control. "His death or his murder?" I ask.

Cathal's eyes flash. "Careful, Darcy."

I'm not scared of Cathal. "Or what?"

His jaw clenches. "I don't wish to discuss my brother or his death." The tone of his voice drips with guilt.

I struggle to understand how anyone can kill their own brother, but I did know his brother, and the guy was an arrogant asshole.

"Fair enough," I say, holding up my hands in defeat. "Back to the matter at hand?"

He nods. "Nina seems like she's so put together."

I shrug. "Yeah, I think she's fine at the moment. They have her condition under control."

He sighs heavily. "Fuck, I can't have a basket case on my hands."

"What are you going to do?"

"I guess I'll have to cut ties."

"I think it's best," I agree, thankful that hopefully after tonight I'll see less of Cathal. Seeing him stirs up emotions and memories I'm not ready to deal with. When we were kids, it was always the three of us hanging out. Cathal, Aiden and me. I hate constantly running into him, as Aiden isn't here anymore, and to make it even harder, he doesn't even remember me.

My emotions surrounding this man are complicated.

"So, enough about Nina," he says, a look of hurt in his eyes at the mere mention of her name. I sense he really loves her. "Tell me more about the great Isiah Darcy." His eyes flash with what I can only describe as playfulness.

I shake my head. "There's not much to tell."

Cathal sighs. "Shall we cut the bullshit, Joe?"

I straighten, my entire body as rigid as a board. "What?"

"Did you really think that I wouldn't recognize one of my best friends?" A tightness spreads through my chest as I shake my head. "How long?"

"Since the party for Bella."

"Why did you pretend like you believed me when I said I wasn't Joe?"

He tilts his head. "I decided to humor you."

I shut my eyes, realizing that I'm going to have to tell Cathal my story and hope that he doesn't rat me out to the Benedetto family. "Because I couldn't risk it."

"You want revenge on the Benedetto family, right?"

I nod.

"Where's Aiden?"

That question is the hardest anyone has ever asked me since his death. No one knows what happened to our family. No doubt Cathal presumed all of us were dead. I feel my throat trying to close up,

122

but still the tears won't come. "In Dumbarton Oaks Park."

Cathal's frowns. "What?"

"Buried in an unmarked grave the night we lost everything to those bastards."

Cathal's eyes immediately fill with tears and, in a way, I envy him. At least he can cry. "Fuck, I'm so sorry." A solemn silence falls between us for a short while before he nods. "It makes sense why you'd want them to pay." I notice the way his jaw clenches. "But did you really think I'd get in the way of that plan?"

I shake my head. "We've not seen each other for fifteen years. I didn't know what to think."

Cathal swallows. "What are you going to do?"

"Destroy them all," I say.

Cathal's brow hitches up. "As in, every Benedetto?"

I nod.

"But Nina hasn't done anything, neither has Bella."

I narrow my eyes. "None of their children have done anything, but they are Benedettos. All of them are the same."

"I beg to differ. Nina and Bella are different. They're not like the rest of the family."

He's right, they're not, but it doesn't change anything.

"You're blinded by rage, Joe."

I shake my head. "Don't call me that!" I snap.

He gives me a pitying look, one that only deepens my anger. "Aiden was everything to you. I get it."

"You don't. You can't."

He nods. "No, I can't understand what it's like to be a twin, but I was close to Aiden, too." His lips purse together. "When you both disappeared, I searched for years for you two. What happened?"

I shake my head. "His death haunts me to this day," I murmur, still feeling the memories of Aiden's death, like a perpetual nightmare replaying in my head.

The pain of having to dig Aiden's grave while my father hurried me along with cold indifference, as if it didn't affect him at all. It still lingers deep in my bones and heart like a dark wound that will never heal.

The sound of my shovel against dirt and freshly turned earth will haunt me forever. Even after all these years, that wretched noise still lingers in my ear like a monster who refuses to be silenced.

But the worst part about that night was the moment he died. It's imprinted in my mind like a terrible nightmare that I can never stop replaying. We had been sitting at home playing video games and had ordered pizza when four men with black hoods broke in and threatened us, asking where our dad was.

To this day, I still don't know the identity of those four men. But, I intend to find out. When we told them he wasn't here, they searched the entire place and before leaving, one of them with dark brown eyes stopped in front of the two of us and looked between us as if making a decision.

And then he shot Aiden right between the eyes without blinking.

Tell your father that's a warning from Gio Benedetto. It will be him next if he doesn't get the fuck out of town.

Aiden's expression as the bullet tore through his flesh was blank and, the blood, there was so much blood. I remember the surreal feeling of time standing still as I gazed into the dark hole I'd dug and looked at his lifeless body wrapped in an old tarp. It's not the way I should have said goodbye, making the pain too deep for words to express. Our promise to stay together no matter where life took us was broken in an instant, and it was too late to do anything about it.

I shake my head. "I can't talk about it. Let's just say the Benedetto family is the reason he's dead."

Cathal nods. "I get that, but you should consider sparing Nina and Bella from your plan. Don't let this anger consume you or damage what you both stood for: mercy and compassion." His eyes are blazing with determination. "You both hated how your father was with people. Don't turn into him."

His words cut deep and my immediate reaction is anger. "I'm nothing like him."

"Then prove it," Cathal says.

I know deep down he's right. All the Benedetto children are innocent, to an extent. Although, Cain, Maria and Luciana are very much like their parents.

It's not them that I'm angry at. It's Gio Benedetto. He's the reason Aiden is dead and buried. Yet, waiting this long for revenge has made my need for it deepen and widen to encase everyone who bears the same name as him.

I look Cathal in the eye. "I'll think about it," I say simply.

He smiles and lifts his glass up. "Cheers to that."

I clink my glass against his and take a long swig, a weight lifted from my shoulders having my friend back, even if it does make me a little uneasy.

13

ISIAH

"Y ou weren't gone nearly long enough," a sweet voice speaks from behind me in the entranceway of the Benedetto's home. "I'm disappointed."

I smirk and turn to her, my gaze settling on those vivid blue eyes of hers. "Your lips say one thing, but your eyes tell a different story, love."

"They don't," she snaps, crossing her arms over her chest.

My lips quirk, and I take a step closer. "I see want every single time you look at me." I lean forward toward her. "Especially since I made you come for me."

My words send an inferno blazing across her cheeks. "Go to hell," she hisses.

A smirk tugs at my lips as I take another step forward. "That's certainly no way to speak to your fiancé, is it?"

I watch as the fight drains from her body, as she has nothing to say in return. There's no denying the fact that in a few short hours, our fates will be bound together—sealed by a contract that will outline the terms of our upcoming nuptials—and there will be no turning back.

I step even closer so that our bodies are flush against each other. "If I didn't know any better, I'd say you missed me."

"I didn't miss you one bit!"

I chuckle, a deep sound. "I can still hear your moans while I made you climax for me, love. I remember you crying out my name."

"God! Will you just stop?" she hisses, her mouth thinning into a tight line. There's no denying the heat radiating from our bodies as my gaze remains glued to hers.

"I hope you two aren't already arguing," Gio chides, approaching.

I take a step back from her and put some distance between us, trying to douse the fire that's ignited inside me. Gio may have laid his cards on the table, but until a deal is set in stone, I won't risk my plan.

"Just some friendly debating," I lie.

"Bullshit," Bella says, glaring at me. "As always, he's been an arrogant son of a bitch."

"Bella," Gio growls, eyes narrowing. "You don't speak to your fiancé like that."

I chuckle. "Don't worry, I quite like how fiery she is."

He arches a brow. "You don't think she'll be too much of a burden?"

"You do realize I'm standing right here?" Bella asks, looking offended that we're talking about her as if she isn't.

Gio shakes his head. "Isiah, will you join me in my study before dinner?"

I smirk at Bella, who won't stop staring daggers at me. "Of course, I'd love to." I notice the way she clenches her fists by her sides. "Lead the way."

Gio does that as we walk away from my fiancée without another word directed at her.

"Motherfuckers," I hear her mutter to herself, making me laugh. Luckily, Gio doesn't hear, as I don't think he'd be so forgiving as me.

When we enter Gio's study, I take a deep breath and take stock of my surroundings to see if there's anything that could help me with my plans. Anything I missed the first time I was in here with Cathal, James, and Cain.

There are shelves lined with books and artifacts that are no doubt old family heirlooms. The desk is large and made of sturdy hardwood, and no doubt passed down from generation after generation. A rich history that I intend to bring to an end. On the walls hang paintings of people I can only assume are ancestors of Gio Benedetto.

I take a seat opposite Gio, and he gives me an expectant look. "We must discuss the logistics of you marrying my daughter."

In other words, he wants to know just how rich he will get from an alliance with me and my organization. "I believe that we'll both benefit greatly from an alliance."

He nods in agreement. "Of course. But what is it you can give me?"

At least he cut right to the chase.

"Money and influence to name just two."

He smirks. "And how about a chance for the two of us to sell into each other's territories?"

"You want to see your heroin in London?" I confirm.

He nods eagerly. "Yes, and you can sell your cocaine here in Washington. Together we can take the two cities by storm."

It's ambitious and if it weren't for the fact I intend to kill this man, I'd say it's a good plan. "Okay, we can figure out the details with my man. I'll have to fly him here to do the deal, as well as my solicitor."

"Smart man," he says, standing and walk over to a dresser with decanters full of liquor. "A drink?"

"Whiskey, if you have it."

"Of course."

He pours us both a drink and then returns, passing me a crystal tumbler with a large helping of whiskey. "How soon would you like to wed my daughter?" And then, to my disgust, he sits down next to me.

Despite my skin crawling at having to be so civil to the man responsible for Aiden's death, I force myself to consider the question. I don't want to appear overly eager. "Well, my man and solicitor should be able to visit within a week. And then say another week to sort out all the paperwork." I run a hand across the back of my neck. "Then there are the marriage licenses. How long do they take here?"

He chuckles. "Don't worry about that. We'll have one within twenty-four hours if we want." Clapping my shoulder, he announces, "One month should be plenty of time, don't you think?"

"I would think so, yes." One month is too long in my eyes, but I can't seem desperate. It means another thirty-one days of playing this false role as a man who actually likes the Benedetto family.

"Perfect. Shall we have some dinner now?" Gio polishes off his whiskey and I copy him.

"Sounds good."

He leads the way out of his study and into the dining room, where the others have already started eating. I'm surprised when I see Cathal Bingley is here, especially considering how our conversation went yesterday evening. It sets me on edge that now my secret is not so secure. Although, Cathal claims he knew the first time we met. The way he was talking, he intended to call things off with Nina Benedetto. Unless he's letting her down gently.

Cathal notices me and smiles. "I hear you've struck a deal for the beautiful Bella?"

Bella grunts. "Not if I have anything to say about it."

"You don't," her mom says simply.

I smirk at her. "We'll be married within a month, love, get used to the idea."

She sticks her fingers down her throat and makes a puking sound, much to her mom's disgust.

Even as she acts like she's disgusted by the idea, I know it's not true. She wants me as deeply as I want her. This magnetic attraction between us is impossible to deny, even if it does blur the lines between me and the woman I intend to destroy along with her family.

"Can we stop talking all about Bella and her wedding!" Luciana exclaims, as always dissatisfied by any topic of conversation that doesn't revolve around her. "Cathal has invited us to his home for a party next week."

"Are we all invited?" I ask in a mocking tone.

Cathal laughs. "Of course. I wouldn't exclude you, Darcy."

"Thanks," I say, leaning toward Bella. "Another night we can spend together."

"Over my dead body!"

I shake my head. "When are you going to stop fighting this and just accept you and I are happening?"

"Never," she says defiantly.

"You're very stubborn," I whisper, snaking my hand under the hem of her dress. "Maybe I should finger fuck that stubbornness right out of you at dinner."

Her eyes widen as she glares at me. "You wouldn't dare!"

It appears my fiancée doesn't know me very well if she thinks that I wouldn't feel her up under the table at a family dinner. "How much would you like to bet?" My fingers slip into her knickers and I rub her clit, making her tense.

She slaps my hand away. "What the fuck?" she hisses.

"Don't pretend like your pussy isn't dripping for me right now," I whisper into her ear. Leaning even closer, I run my tongue along the shell of her ear. "Be a good girl and let your fiancé touch you."

"No way!"

I bite her earlobe. "You forget that I don't care about consent." Sliding my fingers back into her underwear, I slam them inside her and groan at the slick arousal coating them. "You're so fucking wet, love."

"Pig," she says, but some of the fight has gone from her tone and her cheeks are flushed. I can't take my eyes off of her cleavage as it swells with each breath she takes, clearly wound up by me.

"Why are you denying it? You want me as badly as I want you, Bella."

"That's a lie."

"What's a lie?" Nina asks, no doubt noticing her sister's distress.

Bella turns beet red. "Nothing," she mutters,

clearly not wanting to admit that right now she's being fingered by her fiancé for obvious reasons.

Nina glares at me, looking like she's about ready to murder me.

"So, Cathal. I hear you've struck a lucrative deal with the new leader of the Estrada Cartel. Is that right?" I ask.

Gio scoffs, "It's fucking ridiculous, having a Russian at the head of the cartel in North America." He shakes his head. "Next we'll be run by the Irish." He shudders, clearly forgetting that he is literally sitting with the leader of the Irish in Washington. The tension in the room thickens, a suffocating blanket of apprehension and fear. We all know he isn't just talking about the Estrada cartel anymore.

The icy glint in Cathal's blue eyes was enough to show for that.

Gio regrets his comment. "What are you saying about the Irish?"

"I mean that we should be led by our own, that's all. Would you like an Italian taking over your organization?"

It was like a lightning bolt had struck the room; I hadn't seen such a powerful stare from him before, making me reconsider Cathal's strength as a leader. "No, of course not. But the deal was too good to pass up," he says, maintaining calm despite the storm raging in his eyes.

Gio nods. "Business is business."

That same fucking phrase he used when talking

about facilitating a pedophile. My stomach churns and my hatred for this man burns deeper and harder than ever before. Jane better come through with the information I need soon, as I have to start deconstructing everything Gio has built in Washington, just like he did to my family. He's a snake that doesn't deserve anything that he has, least of all a daughter like Bella.

Suddenly she grabs onto my forearm and squeezes hard, probably because this entire time I've been fingering her sweet little cunt and I can feel she's getting close. Her muscles gripping my fingers like a vise.

"Isiah," she hisses my name. "Stop it."

I smirk as I meet her beautiful oceanic gaze, which is full of pleasure and rage. "You know that's not what you want," I whisper into her ear. "You want to come for me right here in front of your entire family."

Her nails dig harder into my forearm as she tries desperately to stop the oncoming tidal wave of pleasure, but it's impossible.

I skate my thumb over her clit and she comes apart beautifully. Her teeth sink into her bottom lip as she makes a soft whimpering sound that's drowned out by the surrounding chatter. As the pleasure erupts through her body, she digs her nails in even harder, making my cock turn to stone at the pain and knowing that I've made her come here, of all places.

It's about time my fiancée gave something back in return, and after dinner, I'm determined to ensure that she finally does. I grab her hand and place it on my cock, noting the way her breathing labors as she feels my hardness against her palm.

"Do you feel how hard I am for you, love?" I ask.

She tries to hide the shudder of pleasure coursing through her body, failing miserably. Her eyes widen with arousal, yet she manages to utter a feeble, "Stop it," in response.

I smirk, pulling my slick fingers out of her cunt before pressing them against her soft lips. All I want to do is make her suck them clean, but I know it would draw too much attention. Instead, I reach into my briefs and jerk my cock a few times, coating it with her arousal. I groan in pleasure at the sensation and then force myself to focus on anything but the sweet temptation sitting next to me.

My ever-growing desire for Bella Benedetto is a complication I never foresaw, and yet it's one I don't mind exploring further—that is, until she's fulfilled all of my sick and twisted desires. Then, just like all the other members of her pathetic family, I'll destroy her and burn her world to the ground.

14

BELLA

There's a knock on my bedroom door thirty minutes after I head up, making me stiffen.

It's certainly not Nina, because she doesn't knock. Nina has a key, just like me. And I sensed she would be staying up pretty late since Cathal is here.

Standing, I walk over to the door. "Who is it?" I call.

"Open the door, Bella." That sinful, dark voice speaks from the other side.

"Go away," I shout back, feeling butterflies flutter to life in the pit of my stomach.

There's an ominous silence before he speaks again. "I would do as you're told if I were you."

I place my hand on the solid wood door, knowing that he can't get to me, not in here. "My dad wouldn't be impressed if he knew you were trying to break into my bedroom."

He laughs wickedly. "That's what you think, but

he suggested that I come and see you and spend some time alone with you."

I glare at the door, wondering if that's true. Is my dad really that sick that he'd send a predator into my bedroom without a thought?

"I don't believe you."

"And I don't care. Open. The. Door."

"Or what?" I ask.

"Or I'll break it down," he says, completely serious.

I realize that there's every chance that this man will make good on that and break the door down. He's a formidable opponent to reckon with.

"Okay," I say simply, unlocking the door and jerking it open.

Isiah stands tall in the hallway with a lethal darkness swirling around him; he cuts a striking figure silhouetted in the moonlight shining through the window at the end of the corridor.

Instead of speaking, he stares at me in silence, as if waiting for me to break it. I hold his gaze, not wanting to submit to him in any way, especially not after how he's talked countless times about dominating me.

"Aren't you going to invite me in, love?" he says after what feels like an eternity.

I shake my head. "I'd rather not."

Isiah rolls his eyes, pushing past me and into my room. He takes a few steps before turning to face me again. His piercing gaze craves my submission and I feel the need to deny him, no matter what. "What do you want?" I ask, my voice barely over a whisper.

He grins as he strides closer, invading my personal space. His fingers slide into my hair as he tips my chin up toward him with his other hand. He stares deeply into my eyes before finally speaking. "I want you."

My heart rate starts to race as I try to back away from him, hating the way my body reacts to his words. Ever since that night in the ladies' bathroom when he fingered me to orgasm, it's been impossible to forget. He reaches for me, grabbing my hips and tightening his grip on me. Slowly, each step pushes me closer to the wall until I'm trapped against it. He leans in closer and presses his body against mine, imprisoning me between him and the brickwork as he holds me in place.

I can feel the heat radiating off of him and it's almost too much for me to handle. Before I have time to think about it, Isiah captures my lips with his own in an all-consuming kiss that leaves me breathless when he finally pulls away.

"You're mine," he whispers before tracing a path down the side of my neck with feathery light kisses that send shivers through my body despite how much I wish they didn't affect me.

Before I can gather myself enough to protest or push him away, Isiah slides one hand around to cup my breast while his other slips between us and snakes its way under my nightgown and into my panties.

"Stop it," I gasp, feeling transported back to that

bathroom and dinner in an instant. As before, this isn't consensual, but I don't have the strength to make him stop. A part of me wants this, and even though I told him to stop, my body cries in protest when he does.

He pulls away and whispers in my ear, "Now kneel."

My breath hitches as I feel his words sink into my skin, sending a jolt of electricity through me.

"No," I say, my voice wavering as I try to sound strong.

Isiah's eyes flash dangerously as his grip tightens on my hips, and then he grabs a fistful of my hair again, yanking my neck back unnaturally to look up at him.

"Since we're definitely going to be married, I'd think carefully about how you play this, love."

I swallow hard. "I won't kneel for you."

"It's your turn, love. I've made you come twice." An evil smirk twists onto his lips and he grabs my throat, pushing me down to my knees and pressing me into the ground with such force that I am left in no doubt of who is in charge. He stares at me for a few moments, watching as I submit against my will to him before finally speaking.

"Good girl," he murmurs, releasing his grip on me. "Now you know your place."

I glare at him. "My place is with my hands around your fucking throat."

"Then why are you on your knees?"

I move to stand, but he grabs the back of my neck, making it impossible for me to rise any further from this position.

"Don't." One word, but it's said in a way that sends a chill through my body. I slowly lower myself back down onto my knees and look up at him, hating the way he smirks with satisfaction before unzipping his pants.

My body heats as he takes out his cock and places it right in front of me, commanding that I take it in my mouth without saying a single word.

A deep ache ignites within me at the sight of it, hard and veiny, a drip of precum at the end begging to be licked off.

What the hell is wrong with me?

"Do you like what you see, love?" he asks, his voice has a raspy quality to it. "I bet your cunt is dripping wet, wishing it was filled up with my cock right now."

"Like hell it is!"

He chuckles. "Unfortunately, I'm not in a position to check yet. But once you've swallowed every drop of my cum, I'll confirm."

"You're a piece of shit, Isiah."

My insults always seem to just rebound off of him as if he's made of stone.

"Open your mouth wide."

I clamp my mouth shut, even though deep down I know it's futile.

His grip tightens around the back of my neck to

keep me still as I try to move away. "Stop trying to fight the inevitable."

For once, his words penetrates my soul as I slump in defeat, knowing that if I don't obey him, he will only keep pushing harder until I do as he says.

Relinquishing, I open my mouth wide, allowing him access to the depths of my throat. His thick cock slides in inch by inch, sending terror spiking through my veins as I gag around him.

He holds me still, refusing to let me escape from his grasp. "You're not going anywhere until you've swallowed every single drop of my cum."

He starts to rock his hips, thrusting into my throat as if he is fucking me. Each movement feels like he's trying to rip my throat apart. My mind flashes with horror as I desperately try to breathe but find it almost impossible. The only thing I can do is endure him and pray that it will be over soon.

"It would be easier if you stopped freaking out and breathed through your nose, love."

I glare at him, which only seems to spur him on. Yet, I can't disobey him in this position and the moment I take his advice, my entire body relaxes. Oxygen flooding my lungs enough for me to not think I'm about to die. And I hate to say as he continues to use my throat, fucking it and grunting above me, my pussy starts to drip with arousal.

His hips rock back and forth, faster and harder, forcing me to moan around his thick girth.

"That's it, Bella. Moan around my cock," he

growls, his fingers tightening around the back of my neck as he shoves himself even harder into the back of my throat. "Fuck. Open that throat for me just like that."

The terror that had once spiked through my veins was now replaced by an inexplicable pleasure that makes me tremble in anticipation of more, despite everything.

I'm no longer under his control; I'm submitting to his will willingly, as he uses me the way he wants. A sickening and yet irrefutable truth.

His labored breathing fills the surrounding air, as I sense him getting closer.

He starts to move his hips even faster, and I feel the swell of his cock grow in my throat as he gets closer to release.

He groans loudly above me, head thrown back, as he releases my neck for the first time. The pleasure is written all over his face as his cum shoots into the back of my throat, making me gag even more as I force my eyes away from his face.

"Swallow it for me," he growls.

And when I look back at him, those ice-blue eyes are watching me intently.

"Every fucking drop."

I swallow, drinking down his seed willingly as my pussy throbs with need. It's shameful. The taste of him fills my mouth, and I can't help but moan. A feeling of power surges through me as I know that I made him come.

"Good girl, Bella. You'll make a wonderful wife," he says.

Fire rips through me as I feel his pleasure subside and reality hits me like a ton of bricks. "You're a fucking bastard."

Time is quickly running out, and I hear Nina's footsteps coming down the hall, forcing me to scramble to my feet. "Shit, you've got to get out of here—Nina's going to be here any second."

Isiah casually stuffs his cock back into his pants and takes a step closer to me, his fingers digging into the back of my neck. His knowing smirk only amplifies the fire I can already feel raging inside me. "Shame I don't get time to taste you, but maybe next time," he murmurs, as if he can sense my disappointment.

My nostrils flare as anger spikes through me, but a part of me is disappointed there wasn't any time. And then he yanks me into him, pressing his lips against mine in one final passionate kiss, no doubt tasting his own arousal on my tongue.

A low rumble comes from his chest, almost undoing me. Right now, I wish I didn't share a bedroom, as I need to come more than I've ever needed to in my entire life.

The door swings open and Nina gasps when she sees us there.

"Don't worry, I was just leaving," he says, giving me a smug smirk. "Sweet dreams, love."

And then he turns around and walks arrogantly

past Nina and out of the room without another word spoken between us.

Nina stares at me in confusion, but I've got no answers for her. What just happened between us I have no explanation for. It was downright wrong and I hate that I enjoyed it.

15

ISIAH

I walk back into Jane's flat two days after I gave her the job to find her buried under a mound of paperwork.

"Man, this shit you sent me after." She shakes her head. "I've uncovered a fucking pedophile ring run by the man you asked me to hack. It's deep-rooted and even has links to the fucking government."

I swallow hard as all I really needed was a way to hurt Gio, not get entangled in something this complicated. "Are you saying he's the ringleader?"

Jane shakes her head. "No, but he's instrumental to the entire thing. He's the way they get the children."

"How?" I ask, needing to know how exactly that sick bastard lures the kids.

"He has connections with about twenty school principals that run schools outside the city. Turns out, they send him kids in return for keeping quiet for their own sick and twisted desire for kids."

"Are you fucking serious?" I ask.

She nods. "I'm afraid so."

"How the hell do pedophiles end up running schools?"

"Beats me."

My chest clenches in anger.

"He gets the school children and has them auctioned off to the highest bidder. Each event is highly exclusive and invite only."

"Jesus," I cringe, feeling sick to the stomach. "Do you know how he even gets the kids from the school?"

"The principal of each school targets a certain child and adds a special something to their food and water to make them sick." She shrugs. "That forces them to miss school the next day. And then he has them kidnapped from their home." She looks up at me again. "Obviously, he has to work with numerous schools to avoid rousing suspicion. If lots of kids kept going missing from the same school, there'd be an uproar."

I shake my head. "And you have the names of everyone involved?" I confirm.

"Every single bastard."

"Good." The hatred I've harbored toward Gio Benedetto is deepening the more I learn about him. Not only did he bring about my twin brother's death, he's also instrumental in a pedophile ring. I should have realized at that meeting with Alastair. It wasn't a one off. He makes a shit ton of money doing it.

"Do you know where the auctions happen?"

She shakes her head. "I can't find it yet, but I'm still digging. Gio knows, and you're close to him. Can't you enquire?"

I run a hand across the back of my neck, regretting how dismissive I was of Alastair at the meeting before, as Gio wouldn't dare even mention the auction to me. "He knows my opinion on the subject and wouldn't be very forthcoming."

"Shit," Jane says, typing frantically at her computer. "I'll find it. It's got to be here."

"Maybe the location changes each time?"

She arches a brow. "It's possible."

"I need to know where the next one is going to be taking place." I slide my hand into my pocket to pull out the envelope of cash. "Can you keep working on this for me?" I pass the envelope to her.

"Sure thing." She takes the money. "I'd do this for free, but a girl's got to pay rent."

I laugh. "I wouldn't let you do it for free."

"So, I think I'll need a few days if I'm honest about digging deeper into this."

"Okay, I'll give you fifteen thousand dollars if you can get me the next location and date. I'm going to throw a spanner in the works, no matter what it takes."

She stops typing and turns to really look at me. "I don't say this very often, but I like you."

The girl is socially awkward, but I've got to admit I like her too. "Thanks, right back at you."

Jane gets an odd look in her eyes. "Anyone who will put their neck on their line to help children is a saint in my books." I sense that she has past trauma of abuse just from the look in her eyes and how important this is to her.

"I'm definitely not a saint."

Even in her silence, I feel her knowing this bond of understanding pulls us together. And then she says it—a phrase so potent and weighted with meaning, it takes me aback. "You're tortured like me," she states, as if she can see right to my soul and the trauma that I harbor over losing Aiden.

I'm taken aback by the emotion that suddenly swells within my heart. We're the same—broken by our pasts and driven by them—even if the source of our pain is not the same. "Perhaps," I reply with a small nod, feeling as if I can trust her, something that doesn't come easy to me.

"Count me in on this journey," she continues, her gaze unwavering as she speaks. "Wherever it takes us."

I nod. "I will."

A thick silence settles between us as I linger and observe the peace that radiates from her as she begins to work again. At that moment, I feel like I belong somewhere for the first time in ages—even if it doesn't make much sense.

"WHAT IS THIS ALL ABOUT?" Bella asks, sitting across from me at the little family run Italian restaurant I know she loves, as Gio suggested I bring her here.

I tilt my head. "Your father suggested we start to get to know each other a little better before the wedding."

"You know, I've been trying to work out why a man from Britain would come all this way just to marry me." Her eyes narrow. "I sense you have an ulterior motive behind wanting to tie the knot, and I have every intention of discovering what that motive is."

A chill runs through me, as clearly Bella is more intuitive than I anticipated. If she unearths my plan, I'd be in deep trouble, but I'm not really worried because I cover my tracks well. "My only reason for marrying you is that it will strengthen my organization with a formidable ally."

"Thousands of miles away?" she challenges.

I nod. "It's best that way. Less competition and your father is doing the same thing, wanting to expand across the pond."

Her eyes narrow as there's no refuting the fact that her father is indeed doing the same thing. "Even so, I don't buy it," she says.

A half smile plays on my lips as I study her closely. Over the past few weeks, I've gotten to know her well and each day, she astonishes me with her courage and intelligence. Sitting opposite her, I wonder if she's aware of how much of a monster her father truly is.

"And I don't care." I grab her hand and squeeze. "You're going to be mine one way or another. It's futile to try to clutch at straws in an attempt to find something to get you out of this wedding, because there's nothing to find."

She crosses her arms over her chest as the server comes over.

"Hey Bella," he says, giving her a dazzling smile. "It's been a while since I've seen you in here."

"Hey Enzo," she replies, hardly looking at him as she continues to glare daggers at me.

"Who's your friend?" Enzo asks, a look of jealousy in his eyes.

It's amusing really, as he's just a boy. Hardly a suitable match for a formidable woman like Bella. That thought makes me pause as I wonder when I stopped thinking of her as a Benedetto and rather as a formidable woman in her own right. She's no different from the rest of them, except annoyingly she is; Smart, independent and selfless, unlike the rest of them, except perhaps Nina, who seems complicated but different from her family.

And as that thought echoes in my mind, so does Cathal's plea to spare her and the Benedetto children. I'm still not convinced.

This world would be a better one if no Benedetto existed within it. Cain is practically a clone of his father.

"This is Isiah," she says somewhat dismissively.

"Her fiancé," I add.

She glares at me. "You are not my fiancé."

The boy, Enzo, looks dumbfounded as he glances between the two of us. "So, he's your boyfriend, then?"

Bella shakes her head. "Definitely not."

"Soon to be husband."

Enzo's brow furrows. "Right, sounds complicated. Can I get you some drinks?"

She smiles flirtatiously at Enzo and I feel a possessive rage claw at my heart. "Sure, you know what I like," she says, placing a hand on his forearm. I'm pretty sure she's doing it to piss me off.

"Bella," I say her name in a deep tone in an attempt to warn her.

Enzo's cheeks flush and he glances at me, turning pale the moment he sees my expression. "Of course, pinot noir, right?" He takes a step away so her hand falls off of his forearm.

"That's right," she says.

Bella shakes her head opposite, glaring at me disapprovingly, but I don't give a shit. This kid has the hots for her and it's pathetic.

"And what can I get you, sir?" he asks, rightfully realizing when he's in the presence of his superior. I'd tear this boy apart if he even tried anything with her.

"Single malt on the rocks." I narrow my eyes. "Macallan, if you have it."

He swallows hard. "I'll check what we've got," he says, rushing away from the table at speed.

"Do you have to be so rude to people?" Bella asks, glaring at me.

I lean forward and grab her hand firmly. "Let's make something very clear here," I say, holding her gaze. "You'll stay away from boys like Enzo now that I'm a part of your life, unless you want to be the reason his head is severed from his body."

Her eyes widen at the threat as she visibly shudders.

"Do you understand?"

Her lips purse, but she just gives me a small nod, aware that she's sitting opposite a killer. She knows what I'm capable of and she knows I wouldn't hesitate to make an example out of a boy like Enzo if he flirted too much with what is mine.

"Now, what are you going to order?" I ask, glancing at the menu.

"I'm not hungry," she mutters.

I glare at her. "Your dad assured me this is your favorite restaurant. Don't be immature."

"Immature?" she asks, that fiery rage blazing to life in her vibrant blue eyes. "You just told me you'd cut a boy's head off and you expect me to have an appetite?"

I roll my eyes as she's being dramatic. "It's nothing your dad wouldn't do." I scan the menu. "I reckon you are into pasta, am I right?"

Her eyes narrow. "Everyone is into pasta."

"I bet I can pick your favorite dish from this menu."

She watches me for a few minutes and then nods. "I bet you can't."

"Spinach and ricotta cannelloni," I say.

Her eyes widen for a split second. "My dad told you, didn't he?"

I shake my head. "No, you can ask him yourself. I'm good at reading people."

She scowls. "I bet that Italian food isn't your favorite, am I right?"

"No, it's not my favorite."

"What is?" she demands.

"Indian food."

Her eyes narrow. "Really? I don't think I've ever had Indian food."

"We'll have to change that. It's popular in Britain."

Her lips curl into a sneer. "I don't think I'd like it."

"How do you know if you haven't tried it?"

Enzo returns then with our drinks, serving them and putting an end to our conversation.

"Thanks," Bella says, making sure she barely makes eye contact with the boy. Clearly, I've scared her with my threat to murder him.

Enzo doesn't linger, rushing away the moment I glare at him.

"Cheers," I say, holding my glass up.

All I get in response is a withering glare. "There's nothing to toast."

"Did you know you can be very rude at times, love?"

She takes a deliberate sip of her drink and regards me with disdain over the rim of her glass. "I don't really care."

I smirk, my lips curving into a sneer. "Oh, I can change that, Bella. I'll show you just how a real man disciplines a woman."

Her lips part at the sexual connotations. "Don't be an asshole."

"I won't hesitate to put you over my knee and give you a good spanking," I reply, noting the husky tone of my voice as my cock hardens at the thought.

She trembles, her cheeks flushed a deep red. "You're never going to get your hands on me, so don't even think about trying it."

I laugh and the cruelness laces my words. "Oh, sweetheart, once we're married, you won't have a choice. You'll simply be my toy to use for my pleasure and nothing more."

Her nostrils flare and she moves to stand, forcing me to grab her wrist. "Where do you think you're going?"

"I'm not staying here and listening to this," she spits.

"Yes, you are Bella." My voice is like steel, and I hold her gaze in a battle of wills. "So help me God."

Finally, she relents and sinks back into her seat. "I've never held so much dislike for someone before I met you."

"Is that right?" I ask, narrowing my eyes. "Shame you have to marry me, then, isn't it?"

Her nostrils flare, but she doesn't respond. Instead, she just downs the entirety of her glass of wine. "I'm going to need more wine."

"Alcohol won't change the fact that you're mine, Bella."

"Give it a rest."

I grab her knee under the table and squeeze. "No. I'll give it a rest once you submit to me."

"I'll submit to you once I'm fucking dead inside."

It's amusing how determined she is to resist, when all along there's been a palpable attraction that neither of us can deny. "You are attracted to me and if you say you aren't, you're a liar."

"Fine," she grinds out, her cheeks flushing red. "You're attractive, but you're also a jerk. I can't stand your personality."

I scoff and hold a hand to my chest. "You wound me," I say in a mocking tone. But I can't help feeling a little hurt by her opinion. I don't blame her though, I'm treating her badly, exactly how Gio would expect me to act. And, in life, I've never exactly been good to women. Having never had a female role model growing up, since my mom died during mine and Aiden's birth, I only had my dad's example to follow, which was pretty rotten.

"Let's eat and get the hell out of here."

I arch a brow. "Fine."

We fall into an uncomfortable silence as the rest

of the evening progresses, and I start to question my entire approach when it comes to Bella Benedetto. As part of me wants her to submit willingly and fall at my feet, though I know it's a highly unrealistic expectation.

16

BELLA

*I*t's been a week since my parents announced my engagement to Isiah, which immediately forced my Auntie Olivia to come and visit.

I love Olivia. She's not like the rest of my family. Nina and I have always gotten on really well with her. She's our dad's sister, who also was subjected to an arranged marriage, but it turned out well for her. Uncle Darius, the guy she married, she actually likes.

"Stop moping, Bella, it doesn't suit you."

I glare at her. "I'm sorry, but I'm just not in a good mood. My parents are forcing me to marry a stuck-up asshole."

She shakes her head. "I've got an idea," she announces.

I grab the box of cereal and pour myself some into a bowl. "What kind of idea?" I ask, adding milk.

"How about a weekend away?" she suggests.

"Does that really fix anything?"

She sighs. "It might take your mind off of things."

I shrug. "Where were you thinking?"

"How about London? You can see your future home."

"Are you suggesting this to depress me more?"

Olivia shakes her head. "At least you'll be away from him. Isiah is remaining in Washington until the wedding, as far as I'm aware." She smiles. "We can take the jet, just the two of us. No men or bullshit about the wedding."

"And you think my dad will agree?"

"I've already cleared it with him. He thought it was a good idea."

I sigh heavily. "Of course he did."

"You know Nina is heartbroken over Cathal. I shouldn't really leave her alone."

The guy was clearly no good, as he's ghosted her since the party the other week.

"Nina is going to have to learn how to toughen up and take care of herself. She's a big girl and when you are married, who will look after her then?"

I sigh heavily, as Olivia has a point. Once I'm married to the stuck-up British bastard, I'll be shipped off to London, and something tells me that Isiah wouldn't take kindly to me bringing my sister along. "You're right."

"See this as a trial run? Nina will cope."

I swallow hard. Even though Olivia is my dad's sister, she doesn't know the details of Nina's struggles with depression and the attempts she made to take her own life. "Sure, let's do it."

Olivia beams. "Perfect. I'll call your father and arrange everything. I just need you to be ready to leave by this evening."

I sigh heavily and nod. "I'll be ready," I say in defeat, spooning my cereal into my mouth despite no longer feeling hungry. A weekend away might be the perfect thing to keep my mind off of Isiah Darcy, even if only temporarily, but London seems like the last place to do it. I know better than to argue with Auntie Olivia, though, when she's got an idea in her head.

THE JET LANDS with a thud on the runway in London, jolting me awake.

"We're here!" Olivia exclaims, holding a hand to her chest. "I've always wanted to visit London."

Oh God. What have I done?

Her enthusiasm is too much, especially as I'm still bummed about my father bringing the wedding forward. In two weeks, I'll be Mrs. Bella Darcy. It makes me want to puke.

"Could you tone it down a bit, Olivia?"

She gives me a sharp look. "You need to stop moping and enjoy your freedom while you still can." Standing, she approaches me and then grabs my hand, yanking me to my feet as the jet comes to a stop. "Time to enjoy yourself and forget all about Isiah Darcy."

"Right, as if that's going to be easy in his hometown."

She rolls her eyes. "London is a huge city. Forget about him and have some fun!"

I sigh. "Fine. What's first on the agenda?"

The smirk she gives me is answer enough. "We're going shopping."

I groan. "Do we have to?"

Instead of dignifying my response with an answer, she just walks down the steps off the plane, leaving me trailing after her. No one can shop as much as Auntie Olivia, and I've never been one with a love of shopping.

After a few minutes, we get settled into the town car waiting for us and begin our drive to Oxford Street to start a grueling day of shopping. As I sit there watching England pass by outside my window; with lush rolling hills and picturesque villages that seem so unlike anything back home, my mind wanders over what surprises London might hold. Hopefully good ones.

"Maybe it won't be so bad here," I say to Olivia.

She smiles. "That's the spirit."

"How long is it to Oxford Street?"

Her brow furrows. "About an hour."

I groan. "I could go to bed right about now."

We both have a nap in the car until it pulls to a stop to let us out in the center of a concrete jungle, which is a stark contrast to the countryside we were driving through near the airstrip.

"We're here, ma'am," the driver man says.

"Great, can you park up at the hotel? We'll walk there from here."

His eyes widen. "It's not walking distance."

"Underground?" she suggests.

He nods. "Sure, you could use the underground."

"Perfect. Come on, let's go," Olivia says, jumping out of the car.

"Where are we starting?" I ask.

The smirk on Olivia's face worries me. "I've got an appointment."

"Appointment, where?"

"You'll see." She hooks her arm with mine and leads me down the street.

We walk for about five minutes until she pulls me to a stop outside of a building with a black door and presses an intercom button.

"What is this place?"

"Haute Couture Bridal," a voice says on the other end.

"You've got to be fucking kidding—"

"Hello, yes, we have an appointment at midday. The name is Benedetto."

"Oh yes, we've been waiting for you." A buzzer sounds. "Come on up."

"Olivia, you said you'd let me forget about Isiah, not come here shopping for my goddamn wedding to him that I don't even want."

"You only get married once, especially in our world. You'll leave your husband in a body bag or vice versa, so you need to do it right, even if you hate the man you are marrying." She waves her hand. "And this is the most exclusive wedding dress shop in London."

Sighing heavily, I follow her up the stairs into a very exclusive and expensive wedding gown boutique.

"You weren't kidding about exclusive," I mutter.

Olivia smiles widely. "So many gorgeous gowns!" she exclaims as a pair of assistants come forward to greet us.

I'm quickly ushered over to the dressing room while Olivia helps me select which dresses she thinks will look best on me. It's like being in a dream with all these beautiful gowns—some sleek and simple, some embellished with delicate beading or lace details that add an exquisite touch of romance to them—swirling around my feet until I am transformed into something fresh from the fairytale world. All of which would be exciting if it weren't for the heavy reality weighing on my heart.

My story is not a fairytale, it's more like a nightmare. My marriage is being forced upon me to a man I can't stand.

"You look gorgeous in every one you try," Auntie Olivia says as I come out in the third dress.

I clench my jaw, attempting to keep my composure as the tears begin to well up in my eyes. "But I don't want to marry Isiah," I choke out.

Olivia gives me a sympathetic look. "I understand why you don't want to, Bella. But unfortunately, you have no choice."

Hot tears pour down my face as I feel the crushing reality of my arranged marriage settle in.

She wraps her arm around my shoulders and murmurs, "It sucks, I know. No one should be forced to marry someone they don't love," she says, trying to console me. "But that's the way it is for us women in the mafia. We don't get to have a say when it comes to our own lives."

"You like your husband, though."

Olivia laughs a hollow laugh. "Did you really think it was like that for us from the beginning?"

My brow furrows. "It wasn't? You and Darius seem so perfect for each other."

She offers me a tender smile. "I loathed him at first, just like how you feel about Isiah right now."

"That seems impossible."

"Trust me," she says with a shake of her head, "it is more than possible. The bizarre thing about hatred is that it can be just as powerful and passionate as love."

"There's no way that I could ever love Isiah Darcy."

She purses her lips. "I wouldn't be so sure, Bella."

The assistant comes to check on us then, interrupting our conversation. "How are you getting on?"

I look at myself in the mirror and shake my head. "Not this one."

Olivia agrees, as she helps me out of it. After trying on a few more styles, we finally settle upon a stunner of an A-line dress made from layers of white tulle that almost shines when the light catches.

The intricate embroidery detail at the bodice along with iridescent sequins speckled throughout the underlay — it almost takes my breath away, but still the dress is overshadowed by who my fiancé is.

"I'm starving," I say as I go to pay for the dress.

Auntie Olivia grabs my hand and shakes her head. "This is my gift to you. You may not be too thrilled with who you are marrying, but you are going to looking amazing, anyway." She hands over her credit card.

The assistant takes it and then says the price, making me almost faint as it's ten thousand dollars.

"You can't pay for—"

"Quiet. I can and I will. Now you can buy me lunch," she says, leading me out of the shop.

"What about the dress?" I ask.

"They're shipping it to a seamstress in Washington who will do the adjustments."

I give her a pointed look. "Please tell me that this entire trip isn't about wedding shopping."

She smiles. "No, only the dress. The rest of the weekend we will sightsee like normal tourists."

"Thank God for that."

"What do you want to see first after we eat?" she asks.

"The London Eye looks pretty cool."

Olivia pales as I know she hates heights, but it's fun to wind her up. "Oh, but I—"

"I'm joking. I know you hate heights. How about Buckingham Palace?" I suggest.

All the tension eases from her shoulders as she laughs. "Sounds great."

I smile at her, but deep down I can't help but feel this heavy weight still bearing down on my chest. This is where I'm going to be carted off to once I'm married to Isiah and it couldn't feel further from home. All I want is to stay in Washington and never marry. If only I had a way to freeze time and keep my life exactly the way it is.

17

ISIAH

"Where is Bella?" I ask as I sit down at the Benedetto family table for dinner.

I never expected to be so easily welcomed into the family, so much so that they'd ask me to stay under their roof. Inviting the wolf into the sheep's pen to feast.

"She's gone to London this evening for a weekend away with Auntie Olivia," Luciana announces tactlessly.

I stiffen at the mention of my hometown. "London?" My attention moves to her father. "And she didn't think to invite me to show her around my backyard?"

Gio smirks. "It's a girls' weekend. I'd hardly think she'd appreciate her husband to be tagging along, do you?"

"A girls' weekend in my hometown." I stand. "I will join her."

Gio's brow furrows. "I think it's best you remain here."

"I think it's best I go and join her."

We enter a staring match, one which I won't back down from.

"Why exactly is it important for you to be with her this weekend?"

I cross my arms over my chest. "I expected to be the one to show Bella around London. Couldn't she have gone to Paris or some other city?"

Gio sighs. "Very well, do what you want."

"Don't tell her. I'll make it a surprise."

Luciana laughs. "Not a nice one. She won't be happy to see you. God knows why." Her eyes drag down the length of my suit in an attempt to objectify me. It's pathetic. She's pathetic, much like the rest of her family.

"Luciana," Viola says, shaking her head. "Stop being so disgusting."

Maria laughs and shoves her in the shoulder. "Yeah, you are acting desperate."

"If you would all excuse me, I've got a plane to catch."

Gio shakes his head. "You can't even stay for dinner?"

"No time to lose," as the thought of tonight's dinner with the Benedetto family without Bella makes my stomach turn. "See you when I'm back," I say, turning and striding out of the dining room.

None of them say a word to stop me as I head

toward the exit, knowing that there was no way I'd stay at dinner with them alone. The only good part about those dinners is seeing my fiancé.

I halt mid-step, my feet suddenly feeling like bricks.

I was looking forward to seeing Bella tonight. When did that happen? An icy shiver slithers down my spine, reminding me of my revenge mission. Nothing has changed, and nothing could change; the only way forward is to watch them all burn.

***

MY CELL PHONE BUZZES, sending my heart racing as Jane's name appears on the screen. "Hello," I answer.

"Hey boss, I've discovered the date and location."

My muscles tighten and my blood runs cold. "When and where?" I ask, hoping that going after Bella wouldn't destroy my mission to take down Gio's disgusting side business.

"One week's time at a club called Insignia."

"Thank fuck for that," I exhale in relief.

"What?" she questions.

I shake my head. "I'm in London for the weekend. Just got in. I'll be back in Washington on Monday."

Jane clears her throat. "Okay, do you want to come over here and we can brainstorm a plan? I know some trustworthy people who can help us out."

My jaw tightens as I contemplate whether Jane is

reliable enough to provide me with the contacts I need. "We'll discuss further on Monday," I murmur before disconnecting the call.

I stalk down the street toward my headquarters, my thoughts darkening with a plan to surprise Bella.

Her family, being useless as ever, had no idea which hotel her aunt had booked them into, making it difficult for me to locate her.

To pull off my plan, I need to enlist the help of the finest hacker on my payroll, Jack Oliver, who should be at the headquarters working. Hacking into her aunt's phone is the only way to find them and ambush them later in the evening.

It feels good to be back on my home turf as I round the corner and step through the revolving doors into my office block. However, the moment I step into our building, I'm assaulted by the image of Henry and five of my subordinates hovering near the entrance.

"What's going on?" I ask.

They all go still at the sound of my voice, turning to face me.

"I didn't know you were back in town, sir," Henry says.

I cross my arms over my chest. "It is an impromptu visit. Are you discussing something important?" I ask as I gaze at the five other men—all high-ranking members in our organization.

Henry glances at Kane, one of our spies. "Kane

has discovered a plot against us and I didn't want to bother you with it like last time."

"What kind of plot?"

"An inside one to overthrow you."

I glare at Kane. "You realize this looks a little like an inside plot? My six highest ranking men meeting together."

Henry steps forward. "We have all the evidence. I can assure you that it's not us."

I groan, this isn't why I'm here. I'm here to ambush Bella Benedetto and make sure she knows there's nowhere she can go that I won't follow.

"Send me the evidence. I've got to go and see Jack."

Henry nods as he and his team step back, allowing me to make my way to Jack's office. Taking the elevator to the second floor, I head down the corridor and stop in front of Jack's door.

He'll probably shit his pants seeing me here, since everyone thinks I'm in Washington and I never visit Jack's office.

Knocking on his door, I tap my heel on the floor, waiting for him to answer.

"Who the fuck is it?" he shouts from the other side.

"Your boss," I say coolly.

The door to his office flings open in a second, and he stares at me for a moment in shock. "I'm sorry, sir. I wasn't expecting you." He steps aside. "Come on in."

The office is messy and filled with computers and gadgets on every surface. When I don't say anything, Jack fumbles over his words, "How—What—Can I help you, sir?"

I nod. "Yes, I need you to hack into Bella Benedetto's aunt's cell phone.

"Have a seat," he says, clearing off a load of papers from it.

"I'm good standing, thanks."

He clears his throat and sits down himself, tapping frantically at his computer. "No problem with hacking the cell phone. Do you have the cell number?" he asks.

I nod and pass him the piece of paper I scribbled the number down on after speaking to Gio on the phone.

Crossing my arms over my chest, I stare at him with an icy glare. "How long will it take?"

He pales when he looks up at me. "An hour tops."

"Okay, send me the details on my cell phone once you've cracked it."

Jack nods. "No problem. I'll try to make it quicker."

I turn and leave Jack's office, walking back to the elevator and riding it up to the top floor to go and find Henry. If I have an hour to kill, I can find out what the fuck is going on with this inside plot.

Henry and the five men are in the boardroom. Files are all over the table. I walk in and their eyes widen.

"So, what's this all about? Who is plotting against me?"

Henry grabs one of the files and passes it to me. I flip it open to see photos of some of my soldiers meeting with the Belyaev Bratva, our main enemy in the city.

"Motherfuckers," I murmur, flipping through the images. "There's quite a lot of them."

Henry nods. "Yeah, but we're handling it."

"How?" I ask.

Kane clears his throat. "We have called an organization meeting for tomorrow morning. The culprits will be tortured and killed without fail."

I clap my hands. "You've all done well catching this. Send me the details for the meeting and I'll be there."

Sam, who is in control of merchandise, nods. "Jackson has been the ringleader on this."

I arch a brow. "I didn't think he had it in him, but he's always been too arrogant for his own good."

"Since I'm here, are there any other issues I need to handle?"

Ahmed, my finance manager, nods. "Yeah, there's some money missing, too. We suspect it's the same culprits, but Jack hasn't managed to track the money back to anyone in our organization."

I must admit that the Belyaev's persistence to keep attacking never made much sense, but now it adds up. They had inside ties that they felt would bring them success. We'll see if we can finally be done with them once and for all after every man who worked with them is dead and buried six feet under.

"Keep working on it and report back to me. I may not be in the city for the next month or two, but this is an important matter and I need to be kept informed." I give Henry a pointed look as I think he took my irritation last time at being called back to London a little too seriously, as this is a much more difficult matter to address than the Belyaev's overstepping their territory.

All six of them reply in unison, "Yes, sir."

I nod and turn around. "I'll be back in Washington on Monday. If anything urgent crops up, call me." Walking out of the room, I can't help but feel on edge.

Is it possible that my quest to get revenge on the Benedetto family is putting my position as king of London in jeopardy?

There was always going to have to be a time where I wasn't in London if I wanted to carry out my plan against the Benedetto family, but I wonder if it's blinding me to what's going on right under my nose.

Clenching my fists, I march out of my headquarters and onto the street. Rage simmering in my veins. Tomorrow morning I intend to make an example out of the men that crossed me, ensure that everyone knows that even when I'm not in the city, I have eyes and ear everywhere.

My cell buzzes and I answer the call. "What've you got for me, Jack?"

"So, it was really easy to hack her phone. They're staying at the Ritz."

"Of course they are."

"And I intercepted some text messages between her and Bella's mom. They're going to some art exhibition tonight at the Tate."

"Perfect, thanks Jack." I end the call. Some of my rage eased at the prospect of being able to see the look on Bella's face when I turn up at the gallery tonight. It's crazy how the prospect of seeing my fiancée, even though she's a Benedetto, can soothe the rage that wants to break free and demolish everything in its path.

18

BELLA

*M*y heart pounds like drums in a war march as our eyes meet, and a surge of anger overwhelms me.

"Why the hell is he here?"

Olivia looks as dumfounded as I feel. "I have no idea how he found us here, Bella," she murmurs.

"This is a damn setup," I hiss.

She shakes her head. "I can only imagine your dad told him we were here in London." Her eyes narrow. "How he found out we were attending an art exhibition tonight, I'll never know."

"Fuck's sake."

Isiah strides toward me in slow motion, every step as precise and calculated as a predator stalking its prey. In the crowd of faces, his is the only one I see. "Surprised to see me, love?"

I swallow hard as Olivia shuffles awkwardly. "How did you find me?" I ask.

The smirk he gives me makes me want to slap it off of his face. "There's nowhere you can go in London that I won't find you. This is my city, Bella."

He turns to Aunt Olivia, his voice dripping with false politeness. "Do you mind giving us a moment alone?"

Bella grabs her aunt's arm. "Yes, she does. We're here together and anything you have to say to me can be said to her, too."

Isiah raises a single brow. "Really? Are you sure about that, love?

The look in his eyes makes me sick to my stomach. "No, I just want you to leave me alone. This weekend was supposed to be a break from you."

"Bella," Olivia gasps in shock that I would be so honest to him directly.

He smirks and looks at my aunt. "Oh, don't worry, I know Bella doesn't enjoy my company, or at least that's what she tells herself."

"It's the truth," I hiss, my hatred for him obvious in every word.

"Continue believing that," he speaks as if he knows better, "even though deep down, you can't cease thinking of how I made you scream in pleasure—"

"Shut up!" I forcefully grab his forearm and haul him away from where my aunt stands. "Are you fucking insane?"

The arrogant son of a bitch just shrugs. "I asked to speak with you alone and you refused."

"That was completely uncalled for."

He grinds. "I gave you adequate warning, though."

I glare at him through narrowed eyes. "What is it you want?"

"I want to show my fiancée around my city." He grabs my hips dominantly, making a shudder race down my spine. "It was foolish to think you could come here and I wouldn't follow."

I clench my jaw as people are starting to piss me off. "It wasn't my idea. Olivia suggested it because she wanted me to go dress shopping with her."

"Wedding dress shopping?" Isiah confirms.

I nod. "Yes, much to my disgust."

"And did you find one?" The look in his eyes is odd, no longer playful.

"Yes, why?"

He shakes his head. "No reason." The answer is short and clipped and I wonder what made that switch flip. "Now why don't we put our differences aside and enjoy all London has to offer together?"

"Because then my aunt will feel like a third wheel."

Isiah smirks. "Hardly looks that way." He nods at her as she dances with an attractive man who has to be half her age.

I gasp. "She's married!" Yanking myself away from him, I head over to intercept her gyrating on this guy, grabbing her wrist. "Olivia, let's go."

"Hey!" She yanks her wrist back. "I'm having

fun." I can tell she's drunk. I lean toward her. "What about Darius?" I hiss.

She waves her hand. "What happens in London stays in London. Believe me, he's had enough fun without me before, too."

Perhaps her marriage to Darius isn't as happy as it appears on the surface. Releasing her arm, I realize that my aunt has basically ditched me, leaving me at the mercy of Isiah fucking Darcy. The man I flew thousands of miles from to get a break.

The smugness of his expression when I return to his side is enough to make me sick to the stomach. "She didn't want to leave, huh?"

"Don't," I say, not in the mood for his gloating.

"How about a drink?" he asks.

I look at him then, my heart skipping the moment our eyes lock. "Sure."

He walks away to find us drinks and I slump back against a nearby wall, trying to regain my composure. How the hell did he find us?

London is a huge city, and it's no coincidence that he found us here at this event. Somehow, he tracked us down and I want to find out how.

When he returns, I've composed myself and take my drink. "Thanks." I take a sip, ignoring the heated look he gives me. "So, tell me how you found us."

"Wouldn't you like to know?"

I grind my teeth together. "Was it through our cell phones?" I ask, knowing that my father has done that in the past when he wanted to track down a rogue man who had taken off with a load of his cash.

His eyes narrow. "Perhaps."

I walk away from him to go and check out the artwork, irritated when I glance back to find him following me. "If you don't mind, I'd like to enjoy the artwork in peace," I say, glaring daggers at him.

He doesn't stop following. "No problem. I'll just enjoy it with you."

"The fact that you are even in the same room is stifling my enjoyment, let alone having you within a foot of me."

Isiah smirks. "Don't be so dramatic, love."

"Don't call me love, I don't like it."

"Does it look like I care what you like or not?"

I roll my eyes and focus my attention on the unusual artwork that seems to line the walls of this gallery. It's not exactly classic art, but apparently Olivia is into the strange modern art.

"So, you like art?" Isiah asks.

I glare at him. "I like to enjoy art in silence." I don't mention that my favorite pastime is painting.

He laughs. "Come on, Bella, why don't we put our differences aside and have a normal conversation?"

I sigh heavily. "This kind of art isn't really my thing, no."

"What kind of art do you like?"

"Classic, beautiful art like Da Vinci and Van Gogh." My brow furrows as I stare at a maroon square painted on a red background, which is then painted on a maroon background. "Anyone could paint that," I say.

Isiah chuckles. "I agree that this modern art doesn't make any sense, at least not to me."

For once, it's weird that we are in accord with one another.

He suddenly grabs my hips, his touch sending a shot of fire through my veins, despite everything. "How about we get out of here?" he whispers into my ear, his tone dark and sinful, warning me that I shouldn't agree.

And yet when I pull back and glance into his eyes, I feel an intense desire to agree.

"Where would we go?" I ask.

His eyes flicker with playfulness. "I'll give you a real tour of the city."

I can't help but sink my teeth into my bottom lip as this man makes everything sound dirty, or perhaps it's just my mind interpreting everything that way since we became intimate, despite my lack of consent. Despite all the warning bells going off in my mind, I nod my head, as if my body and mind are no longer in conjunction with one another.

He grabs my hand forcefully. "Come on then," he says, leading me toward the exit of the art gallery.

One glance back at my aunt and I see she's still entangled with that young guy, seemingly forgotten all about her niece she's supposed to be cheering up on this trip.

Sighing heavily, I allow Isiah to lead me out into the busy streets of London. "Where are you taking me?" I ask.

He flags down a cab. "Number one rule of this tour, no questions."

I narrow my eyes at him. "You are very infuriating, did you know that?"

He opens the door to the cab. "I rather enjoy annoying you, love. Now get in."

I grunt and slide into the back of the cab, smiling at the driver. "Hi," I say.

He smiles back. "Hey."

Isiah gets in and gives the driver a death stare for even looking at me. "Regents Park," he says.

The driver nods and starts to drive, and I give Isiah a withering look, as he's being a dick. I literally just said hi to our driver. It's not like I was flirting with him. Ever since his warning about Enzo, I do feel on edge around other men with him near. The guy is a loose cannon, ready to go off at any moment.

"What's in Regents Park?" I ask.

Isiah clicks his tongue. "What did I say the number one rule was?"

"Are you serious?"

"Deadly." There's no humor in his tone.

I roll my eyes and cross my arms over my chest. "Fine, I'll just sit in silence then."

He chuckles and slides a hand under the hem of my skirt, high onto my thigh. "I can think of something more entertaining to do on the drive over."

My entire body turns stiff. "Don't you dare," I warn.

He ignores me, though, and thrusts his fingers into me. His movement is so sudden that I gasp, my grip on the leather seat tightening as he works against me. He moves fast, in and out, until I'm trembling with pleasure and desire so strong it renders me speechless and yet there's that underlying hatred always there. My breath comes in desperate gasps while his other hand tugs at the ends of my hair.

My head spins from the sensation and I'm torn between wanting more and wanting to push him away. He knows he's pushing boundaries, yet still he persists, showering kisses along my neck as his finger-tips keep working inside me. Every touch sends a wave of pleasure to my core, making me forget all about the fact that I don't want this.

The cab driver looks at us in the rearview mirror with a disapproving frown, getting Isiah's attention.

He gives him a warning glare. "Eyes on the road, mate." His accent is heavy as he says that. What I can only say is it has a London twang to it.

The driver pales and focuses on the road ahead, but I use Isiah's distraction to my advantage, tearing his hand away from my pussy.

"I told you, no. Keep your hands to yourself."

He laughs. "That's why you were moaning, is it?"

"I wasn't moaning."

I can't believe how arrogant he is. Every day, he surprises me with his utter bullshit.

He wraps his palm around my throat and squeezes, and then when I think he can't be any more of an asshole, he slides his other fingers back into me. "You know how this goes, Bella. I own you, pure and simple."

I notice the driver glance back here again, a look of horror on his face as he sees what Isiah is doing.

"Driver, do you want me to fuck you up?" he asks, not taking his eyes off of me.

"N-No," he mutters.

"Then eyes on the fucking road."

I shudder at the intensity in his gaze as he fingers me lazily, drawing that pleasure he seems to so expertly coax from my body to the surface. His tongue draws a line across my collarbone before dipping lower between my cleavage, eliciting a wanton moan from my lips, despite myself. When I feel like I'm about to come apart, the cab comes to a stop.

Isiah slowly withdraws his fingers from my pussy and leans back into his seat with a satisfied smirk on his face. His gaze holds mine as if daring me to confront him over it, not letting me come before he throws some money at the front seat for our driver. "Keep the change," he says simply, before getting out of the cab.

"I'm sorry," I mutter to the driver.

He shakes his head. "Don't be," he says simply, and once I'm out, he races away at breakneck speed.

"I think you scared him half to death," I say,

glaring at the man who, unfortunately, I have to marry in less than one month's time.

"Good," he says simply, shoving his hands into his suit pockets. "He's lucky he isn't dead for looking at you the way he did."

"You are insane. He looked at me like any normal human being."

Isiah closes in on me. "No, it's just that you are too innocent to see that almost every man you come across looks at you like a piece of fucking meat. And you are mine."

I roll my eyes and step aside, walking away from him and into the park. "Whatever. Why did you bring me here?" I ask, as it just looks like a huge expanse of gardens, but it's not exactly the best time to enjoy it in the dark.

"There's somewhere I want to take you to." He holds out his hand. "Trust me."

I narrow my eyes, untrusting of this man, especially here in a dark and deserted park. "Right, like I want to trust you after what you just pulled."

He smirks. "Don't tell me you didn't enjoy it?"

I don't answer that and instead take his hand, hating the way heat spreads through my entire body in an instant. He leads me into the park, walking past a playground and down a meandering path toward an unmarked gate.

"What is this place?"

He doesn't answer and instead pushes open the gate. "It's more beautiful in spring, as all the flowers are out. The wisteria is stunning, but perhaps I'll bring you back in the spring."

My stomach churns. "If I survive that long married to you."

He laughs as he leads me under the tunnels with the bare wisteria trunks trailing over it. There're dim lights scattered around the secret garden as he leads me to an old wooden bench.

"Have a seat," he says.

I tear my hand away from his and sit down, placing my hands in my lap. The setting is oddly romantic, and that just puts me more on edge than ever before with this man. I still don't know why he's so set on marrying me, a daughter of an insignificant man thousands of miles across the sea.

My family holds a certain level of influence, but Isiah Darcy wields far more power—it's as if he's been handed his authority. I'm determined to discover his secrets, but I'm at a loss as to how.

"I come here when I want to reflect on things," he says, gazing into the center of the lawn, which has a large fountain in it, but it's not on. No doubt because the place is deserted. There are not many lights, which suggests people don't often come here at night.

"It's beautiful," I say, taking in the surroundings.

He flashes me one of the sincerest grins he's ever given me. "It is, isn't it? The only thing I don't like about the city is that you can't see the stars." He gazes up at the night sky, and I do the same.

I look up and nod. "Yeah, I remember we went on

holiday once to Arizona, staying in the desert, and the stars..." I shake my head. "I've never seen anything like it."

"The stars are often visible at my country house."

I arch a brow. "You have more than one house?"

He laughs. "I have numerous properties, yes. Doesn't your father?"

I shake my head. "No, I don't believe he's as rich as you are."

"Not many are."

"Is your house far?" I ask.

"Just over an hour out of the city in Letchworth."

I swallow hard, wondering what it's like. This country, completely foreign to me, is going to become my home. "And when we are married, where will we live?"

"You can live where you want. In my penthouse or the country house, as both are big enough." He shrugs, as if it doesn't matter where I am. "I spend weekends at the country house and the weekdays in the city. When we leave here, I'll show you my apartment."

The way he says it suggests he intends for us to live separate lives. A notion which should thrill me, but for some reason, I have a sinking feeling in the pit of my stomach. And the idea of going back to his apartment makes me shudder, but if I want to learn why Isiah is so set on this union, I need to try to get closer to him.

We sit there in contemplative silence as there's something about Isiah Darcy in his determination to marry me that I feel has a sinister twist to it. One I'm determined to uncover before it's too late.

19

ISIAH

I follow my prey down the corridor toward my penthouse, knowing that within minutes I will have devoured her. Ever since I'd met her at the party, the need for her has been a searing fire within me - an insatiable hunger that can only be satisfied with her surrender. She has become somewhat of an obsession, and I absolutely refuse to wait for our wedding night to take her.

Bella walks ahead of me, unaware of the devastating effect she has on me, a siren's call that can't be denied. The sway of her hips in those high heels sends my thoughts spiraling to dark places, and I've every intention of bringing those thoughts into reality before the night is through.

She stops in front of the door to my penthouse apartment and turns to look at me, lips pursing as she meets my gaze. "You better hurry up before I change my mind."

I smirk. "There's no going back now. You are on my turf."

Her brow furrows. "I can still change my mind. It's not like I'm your prisoner."

"That's what you think."

I notice the way her lip quivers as she takes a step away from me. "You're crazy."

I stand in front of the eye recognition software to open the door and it clicks open. My apartment is burglar proof, fitted with the best security system in the world.

"After you," I say, signaling for her to walk inside.

She stares at me for a few moments before finally giving up and stepping into my lair.

My cock is hard and heavy in my slacks as I follow her inside. "Would you like a drink?" I ask.

She turns and holds her arms in front of her defensively. "I guess."

"Pinot noir?"

She nods. "If you've got it."

I laugh. "I have everything. Follow me," I say, walking down the corridor toward my wine room.

Bella follows, keeping a good distance between us. It's probably wise, as I'm ready to pounce at any moment, the lust taking over my brain.

"Take your pick," I say, opening the door to reveal hundreds of bottles of wine lining a room with floor to ceiling racks.

Her eyes widen. "I wouldn't know where to start!"

"Would you like me to pick one?"

She nods in response, hugging her arms tight around herself. I'm surprised how vulnerable she looks.

I select the finest pinot noir I have and nod toward the door. "Let's go and find some glasses." It's rare that I drink wine, but I'll make an exception tonight. The bottle is, after all, worth over ten thousand dollars.

Once I'm in the open plan kitchen, I select two glasses and pour us each a drink, watching Bella as I do. She's different right now. Shy and quiet. It only excites me more because she's always been so fiery and now she's in my den, she knows to be scared.

I pass her a glass and she takes it with a trembling hand, hesitating before taking a sip, her eyes never leaving mine. She looks into my soul as if searching for something, but I know exactly what she's looking for—the reality of what the night will bring.

"So, you live here alone?" she asks, glancing around the penthouse apartment.

"When I'm in London, yes." I take a sip of wine. "And I won't be alone for long, will I?"

Bella's lip trembles. "I really don't want to live here."

I laugh. "What do you think happens when we marry? I certainly am going to be living in London, love."

Her brow furrows. "Why don't we just live apart? The marriage is nothing but political, anyway."

I click my tongue. "Now that is where you are greatly mistaken." I place my glass down on the island and walk around it, closing the gap between us. "Our marriage is going to be more than political. It's going to be highly erotic."

Her lips purse together. "No it's not."

"You will do your duty as my wife and service me whenever I deem necessary."

"Like hell I will."

I smirk. "You know, I actually enjoy it more when my partner is reluctant. It makes it all the more thrilling and then so much more satisfying when she finally starts to scream my name while I fuck the reluctance right out of her."

Her nostrils flare. "That's sick."

I shrug and grab her hips. "Do you think I care whether you think I'm sick or not?"

She shakes her head. "No, because you are sick in the head. You don't care who you hurt to get what you want, just like my dad." Her jaw clenches. "And my mom."

Her opinion about her parents strikes me hard, as it's the same one I have of them. And yet she is throwing me in with them. I wonder if it should give me pause, but right now my cock is too hard and I've waited too long to have her to care about anything but that task.

My hand moves under the hem of her dress and I tear her thong in two, ripping it off of her.

She gasps as I run my fingers teasingly through her slick flesh.

"Isiah," she murmurs my name.

"Yes, love?"

"Please don't."

I smirk and press my fingers deep inside her pussy. "Don't what?"

Bella's teeth rake over her lower lip, drawing my eyes to them. "You know what."

"I'm going to fuck you tonight, love, and there's nothing you can do or say to stop me."

She gasps, trying to push away from me. "No."

"Yes," I mutter, grabbing her wrist and forcing her hand onto my cock. "You make me so fucking hard all the damn time. I need your cunt wrapped around my cock before I go insane."

Her eyes dilate, but she still tries to act like she doesn't want this. "I'm a human being, Isiah. You can't just fuck me when I tell you no."

I narrow my eyes. "Do you think I'm the kind of man who gives a shit about consent?"

She gulps.

I grab hold of her waist and before she can scream, protest, or use her fists to fight me off, I'm lifting her up into the air and carrying toward my bedroom. Synapses fire within my brain as adrenaline courses through my veins. She's mine for the taking and has been since the day I set eyes on her.

Bella fights then, managing to wriggle free of my

grasp and escape. She darts away from me, running down the hallway toward my living room.

The adrenaline races harder through my veins and I smirk, the thrill of the chase only adding to my desire. She's tempting a fucking animal right now.

I turn and follow—my footsteps pounding in rhythm with my beating heart as she desperately looks for a way out. There isn't one.

"You know it's more thrilling when you run, love."

Just as she reaches for the doorknob of the apartment, which is locked anyway, I catch up and scoop her up into my arms. She struggles against me, but it's no use—I'm too strong for her.

Lifting Bella over my shoulder, I press my teeth into her thighs hard and then press a kiss over the same spot, making her whimper. I carry her over the threshold of my bedroom as she continues to fight.

Only once she realizes she's never going to win does the fight leave her body. I feel her sag deeper against my shoulder as I drop her onto my bed, crawling over without hesitation. Pinning her beneath me with my weight as I grind the hardness in my trousers against her center, groaning. "You don't know how long I've imagined this moment."

"And was I always reluctant in your warped fantasies?" she hisses.

I smirk. "A lot of the time, yes. At least at first, but once my cock was inside you, you soon warmed up to the idea." I sink my teeth into her neck and groan.

"You screamed my name while I tore open that tight virgin cunt and made you bleed for me."

She gasps in shock, but her thighs clench together. "You're disgusting."

"Stop the bullshit, love, and tell me the truth. You want this, we both know it, so who are you trying to fool?"

She doesn't answer, and that in itself is answer enough for me. My hands are everywhere at once, ripping apart the buttons at the front of her dress and then tearing it from her body.

The violence of my actions makes her gasp. "Stop this, Isiah."

"Fight me, Bella. I like it when you fight."

I know I'm sick. I have been for a very long time. My desire for non-consensual sex is predatory and not right, but I can't help myself. Especially not when it comes to Bella Benedetto.

A cruel smile on my face, I tell myself this is revenge. She's a Benedetto. And yet I know it's not the reason. I can't deny the sick thrill that goes through me at the thought of taking an innocent woman's virginity against her will. Because somewhere along the line, the person I was got broken and twisted by the darkness I've wallowed in for far too long. Bella is lightness and innocence and I'm just a dark, endless pit that swallows anything good whole. It's why revenge is the only thing I can cling onto, as I don't have anything else.

"That's because you're clearly a psychopath," she spits.

I rip open her bra, driven by my own dark cravings. My mouth waters as I see her firm breasts and hard nipples for the first time. "Let's see if you're saying that once I'm through with you." I hold her gaze for a few seconds.

She's about to open her mouth when I close mine around her nipple and suck, making her hips rise off the bed and a gasp tumble from her lips.

I move to the other nipple and repeat the same movements, feeling her nipples stand out against my tongue.

Bella's teeth sink into her lip as I cover her body with mine, pressing against every inch of exposed skin. She parts her thighs for me without resistance as my fingers slide between her legs, making slow circles around that tiny bud of pleasure. "Tell me how it feels," I whisper, holding her gaze.

She narrows her eyes in defiance. "Fuck you!"

A chuckle escapes me as I refuse to be deterred. "Suit yourself." Forcefully, I shove my fingers past her clit and deep into her cunt, groaning when I feel how wet she is.

She grabs my arm and digs her nails in, but still can't hide the labored breaths and reddening cheeks that betray just how much she is enjoying this sinful game we are playing.

"Your pussy is dripping wet and practically screaming for me to fuck it."

"It's no wetter than it normally is."

I chuckle and press my fingers deeper into her cunt, making her gasp and arch her back in pleasure.

"Let's put that to the test, shall we?" I whisper before smashing my lips against hers, taking all of her breath away as I thrust my tongue into her mouth.

My hand moves down her body, finding her thighs and pulling them apart, while keeping my body between them.

Reaching between our bodies, I unzip my trousers and free my cock, before pressing the head of my cock against her soaking wet entrance.

"Isiah, don't," she warns.

"Or what, love?"

"This isn't right," she mutters.

I bite her lip and then kiss her cheek before whispering in her ear. "If you were hoping for romance and waiting until our wedding night, then you've read me all wrong."

In one violent thrust of my hips, I push through her virgin entrance and slide deep inside her.

She screams and I press my lips over her mouth to swallow them, feeding off of her pain. My tongue delves into her mouth frantically as I search it with all the passion and rage and emotion I feel in this moment. This woman is a part of the family that destroyed my life.

I thrust again and again, faster and harder each time until I'm slamming my hips against hers with a force so powerful it shakes the bed.

And yet once she gets over the initial pain, she relaxes beneath me. Her whole body turning soft below me. Her cunt grasping my cock like a fucking glove.

I grip her hips so tight I know I'll leave bruises on her flesh. In fact, I relish the idea. Driving deeper into her pussy, I feel her muscles get even tighter as she gets closer and closer to the edge.

There's no way I'm letting her climax that easily, halting my thrusts instantly and pulling out of her, groaning when I see a small amount of blood on my cock.

"Fuck, love. You've bled on me."

She whimpers, looking at me in a way I've never seen before. It's pure, unadulterated desire. "What are you doing?"

"It's too soon for you to come." I pull my jacket off and chuck it aside before stripping the rest of my clothes off fast, wanting to feel every inch of her pressed against me.

Crawling over her body, I slam back into her. "Is that better?" I ask.

Her eyes widen. "Isiah," she gasps my name in response.

I capture her lips in a passionate kiss before beginning to thrust again. Her nails dig into my skin as I move deeper and harder inside her with each stroke.

I carefully judge when she's close to orgasm and then slow down, denying her pleasure until the urge passes, teasing her mercilessly. "You only get to come when I decide you do, Bella."

She grunts in frustration. "I hate you."

Flipping her over onto all fours, I spank her firm, round ass cheeks. "And I don't believe you."

She arches her back almost in invitation and seeing her in this position for me makes my balls ache for release. My cock is dripping with her arousal and my own as I drag the head through her soaking wet entrance.

"If you hate me so bad, would you like me to stop?" I ask, bumping the head of my cock over her clit.

She cries out and shakes her head.

"Use your voice to answer, Bella."

I can feel her annoyance practically tingeing the air, but she's too desperate. "Don't stop," she gasps.

The satisfaction I get from hearing her practically beg me to keep fucking her does something to me on a primal level.

The growl that tears from my throat is animalistic as I thrust every inch of my cock as deep as possible into her, losing control as I fuck her relentlessly, my thrusts no longer teasing but entirely savage.

"Isiah!" she screams my name.

I spank her ass. "That's right, love, scream my name," I say, feeling my release coming like a firestorm I can't stop.

Bella trembles violently, warning me she's literally on the precipice. Her muscles clenching around the girth of my cock so tight it's as if she's trying to milk me for every drop. "I'm coming!" she cries out.

"Good," I reply, spanking her tinged pink skin. "Come on my cock like a good girl," I say, my voice strangled as I barely hold on for a second longer. My release is so intense as I spill every drop of cum deep inside her cunt bareback.

The subject of whether she's on a birth control didn't come up, and to be honest, it doesn't fucking matter. In a few weeks, we'll be married and I will take advantage of my position as many times as possible.

I collapse onto the bed next to Bella, utterly spent. She follows suit but won't look at me as her chest heaves up and down frantically. As I gaze at her, I'm sure she's never looked so beautiful. The silence stretches between us eternally and I know that I won't be the one to break it.

Despite the fact that Bella is supposed to be my enemy, deep down inside, I can't help this irritating feeling of fondness for her. She's nothing like her family.

Every time we touch or argue, it feels like there's an invisible connection between us. A connection that will need to be severed if I'm going to get my revenge on the Benedetto family, which includes her.

BELLA

My eyes flutter open, and instantly I panic at my unfamiliar surroundings, bolting upright in the bed. And that's the moment when every memory of the night before comes flooding back. A mix of confusing emotions comes flooding in, making me unsure whether I want to laugh, cry or scream.

My stomach rolls with sickness. Last night, Isiah took my virginity like some kind of animal, as if it were his right, and that's not even the most disgusting part. It's the way I ended up begging like a whore for him to fuck me.

What the hell is my problem?

Swinging my legs out of the bed, I rest my head in my hands, noticing my head is pounding. I drank far too much last night and I desperately need a drink of water. I grab my cell phone off the nightstand to find

I have no messages from Olivia. Clearly she isn't concerned that I didn't return last night.

I walk over to the door and grab a robe off the back of it, wrapping myself in it and slipping my cell into the pocket before leaving Isiah sleeping. The apartment is huge as I try to remember which way we came in and past the kitchen. Once I'm almost all the way back to where I'm sure we entered, I notice a door is ajar to my left.

Out of curiosity, I push it open and step inside. All the blood in my body drains as I'm confronted by a huge police-style board with pictures of my entire family pinned to it.

"What the fuck?"

I advance further, noticing that there are notes under each of our names. My brow furrows as I step closer and read the text under my name.

Twenty-two years old. Virgin. Easy target.

I clench my fists by my sides, rage coursing through my veins.

Easy target?

I fumble in the pockets of my robe and grab my cell phone, snapping photos of Isiah's creepy board.

"What the fuck are you doing in here?" Isiah's voice is calm and yet somehow more deadly than ever before.

I let out a yelp, almost dropping my cell phone as I spin around to face him. "I was trying to find the kitchen to get a glass of water. But I think the more important question is why the hell is my family on some kind of murder board in your apartment?!"

I shudder as I realize whatever Isiah's intentions are toward me and my family, it's not good. He wants to hurt us, and I'm determined to find out why.

He watches me quietly for a few beats before stepping closer. "Get. Out." He says the two words separately, glaring at me.

"Not until you give me an explanation."

He shakes his head and starts forward again, grabbing my arm and dragging me out of the room. "Go back to Washington today, Bella."

"No. Aunt Olivia and I are here until Monday, so you can go fuck yourself!" Rage so prudent runs through my veins and it's unlike anything I've felt before. "Don't think this isn't going straight back to my dad." I hold the cell phone up and instantly regret it as his eyes darken.

"On second thought, I'm not letting you out until you delete whatever is on that mobile phone." He shuts the door behind him and every muscle in my body tenses.

I fumble with the phone, trying to send the images via a multimedia message to my family chat, but my hands are shaking too much. "Stay away!" I shout as he advances toward me.

Before I can steady my nerves, he's grabbed the phone out of my hand and thrown it against the wall, smashing it into pieces. "That solves that issue."

"You bastard!" I slam my fists into his hard chest over and over, rage and fear mixing together as I struggle to contain my emotions.

Isiah just stands in front of me like a wall of stone, taking punch after punch. "You can hit me all you like, love. It won't change anything." He grabs my wrists then and I feel the fight whoosh out of me, sickness replacing it as I wonder what the hell Isiah Darcy wants from my family.

Why is he targeting us?

"Why are you doing this to us?"

"Doing what?" he asks.

I signal to the board. "What's your ulterior motive for marrying me?"

He shakes his head. "I just like to have a good understanding of people who I'm about to become partners with. It's that simple."

"Bullshit!"

He yanks me closer and wraps his large palm around my throat, squeezing. "Do you want me to discipline you again?"

I shudder. "Definitely not."

"And do you think I will listen to what you want?" His tone is cruel and vindictive.

"No." I know after last night that this man just takes whatever the fuck he wants, and nothing will stop him.

"That's right," he says, pressing his lips to my jaw and kissing me there. "I don't listen, I take." He yanks open the robe I'm wearing and slams his fingers between my thighs, making me yelp as I'm still sensitive from last night.

I bite back a moan. "What are you going to take now?" I whisper, dreading the answer.

Isiah smirks and his eyes rake over my body hungrily. "I'm going to fuck you on this desk."

Only he would be that perverted, fucking me in front of a creepy board with photos of my family pinned to it. I shiver in anticipation as he kisses my neck slowly, trailing his lips down my chest.

Slowly, he drags his tongue around my nipple, making it impossibly hard. And then he does the same to the other, making me pant for oxygen. "This is so wrong," I mutter.

He smirks cruelly. "No, it's right. You're my fiancée, after all. It's only my right I get to give you a test drive."

I punch him hard in the chest, but it hardly seems to affect him. "I'm a human being, not a fucking car."

He bites my nipple and I scream, the pain oddly pleasurable.

What the hell is wrong with me?

None of my reactions to this man or his actions makes any sense whatsoever.

"Stop thinking so much," he growls and then turns me around, his body pressing up against mine as he slides his hands down my arms. "I can practically hear you debating with yourself."

He forces both of my hands down on the desk, his

chest still pressed against my back. Nipping my earlobe, he murmurs, "You know your cunt is throbbing to be filled with me again, despite your pathetic insistence that you don't want me."

I'm completely at his mercy now; the intensity of it all sends shivers down my spine and I can feel how wet I am between my thighs. Isiah slides his own leg between mine and parts them, pressing his huge cock against my slick entrance, making it hard for me to breathe properly as I wait in trepidation for him to push forward, torn whether I want it or not.

I can't help but feel a spark of pleasure in the midst of all this pain and humiliation.

He takes one hand off my wrists and grabs a fistful of hair, yanking my head back so that I'm unnaturally forced backward. His lips press against the back of my neck as he speaks softly into my ear. "You have no choice."

My breath catches in dread but also excitement as he continues moving forward, pushing himself slowly inside me until I'm filled with the huge, hard size of him.

My body trembles beneath him as he moves in and out slowly— savoring each moment—intensifying every sensation in its wake.

He moves faster and I gasp, my orgasm quickly building as my nipples brush up against the cold wood of the desk. There's violence in the way he moves, his hips slamming into me as if he's trying to break me apart.

"That's it, love, take my cock just like that." He spanks my ass cheek hard, making me yelp in surprise. And then he does it again, over and over, until my skin is stinging.

I try to push him away, but his grip on my hair tightens, pulling me back with each thrust until I'm screaming in pleasure. I'm so lost in ecstasy that I've almost forgotten about the sick board he has on his wall with my family's photos on it.

His hands move from my hair and then he pushes me face first onto the desk with force. I didn't believe it was possible for him to fuck me any harder, but he does, driving into me like a mad man.

My climax rushes toward me at an unprecedented speed, making me moan as all my hatred disappears. All that replaces it is pure pleasure. I'm floating through time and space, being transported to some other realm where only pleasure exists.

Isiah groans loudly behind me, digging his nails into my hip so hard it hurts. And yet it only sends me over the edge faster as I scream his name, "Isiah! Fuck!"

"Now," he growls, his voice low and dangerous, "you're mine."

And then he groans as his own orgasm takes over, gripping onto me tightly as he unleashes his seed deep inside me. The same terror I felt the night before rushing in as I remember we didn't use protection then, either. And yet, I doubt he cares. We'll be married in less than a month, so he won't give a shit if I'm pregnant beforehand.

Once the aftershocks of my orgasm wear off, my vision clears and I see that fucking board. My rage hits me renewed and I take the moment of his distraction to escape him, rushing back into the bedroom as fast as possible.

He follows slowly, watching me as I run into his closet and find some clothes in there since Isiah destroyed mine. As I expected, there are a few items of female clothing, so I select a dress and throw it on. And then I return to the bedroom to get my shoes.

"What are you doing?" he asks.

"Getting the fuck out of here and away from you!" I grab my purse and rush toward the exit.

He grabs my arm as I'm passing. "I hope my cum is dripping out of you all fucking day as a reminder of what we did," he says, coldness gripping every muscle in my body at how nonchalant he is.

Yanking my arm from him, I rush away from the beautiful devil behind me, feeling more mixed up than a wash on high spin. And then I rush into the street, hating that I do indeed feel his cum dripping down my thighs with every step I take.

I need to get back to the hotel desperately and shower for hours to get him off me, but I fear he's ingrained in me more permanently, despite what I've learned. That all along, I was right.

Isiah Darcy has some kind of vendetta against my

family and that's why he's marrying me, but the question is what has my family done to him?

21

ISIAH

I fucked up.

And as I stand amongst my men, an unchecked rage is simmering below the surface. It doesn't bode well for the traitors. I intend to tear them apart limb from limb until there's nothing left but pure blood and carnage.

Allowing Bella into my home before we were married was a big mistake, one that could come back to bite me in the ass, if Gio believes his daughter. It's unlikely as he knows how badly she wants out of this engagement. I'll lie and tell him she's trying to find anyway to get out of our upcoming nuptials and has grown desperate after she found nothing in my apartment.

At least the proof was destroyed before I took my rage out on her, fucking her until she was screaming for release. Once we finished, she rushed back to the bedroom, got dressed, and fled my apartment as fast as she could.

"Sir?" Henry says my name in question.

I shake my head. "Sorry, what?"

"I said, would you like to take the lead on this?"

I clench my jaw. "Yes."

He passes me the file of evidence and I step in front of my men, clearing my throat. "It has been brought to my attention that we have a serious problem within our organization."

Jackson shuffles nervously, no doubt on edge, since he knows what he's done.

"Jackson, will you step forward?"

He glances at Archie, one of the men he betrayed us with, before stepping forward. "Yes, sir?"

"Closer," I say.

His Adam's apple bobs as he walks up to me and stops a foot from me.

I slam my hand into his neck and squeeze so hard his eyes bulge out of their sockets. "You are a traitor and do you know what I do to traitors?" I ask.

Archie, Derek, Liam and Ben all try to scatter, but my loyal men are on them before they have a chance to escape.

Jackson can't reply because I'm cutting off his airways, and once I'm sure he's close to passing out, I release his throat.

"Can anyone tell me what I do to traitors?" I ask.

Jack, the hacker, steps forward. "You make them pay."

"Indeed. I'm going to have fun with all five of you."

I grab Jackson by the shoulders and drag him to the center of the room, where a rack of torture tools await.

His eyes widen when he realizes what I'm going to do to him, and I can see fear written all over his face. It's something I've learned to feed off thanks to my dad's lessons. I force him down into the chair and two of my guys help me by chaining him to it.

Grabbing some electrodes off of the rack, I hook him and give him a low voltage shock at first, enjoying the way he screams in pain.

The four other men have turned white as a sheet as they watch me work, and yet I've hardly gotten started. As I watch Jackson writhe in agony, I realize I'm dead inside. It's been the same ever since I lost Aiden, spiraling into darkness as my father pushed me further. The darkness feeds on my unresolved grief, and the need for violence become more poignant the more time that passes.

It's the reason I can't let Bella Benedetto get in the way of my revenge.

I turn to the rest of my men, some of whom watch with fear in their eyes, others who watch with sheer glee as there're as dark as I am. "Do you see what happens to scum that betray Isiah Darcy?" I ask, the coldness in my tone almost shocks me.

A lot of the men nod.

"I can't hear you!" I shout.

"Yes, sir," they reply in chorus.

"Good." I turn my attention back to Jackson, grabbing a knife off the rack. "Let's see how rats squeal when they're being gutted."

Jackson shudders, eyes wide. "Please, Isiah. I didn't—"

I grab his chin and force his mouth open, pulling his tongue from his mouth and cutting it out. "I don't listen to excuses from rats." Blood pools in his mouth as his head sags to the side from the pain, his entire body trembling violently now.

I slice my sigil, a raven flying through a ring of fire, into his chest. The signature move my father came up with and I've carried on ever since. He screams but the sound is muffled by the fact he has no tongue.

If Bella could see me now, I wonder what she'd think? Does she know how dark and depraved her fiancé truly is?

I may have taken her against her will last night, but that's not a patch on what I'm capable of. I shake my head, wondering why she seems to keep making an appearance in my mind at such random times.

"I want anyone and everyone to know that rats like this one get made an example of." I slide my knife through his abdomen as his guts spill out, and still, I feel nothing, even with the carnage and blood.

A few of the men gag behind me, no doubt the hackers and weaker men on the team. And sure enough, when I glance around, Jack is bent over double, his puke all over the floor.

"Anyone who can't handle this, get the fuck out of here. I don't need wusses at this meeting!" I give Jack a pointed look and a few of the other men, and they all make a move for the exit. "As I've barely gotten started yet."

Many of the men don't expect this violence from me. To them I walk around in a suit looking like some kind of billionaire businessman, and that's the part I play within the organizations we run to launder our illegal cash. No one knows the lethal monster hiding beneath the suit and perfect hair.

Once Jackson takes his last breath, I nod at my men to remove his bloodied, lifeless body from the chair and then walk over to the four other men. "Which one shall I end next?"

There's silence in the room as I walk up and down, twirling the bloody knife in my hands.

"Let's make it simple and go alphabetically." I point at Archie, who literally pisses his pants.

I wrinkle my nose. "You're a disgrace," I say simply, yanking him forward and forcing him onto the bloody chair that Jackson was sitting in. "And I intend to make an example out of you."

"Please, sir, I can tell you secrets about the Belyaev —" My arm moves methodically as I plunge the blade of my knife into Archie's femoral artery, my eyes never leaving his face. The stench of fear fills the room as I turn to see the three other rats watch, their bodies trembling. "Lesson learned, boys," I snarl, observing the whimpering trio behind me. "There is no escape from my justice."

As I wrench the weapon free of Archie's body, I relish in the violent force of the blood spray. This suit is worth fifty-thousand dollars and I don't even care that it's being ruined by this bastard's blood. Fifty thousand dollars' worth of fabric is nothing compared to the satisfaction I get from this moment, and I smile in grim satisfaction as I slam the knife through Archie's throat, watching as he chokes on his blood.

Cold indifference rushes through me as I watch the light leave his eyes. "Two down, three to go." I tap the end of the knife against my lips. "What exciting ways can I kill the rest of you?" I ask, walking over to them.

Ben is next, and I torture him slowly, pulling his nails off first to inflict the maximum pain. And then ending him with a knife to the skull.

Derek is the penultimate and my blood lust is out of control, as I take my time, cutting bits of him off as well as breaking bones, and enjoying the way he screams like a fucking pig being slaughtered.

By the time I get to Liam, I'm feral. Lost to the violence of my actions as I grab a saw off the rack intending to hack each of his limbs off. It isn't until Henry appears in my field of vision that the rushing in my ears dulls. "Sir, are you sure it's necessary to make so much mess?" he asks, glancing at the saw. "You've made your point," he murmurs quietly.

"Fine," I say, grabbing the gasoline and dousing him in it. "Quick and painful," I say, meeting my second in command's concerned expression.

And then I strike a match and set him on fire, burning him alive as punishment for trying to double-cross me. His agonizing cries are a hauntingly beautiful end to my symphony, serving as a reminder of what happens when someone goes against me or my organization that they suffer the consequences—no second chances.

Finally, his screams die down to nothing and a poignant silence fills the air. The rage dulls a little and my vision focuses on my handiwork, which is a horrific scene of carnage. Most normal people would be sickened by it, and even my men, who are hardened criminals, find it difficult to swallow. I see it in their eyes when I turn around. They are horrified.

"Let this be a lesson for all of you. I'm not the kind of man you want to cross, so anytime you even think about being disloyal, remember what I did here today." I nod toward the exit. "You're dismissed."

I've never seen my men move at such speed, all of them, except Henry, rushing out of the basement of the warehouse. The scent of burned flesh tingeing the air.

"That was intense," Henry says, that concern clear in his eyes.

"People still don't take me seriously since I took over from my father. It was time I showed them just how far I'll go to keep myself in power."

He nods. "I understand that and they deserved it. I'm just..."

"Just what, Henry?"

His brow furrows. "Concerned about you."

"Don't be," I say.

He swallows hard. "You were about to hack Liam to pieces with a saw."

"And?"

His lips purse together, as he's known me since I was fifteen years old. We've been through all the ups and downs as my father built everything here in London and rose to power. "I've never seen you like this before. Does it have something to do with the Benedetto family?"

I clench my fists by my sides at the mention of them, my rage was inflamed by Bella running out of my penthouse this morning as if fleeing a savage animal. Perhaps that's all I am.

"Perhaps," I murmur, shaking my head. "Being back in Washington brings everything back to the surface and all I feel is rage all the time," I admit.

Henry nods. "It shows, sir, but I don't think we have to worry about any traitors for a while." He arches a brow. "Perhaps never after that demonstration."

I glance at the carnage I've left in my wake. "Can you get this cleaned up? I need to get back to Washington right away." There's no point in me staying here. I need to get ahead of Bella and see her father first and tell him she's trying to find any reason to get out of the engagement, including some notes I had on the family, which was merely research before I decided I might like to marry into it. Gio will understand that.

"Of course, sir. I'll get some men onto it."

I clap him on the shoulder. "Thank you. What would I do without you?"

He shrugs. "Who knows?"

I laugh. "Call me if there are any more problems." I turn to walk away.

"You've got it. Have a safe journey back, and sir..."

I stop and turn to face him. "Yeah?"

"Try not to lose yourself over there."

"I'll try." Even though I know that I haven't been myself for fourteen years. I lost myself when my brother died and my father forced me to dig his unmarked grave. I fear there's no coming back from it, as the person I once was is buried too deep inside.

22

BELLA

"Where have you been?" Olivia asks as I walk into the hotel room. "I've been worried sick."

I tilt my head. "Not worried sick enough to call," I say, remembering the way she completely ditched me at the art exhibit.

Her lips purse. "I've been trying to call for the last hour and all I've gotten is a deadline."

"My phone got smashed to pieces by my fiancé."

Her brow furrows. "Did you have an argument?"

"When don't we have an argument?"

She rushes over to me and places an arm around my shoulders, guiding me to the sofa to sit down. "Tell me what happened."

"The guy is a psychopath."

She bites her bottom lip. "What did he do?"

I feel heat coil through me because I can't tell her what he did. It's too humiliating. That he took my virginity even when I said no multiple times, and by the end, I was practically begging him for it. And then again this morning after I saw that board about my family.

"He has some weird detective style board in his apartment with the entire family mapped out on it with photos and everything."

Olivia's brow furrows. "What?"

"I'm serious. The guy has it out for our family and I'm part of his plan. I just don't know why."

"You have to tell your father."

I sigh heavily, knowing deep down that he won't believe me. "I don't have any evidence. Isiah made sure of it when he grabbed my phone and smashed it against a wall."

She gasps. "He didn't hurt you, did he?"

The bruises on my hips and the ache between my thighs are reminders of the pain he inflicted, but I shake my head in response. "No."

"That's something, at least. Let me talk with your father."

I tilt my head. "Do you think he will listen to you?"

Olivia's throat bobs as she swallows. "It's worth a try, isn't it?"

I know from the look on her face that she's not convinced my dad will listen to either of us. "We're fucked," I say, slumping back and shutting my eyes. "Isiah Darcy is dangerous. I always knew there was something off about him from the day we met."

"You have to get your dad to listen to you. No matter what it takes."

She's right, and yet I know it's impossible even before I try. Dad doesn't listen to women. A fatal flaw he's had all his life and something tells me it will be the Benedetto family's downfall.

"If he doesn't listen, then it will be down to me to work out what Isiah's game is."

My aunt worries her lip between her teeth. "You need to be careful, though. Men like Isiah..." she trails off. "They'll do anything to get what they want."

"You sound like you're speaking from experience."

She meets my gaze. "Things between Darius and I aren't great, Bella. I know you think we're happy, but it's all a façade. The man is a violent drunk who degrades women."

"And that's why you cheated on him last night?" I confirm.

Her expression turns sorrowful as she shakes her head. "Despite all the shit that bastard has put me through, I couldn't go through with it."

I find that hard to believe. "So why did it only occur to you this morning to try to find out where I was?"

"I assumed you were with Isiah and went to bed drunk and exhausted. When I woke to find you not here, I panicked, and that was an hour ago."

"I'm glad you made me come here."

Her eyebrows raise. "You are?"

It sounds insane, especially after the way Isiah

treated me last night, but I am glad I saw that board as it only cemented the opinion that Isiah Darcy has an ulterior motive for marrying me. "Yes, because now I can find out what Isiah is hiding. I had a suspicion, but nothing concrete to go on."

Olivia shakes her head. "Seriously, Bella. If he's as dangerous as you say, it's a good idea not to make things worse."

I know she's probably right, but what if he intends to destroy my family? I may not be close to them, but there's no way I'd stand by while he does that.

"I have to get back to Washington as soon as possible," I say, sighing heavily as this trip has turned into a nightmare. "I need to talk to my dad and try to convince him that Isiah is up to no good."

Olivia nods in agreement. "Of course. We'll take the jet back this afternoon."

I wince. "Is that the earliest?"

"Unfortunately, I've already paid for a spa treatment at the most exclusive spa in London." She purses her lips. "What's a few hours?"

I roll my eyes. "Can you never take anything seriously?"

"You definitely need a good massage to loosen you up, ready you for a showdown against your dad."

She might be right that it would do me some good, but despite only knowing Isiah for a few weeks, I've learned that he's always one step ahead. The last thing I want is for him to beat me back to Washington.

"What if he gets there before me?"

"Who?"

"Isiah. He will head back and try to get to my dad first."

"Don't you think it's going to look suspicious if he heads straight back to Washington this morning to see your dad?" Olivia asks.

I shake my head, as I know how good Isiah is at manipulating my dad. The man hangs off every word he says, and it's pathetic. "No, he'll have a way of manipulating the situation somehow."

"Do you really think that he's going to just head straight back this morning?"

"Possibly not." My shoulders slump. "What time is the appointment?"

"Ten o'clock this morning for two hours." Olivia's eyes narrow. "We can be on the plane by two o'clock this afternoon at the latest."

I sigh. "Okay, I'm not going to say I'm happy about it, but let's do it."

She claps her hands and jumps up and down, making me want to puke. This is so insignificant right now, but I accept that she's probably right. A few hours won't make a difference.

"Get ready and we will head downstairs to the spa." Olivia pulls her cell phone out of her Gucci purse. "I'll arrange for the jet to be fueled and ready for a two o'clock take off, okay?"

I nod and go into the bathroom to get ready, staring at myself in the mirror. The girl staring back is hardly recognizable. I feel like last night I lost a part of myself when Isiah took me against my will and I submitted to it in the end. The fight left me and pleasure replaced it, as sickening as that admission may be.

Olivia bangs on the door impatiently. "Do you realize we're going to be late?"

I roll my eyes and grab my robe off the back of the door, carrying it out. "I'm ready."

Olivia arches a brow at the fact I've not changed from the night before, but I don't really give a shit right now. She leads the way to the hotel spa, which should be a relaxing space with the soothing music playing in the background and the scent of essential oils, but there's nothing that could make me relax at the moment, not even a massage.

This is a waste of time. Precious time that I could be using to ensure that I get to my dad first. I have this sinking sensation that Isiah will want to get ahead of me on this.

"Welcome to the spa. Do you have an appointment?"

Olivia beams at the staff member who greeted us. "Yes, Benedetto at ten o'clock."

He checks a clipboard he's holding and nods. "Yep, we've got you down here for two spa treatments. Bella is in room two and Olivia is in room three. Here are the keys. If you go and change in to your robes, your masseuse will be with you in ten minutes."

Olivia squeaks as she takes her key. "Thank you." And then she's off.

I take mine with less enthusiasm. "Thanks."

I head into my room, which is overly lavish and smells even more strongly of essential oils. And then I get dressed in my robe, wishing that I could get the hell out of here and onto that plane right now instead.

Impatience plagues me as it feels like I'm waiting a lifetime, not ten minutes, for the masseuse to arrive, staring at the fucking floor through a hole.

"Sorry for the wait."

I freeze, terror striking deep within me as I know that voice. Trying to scramble off the masseuse table, I don't get very far when a palm wraps around the back of my neck and yanks me away from the bench and into him. "You were booked in for a fucking massage with a man, Bella," he growls, voice like ice.

"I didn't book this fucking massage. I didn't even want it!"

Isiah's warm breath ghosts over my face as he's so close—too close. "It doesn't matter. You belong to me, and I won't have any other man touching you. Do you understand?"

"Then assign me a fucking female masseuse to give me one."

His eyes narrow. "I don't want anyone else touching you, man or woman."

"You've got a screw loose."

He tilts his head. "Maybe."

There's one silver lining to the fact that Isiah is right here in this room with me. He's not on his way back to Washington to try to get ahead of my story about his fucked-up board in his apartment.

"Are you here to explain what I saw this morning?" I ask.

"You saw nothing but my research into a family I'm considering an alliance with."

I shake my head. "I know what I saw, and that was fucked up. How did you even know I was at the spa this morning?"

"I'm the king of fucking London, love. I know everything that goes on in my city."

"Bullshit. The city is too big for you to know everything." Her eyes narrow. "Are you tracking my aunt's phone?"

He smirks and opens my robe without a word, making me heat as he takes in my almost naked body. All I'm wearing are my panties. "It's lucky I got here before that masseuse came in here. If I'd found him with his hands on you, he'd have lost them, and that would have been a very bloody ordeal."

Dread creeps down my spine as I notice the coldness in his eyes. He isn't joking. "That's ridiculous. He's just doing a job."

"I don't care." Isiah forces me around and pushes me back down on the table, face first. "Only I get to touch you."

"No, we're not married," I say, trying to overpower him, but he's too strong. "You don't have any right to touch me."

He laughs, a cruel and vindictive sound that sends terror right through my heart. "I owned you from the second we met, love." His hands land on my ass cheeks in a firm spank. "Your eyes gave away what you wanted, even if your mouth denied it. You wanted me then, and you still want me now... even when I treat you like shit."

"That's not true!" I hate the way my stomach clenches knowing I'm lying. Despite everything, that attraction I felt the first day we met just doesn't want to quit.

Isiah's fingers skate down my spine, making me shiver, pausing at the waistband of my panties. And then, he tears them off without warning, and suddenly his hot tongue is probing at my soaking wet pussy. Pleasure rips through me like a thunderbolt.

"Isiah!" I cry out his name, unable to deny the pleasure coursing through me, despite the hatred I feel for him.

He devours my pussy, licking deeper with each thrust of his tongue. "So delicious and all mine," he murmurs, fingers digging into my stinging ass cheeks. And then he does something that takes my breath away and shocks me to the core. His tongue circles my asshole, making me tense.

"What are you—?" I try to ask what he's doing but am silenced by a sharp swat.

"I'm licking your tight little asshole, love. I intend

to fuck it soon enough," he murmurs as his lips brush my sensitive flesh.

"No chance," I say, trying to scramble away from him.

He grabs my hips before I get anywhere and yanks me back toward him, and then he's licking my asshole again. I hate how good it feels, the illicit thrill of him doing that to such a forbidden part of my body. "You know you don't get a say in the matter, Bella," he growls against my skin, sending shivers down my spine.

The way he says my name sounds so dirty as he continues to lick me, sending a new kind of pleasure through me. My pussy is dripping onto the massage table and no doubt making a mess.

He pulls away from me and I glance over my shoulder to see him grinning wickedly. "I'd say by the way you're wetter than I've ever seen before, you're quite into the idea of getting fucked in your tight little asshole." His voice is low and husky, sending a new wave of pleasure through me.

I sink my teeth into my bottom lip, wishing he'd just make me come and fuck off already. It's an odd sensation, wanting him to pleasure me and yet hating being in his presence. "Why can't you just leave me alone?"

He tilts his head. "Because I came to London to spend time with my fiancée, and that's exactly what I intend to do." And then he pinches my clit, the pain and pleasure that courses through my body is untenable.

He lifts my hips off the massage table to get better access to me and then he devours me with his tongue. He licks and sucks, exploring and teasing at my ass and pussy in succession.

And then he shoves his fingers deep into my pussy, continuing to lick my ass as he does, driving me wild with the need for release.

I'm writhing on the massage table now, my head thrown back in ecstasy as he presses down on my G-spot. My moans grow louder, Isiah's name spilling from my lips like a prayer repeatedly, making me hate myself in the process. He pulls his fingers out and sucks on my clit, dragging his teeth over it until I'm breathless.

"Please," I moan, hating that he's reduced me to this. I'm begging him to make me come and it makes me sick.

He chuckles. "Are you begging, love?"

I bite the inside of my cheek. "Just make me come."

"Maybe if you ask nicely," he says.

I shake my head, trying to stave off the rage simmering like an inferno within me. "Please make me come," I say.

And then he thrusts two fingers back inside, his tongue probing at my ass. That's all it takes to bring my orgasm crashing down on me, exploding through me like a wildfire, consuming everything in its path.

As wave after wave of pleasure washes over me, Isiah doesn't stop licking and sucking every part of me until every last drop of my arousal is consumed.

Once he's finished, he releases me and reality hits me. "Get out," I say, scrambling to my feet.

He shakes his head. "I'm not going anywhere. We're spending the day together in London."

I shake my head. "I'm leaving on a jet at two o'clock."

His eyes narrow. "Why?"

"You know why."

"Well, we'll see who gets there first."

I start toward him, forgetting I'm totally naked. "You better not go near my house."

"Or what?"

I'm shaking with anger as I grab my robe and throw it on. "We'll be leaving sooner, and I doubt your jet will be fueled and ready. Now get out of my way." I push him aside.

"See you in Washington, love. May the best person win." He winks.

I grunt in anger and head next door to Olivia's room, knowing forcing her to leave early is going to be difficult, but I won't let Isiah beat me back to my dad. He's unbelievable at times.

23

ISIAH

*B*ella comes rushing into her father's study, her shoulders slumping the moment she sets eyes on me. She was close, but not close enough.

"I thought you were still in London," I say, trying to remain casual.

After all, I've already told Gio my side of the story.

Gio stands. "So did I. Don't tell me that you flew back early all because of this silly little argument you had with Isiah."

Her eyes narrow to slits as she balls her fists by her sides. I've got to admit she's adorable when she's angry. "Argument? The man has a fucking board with all our faces on it in his home!"

"Isiah said it was more of a notepad on a desk than a board and that you were blowing it out of proportion in an attempt to get out of this wedding."

He runs a hand across the back of his neck. "Is that true?"

She shakes her head and marches closer. "No, he's lying to you."

"Do you have any proof?" Gio asks. "A photo, perhaps?"

I can feel the heat of her rage seeping from her pores as she glares at both of us. "I had a photo until Isiah threw my phone against the wall and smashed it to pieces."

"Who's lying now?" I say in a cool voice.

"That seems highly unlikely, Bella."

Bella growls like a feral animal. "You are fucking crazy if you think you can trust that man." She thrusts her finger in my direction.

"You're being hysterical," Gio says.

I can hardly contain the smirk that graces my lips as I watch her turn a scarlet red in pure rage.

"You're a fucking idiot!" she shouts, shaking her head. "If you won't do your duty to protect this family, then I'll have to!" She storms out of the room.

Gio sighs heavily. "I apologize about that. Don't let her outburst put you off, though. Most of the time, she's not so emotional."

Bella is right, the guy is a fucking idiot, thankfully. If he would only listen to his daughter, he would save himself and his family from devastation and ruin. I hate that it makes my admiration for my soon to be wife grow. She's been on my mind far too much lately and it's becoming a little irritating. As she's supposed to end up dead and buried just like the rest of them, just like Aiden was at their hands. Yet the idea of ending her is becoming less appealing by the day.

"Of course not. She doesn't faze me," I say, but it's a lie.

Gio smiles. "No, I don't suppose she would. I hear rumors that you dealt with some rats rather brutally over the weekend."

"Where did you hear that?" I ask, wondering if he has someone spying on me.

"News spreads fast in London and I have my ways to hear it."

I arch a brow. "Are you spying on me, Gio?" I ask, keeping the question lighthearted.

He laughs, shaking his head. "Of course not. I simply have a couple of contacts in London who keep me informed."

That basically means he's spying on me. If this were anyone else, I'd get angry and make an example out of him, but I need to remain in his good books, at least for now. I want to watch while everything he's built crumbles in front of his face and then I'll end his life.

Not that it would do much for him having someone spy on me, as they'll never learn the truth. I've kept the truth about my identity and intentions too well hidden.

"Fair enough," I say, standing. "If that's all—"

"Actually, I have an event I'd like you to attend at my club, Insignia, on Saturday."

My heart starts to beat harder and faster because that's the kiddy auction he's talking about. "What kind of event?" I ask.

"It's merely a party with some politicians. A work event to make more contacts."

I nod in response, which means that the auction isn't being held in the main club. It can't be, as I know Gio wouldn't invite me knowing my opinion on the matter. "Sure, I'll be there."

"Great, I'll ensure Bella accompanies you as your date." He claps me on the back, the physical contact from him making me feel sick. And yet, I plaster on a fake smile. "You two need to try to get over this rivalry you seem to have going on before the wedding in three weeks."

"I wouldn't call it rivalry."

"No?" Gio questions.

I shake my head. "Merely foreplay."

He laughs, and although I knew he'd find it funny, it surprises me anyway as we're talking about his daughter. Most fathers worth anything wouldn't like a man talking that away about his daughter. "Fair enough. I'll see you later." He nods toward the door.

I stand and take my leave, a flurry of thoughts racing through my mind.

I had planned to break into Insignia and stop the auction, but now I'm invited to Gio's party. It makes it all the more complicated. It'll be nearly impossible for me to sneak away from the party and into the auction without being seen, especially with an already suspicious fiancée by my side.

Gio really knows how to throw me a curve ball, and somehow, I have to navigate my way around it.

I PACE the length of Jane's room, trying to figure out how we're going to infiltrate the next meeting of these sick fuckers and bring them down when I've been invited as a fucking guest. It complicates things, as I sense the auction is going to be in a part of the club that's off limits. The corruption involved goes much further than just Gio's and his criminal outfit. It has government ties and that makes it trickier than anything I've tried before.

I can't work out whether being invited to the party, which is no doubt a guise for the auction, is a bad thing or good thing. A wrong move could jeopardize my entire plan to get revenge on the Benedetto family. And yet, I have to do this. How many children is Gio going to get away with hurting before he's brought to justice?

Jane sits with her back to her desk in her gaming chair, watching me. "So, what are you going to do?"

I shake my head. "I'm thinking."

She clicks her tongue. "I thought a man like you." She gives me a once over. "Would have a plan in place already."

"Being invited to the party complicates everything." I stop in my tracks. "And what do you mean, a man like me?"

"You look put together, so I assumed you had a plan in place once I got you the information, no matter the circumstances." Sighing heavily, she turns back to her computer and types on the keyboard. "I guess I misjudged you."

"Do you realize who I am?" I ask, clenching my fists by my sides.

"Isiah Darcy, criminal boss of the most powerful organization in London." She glances over her shoulder, grinning. "Yep, I know."

"How?" I ask, advancing toward her. "I haven't told you my name."

"Do you really think that a hacker like me would work with someone without knowing the person's identity?"

Although I've always felt at ease with Jane, I don't like the fact she knows who I am, even if it's not my true identity. "No, but tell me how you did it so I can avoid anyone else doing the same."

She smiles and grabs a cell phone case off her desk. "Put this on your phone and it will block anyone from hacking it."

I arch a brow. "You hacked my phone?"

She nods. "It was a little too easy for a man like you."

I swallow hard and take the case, fitting it to my phone. "Do you have any ideas for stopping these bastards?" I ask, nodding at the screen where she's mapped out everyone involved in the sick and twisted business Gio has his hands in.

"Yes, in fact, I do."

I perch on the edge of her desk. "Perfect, let me hear it."

"So, the people running the ring are two senators and Gio Benedetto as far as I can tell. They're the ringleaders, so to speak."

I nod in response. "And that helps us how?"

"They each have a bank account dedicated to the business we're trying to take down. They aren't in their name, but they are the beneficiaries. I'd say we take all the money in those accounts to start."

I sigh heavily. "They'll just replenish it." Gio is worth billions, so a few million or whatever is in those accounts will be like losing change to him.

"Not if we wire the money back via an illegal source, forcing the bank to put a block on the accounts."

Jane is smart, I'll give her that. "That could slow them down, but they have too many contacts. They'll unfreeze the accounts in hours, most likely."

She purses her lips. "Fuck."

"I think it's going to have to be a more physical approach."

Her face pales. "I know some guys who could help." She twirls her fingers in the ends of her hair. "A few of them wouldn't even want payment if they knew kids were involved."

"And you trust them?"

She shakes her head. "Not exactly, but they don't need to know your name or even see your face."

My brow furrows. "Are you suggesting that I let them do my work for me?"

"Well, you are a guest at the party, right? How are you going to break the kids out?"

She makes a good point, but I don't like entrusting something this big to men I don't even know.

"These men, they are vigilantes?"

"Yeah."

I sigh heavily, pinching the bridge of my nose. If I were in London, I'd have my men do it, but it's not like I can fly a bunch of them over without too many unanswerable questions cropping up. "Set it up," I say, wondering if I'll regret it. "I've got no other idea how to do this, so get me the men and give them the instructions on how to infiltrate the club." I draw in a deep breath. "Whatever it costs, I don't care."

Jane smiles, and it's an odd smile. "For a mobster, you sure care a lot about innocent kids."

"I may be a mobster, but I'm not a monster." I pin her with a determined glare. "Gio on the other hand..." I shake my head.

"Something tells me he did something to you that was very bad indeed."

I swallow hard, as there's no way I'm going to tell Jane about my true identity or Aiden's death at the hands of their family. "He took something from me," I grit out.

244

She nods as if she understands. "Someone you loved very much."

My gaze snaps to her face and I shake my head. "What do you know?" Suddenly, adrenaline courses through my veins as I wonder if I'm going to have to silence her forever.

"Nothing, I just saw that haunted grief in your eyes. It's a feeling I know all too well."

I clench my jaw, as I've never been an open book, but this girl just seems to see right through my shields. It puts me on edge, but unfortunately, I need her. "Fine. So, you'll arrange it with the men?"

"Of course, and I'll be stationed outside in my old van as your eyes and ears. I'll be linked to the guys and you and I'll hack the CCTV so I can see what's happening."

"We will meet Saturday afternoon here so you can give me the equipment and run over the plan you've given to the guys."

She does a mock salute. "Aye aye, captain."

I glare at her. "See you then." Turning around, I leave Jane's apartment, feeling a little on edge. Stopping the auction will be the first big move I've taken against Gio. I just hope it goes to plan, even as dread settles in my bones. All this time I've known Gio is bad news because he killed my brother, but there's nothing more deceitful than a villain, and it appears Gio is the worst villain I've ever known.

24

BELLA

"You look stunning," Isiah says as I stand in the entryway of my house, wishing I wasn't being forced into this.

"Whatever. Let's get this over with."

Dad appears. "Isiah, I'm glad you made it." He takes his hand and shakes it like the gullible idiot that he is. "Are we ready to go?"

Isiah looks confused. "Your wife isn't attending?"

"No." He clears his throat. "Viola doesn't like attending these events."

Mom hasn't been to Insignia with Dad in years. I don't know why. She used to, but one time they had a big argument after it and ever since she's never attended another one.

"What are we waiting for, then?" I ask, glaring at the two men I'm having to accompany to this bullshit party.

Isiah grabs my hand. "Nothing, let's go." He

forcefully leads me out into the driveway ahead of my father, leaning in to whisper, "Do you often go to these parties?" There's an odd tone to his voice.

"Never. This is the first I've been to."

Strangely, he relaxes the moment I say that. "Good."

My brow furrows. "Why's it good?"

He shakes his head and leads me over to the limousine waiting to take us to Insignia in the center of town. The driver is standing with the door open and I slip inside, hating that Isiah is right behind me, too close for my comfort, especially with my dad joining us. He slides in opposite and barely pays us any attention as he types on his cell phone.

Isiah leans toward my ear. "How about a repeat of last Saturday night after the party?"

I shake my head despite the heat building between my thighs at the mere reminder. "In your dreams. With my dad here, there's no way you're pulling that shit again."

His lips graze my earlobe. "What? Making you scream my name in pleasure and climax multiple times? So terrible," he purrs.

I glare at him. "You know that's not what happened. I said no, and you didn't care."

"Keep telling yourself that you didn't want it, love, if it makes you feel better."

"I'll tell you what would make me feel better," I say, meeting his heated stare. "Strangling you to death."

He laughs.

"It's not a joke."

"Sorry, love. It's just very hard to take you seriously when you threaten to kill me."

It's as if his mission in life is to piss me off. Instead of making a retort, I shift further away from him on the seat.

Dad glances up, smiling. "You two do make a wonderful couple."

I glare at him. "No, we don't. We can hardly even have a civil conversation. That's not a wonderful couple." I ball my fists by my sides. "How come you and Mom got to choose who you married?"

"Your mom and I were luckily a perfect match, both for the family and for each other." He tilts his head. "We met through our families and liked each other, and they approved of the match."

"Lucky for some."

Isiah clears his throat. "Don't worry, love. Once we're married, you won't be able to help falling for me." He winks, and I literally wish I could strangle him.

"Why are you so arrogant?"

He shrugs. "Part of the job description."

Gio laughs. "Yeah, it wouldn't do for him to be weak and meager, would it? The guy practically rules London."

I clench my jaw and stare out of the window, knowing that even though he's my dad, he'll never come to my aid. It's as if he doesn't care what happens to me or how I'm treated by Isiah. All my life, it's always just been Nina and me looking out for each other. The rest of my family I've never been close to, and yet I'm sure Isiah wants to do us harm. Which means if my dad isn't going to listen to my warnings, I have to find a way to stop him myself.

The limo pulls up at the curb in front of Insignia, my father's lavish and recently redesigned club.

The club is an exclusive, luxurious establishment, and the outside of it alone shows that. The entrance is a grand spectacle of gold and marble, with lush red and gold curtains cascading down the sides. Two marble pillars stand sentry on either side of the doorway. As always, Dad has gone overboard with the design.

From the sidewalk, there are marble steps with a red velvet carpet through the middle, leading to the entrance, which is guarded by two black-uniformed doormen.

The driver opens the door and I scramble out first, hoping to get away from Isiah, but it's a false hope. Isiah is out before I can take more than three strides, grabbing me by the arm. "Where do you think you're going?"

"Into the party," I say simply.

He yanks me toward the entrance of the club and straight past the guards without even glancing at them.

"Not without me." Isiah's grip tightens around my

arm as he drags me inside, his voice more demanding than ever. "You're my date. Act like it."

I shoot him a venomous glare before allowing him to drag me inside. Music thunders in my ears, while laughter and chatter fill the air. I'd been to this club before—the third time my father had invited me along to one of his parties.

Stepping into the main club, I stumble as Isiah's grasp abruptly slips away as someone greets him warmly. Immediately seizing my chance to escape, I hurry away without looking back. Freedom!

At one end of the room there's an area filled with plush sofas; people rest there while they sip their drinks and talk in low voices. At the opposite end is a stage where a live band plays, the music reverberating off the walls and giving life to the bored crowd dancing in front of them.

I want no part in this and I quickly walk away from it all toward the restroom instead, choosing to find solace further away from the crowd, far from Isiah's prying eyes. My night will be spent counting down the minutes until I can finally go home.

As I'm about to make it to the restroom, someone clears their throat. "Not so fast, love." A heavy hand clamps down on my shoulder, and then he slams me into the wall, the force of which takes my breath away. "Did you really think you could escape and hide from me?" His ice-blue eyes look alluring in the lighting of the club, a fact I hate to admit.

I shrug. "It was worth a shot."

He moves his hand to my throat and squeezes, asserting his dominance over me. "It's about time you stop playing games and accept the facts. You're mine, Bella Benedetto, and there's nothing you can say or do to change that fact."

I hate the way my stomach flutters hearing him say that. It's pathetic as this man is clearly unhinged and has no respect for women, and yet since he took my virginity, it feels like I'm connected to him in an irreversible way.

"I'll never willingly be yours."

He moves his body against mine, his hard muscles pressing against the length of me. "Are you sure about that?" he murmurs into my ear, lips teasing at the shell before gently skating down the side of my neck. "As the way you shudder at my touch suggests otherwise."

Fed up with his antics, I bring my knee up into his crotch.

He grunts and releases me, doubling over in pain. "What the fuck?"

I dart around him and into the ladies' room, trying to lock to the door behind me. And I fail, as he slams through it before I get to the lock. "Big mistake, sweetheart."

He stalks toward me like an angry wolf ready to rip apart a sheep from limb to limb.

"Stay away from me."

He tilts his head to the side. "Why would I do that when you just assaulted me?"

I bite my bottom lip, knowing that nothing can save me from his wrath now. His ice-blue eyes are swirling with rage as he stalks toward me. And then he surprises me by kissing me, stealing the oxygen from my lungs with one move as my heart thunders in my chest.

I melt into him, the passionate hatred I feel for him fueling my need to kiss him back, as I slide my fingers into his hair, enjoying the feel of his warm body against mine.

When we break apart, I'm in a daze, staring into those eyes I've come to hate and yet love all at the same time. "What the hell was that for?" I ask, stepping back from him.

He smirks. "Your feisty attitude gets me hot under the collar."

I shake my head. "And your arrogance drives me to despair."

"Is that true, Bella?" he breathes, stepping closer to me again. "You kissed me like a girl who's desperate to get fucked again."

My entire body tingles at his words as I shake my head. "We need to get back to the party." I try to move toward the door, but he blocks me.

"But do we really?"

I hold his gaze. "Yes."

"Okay, on one condition."

I narrow my eyes. "No conditions."

He chuckles. "I need another kiss before I let you go." Isiah leans toward me, expecting me to initiate.

I swallow hard, drawn to him despite everything. And then I press my lips to his in a quick, chaste kiss. As I'm pulling away, he laces his fingers in my hair and deepens it, his tongue sliding against my own. And then, he pulls back a little and looks into my eyes as if he can read me like a book. "Your cunt is dripping wet right now. I can see how turned on you are just looking into those pretty little eyes of yours." He drags his tongue down the side of my face, a move that should disgust me, but only increases the desire pooling between my thighs. "Now, let's go back to the party." With that, he grabs my arm and hooks it under his, before unlocking the bathroom door and leading me back out into the club.

"You really do make me despair," I say.

"Good," he mutters back.

And with that, the conversation is over as someone who knows him spots him and calls us over.

"Isiah, it's lovely to see you. I hear that there will be wedding bells soon," a short, middle-aged man says, smirking at me. "Such a beautiful prize you've won." His brow furrows. "But I assume you are not attending the auction?"

The lady next to him elbows him in the ribs. "You know that's not common knowledge."

"Oh, come on, Helen. I'm sure Isiah knows about it. He is very close to Gio."

I straighten, wondering what they're talking about, as Isiah's jaw clenches so hard it looks like he's trying to break it.

"I don't know what you're talking about," he says, eyes narrowed. "Now, if you'll excuse me. I have important people to talk to."

The two people's faces fall and they look very offended, as Isiah guides me away from them. Once we're out of earshot, I yank him to a stop and turn to look at him. "Why were you so rude to that couple?" I ask, unsure what his problem with them is.

"Let's just say they don't deserve civility," he replies, a steely edge to his voice.

"What do you mean?"

He shakes his head. "Don't pretend you're unaware of your father's activities at this club."

I feel my stomach sink as I honestly have no idea, but I sense it isn't good.

"I may be a criminal and do unspeakable things, but I draw the line at the shit he's got going on in the basement tonight."

I move closer to him, placing a hand on his arm. "Tell me what he's doing."

He glances at my hand, which rests on his arm, and then back into my eyes. "Your father is selling kidnapped children to pedophiles."

Those words feel like a physical blow, echoing through my skull like a hammering gong in a temple. I stare at Isiah in disbelief, tears shining in my eyes, my throat closing up as the stark truth of what is happening beneath us is too much to bear. I want to tell him he's lying or that he's wrong, but deep down, I know the truth.

He's trading in slavery, exploiting innocent lives for his own gain. People who deserve nothing more than love and support are bought and sold like objects to be abused by twisted predators—all under the guise of a normal club on the surface, but below ground... I can hardly bear to think of it.

ISIAH

I'm getting too sloppy with Bella as I stare at her, unable to believe the words that slipped out of my mouth.

"What did you say?" Bella asks.

I swallow hard. "You heard me."

"Are you saying that right now my dad is selling children to pedophiles in the basement?"

Why the hell did I say anything?

It's clear that this electric, toxic thing between us is getting out of control. As if I can't help myself but share things with her, which is dangerous. And yet, if she's going to be my wife, maybe it's a good thing that I'm being honest. "Yes." There's no backtracking now. Bella heard me loud and clear.

"That's sick."

I nod in response. "I agree."

"Then why are you here?"

I crack my neck as far as Gio knows I think this is

a standard party, and I'm completely unaware of the sick auction playing out below. "Your father invited me to the party, not the auction," I say simply.

"It always happens here?" she confirms.

I shrug. "Possibly."

"Explains why my mom won't come here anymore." She slumps into a chair at one of the tables. "Fuck." She holds her head in her hands. "Anyone that sick in the head needs..." she trails off, swallowing hard.

"Needs what?" I press, wondering if she agrees with my opinion that her dad needs to be stopped for good.

"It's bad to say, because he's my dad. But anyone who hurts children needs to be murdered and die a painful death."

I force my expression into neutral, unable to agree with that outright. It's like she's trying to lead me into a trap, as she's suspicious about my intentions already, let alone me agreeing that her dad deserves to be killed slowly and painfully.

When her dad suggested she come, I did wonder if she knew about the auction. It's clear she has no idea. "Do you want a drink?" I ask.

She nods. "I think I need one."

My feet move me away from Bella, desperate to get away. My fists clench tight, white-knuckled, as I struggle not to succumb to the rage brewing inside me, as one question repeats over and over in my mind.

Why the hell did I tell her?

The bar is crowded, and as I make my way to the front, I turn to my right and spot Alastair. My blood boils the moment he notices me and gives me a smarmy smile.

"Hey, Isiah. How are you?"

I grind my teeth together in an attempt not to smash this guy's face in. It was merely two weeks ago when he demanded two kids be delivered to him, and now he's here, no doubt, to bid on more innocent children.

"Fine," I mutter, moving my gaze back to the bar, as I can't stand looking at him. The guy should be behind bars, not a senator in the fucking government running the country.

The bartender notices me. "What can I get you?"

"Whiskey on the rocks and a pinot noir."

"Put it on my tab," Alastair chimes in, but I shake my head, refusing to accept his charity.

"No, I can buy my own drink. Thank you." My voice drips with loathing as I give him a cold stare.

The guy laughs it off, clapping me on the shoulder. "I know you can, but I want to get it for you."

The mere sensation of his touch sends a wave of nausea rolling through me, and all I want to do is break his arm in two. But I maintain control. There's no other choice. Losing my cool now and attacking Alastair for no reason will be suspicious, especially considering right now I've got three men breaking in downstairs to steal the children this asshole wants to bid on.

"Thanks, but no. I'll pay." I pull a fifty-dollar bill out of my pocket and pass it to the bartender as she returns with my drink. "Keep the change."

She smiles warmly. "Thanks."

I take my drink and take a sip, relishing the warm burn of alcohol. And then I grab Bella's wine and turn to Alastair. "Good to see you," I lie, holding up the glass of wine. "I need to deliver this to my fiancée."

He smiles. "Oh, of course. The beautiful Bella." He winks, and I hate how badly I want to destroy this man and can't. The need for violence tearing at my insides.

"See you around," I say, before turning and walking in the opposite direction.

"Boss, we've got a problem," Jane says in my ear.

I come to a halt, adrenaline pulsing through my veins as I press the intercom in my ear. "What kind of problem?" I hiss.

"The guys are struggling to find a way to get close to the kids." There's a few moments' delay before she says, "It could get messy."

"How messy?"

She doesn't answer right away, which only winds me up.

"Jane. Answer me."

"The guys are suggesting the only way to get them

out safely is a distraction. They're going to start a fire and nothing I say or do will stop them."

I pinch the bridge of my nose as a fire in the basement will tear through this entire club. "How long do I have?"

"Five minutes maybe, ten tops."

I sigh heavily. "Fine, keep me posted."

The moment the line goes dead, my mind goes to my fiancée and getting her out safely. If this place is going to go up in flames, then getting her out is a priority. As I scan the crowd for her, I wonder why it's a priority. After all, she has to come to an end like the rest of her family once I'm done.

I swallow hard and ignore the nagging at the back of my mind, hating that I can't find her.

Where the hell is she?

I backtrack toward where I'd left her to get a drink, and rage kicks me in the gut when I see she's over in the corner, talking to James Wick. Marching over there, I'm ready to murder him for looking at her, let alone talking to her.

"What the fuck do you think you're doing, James?"

He straightens at the sound of my voice. "Isiah, what an unpleasant surprise."

Bella laughs and I'm about ready to grab her and haul her over my shoulder like a caveman so I can take her back to the Waldorf Hotel and give her a good spanking.

I tilt my head. "Do you realize Bella is my fiancé?"

He squares up to me, as we're about the same height. "Yes, and your point?"

"My point is she belongs to me, so stay the fuck away from her." I shove him hard in the shoulder.

He shoves me back. "Nothing is set in stone until the wedding day." There's a taunting look in his eyes that makes me want to claw them out of his skull.

Grabbing a switchblade out of my jacket pocket, I open it and press the sharp tip to the underside of his chin. "Do you know what I do to men that touch what is mine?"

Bella starts forward, grabbing my arm. "Isiah, don't!"

I shrug her off, as she needs to learn what happens to men she shamelessly flirts with. When I threatened that boy Enzo at the restaurant, I meant it. I don't do well with sharing.

James tries to act tough, holding my gaze, which only angers me further. I slice the skin, cutting the underside of his chin deep enough to make him bleed badly.

His eyes dilate with pain. "What the fuck?"

"I'm only getting started."

He takes a step back as Bella tries to push me away. "Stop this insanity," she says.

James suddenly stiffens. "Does anyone else smell smoke?"

As if on cue, Jane's voice echoes in my ear. "Get the fuck out. It's going up like a tinderbox."

I sniff the air, trying to remain calm despite the

storm brewing within. "Yeah, where's that coming from?"

Bella notices the source and it's coming from the air vents. "It looks like it's coming from the basement." Her eyes go to mine and there's something in her expression. I can't work out if it's an accusation or just an understanding that it's coming from the auction, but she doesn't say anything.

Does she realize that I'm behind it?

There's no way I'd put it past her. She's smart. The fire alarms sound then, and I grab Bella's arm. "We need to get out of here now."

Gio appears from a door which I assume leads down to the basement. And a number of men and women come flooding out too in a huge plume of smoke. I take the moment to make a mental note of the pedo's faces as I will ensure none of them are breathing by the time I'm through with my work here in Washington.

"Fire!" Gio shouts, panic dripping from his voice. "Everyone needs to remain calm and get out of here in an orderly fashion."

As expected, panic ensues as everyone rushes for the exit.

"Do you know another way out of here?" I ask Bella.

Her lips purse and she nods. "The back, through the kitchen."

"Let's go," I say, yanking her in that direction.

She doesn't fight me as I rush her toward safety, my fight with James forgotten, for now.

We hustle through the kitchen and down a long, dark hallway, rounding a corner to a service exit. I open it and we burst out into the fresh air and into a staff car park at the back. And, instantly, I notice the guys Jane employed.

They're bundling six kids into the van Jane is in, masks on their faces.

Bella stops dead in her tracks when she sees them. "Are those..." She doesn't finish her question, shaking her head as tears pool in her eyes. "We need to help them." She tries to move forward, but I grab her wrist and stop her.

"What do you mean?" I ask.

"The children! We need to save them."

I shake my head and grab her cheeks, looking into her beautiful blue eyes. "They're safe."

Her brow furrows as she glances between me and the van. "Are you the one who started the fire?"

I shake my head. "No, I was with you the entire time."

"You know what I mean. Did you plan this? A kidnapping."

I clench my jaw, as I can't admit it. "I don't know what you're talking about."

She grunts in frustration. "If they are safe, it means you know those men!"

I crack my neck, feeling the tension building in my shoulders. "Let's just say I'm not the kind of man who can watch as children are sold like they're nothing more than merchandise."

The admiration that briefly flashes in Bella's eyes vanishes almost as soon as it appears.

"You've lost your mind, Isiah," she hisses. "My dad will murder you."

My lips feel dry as I lick them, hating how out of my depth I feel having to explain this to her. This wasn't part of the plan. "Not if you don't tell him."

Her delicate features are so fiercely set, it's almost as if she's been carved from marble.

The last child is bundled into the van and the door is shut. Within seconds, the vehicle speeds away, taking those innocent children to safety. Jane intends to drop them all off at their homes to ensure they're safe and back where they're supposed to be. None of us trust anyone in this city to do the right thing, not after the corruption we found within the government.

Bella doesn't say anything for a few moments, just keeps looking at me with intensity in her gaze.

"I won't tell him," she finally says, more to herself than to me. She looks right into my eyes. "But you can rest assured that I'll find out your true motive for marrying me," her voice drips with threat. "And when I do, I will make sure to put an end to whatever twisted plan you have against my family."

It's a rarity that anyone surprises me, but I find Bella's strength remarkable, especially after everything I've put her through. And, I wonder, as I stare into her eyes if I've finally met my match.

Could Bella be a threat to my entire plan for revenge?

I couldn't allow it. Revenge against the Benedetto family is all I've been living for since Aiden was taken from me. Grabbing her hip, I pull her close. "Have at it, love. I've got nothing to hide." Pressing my lips to the juncture between her neck and shoulders, I murmur against her skin, "Your deliciousness is enough of a reason to marry you, Bella."

Satisfaction races through me as she trembles. And then I sink my teeth gently into her skin, making her moan at the exquisite sting. "And I will have you, no matter what happens." Moving my lips to her ear, I mutter, "If you tell your father what I did today, I'll just kidnap you and make you my fucking pet. Do you understand? There's no escape from me because I own you, mind, body and fucking soul."

Her breathing is labored as she meets my gaze, her lips parting as desire overwhelms her. Bella has her own inner strength and yet she's addicted to dominance. I see it in the way she melts every single time that I'm assertive with her, and that has to be enough to maintain control of this situation.

Bella is getting too close for comfort, and I can't let her learn the truth.

26

BELLA

I have been dreading this day for an entire month, the longest month of my life. And my suspicions about Isiah and his intentions toward my family have only grown exponentially since seeing the board in his London apartment and then learning he was involved in the fire in the basement of Insignia.

And yet, the last one I can't help but admire him for. He risked everything to save innocent children, an oddly selfless act for a man who always appears cold and aloof.

Even so, I've voiced my concerns about Isiah's reason for marrying me to my father over and over, and every time he dismisses me. I know deep down Isiah is hiding something huge.

Today I'm going to be forced to walk down the aisle and say "I do" to a man who clearly has it out for my family.

I stand in front of my dressing mirror, barely able to recognize the woman staring back. In a month, it feels like my whole world has been turned upside down, and all because of one man. A man I hate.

All I want to do is run far away and never look back, but I'm not stupid enough to believe I'd make it very far. Both my dad's and Isiah's powers and influence are too much to contend with.

A soft knock sounds at the door and Nina opens it, giving me a sad smile. "I can't believe this is happening," she mutters.

I shake my head. "Me neither."

Her eyes travel the length of my body, taking in the sight of my wedding dress. "You look absolutely stunning."

It's a beautiful dress, made from a soft white tulle fabric adorned with intricate ivory floral lace applique. My waistline has been cinched by an exquisitely beaded band of exquisite crystal beadwork along the edges and throughout the bodice. The sleeves are long and fitted to my arms, constructed from layers of lace and cascading over each shoulder. Meanwhile, the skirt falls to floor length in a light silhouette that sweeps gracefully as I walk. It truly is a gorgeous dress and I can't help but feel sad that I'm wearing it to marry Isiah Darcy, a man I despise.

Nina is wearing a beautiful pale pink dress as my bridesmaid.

"How are you feeling?"

I give her a look that says don't ask.

She nods. "I thought as much." Walking forward, she sighs heavily. "It's ironic, isn't it?" she asks.

"What is?"

"You don't want to marry Isiah and you have to and I wanted to be with Cathal and he doesn't want me." She shakes her head. "Are we doomed to never get what we want?"

I know that ever since Cathal broke things off with Nina, she's been spiraling into darkness again. He made her better when he was around, but now...I hate to think what will happen when I'm no longer living here, thousands of miles away.

"Yeah, pretty fucking shitty, if you ask me."

She laughs, but it's humorless, placing her hands gently on my shoulders as she tries to console me.

"Come on," she says. "Let's go and get this over and done with."

I swallow hard. "I'm being married to a monster."

"Did you ever expect any different?"

As I think about that question, I realize this is what I've expected all my life, so why does it feel so wrong?

Taking a deep breath, I shake my head. "No, I supposed I didn't."

I grab the bouquet of white roses and then walk out into the hallway with Nina.

The sound of the organ music fills my ears and sends a chill down my spine.

The wedding venue is nothing short of stunningly

beautiful; it looks as if it's been taken right out of a fairytale book. The walls are draped in white silk fabric with golden accents adorning every corner, while crystal chandeliers provide a soft glow to the already romantic atmosphere. A red carpet leads us to where Isiah stands alongside Cathal, who he asked to be his best man.

I know it's difficult for Nina to see him, as she barely looks in his direction.

The look in Isiah's eyes is cold, yet calculating as he watches me approach him with Nina close to my side.

I try not to tremble as I stop and stand in front of him, attempting to compose myself for what's about to come next—exchanging vows, signing documents and entering into an eternity of what could only be described as modern-day slavery—but no matter how hard I try, I can't help feeling utterly terrified.

The priest begins reciting from the *Bible*. Though my mouth moves mechanically in time with his words, I can't take in any of it.

Until I hear him murmur, "You may now kiss the bride."

The force of Isiah's kiss stuns me, twisting my insides with dread and humiliation. He kisses me long and hard, like a warning—I belong to him now.

It's embarrassing the way he's kissing me in front of hundreds of guests, all eager witnesses to a union that only one of us wanted. But no one cares. This is how it's done in the mafia and always will be.

Finally, the kiss ends and Isiah grabs my hand to lead me away from the altar. Despite his tight grip on my fingers, I feel an inexplicable sense of relief—this ordeal is finally over.

As we make our way out of the church and into a limo waiting outside to take us to the reception, I can feel Nina's gaze on me. She smiles softly, giving me one final hug before I get into the car.

I take one last look as the car careens down the dirt road, leaving the darkness of my past and family behind, only to replace it with more.

But I'm still not free—as far as the law and the world are concerned, I'm still Isiah's.

His hand suddenly slides up my arm, his fingers wrapping around my wrist as he pulls me closer to him. His fingers feel like hot irons on my skin, burning through the thin fabric of the sleeves of my dress.

He looks into my eyes. The ice-blue hue of his are so vibrant and his face is so close that I can feel his breath ghosting over my sensitive skin. Our eyes lock and a smirk curls up his lips as he whispers, "You're mine forever now, love."

The words send a chill down my spine, but I remain unmoved. I raise an eyebrow and reply softly yet firmly, "I'll never be yours in the true sense of the word."

The smirk remains firmly in place, and it takes all my willpower not to punch it right off of his face. "We will see."

I shake my head, ignoring the searing anger that

tries to tear forth. I won't engage in any more point-less arguments with this man. He's impossible. "I will find out why you wanted to marry me, if it's the last thing I do." I glare at him then, anger burning like a bonfire in my heart. "And then I'll stop whatever plan you have against my family dead in its tracks."

He just smirks at me, totally arrogant. Neither denying nor affirming that there is a plan to stop. "I can't wait to get you into my bed tonight, love."

"I'd rather throw myself off a bridge."

He chuckles. "I highly doubt that."

Finally, the car comes to a stop outside of the Waldorf Hotel. The same hotel that we're booked into for the night before flying to the Maldives for our honeymoon. An aspect I begged my father not to force on us, but he and Isiah were having none of it. The idea of being confined to a tiny island with this man makes my skin crawl.

I get out as fast as I can, trying to put distance between me and my husband, but he is too fast. He grabs my wrist when I'm a mere two steps away from the limousine and pulls me to his side. "Where do you think you're going, wife?"

"Anywhere away from you."

He almost tenderly pushes the hair away from my face and leans down to whisper in my ear, "There's no escape now, love."

The sinister tone of his voice sends tremors through my body. To any onlooker, it would be as if he's being loving and attentive to his new wife, but that couldn't be far from the truth.

"I hate you."

He forces my hand onto his arm. "Stay close and don't try anything," he says.

I dig my nails into the fabric, trying to find some way to hurt him, but it's no use. This man is made of steel and there is no hurting him, at least, not in any way that I've discovered yet.

The events hall is packed already with guests who weren't invited to the ceremony, but have been invited to the party, all of whom are my dad's friends. Proof that this wedding and party has nothing to do with me or my marriage to Isiah. It's all about connections and politics and it makes me sick.

Ever since Isiah revealed the shit my dad is into, I can hardly look at my father the same way. He may not be the one physically abusing the children, but he has a hand in kidnapping and selling them for fuck's sake.

And Isiah doesn't agree with it. It makes me wonder if that has something to do with his plot against the family, but my instincts tell me it's just the tip of the iceberg.

"Isiah, congratulations," a man says, stepping forward.

He smiles, and it's such a false smile it makes my stomach churn.

Am I the only one who sees through him?

"Thank you, David." He glances at the woman on his arm. "Is this your wife?"

The woman laughs. "No, I'm his girlfriend."

My brow furrows. "What?"

David clears his throat. "She's joking," he says, giving her a pointed look.

"Alison and I'm not joking." She holds a hand out to me and I shake it. "This one has been promising he'll leave his wife for over three years now."

I arch a brow. "Then why don't you leave him?"

David straightens. "Do you realize I'm right here?"

Isiah smirks. "Don't bother. There's no reasoning with her."

I glare at him. "I hope you don't think that's acceptable behavior."

He turns to me. "If a woman isn't putting out, then what's a man supposed to do?"

I clench my fists by my sides. "You aren't the type of man who cares whether a woman consents or doesn't."

The accusation hangs in the air between the four of us, making David and Alison visibly uncomfortable.

Isiah, being the arrogant son of a bitch he is, laughs it off and shakes his head. "I've never done anything to you that you didn't want." He seems untouchable, like a wall of steel, as if nothing can penetrate him.

"That's a lie," I spit.

Isiah doesn't back down, though. His ironclad grip tightens on my hip as he says to the couple, "It was lovely speaking with you. Enjoy the party."

He guides me away from them, though I fight against him with every step.

I yank away from him and slam my fist into his chest, which hardly seems to faze him, as if he's made of stone. "You're an arrogant liar."

He tilts his head to the side. "I'm not lying."

"I told you no countless times in your apartment."

"Your mouth may have said no, but we both know that's not really what you wanted."

I feel a murderous rage building in my chest as I look at this man who believes he can control me. "You're impossible," I mutter, turning away from him to put distance between us.

But he grabs my wrist and yanks me back into him, pulling my body against his solid chest. "You're not going anywhere," he breathes, placing his hands on my hips.

His touch sends sparks of pleasure through my veins and makes my stomach clench with desire. I hate that I still react this way from his touch after everything he has done to me.

"Get your hands off of me," I say, keeping my voice level despite the fact that deep down, I'm shaken by my husband. No matter how much I try to remain strong and not give in to his ways, the passion between us is impossible to ignore. And then someone

BIANCA COLE

speaks over the microphone. "It's time for the newly-weds to have their first dance."

I grind my teeth when I see Cain standing at the microphone, smirking at me. Smug bastard.

"Indeed, I think he's right," Isiah mutters, leading me toward the dance floor.

The look in his eyes concerns me, as it's full of evil intent. He grabs me by the waist once we're on the dance floor and takes my hand, drawing me close to his body. "Try to keep up, love."

"I don't think I'll be having any trouble." The music starts and Isiah whisks me into a waltz across the dance floor, but I match him step for step.

We spin around the room, our eyes locked, and I'm almost mesmerized by him despite everything. We move as one like a perfectly choreographed dance and every time his hand presses into my lower back or his fingers intertwine with mine, I can feel the electric current between us. Every inch of my body tingles with anticipation as he guides me through our next few steps in perfect time to the music.

He presses his lips to my ear and murmurs, "You look like your mind is elsewhere, love."

I shudder at the tone of his voice, whenever he touches me I can't help my mind from wandering to thoughts of the way he took my virginity. It was savage and brutal and yet I've fantasized about it far too many times, bringing myself to orgasm with my vibrator.

It's almost like a scene out of a fairytale with

everyone's eyes on me because we're the bride and groom. But this isn't a fairytale—it's reality—and I know that I can't let my guard down.

Isiah pulls me closer to him as we reach the end of the dance, so close that our noses touch. His voice is low and intoxicating when he speaks, "Let go for once."

I drag my tongue over my bottom lip. "Let go of what?"

"The futile desire to remain in control, no matter the cost. Let me show you just how good submission can be."

I nod in response, knowing that there's no use fighting it any longer. Spending hours at this reception won't make a difference. We might as well leave sooner rather than later, as there's no point putting it off.

"We will have to thank everyone," Isiah says.

I swallow hard. "I'd rather not."

His eyes narrow. "It's rude not to say goodbye to all these people."

"Fine." I nod toward the stage. "Make it quick."

Isiah pulls me close again. "Nothing about tonight is going to be quick. It's going to be the longest, most memorable night of your life."

With that, he leads me up to the stage, but I can hardly think straight. My entire body quivers with anticipation of what's coming. Even though I try to profess that I hate this man, my body craves his dominance. And with that thought, I remember the first vulgar thing he said to me.

Wait until you've been dominated by a real man in bed and see if you are still a feminist, love.

I fear that any feminism I had has been obliterated, as no sane feminist would want a man that treats her the way Isiah has treated me so far.

27

ISIAH

*I*t's surreal to think that I'm married to my enemy's daughter. Tied to her in the eyes of the law, and for some reason, I don't feel as dirty as I expected. In fact, getting married to Bella and being able to call her mine is the highlight of this entire fucking revenge plot so far.

The fire hasn't gone out in her eyes, as I sit down in a seat on the jet opposite her, since I decided we'd make a head start and go straight to the Maldives for our honeymoon. We had been booked into the Waldorf Hotel, but I wanted to get Bella out of Washington. Satisfaction coils through me, as I've got one week alone with her on a private island for our honeymoon, and I intend to make the most of it.

"How are you feeling, Mrs. Darcy?"

Her eyes narrow. "Don't call me that."

"What? It's your name now." I lean forward,

clasping my hands together and staring at her. "You belong to me now, Bella."

She shudders at that, either from arousal or fear, both of which excite me. "I don't belong to anyone. I'm a human being. You can't own me."

"You're wrong. In our world, marriage may as well be slavery." I stand and walk behind her seat, setting my hand on the back of it. I lean down to whisper in her ear. "Before long, you'll be screaming my name. And every single time I ask you who you belong to, you'll tell me my name repeatedly, and if you don't I won't let you come."

Bella gets out of the seat and turns to face me, a flame of anger burning in her eyes. "You've no right to speak to me like that," she hisses. "I'm not a puppet you can use for your own pleasure."

I chuckle darkly, watching her. "That's what a wife is. A puppet." I step toward her, and she backs away, clenching her fists by her sides as she realizes I'm backing her into a corner. There's nowhere for her to go.

Once her back hits the wall, I notice the way her lips part. Even now, as she fights it, her body is craving what I can give her. Pure pleasure. It's clear that she wants me as badly as I want her, and it's intoxicating.

I place my hand gently around her throat and squeeze. "And you may scream and shout that you don't want to be used, but deep down, I can see it in your eyes. You want me to take you against your will."

I drag my lips across her cheek. "And in time, you will submit to me willingly."

The fire in Bella's eyes flares brighter, and a vein pulses in her temple as she straightens and meets my gaze, even while my hand remains wrapped around her throat like a collar. Her hands tremble ever so slightly as if she is fighting the urge to reach out and touch me—or push me away.

"Do you really think that? That I will just bow down to you?" She spits the words at me, venom dripping from every syllable.

"You may not believe it now," I say calmly, relishing the tension between us that threatens to boil over into something more physical any minute. "But it's inevitable. You won't be able to fight the chemistry between us as I force you to submit over and over." I slide my tongue down the edge of her face and she shivers, her entire body shaking.

My smirk widens as I realize that Bella is fighting against her own desires just as much as she is trying to defy mine. The jet starts to move and the hostess on the plane clears her throat.

"I apologize for interrupting, but you must be seated for takeoff."

I glare at her and release Bella's throat. "Fine." I grab her hand and lead her over to the seat I'd been sitting in. "You will sit on my lap, love."

The hostess looks like she wants to tell me that's not allowed, but when I glare at her, she backs off and walks away.

"Let go of me," Bella says, trying to wriggle out of my grasp.

Which only makes me tighten my grip on her. "No," I reply simply, pushing her down onto my lap so she's facing me.

She squirms on my lap, which is a mistake, as she's only making me harder than nails the more she tries to fight away from my touch. I stroke her thigh slowly and deliberately, making it difficult for her to move away as the pleasure outweighs her desperate need to disobey me.

A soft, hardly audible moan escapes her lips as I move my hand between her thighs and hike up the hem of her wedding dress. "Be a good girl and moan for me, love."

She's about to say something when I slam my fingers deep into her soaking wet cunt. The moan that escapes her lips is tantalizing as I move my fingers in and out of her.

"You are so wet, Bella," I groan, hating the raspy quality of my voice as this girl has me twisted up over her. "Is it because you can't stop thinking about my cock?"

Her lips purse and her eyes flash with a mix of anger and desire. "Definitely not."

"It sure as hell feels like it." I grab the back of her neck and yank her lips to mine. "I can't wait to be deep inside you."

She shudders as I slide my tongue into her mouth, kissing her like I've never kissed someone before. It's all-consuming. The desire I feel for my wife is addictive and I fear that's a bad thing. She's a Benedetto. A part of my revenge plan, which means I need to break my addiction. For now, I'll indulge in her.

"Isiah," she murmurs my name as we break apart.

"What is it?"

Her lips purse and she shakes her head. "Nothing."

I know that deep down she's been waiting for this all night.

She gasps as I move my fingers deeper inside her, hitting the spot I've quickly learned drives her wild with need.

"This isn't going to stop on this airplane," I whisper against her ear. "Once we get to the island in the Maldives, I intend to make you moan non-stop for an entire fucking week. You'll be so well fucked, you won't be able to walk back onto the plane." I nip her earlobe with the edge of my teeth. "I'll have to carry you, and even then I won't show you mercy, love. I'll fuck you the entire way home."

Bella shudders, her eyes dilating with a mix of fear and desire at my words. Increasing the pressure as I finger her makes her whimper softly, and I know if I keep pushing, she won't be able to last much longer before she comes undone, but I don't want that.

I withdraw my fingers, enjoying the way disappointment flashes across her face. And then I spin her around so that I can unlace her dress as it's getting in the way. She may constantly deny her desire, but that disappointment tells the truth more than her words ever do.

"Are you desperate, love?" I ask, as I unfasten it as quickly as I can.

"I'm not desperate for anything from you," she replies, as the dress drops to the floor

I spin her around and grab a fistful of her hair and yank her close, my lips skating over her jaw. "Such a liar. And yet I love that you lie. It makes it so much more satisfying when I see the truth in your eyes." I drag my teeth over her skin gently, wanting nothing more than to devour this girl in every way, consume her until she's nothing but a shell.

Releasing her hair, I grab the bag at my feet.

Bella's brow furrows. "What are you doing?"

I smirk at her. "You'll see soon enough."

Reaching into the bag, I pull out a vibrator first.

Her lips purse together.

"Let's see if you can still lie after I've played with you for an hour."

Her throat bobs as she swallows. "That's a long time."

"Indeed, and by the time I'm through, you won't be able to stop begging me for my cock."

She shakes her head. "That will never happen."

Instead of responding, I turn on the vibrator in my hand and press it against her clit.

Her entire body jolts at the pleasure tearing through her body as she gasps, arching her back.

I take it slow with her—pushing her closer and

closer to orgasm until she's on the precipice of coming apart. And then I switch it off and pull it away.

The gasp that leaves her lips is tantalizing as she gazes down at me, flushed and more beautiful than I've ever seen her. "Why did you stop?"

I tilt my head. "Because you were going to come, and I'm not going to let you until I buried balls deep inside this perfect little cunt." I slip a finger inside her, groaning at how wet she is.

Her nostrils flare as rage mixes with lust. "You're disgusting."

I place the vibrator down on the arm of the chair and reach into the bag, grabbing an anal plug and lube. Her ass is fucking perfect and I want to be the man to ruin it, stretch it apart with my cock and introduce her to a pleasure she never knew existed.

Grabbing her hips, I lift her off of my lap and forcefully bend her over the arm of the chair. "So fucking beautiful," I muse, almost to myself, as I take in the sight of her dripping wet cunt and tight little asshole. "And all mine."

She looks at me over her shoulder. "I'll never be yours."

I smile and reach for the lube, squeezing a generous amount on my fingers. "We'll see."

I spread her ass cheeks and rub the plug against her tight hole, feeling the heat radiating from it. I circle my finger around it before pushing my thumb inside, stretching her out first.

She grunts at the sudden intrusion of a foreign object in her ass but quickly adjusts, panting as I gently thrust into her body with two fingers. Slowly, her body relaxes as she begins to pant, accepting three fingers into her ass. Her pussy is dripping wet and running down her thighs.

"Isiah," she gasps my name as I add a fourth finger.

"Yes, love?"

She shakes her head. "What are you doing to me?" The exasperation in her voice makes my cock harder than ever.

"Making sure that you never forget this night, love. I'm going to use every single one of your holes until you can no longer think straight." I finger her harder, stretching her ass until it's relaxed enough to accept the plug, so I pull my fingers out and add lube to the anal plug.

I brush my fingertips over the smooth metal of the plug, pressing it firmly into her ass and relishing her contented moan. Her body writhes in pleasure as I move my deft fingers over her clit.

"My little slut loves her plug, doesn't she?" I muse, as her hips grind backward as if she wants her ass fucked.

Bella doesn't respond, as she's lost to the sensation.

I grab the vibrator, pressing it onto her clit as I slip my fingers into her wetness. Her back arches as she gasps out loud, the sound a reminder of why I love dominating girls like Bella. "You're such a filthy girl," I say, thrusting my fingers in and out of her soaking wet cunt. "I bet you'd love my cock deep in your asshole."

I'd promised her an hour of teasing, but it's impossible to resist her while she melts for me.

She's so ready for me and the need to fuck her wins out over teasing her, as I remove the vibrator, chucking it on the chair.

A whimper of protest leaves her lips, but she'll soon be satisfied. Fumbling with the zip of my trousers, I release my throbbing cock and slide the head up and down her wetness before settling against her swollen clit.

"Isiah, please," she begs.

I grind my teeth together as her begging has me on the edge of snapping any sense of control I currently have. "What do you want, love? Tell me."

She glances over her shoulder at me with those vibrant blue eyes. "Fuck me," she utters, hardly audible, and yet the word reverberates through me.

"You're mine," I whisper, thrusting forward with one powerful motion. I growl in pleasure as she wraps around me like a vise. "And always will be."

The plug in her ass makes her tight channel even tighter and I can't control myself any longer—I ram into her again and again until the beast within has taken control.

She trembles beneath me as each sensation tears

through her body, pushing her even closer to the edge.

"You are so fucking tight," I murmur, gently dragging my fingers down her spine. Once I get to the base of her spine, I spank her ass cheeks in quick succession, making her gasp in surprise. Her body shakes with pleasure as she gasps my name over and over again, each time getting louder.

Abruptly, I force myself to stop and pull out of her, only long enough to flip her onto her back on the chair, forcing it to recline.

Bella stares up at me, cheeks flushed and eyes dilated to the point there's barely any blue left.

"Do you want my cock in your ass?" I ask, grabbing the lube and pouring it onto my cock.

Her lip trembles as she glances at my cock and then back at my face. "It won't fit."

I smirk, stroking my cock at the mere thought of forcing my way into her tight little hole. "Trust me, love, it will fit." I grab the metal base of the plug and slowly pull it out, groaning at the way her muscles cling to it. Grabbing her thighs, I force them up high so that her ass is visible to me and then I align the head of my lubed coated cock with her already stretched hole. "You are gaping for me already," I say, my voice laced with desire.

"It's going to hurt," she says, a hint of fear in her voice, and I can't work out if it's a statement or a question.

"At first," I say, placing the head of my cock at her

tight hole and easing it inside, inch by inch.

Initially, she turns tense. "It hurts!"

"Relax," I say, looking into her eyes as I keep a steady, slow pressure.

Her breathing hitches as I go deeper, pushing myself all the way until she's filled with every single inch of me. "Are you all the way inside?" she asks, sounding in awe.

"Every fucking inch is in your ass."

She moans, eyes sliding shut as the pleasure takes over all other sensations.

I tighten my grasp on her thighs and move my cock out of her a few inches.

She shudders.

"See," I breathe, forcing her to look at me. "I told you I'd make it fit. And I'm never wrong."

She rolls her eyes, but there's a hint of a smile on her lips. And then the moment I slam back inside her, everything but pleasure disappears as she moans.

Slowly, I fuck her. Each thrust builds upon the last until it's enough, and we're both moaning our pleasure to the night sky.

My hips are relentless as I work my way deeper and deeper inside her tight heat. Her ass clings to me like a glove, milking me for all it's worth as I ram into her over and over again. I pick up the pace, pounding into her hard and fast as I get closer to my own release.

For the first time in my life, I feel out of control. Bella makes me lose control—a dangerous notion.

I focus on driving us both to release, pushing Bella to the brink. I lean down and capture her cries with my lips and as I suck on her tongue, I feel her begin to quiver around me.

"Come for me!" I growl into her ear as I increase the power of my thrusts even more. Her entire body tenses up beneath me before wave after wave of pleasure flows through her body—triggering her orgasm.

"Isiah!" Bella screams out my name, coming hard and long. I fuck her through it and kiss her lips, swallowing her moans as her channel grips me so tightly it builds my own orgasm. The sound of her voice in the throes of passion is the sexiest thing I've ever heard.

My release hits me hard and fast and I erupt inside her, filling her ass with my cum. "Fuck, that's it, love. Take all of my cum in that tight fucking ass of yours."

She moans at that, eyes rolling back in her head as I fuck her through the pleasure.

Finally, once I'm spent and we've come down from our mutual highs, I pull out of her. The sight of my cum dripping out of her gaping ass makes me insane. As I grab the plug and gather as much as I can of the cum, pushing it back inside with the plug. "I want all of my cum to remain inside you. Do you understand?"

Her lips purse as she nods her head. Bella is still trembling against me, eyes half-lidded with pleasure, and it feels like something has changed between us tonight. And I'm not sure I like it.

I can't control the pull between us, no matter how hard I try. After Aiden's death, I thought I'd never feel anything for anyone again. But I can't seem to resist Bella, even with all the risks—it's so dangerous to let her in.

All I should feel toward her is hatred, but even with all the risks involved, there are moments when she's so captivating it makes me want her more.

I thought perhaps having her in London would end this madness, but the desire for her just grows exponentially. At this rate, I'll be professing my love for her in no time, something I fear more than anything in this world.

Bella angles her chin upward as if she wants me to kiss her, but I don't. Sobered by the sickening thoughts of love. Instead, I straighten and nod toward the back of the aircraft. "Go into the bedroom and get on all fours on the bed and wait for me like a good girl."

Her throat bobs as she swallows. "What?"

"You heard me. I intend to fuck you until you're so exhausted you can't keep your eyes open."

Her eyes fill with a combination of fear and desire as she follows my instruction with a timid nod.

This week is going to be a wild ride, as she starts to submit to me completely. Fearful anticipation flutters in my chest, but it's too late—I'm already falling for her, no matter how much I try to avoid the fact. I chase after my wife, determined to show her the true meaning of pleasure before we reach the Maldives.

BELLA

My eyes flutter open, and instantly I sit up straight, glancing around the unrecognizable room frantically. My stomach knots as I blink my eyes against the sunlight streaming through the window.

Once they've adjusted to the light, I can see the azure sea twinkling outside of the villa. Taking a deep breath, I try to orient myself, wondering how I got to the water villa and somehow don't remember arriving.

The night before on the airplane was insane. I remember the way Isiah took me over and over again, fucking me for what felt like hours, until I collapsed on the bed in the back of the jet and fell asleep.

I must have been so exhausted that I didn't even wake when the plane landed, which is crazy. Heat floods my entire body as I remember how dominant he was, forcing me over the chair and using toys on me before fucking me in the ass. That was only the start of it, as he spent a couple more hours fucking every one of my holes and making me come so many times, I lost count.

Trying to sit up, I feel so sore between my legs. I get out of the bed and slowly make my way to the window, finding my body is aching all over, particularly my ass. The sparkling azure sea is glittering below me and for a millisecond I feel content due to the awe-inspiring beauty until I remember why I'm here.

My honeymoon.

A honeymoon after marrying a man I can hardly stand.

I force my gaze away from the sea and turn back to the room, noticing my cell phone on the nightstand. Isiah must have put it there. I march over and grab it, hitting Nina's number in my contacts.

She picks up on the fifth dial tone. "What the hell?" She sounds sleepy.

And that's when I realize we're like nine hours ahead of the US and it's almost midday. "Shit, sorry. I completely forgot about the time difference."

She sighs heavily. "Don't worry. What's up?"

"Isiah is a pig."

She laughs. "Tell me something I don't know."

"He fucked me non-stop on the flight over and at some point, I passed out. And now I'm in the hotel room with no recollection of how I got here."

Nina gasps. "Really? Do you think he drugged you?"

I shake my head, although Isiah is an asshole, I doubt he'd do that. "Unlikely."

"Was the sex good?"

"Nina! Is that all you took from what I told you?"

She chuckles. "Pretty much."

"The man's a beast. Let's leave it at that." I can feel heat unfurling within my veins from the memories flooding my mind.

"Sounds like fun." She pauses for a moment. "I wish I was having fun with Cathal."

I hate how broken she sounds. "He's a waste of space for ditching you."

"It's because I don't deserve a man like him."

"Bullshit. Don't let me hear anything like that from your mouth again. You are too good for him."

"I miss you already," she says.

I miss her too, and the fact is, this is our reality now. After a week in the Maldives, we will return to Washington for a couple of weeks before heading on to London. At least, that's what my father told me.

"I wish this had never happened."

"What? Marrying a sex beast?" Nina asks, chuckling over the phone.

I roll my eyes. "You know that this is how it will be once I'm in London?"

There are a few moments of silence. "Yes."

It's a simple answer, but her tone speaks volumes. When she met Cathal, I really hoped she'd found her someone. A man she could rely on to hold her up during the ups and downs, but he was a flake. He talked the talk, but when it came to it, he was a pussy.

"I better get going," I say, feeling the heaviness between us. "I'll see you in one week. If you need to talk, call me anytime. Okay?"

"Okay," she says, sounding flat.

At that moment, I wish I hadn't called her. As I feel like I've just dragged her down. I end the call and throw my cell phone on the bed, heading over to my suitcase, which is sitting in the far corner of the room.

I search through the clothes that I've brought with me, trying to find something suitable for this afternoon. After a few minutes, I opt for a white cotton blouse paired with a denim skirt and strappy sandals.

Once dressed, I make my way out of the villa and over toward the door, pulling it open and stepping outside into the warm midday sun. The heat is almost overwhelming as it wraps around my body like an embrace.

I take my time walking down the wooden bridge that links the water villa to the beach, which is deserted. As I gaze across the beach, I notice a figure getting closer, coming in this direction.

It could only be Isiah, since he rented the entire private island. Other than some staff at the restaurant and also the spa, there's no one here but him and me. I hate the way my stomach clenches at that thought.

As he gets closer, I feel my mouth water at the sight of him. He's wearing a pair of board shorts and topless as he jogs across the sand, sweat coating his chest and making it glisten in the sun.

As he turns off the beach and onto the bridge, I realize I'm staring and try to snap out of it.

"Morning, love. Like the view?" he asks, smirking at me.

I glare at him. "Yes, I like the view of the beautiful tropical island."

He tilts his head. "Of course, what else would I be talking about?" he asks, arching a brow.

"I'm going to explore," I say, trying to walk around him.

He grabs my wrist. "Yeah, you can start by exploring my cock."

"Fuck off," I say, yanking my wrist from his grasp.

Isiah steps into my path, blocking the walkway with his body and glaring down at me. "It's not a request, but an order." He grabs his crotch, drawing my eyes to the hard bulge. "I went for a run to try to blow off steam, but I'm still as hard as a rock and it's your fault."

My eyes widen. "How is it my fault?"

"Because ever since I fucked your ass, I can't think of anything else. Your ass is heaven and I intend to spend a lot of time fucking it." He pulls me close, his sweat getting on my clothes and yet somehow I don't mind.

What the hell has this man done to me?

"Now be a good girl and kneel for me."

I pull back and look into his eyes. "What?"

Isiah grabs my chin, forcing me to look into his eyes. "Do as I say," he whispers firmly. "Kneel and do your duty as my wife."

"Duty?" I spit, hating how this man can fill me with desire one minute and then hate the next.

"Yes, duty," he says, his voice firm. "It's what a wife is supposed to do. Tend to her husband's desires."

I'm shaking with anger now. "Bullshit. I won't be treated like a slave."

He tilts his head. "When are you going to realize that defying me is pointless?" Suddenly, he grabs my shoulders and forces me to my knees. "Take my cock out and suck it."

I spit at him, which results in him grabbing hold of my hair hard and yanking my head back unnaturally.

"You can pretend all you like that you don't enjoy being taken advantage of, but it's not true. It's a bit pointless always trying to convince yourself that you don't want me. Why don't we cut the crap and just enjoy ourselves?"

This man has got some nerve, and yet as I look into his beautiful eyes, I want to do as he says. A powerful desire to submit to him here on this island where we're the only two people takes hold of me.

And so, I release his cock from his swim shorts.

He's as hard as steel as I wrap my fingers around him, glancing up at him and licking my lips in an attempt to tease him. Slowly, I drag the tip of my tongue over his head, lapping up the precum beading at the slit. All the while, I hold his gaze, knowing how dangerous teasing a beast might turn out to be.

Isiah's eyes darken as he glares at me. "No teasing, love."

Instead of listening to him, I continue my taunting. Only gently licking and sucking at the most sensitive parts of his manhood.

As if like a flick of a switch, everything changes. He takes hold of my head and thrusts himself into my throat, fucking it like an animal. His grip is tighter than a vise and I struggle to breathe, gagging all over him. And yet desire pools between my thighs. Every part of my body wants to pleasure him, which makes little sense.

I feel his cock twitch inside my mouth as he swells, warning me he's getting closer to orgasm.

"Open that throat for me like a good girl and swallow every drop," he growls, forcing his cock even deeper into my throat.

My throat works around Isiah as tremors ripple through my body, his hot release spilling into my mouth. He commands me to swallow every drop and I obey, a hot flush of shame coloring my skin. Isiah watches me as he pushes forward one final time before pulling out.

He looms above me with a look of absolute domination and supremacy on his face, making my heart thunder wildly.

"See," Isiah says in a dark tone, and I'm reminded why trying to deny what lies between us is nothing but foolishness. "Why deny who you truly are? A natural submissive. My submissive." My breath jams in my throat, heart racing wildly as I wait for what is coming next. Isiah remains silent and still until, finally, he speaks again. "You're mine now."

The intensity behind his words and the way he holds me captive in his stare and delves deep into my soul leaves me shivering with helplessness.

Slowly, he steps away from me, letting his last statement linger in the air like a solemn promise; I'm his now. All I can do is watch his retreating figure as he leaves me on my knees like some kind of whore.

I remain there, trembling and overwhelmed by the complicated feelings that swirl inside me for a long time. There's something about the way he takes control that makes my heart beat faster but also sends chills down my spine. Part of me hates being so helplessly entranced by him, but part of me loves it too.

How can I feel such a powerful connection toward him yet hate the man at the same time?

Everything about Isiah Darcy is a contradiction—dangerous and alluring, intoxicating and frightening. He has cast his spell on me and now I'm spinning aimlessly, unable to escape its grasp. What will happen when our dance is finished? Until then, I'm caught in this whirlwind of opposing emotions.

All I know for sure is that whatever happens next, it will be because of him. I fear that whatever sinister plans he has for me and my family could be far worse than anything I've imagined.

BELLA

*J*siah doesn't return to the villa until nightfall. The moment he enters, I notice the haunted look in his eyes. I've seen that look a few times before.

"Where have you been?" I ask, standing up to face him.

His eyes narrow. "Why do you care? I thought you'd be glad to get away from me."

I swallow hard, as although I try to tell myself that's the case, I've been going crazy wondering where he is and why he's not with me.

Slowly, I shake my head. "I'm not glad. You may drive me crazy, but this is our honeymoon. Aren't we supposed to spend it together?"

His jaw clenches as he rubs a hand across the back of his neck. He's still in his board shorts, but he's wearing a shirt now. "This isn't a normal marriage,

Bella. Did you expect we'd be holding hands and skipping off into the sunset?"

I narrow my eyes. "There's no need to be an asshole about it," I spit.

He sighs and comes to sit on the sofa next to me. "There's no need to sugarcoat what this is."

"There's no reason we can't try to get along, since this is our reality now."

His eyebrow hitches slightly in surprise. "And that's what you want?"

I nod in response, as I know the only way to uncover his plan is to get closer to him. The more he trusts me, the easier it will be. "How about we have some dinner at the restaurant and talk?" I suggest.

His gaze is heavy and intense as he studies me with a scrutiny that nearly takes my breath away. Finally, he speaks again.

"Fine, I'll go and have a shower and get ready." He radiates distrust as he stands and walks away from me. And it makes me wonder what happened to him in the past to make him the way he is, and does it have something to do with my family?

I hate the desire that claws at me to follow him, but I remain seated, waiting patiently for him to get dressed. If I'm going to gain his trust, we can't be having sex constantly.

After what feels like an age of twiddling my thumbs, Isiah appears dressed in a tailored navy-blue suit. His brown hair is styled meticulously without a strand out of place, and he looks absolutely stunning.

He's all sharp angles and power, his broad shoulders looking almost too strong to be contained in the slim material of his jacket.

Despite seeing him like this every time we've met, I can't help but admire him right now. Finally, I bring my eyes back to his face and the look in those beautiful blue eyes flecked with gold takes my breath away. I quickly shift my gaze away, not wanting him to see the expression on my face or he'll detect the tumultuous feelings playing havoc within me.

"Stop blushing like an idiot and come here," he demands.

I glare at him while simultaneously my desire hits me. He opens his mouth and ruins it all. "Do you have to be so rude?"

He smirks. "I sense you enjoy it really, all the push and pull." He arches a brow and I hate that in a way he's right. Our sparring is part of the reason he's so intoxicating. "Come on, love." He holds out his hand for me to take and I stare at it for a little while, before moving forward and slipping mine into his.

Electricity races through my veins at his touch, and a soft gasp escapes my lips. In turn, a soft smile graces his beautiful lips, but he doesn't make any more annoying comments. Instead, he leads me out into the beautiful night as stars cast a twinkling display over the water. "I'll never get over the beauty of this place. It's what life should be about."

Isiah tilts his head. "How do you mean?"

"Everyone wants more money, more power, more

material things." I sigh heavily. "Why would anyone need anything other than that?" I signal at the star speckled sky, which is the clearest I've ever seen.

The look on Isiah's face is one of turmoil in itself, making me wonder if he's feeling as mixed up as I am. I'm sure no one has ever looked at me in quite this way before. "You are not what I expected at all, Bella." His voice is soft.

"In a good way or a bad way?" I ask.

"Good way," he says, his voice a little haunted. He clears his throat. "We best get a move on," he says, trying to change the subject.

We enter the restaurant with only one table for us to enjoy, since we are the only two on the isolated island. The restaurant is located in a small, cozy wooden hut nestled away amongst the trees. Candles light up the room, giving it a romantic atmosphere as soft jazz music plays in the background. A red and white checked tablecloth covers a large round table set for two with china plates and silver cutlery carefully arranged on top.

It's so surreal being in a place where we're the only two people, and yet I like it. It feels like true free-dom. And yet it also feels empty because there's not the usual clinking of glasses and cutlery or smell of delicious food surrounding us.

"Good evening," the server says, approaching us. "Here is the menu. If you have any questions, please don't hesitate to ask." He places a large board down on a stand with handwritten options.

"Thank you," Isiah says, glancing at me. "Can we get a bottle of pinot noir to begin with?"

"Certainly, sir," he says, scurrying off to fetch the drink.

"What about your whiskey?" I ask.

Isiah shrugs. "I drink wine on occasion."

"I see. What wine do you usually go for?"

He grins, a mischievous sparkle in his eye. "Pinot noir is good, but nothing can beat a good cabernet sauvignon."

"I'll admit I knew I liked pinot noir, so I've never really experimented with other wines."

He raises a brow. "I'll have to change that then. So, tell me, love, as we're trying to have a civil dinner together," he says, leaning forward. "What kind of things interest you?"

It takes me aback a little that he's showing any interest in me and what I like. "I enjoy reading and watching movies." I pause a moment, thinking. "Also, I love to paint, but my father said it was a stupid waste of time and banned me from doing it in the house anymore."

A flicker of anger ignites in Isiah's eyes. "That's a stupid fucking thing to say."

My brow furrows. "You don't agree?"

He shakes his head. "No, I think that doing what makes you happy is all that matters. And art isn't a waste of time. It's the perfect way to express yourself." He purses his lips. "You can paint while we're here."

My stomach twists with butterflies as sometimes

this man's actions and words make no sense. "Really?" I wonder if this is a cruel trick of his.

"Yes, I'll get you canvases and paints delivered to us in the morning. What do you like to paint?"

I sigh. "It's been so many years, but I used to like to do portraits, since there's not exactly a lot of nature to paint in Washington."

A devious smirk twists onto his lips. "You can paint me in the nude, if you'd like?"

My pussy throbs at the thought, knowing it would be far too distracting to try to paint him. "I fear I'd never actually finish."

"And why is that?"

I lick my lips. "You know why." My body is burning with heat.

"Because you'd be too distracted by my cock and wouldn't be able to resist sitting on it instead of painting me?"

"Do you always have to be so crass?"

"Do you always have to avoid admitting that what I'm saying is true?"

"Fine, yes, it's unlikely I'd ever finish it because we wouldn't be able to resist having sex."

Isiah smiles, but it's not an annoying smile. "Finally."

I shake my head. "What about you?"

His expression turns serious. "What about me?"

"What interests do you have?"

As if a wall comes down, his entire countenance changes. "I don't have time for interests. All of my time is taken up with work." He rubs the back of his neck. "I want to talk about you."

"I'm not sure why. There's not a lot to talk about."

The server returns then with the wine and shows the label to Isiah. "Is this suitable?"

He nods. "Yes."

"Would you like to taste?"

"Bella can taste it," he says, looking at me. I'm surprised he allows me to, as in this sexist society it's always the man they ask.

"Certainly," the server says, pouring me a small amount into the glass.

I take a sip. Honestly, not a connoisseur of wine, but it tastes amazing. "It's good."

Isiah smiles at me and it makes my stomach flip.

"Great, have you decided what you'd like to order from the menu?" he asks.

I nod. "I have."

"Yes, I'll have the lobster," Isiah replies.

I purse my lips, as that's what I was going to order, and now it looks like I'm copying him. "Lobster for me too."

"Okay, thank you." He removes the menu board, leaving us alone again, much to my dismay.

Tonight is increasingly confusing, as Isiah isn't acting how I expected. He's been civil and attentive, and that makes me suspicious. Does he know I'm trying to get close to him in order to figure out his plan?

The rest of the dinner continues much in the same way as it started. We discuss books that we've both read. As it turns out, we have more in common than I ever believed possible. When he gets a chance, he likes to read thrillers and so do I. Also, he's visited many exotic places in the world on business that I'd love to visit.

By the time the meal is over, I'm questioning why he's been so terrible to me all this time when he can be so charming.

"Let's get back to the villa," Isiah says.

I nod and take his hand as we walk in comfortable silence back to the villa and straight into the bedroom. My heart beats erratically as I'm sure he's going to turn into that dominant, arrogant man that I hate, but my body loves.

He kisses me softly and then walks into the bathroom, leaving me standing there.

I undress and get under the sheets, waiting for him. After a few minutes, he returns in just his briefs and gets under the covers.

I yawn as I roll over to look at Isiah lying next to me. "What now?"

He yanks me toward him and kisses me passionately in a way that steals my breath. I kiss him back, enjoying the way he consumes me, as if I'm as important to him as air. When we break away, he smiles softly. "Sleep, love. You're tired and we have plenty of time to explore each other for the rest of the honeymoon." The glint in his eyes is wicked. "Sweet dreams." And then he lies down and rolls over so his back is to me. I can't understand why that gesture makes my heart ache.

Did I expect him to cuddle me while I fall asleep?

I shake my head and rest against the soft pillow, placing my arm against my forehead. Clearly, being here with him is clouding my judgement and I need to get a grip before he unravels me entirely.

ISIAH

*a*s I finish the preparations for Bella's surprise, I wonder what the hell has gotten into me. I don't do this kind of thing for anyone, and yet here I am setting up the little cabin up on the hill as a fucking art studio so my wife can paint.

She should be on her way up here now, as I asked her to meet me here at sunset. Ever since we arrived here, I've felt off because of my concerning feelings for Bella. It's why I had to get away from her that first day, all I did was walk around the island, trying to run away from her despite the fact we're the only two people on this island, except for the staff.

I walk out onto the porch of the hilltop cabin, surveying the view, which is utterly breathtaking. The crystal-clear waters of the lagoon below seem to glimmer in the late afternoon light, and gentle waves lap against the golden sands of the beach. To the left of the cabin there's a vast rainforest filled with towering trees that stretch upward to meet a horizon painted with brilliant oranges and pinks. The sun hangs low in the sky, casting a glowing golden hue over everything it touches.

My heart flutters in my chest as I realize my feelings for Bella are becoming complicated, to say the least.

I can feel the tension in the air, the anticipation of what is to come and whether she'll like what I've done with the place. Turning back to walk inside, I walk around the room, making sure everything is ready. There are windows on all four sides of the small cabin and at each one I've set up an easel, canvas and stool, so she has the option to paint any view that takes her fancy.

To the left of the door, I've set up an old wood table with all the supplies she'll need stacked on the table, an array of different types of paints, paper, and brushes. Hopefully, I've thought of everything.

It's ridiculous how nervous I feel as I glance at the setting sun again, noticing how low it is. Bella should be here any minute.

"Isiah?" I hear her sweet voice calling my name and it makes something inside me flutter.

I walk to the doorway to meet her, my heart pounding hard and erratically against my rib cage. "Hey, love."

She smiles at me and it lights my entire world ablaze. "Hey."

"I've got a surprise for you."

Her eyebrow arches, as I know she's still distrustful of me. And naturally, I never trust anyone, so I'm distrustful of her as well. However, it doesn't stop me from wanting to make her happy. "Is it a good surprise or a bad surprise?"

I laugh. "Stop being ridiculous and come and see."

She strolls cautiously over to the door and steps inside, her eyes instantly widening. "What is this place?"

"I asked the staff where I could set up an art studio for you and they suggested this had the best views."

"You did all this for me?" she asks, unable to mask her tone of surprise.

"Well, I sure as hell didn't do it for me. If you saw how bad I am at painting."

She laughs softly, walking further into the room. "This place has the most stunning views," she says, looking out of the window on the far side. "I can definitely get creative here." Her throat bobs as she swallows. "Thank you," she breathes, a softness in her voice as she looks at me in a confusing way.

"You're welcome, love," I say, unable to take my eyes off of her. She looks like an angel as the light from the windows casts a glow on her olive skin.

She brushes her fingers gently over the canvas. "It's been so long since I've painted."

I walk over to her and pull out the stool. "Paint now, then."

Her eyes widen. "Really? Don't we have to get to dinner?"

"I've arranged for them to bring it up here, so we can spend as much time as you need."

I see excitement ignite in her eyes as she rushes toward the table with the supplies, selecting paints and putting them on a pallet. The mere look on her face makes me fall for her more, and I realize these feelings could jeopardize my quest for revenge.

In this moment, though, I can't find it in myself to dwell on it further. Instead, I just want to enjoy this time with Bella and watch her in her element.

It's as if she's forgotten about everything else around her as she sits and starts to paint with oil paints, depicting the scene in front of the window as the sun begins to dip behind the glistening blue ocean. She works fast and I must admit I'm in awe of her skill.

If I could paint like that, I think I'd enjoy it too.

There's a notable change in her whole countenance as her shoulders become more relaxed, and I know that I could lose time just watching her paint.

An hour or so later, when she's almost completed the painting, now working from memory since the sun has set, the food arrives.

"Thank you, Akhil," I say, smiling at the server from the restaurant, who has been very accommodating. "Can you just set it down there?" I nod at an empty spot on the workbench.

He bows slightly and then does as I say. The

arrival of food finally breaks Bella out of her own world, as she glances over at Akhil.

"Hi, Akhil," she says, beaming at him.

"Hello, Bella." He bows. "Enjoy your meal. We will collect the empty dishes in the morning."

With that, he leaves, and Bella finally stands from her stool, shaking her head. "I'm sorry, I've been terrible company."

"No, you haven't," I reassure her. "On the contrary, I've enjoyed watching you paint." I walk over to the canvas where her painting is and study it. "You are a talented painter."

She blushes and shakes her head. "You don't have to say that."

"No, but it's the truth." I take her hand and lead her onto the porch of the cabin. "Take a seat and I'll fetch the food."

She sits and I go back and grab the tray Akhil brought up, setting it on the little table. "This is even more beautiful than the restaurant," she muses, gazing around the starlit rainforest and sparkling sea further away.

"I agree. If it hadn't been for me mentioning at breakfast to Akhil that I wanted to find somewhere for you to paint, we never would have found it."

Bella smiles and our eyes meet, locked together for a little too long as hope flares in my chest. Ridiculous as it may be after the way I've treated her only days ago, I hope that she might feel something for me the way I feel for her.

There's something so intriguing about my wife. She's a far cry from the people who raised her, intelligent, kindhearted and creative, everything I value in a person and the polar opposite to her father.

When I received the invite to the party for suitors for Bella, I expected to meet a spoiled, stuck-up mafia princess who would be easy to hate. This woman is the opposite of anything I imagined.

"What are you thinking?" she asks, searching my face.

I swallow hard. "I think we should eat." I pull the lid off the tray to reveal a delicious fish curry.

"Curry again?" Bella says, eyes wide.

I smile. "Not a fan?"

Her brow furrows. "I enjoy it, just not every day."

I let the staff pick the food, asking them to prepare fresh local food, which does indeed involve a lot of curries. "I'll mention to the staff you'd like more variety."

"Oh no, wouldn't that offend them?"

I shake my head. "Certainly not, considering how much I'm paying for this trip."

She sits back and nods. "Okay, but I wouldn't want them to think I don't like the food. It's delicious. I just enjoy variety."

We eat the delicious meal and admire the beauty of our surroundings, neither of us talking much. There's an unusual tension in the air that I can't quite comprehend.

"Shall we take a walk on the beach?" I ask, gazing down the hill toward our villa.

"Sure, that would be nice," she says, standing from her seat and stretching.

I notice her glance toward her painting, still sitting on the canvas, half finished. "We'll return in the morning so you can paint more."

Her smile is the most genuine I've seen from her. "Okay, thank you for this," she says, nodding at the cabin. "It's been too long since I put a brush to canvas."

There's a twinge of something in my chest, and it feels like a warning as I nod. "You're welcome, love." I take her hand and lead her down the winding path through the overgrowth to the beach below. Before long, we're walking on the sand, watching as the soft waves caress the shoreline. The moonlight reflects off of the small ripples of water, creating an ethereal glow that illuminates Bella's face as she looks out at sea with wonderment in her eyes.

"Let's sit," I say, choosing this spot to sink into the soft sand below.

Bella sits next to me and places her head on my shoulder gently, making me tense at the closeness. "It's paradise here."

I'm not used to being this close to someone, but slowly I relax and allow her to remain in this position. I swallow hard, knowing that anywhere she is, is paradise for me. A concerning feeling, but one that I know with utter certainty. Bella is mine. And I won't rest until I possess every part of her, mind, body, heart and soul.

She looks up at me then, catching me staring at her as if she's the most precious thing on this earth. "Why are you looking at me like that?"

"Because you are so damn beautiful." I kiss her then, not wanting her to scrutinize my look any further, as I really don't know how to explain what is going on between us.

I'm supposed to hate this woman and make her life miserable, instead I'm making a fucking makeshift art studio for her.

The kiss grows more passionate as I feel her heart beating in sync with mine, our souls merging as one. She wraps her arms around my neck and pulls me even closer, urging me to deepen the kiss further.

We break apart for a breath of air, but it doesn't last long as I can't keep myself away from her. I lean into her again, forcing her to lie down on the sand, and this time my hands explore her body as my hunger for her grows with every passing second.

I pull back only slightly and take a moment to look at Bella—the intensity of my longing for her is almost too much for me to take. "I'm going to fuck you," I breathe, loving the way her eyes flash. "Own every part of your body," I say, kissing her neck and enjoying the moan that escapes her lips.

"Isiah," she breathes my name and I can feel the desperation to be inside her heightening.

Grabbing her hips, I pull the hem of her skirt up

and slide the string of her thong out of the way. My fingers delve into her soaking wet cunt and drive in and out, making her moan even louder.

"You are so fucking ready for my cock," I say, partially in awe that she's completely soaked.

"I need you," she murmurs, and that obliterates any control I had. Quickly, I free my cock from my trousers and slide inside her as deep as physically possible. And then I kiss her, sliding in and out more tenderly than ever before, but still deep and forceful. This moment is different than any that has come before, in that she's not resisting my advances. Instead, she's begging me for it.

We move together, each thrust pushing us further and further into a climax that neither of us can escape. Our passion gets too intense and I start to lose control, fucking her harder as my brutal, animalistic side always comes out. She cries out my name as I slam in and out of her with a ferocity I didn't know I was capable of.

My breath is heavy as she wraps her legs tightly around me, allowing me deeper access to her body. I reach between us, stroking her clit as we both reach for the stars—it doesn't take long before she's shuddering violently beneath me, reaching her orgasm.

And the way her muscles grip me hard shatters me into pieces. I growl against her skin as I come apart, my cock pulsing as I shoot rope after rope of cum deep inside her. I don't stop until I'm certain her pussy is well and truly bred. The idea of her getting pregnant with my baby at this moment drives me wild. Bella would be so fucking beautiful growing big and round with my child.

It's a ridiculous notion, since I have never even thought about becoming a father. The idea always repulsed me a little, and yet I can't help but think of it now. With her, I want everything. Something I never even dared to consider.

What the hell is she doing to me?

ISIAH

*I*t's clear that my desire for Bella is untamable, but even more concerning is the way she's making me reconsider my intent to kill her along with the rest of her family.

Her paintings are beautiful. I have encouraged her to paint every day, partially because she loves it and partially for selfish reasons, as she lights up when she paints. Her already goddess like appearance becomes otherworldly and I could watch her paint every day until the day I die. In fact, that's exactly what I intend to do. There's a certainty inside me that I can't harm my wife, no matter what her last name used to be. She's a Darcy now and I will protect her as my only family. However, the same can't be said for the rest of her family.

I don't exactly like the way she's making me feel. I don't feel, not since Aiden died. It's as if she's deconstructing the walls of steel I've built around my heart and soul.

Slowly, it feels like she's coming around to the idea of us, too. The sex is even better now that she's stopped resisting and coming around to the idea of being my submissive.

Ever since dinner on the first night, she's been different. We've had many pleasant days, chatting as if we were good friends. I regret not booking two weeks rather than one, as the days are counting down and we only have two more until we'll be on our way back to Washington. The question is, will it remain this way once we're back home and no longer in paradise?

Bella walks beside me in contemplative silence. And, I hate that this is going so well, as it makes it even more difficult to consider destroying her along with the rest of her family.

My intention was to marry her, and then kill her along with the rest of her family, and yet I can't imagine harming a hair on her head.

"Are you enjoying it here?" I ask, genuinely wondering how she's feeling about this holiday and our marriage.

She glances at me, smiling softly. "It is beautiful. And you can be pleasant company when you're not acting like an asshole."

I chuckle. "Does that mean you're starting to like me?"

"Don't push it." She gazes toward the water villa

that we're quickly approaching. "This place is paradise. And I love walking around the island. It's so small."

It's paradise being with her, something I never expected. Ever since Aiden died, I've been singled-minded. Focused on nothing but my revenge plan to make the Benedetto family pay. However, being here with Bella has made me think about life after I exact my revenge and sickeningly, I like the idea of it involving her.

"I'm exhausted," I admit.

She shrugs. "I'm not too tired."

I arch a brow. "What are you suggesting?"

Her cheeks flush. "Nothing."

It's clear that ever since we arrived here, her willingness to have sex has grown each day. And now, I can tell she's basically dying for it.

"Come on," I say, grabbing her hand. "I need to get cleaned up."

Her brow furrows. "It's still early. There's another two hours until the sun sets."

Rubbing my hand across the back of my neck, I shake my head. "After walking, God knows how many miles, I'm ready to put my feet up for a couple of hours."

She sighs. "Fine, I guess we have done a lot of walking."

"Maybe you can give me a foot massage."

"As I said earlier, don't push it."

I chuckle as we walk together side by side along

the last stretch of beach to the bridge that leads to our water villa. Bella pauses on the wooden walkway and gazes down at hundreds of colorful fish below. "They are so beautiful here. I've never seen so many fish in one place before."

I stare at her, rather than the fish, wondering how on earth I'll ever bring myself to destroy her along with her family. She's too perfect and all mine. Perhaps forcing her to remain chained to me for the rest of her life can serve as punishment. A twisted attempt at revenge. Her family, however, won't get off so lightly.

"Isiah?"

I shake my head. "Sorry, what?"

"I said, do you know what that blue one is called?" She's pointing into the ocean.

I follow where she's pointing. "That's a parrotfish."

She tilts her head. "How do you know all these fish?"

I shrug. "I've got a good memory." I've been told my memory is pretty much photographic. I think it's given me an upper hand in the underbelly of London, as I never forget a face. Squeezing her hand, I pull her away from the edge. "Come on, I'm dying for a shower."

It's impossible to ignore the flash in her eyes at that comment, but I wasn't even suggesting sex. Although, I wouldn't complain. Bella and I fucked in three different locations across the island and yet she's insatiable and so am I. The more I have her, the more I need her.

Fuck.

Need is such a dangerous word.

We walk into the villa and I head straight for the bedroom, throwing down my phone before unbuttoning my shirt.

As expected, Bella follows me, sitting down on the bed and staring at me expectantly. A part of me knows I need to shut this down before I'm irreversibly hooked on her.

"Do you want something, love?"

She licks her lips as I chuck my shirt down. "No, just watching."

I laugh at that as she's changed a hell of a lot on this trip. Slowly, I unbutton my trousers, keeping my eyes on her. And that's when my cell phone makes a noise.

Bella grabs it and looks at the screen, brow furrowing. "Why is Cathal contacting you?"

I freeze, hoping that the idiot hasn't texted me about Nina. "I don't know." Walking closer, I hold my hand. "Let me see."

Bella's eyes narrow as she jumps to her feet, taking a step back. "Tell me why you look guilty as hell."

"I don't. Now give me the phone."

She shakes her head and rushes out of the room with the phone.

"Fuck's sake," I say, rushing after her.

She manages to get outside and shut the door,

which locks automatically. And then I see her reading the text, her expression turning solemn. When I finally get it unlocked, her entire countenance has changed. Gone is the flirtatious and happy girl who had appeared during the days we've spent here.

"Give me the phone," I demand.

Bella looks into my eyes and shakes her head. "How could you?"

I swallow the bile that is trying to rise in my throat at the utter despair in her brilliant blue eyes. "How could I do what?"

"Meddle in something you had no right meddling in!"

I can sense her despair is quickly turning to anger. "If you're talking about Cathal and your sister, he asked me my opinion on her and I told him."

She places the phone down on the table. "And what exactly is your opinion of her?"

"That she'd make a very difficult wife because of her condition."

Bella starts forward. "Her condition?!"

"It's no secret that your sister has tried to kill herself on numerous occasions."

She shakes her head. "Nina has struggled with handling her emotions and depression for a long time, but Cathal made her happier than I've seen in ages and then he ditched her out of the blue." Once she gets to me, she prods me in the chest. "Turns out it wasn't completely out of the blue. It's because you prompted him to ditch her!"

I grab her wrist. "Don't be so hysterical. I merely told my friend my honest opinion."

"Friend?"

My heart skips a beat as I realize I misspoke. As far as Bella is aware, I've only met Cathal on a number of occasions.

"We've become friends during my time in Washington."

Her eyes narrow. "I didn't think you liked him."

I arch a brow. "What gave you that impression?"

"It doesn't matter. What matters is you've ruined Nina's chance at happiness!"

I release her wrist and turn away from her, as I know part of my motivation in warning Cathal of Nina's affliction was to hurt Nina. After all, I want to hurt all of them, including my wife. "You can't blame me. You can't have expected it to work out between them once he realized how she is."

When I turn around, Bella's face is beet red, and I know I've said the wrong thing. "You fucking bastard!" she shouts. "My sister is a beautiful, kind and loving woman that Cathal would have been lucky to marry!" Bella tries to storm out of the room, but I'm too fast. I get in front of her and block her path.

"Where do you think you're going?"

"Away from you. As if everything you've done hasn't been bad enough, you have to ruin my sister's love life! There's no way I can stay in here with you. What has Nina ever done to you?"

She's a Benedetto.

It's the plain and simple truth of it. I know that's not an answer I can give, but warning Cathal away from Nina wasn't entirely selfish. Although I did want to get Cathal away from the family before he recognized me for certain but that ship had already sailed the day we met.

"Stop standing there saying nothing and get the fuck out of my way!"

The dominant part of me wants to force myself on her. Make her stay and do dirty, twisted things to her. And yet, the logical part of my brain knows that what I did to Nina could have burned any bridge that was starting to form between us. "Bella," I say her name softly, reaching up to tuck a hair behind her ear.

She recoils from my touch. "Don't touch me."

"I didn't do it to hurt you."

Her entire body shakes with emotion. "You might as well have. Nina is my world, and you destroyed her chance with Cathal." She launches toward me and slams her fists repeatedly into my chest. "I hate you!"

I catch her wrist and shake my head. "We both know that's a lie."

Her eyes narrow to slits. "It's not a lie. How can you expect me to feel anything but hatred toward you after what you've done?"

"I won't apologize for being truthful to Cathal. Everyone is entitled to their opinion. Cathal asked me about mine, and I gave an honest answer. If that's a crime, sue me."

"You don't know Nina at all, so how can you be

truthful?" She releases an exasperated sigh. "Get out of my way."

Finally, I relent and step to the side, despite a part of me wanting to bend her over the bed and have my way with her. At least that way, I can use some of her passionate anger. I know doing so might burn any chance of getting things back to how they've been over the past few days.

I watch as she rushes down the bridge across the water, fighting the instinct to chase. Bella Benedetto is starting to get under my skin and I fear that she could derail everything I've worked so hard for. She's smart and doesn't trust me, which makes her lethal.

I need to get a grip and refocus on what is important, which is getting revenge for Aiden's death; a feat I fear will be easier said than done.

BELLA

My feet plunge into the warm water as I leave the sandy shore and I allow the rolling surf to take me in its embrace. The glittering sea is a balm to my turbulent emotions that have been unleashed on learning the truth about Isiah. Fury thrums through my veins as he meddled with Nina's love life and ripped her away from Cathal.

It seems every time I get close to believing that he can be civil and a decent human being, some new evidence emerges of his wrongdoings. His villainy knows no bounds, and I'd never forgive him for what he did to Nina and Cathal. I swim further into the open water, letting it lap against me in an effort to soothe my rage.

Nina's love for Cathal was absolute and my husband's selfish and thoughtless actions shattered that. He is the reason that Cathal ditched her all of a sudden, out of the blue.

How could I ever forgive Isiah for destroying Nina's chance at happiness?

My rage slowly diminishes with each stroke I take as I swim further into the vast ocean, affording me a newfound clarity.

I can't remain married to Isiah—not after what he's done to Nina. I have to find a way out, even if it means leaving everything familiar behind me. There must be a way for me to escape this cruel fate and find solace away from Isiah.

I whirl around to face the distant shore, filled with apprehension, when I realize how far away I truly am. But then, something in the corner of my eye makes me pause.

A figure swimming toward me with great speed.

Isiah.

The fury on his handsome face is unmistakable when he finally reaches me. "Bella! Are you fucking insane?"

I glare at him. "Fuck off, Isiah. I'm trying to get away from you," I snarl back.

He shakes his head. "You shouldn't be swimming this far out. There are sharks!"

I scowl at him, feeling a heat rise through my body as anger courses through my veins. How dare he try to tell me what to do? I'd been so peaceful and content in my isolation, but his intrusion has ruined it.

I know it's stupid to be this far out in the ocean— the Maldives have the highest concentration of sharks, after all. But the thought of his smug face if I agree makes me feel sick, so I shake my head.

"I know what I'm doing! And you don't get to tell me what to do!"

The rage that crosses his features scares me more than any shark could as he powers the last ten yards to me, grabbing my hip. "There's a fucking tiger shark lurking no more than twenty yards behind you. Tell me you know what you're doing again, and I'll just leave him to eat you."

I freeze, wondering if he's telling the truth. Turning to glance behind, I notice the fin poking above the water, swimming back and forth, clearly not aware of our presence...yet. "I'm still so angry at you," I say, moving my gaze back to my husband. The man who ruined Nina's chance at happiness.

"Well, be angry at me once we're on land and away from a blood hungry shark." He nods toward the shore.

I agree, reluctantly, and begin to swim in that direction.

Isiah remains behind me, covering me from behind. Until he suddenly pulls me to a stop, pulling my body close to his. "Stay very still."

I freeze, glancing around in search of the threat. And that's when I see another fin heading right toward us. "Shit."

Isiah pulls me behind him and blocks me with his body. Heat coils through me that this man would put himself in harm's way to save me. He swam out here, aware of the sharks. "Stay still."

"I don't think I could even move if I had to."

"Ssh," he says.

And then when I'm sure we're going to die from a shark attack, he dives under the water, leaving me in the path of the fucking thing.

This it is.

I'm going to die and my good-for-nothing husband has ditched me.

I scream, my muscles unwilling to move as my brain screams to swim away.

Suddenly, the shark starts thrashing around. My brow furrows as I duck under the water to see Isiah squaring up to it as he punches it repeatedly in the nose.

What sane person does that?

I scramble back to the surface expecting the crystal blue sea to be tinged blood red with Isiah's blood, but instead I watch as the fin of the shark turns in the opposite direction as the shark swims away.

A flood of awe and thankfulness hits me, and I hate it. I don't want to feel anything but hatred toward the man, but it's difficult when he just saved my life. He comes to the surface and draws in a deep breath of oxygen, swimming over to me.

My mouth gapes open as I stare at my husband in awe. "That was crazy."

"You are fucking crazy, and I will be punishing

you for this stupid, reckless behavior back at the villa."

"Punishing me?" I ask, shaking my head. "You're the one that needs to be punished for messing with Nina's love life!"

"You may be mad at me for that, but I had my reasons."

"What possible reason could that be? You don't even know Nina."

"I know about her struggles with her mental health."

My eyes narrow as I wonder how that has anything to do with it. "So, because she struggles with her mental health, you think she doesn't deserve to be loved?"

His jaw clenches. "Cathal went running the moment I told him about it. Is that the kind of man who can handle your sister or give her the love she needs?"

I hate how much sense that makes. Cathal clearly wasn't the right person for my sister, but I fear that Isiah didn't give him enough chance to figure out if his love for her could outweigh his fear of her condition.

"Come on, let's get to shore before anymore sharks appear," he says.

A part of me wants to keep arguing the matter, but instead I nod and start to swim to the shore, desperate to get out of the sea. As we paddle toward shore, the sun is setting above us, casting an orange glow over the ocean.

Exhausted, I fall onto the sand and gaze up at the sky as it slowly turns from blue to dark. Isiah lies down next to me, not saying a word as we both remain quiet and the stars being to shine in the night sky.

All the while, I can't shake this feeling that Isiah intends to harm me and my family in some way. All signs point to it, including him meddling in my sister's love life.

I glance over at him, hating how unnaturally beautiful he looks under the soft glow of the stars. "Why did you do it, really?" I ask, knowing that Isiah Darcy doesn't do anything without an ulterior motive. "Does it have something to do with your intention of destroying my family?"

Instantly, I notice the tension in his body as he glances toward me. "I don't know what you're talking about."

I push up onto my elbows. "Don't bullshit me. I know there's something you have against my family. You meddled in Nina's love life and I know for a fact you orchestrated the destruction of that auction at Insignia, which was premeditated." I realize at this point I'm speaking way too fast, rambling almost, because this man makes me nervous and angry and, at times, insane. "And while I wholeheartedly agree with what you did at the club, I'm not an idiot. The photos on that board in your apartment were part of some sort of plan. I know it."

He watches me in silence for what feels like forever, before finally opening his mouth. "I do have something against your father. I want revenge for something he did to me."

I stiffen, wondering if Isiah was perhaps a victim of one of those auctions. "You weren't sold as a child, were you?"

He laughs, shaking his head. "No."

My brow furrows. "Then, what happened?"

The walls come done all of a sudden as his eyes become glazed over. "I've already told you too much." He pushes himself up from the sand and I'm sure he's going to leave again; disappear like he did that first day on the island. Instead, he offers me his hand. "Let's go and get something to eat."

I sigh heavily. "More curry?"

He smirks. "I knew you were getting fed up with curry, so I ordered something special in."

I arch a brow, wondering what he would have ordered. Instead of questioning him, I take his hand and allow him to lead me to the restaurant further along the beach.

We get to the restaurant and the same man who has served us most of the nights greets us at our table. "Good evening, Mr. and Mrs. Darcy."

"Evening, Akhil."

"As requested, we have your meal ready. We'll bring it out to you shortly." He tilts his head. "What would you like to drink?"

"I'll have a whiskey tonight," Isiah says, glancing at me.

I nod. "I'll try one too."

Isiah looks surprised but smiles as Akhil leaves to fetch our drinks. "Since when do you drink whiskey?"

"You've drunk wine most nights, it's only fair that I try your favorite drink."

"It's much stronger than wine."

"Are you suggesting I can't handle it?"

He shakes his head. "I think you can handle anything, love."

I hate the way that statement makes me feel, especially coming from a man who told me he thinks women are merely instruments for a man's pleasure.

"That doesn't sound like you."

"What do you mean?" he asks.

"I distinctly remember you stating that a woman's input in any matter other than how to look after children was useless."

His smirk widens. "Perhaps I was telling your father what he wanted to hear. After all, he was the one who decided who you married."

The man is crafty, and it makes me wonder which parts of his character I've seen are real, if his opinion on this matter was merely a way to trick my father. I need to broach the subject of what exactly he wants revenge for and what he intends to do to my family.

Akhil places our whiskeys down on the table. "Shall I bring your starters?"

Isiah nods. "Yes, please."

He scurries off to go and fetch them and a silence falls between us.

While I might abhor my father, the rest of my family, as stupid as most of them are, have done nothing to wrong Isiah. "You really hate my father, don't you?"

His eyes flash and he shakes his head. "Enough talk of your family. The food is coming."

"Mozzarella in *carozza*," Akhil announces, as he sets down two plates of delicious breaded cheese in a homemade tomato chutney.

I smile at Isiah for a moment, forgetting all my suspicions and worries about the man before me. "It's my favorite starter." I tilt my head. "How did you know?"

"I have my sources," he says, taking a sip of his whiskey.

I don't question him, while I like fish and curry, I've been getting sick of it. So, I delve into the delicious cheese and take a bite, groaning at how good it is. "This is amazing."

"Good, otherwise I would have had to kill the chef."

My eyes widen and he starts to laugh, a deep and rich sound that surprises me. "Don't worry, I'm joking."

I sigh a breath of relief. "Thank God."

We eat in silence, enjoying the sound of the waves in the distance. Once finished, Akhil returns and clears our plates.

"What's for the main dish?"

"I'll give you one guess," he jests.

"Spinach and ricotta *cannelloni*?"

He shakes his head. "No, as you only love it from San Marino in Washington."

"Who have you been speaking to?"

"I asked Nina for a few pointers at the wedding reception."

I shake my head. "Nina should keep her mouth shut."

"If she did, you wouldn't have lasagna *al forno* for dinner, would you?"

I groan, my stomach rumbling despite just polishing off a good helping of fried cheese. "If it's as good as the mozzarella in *carozza*, then I'm excited."

Akhil returns with one of the best lasagnas I've ever had, even in Italy. And I polish every bite off until I'm so full I can hardly move. I hate the way he's acting so thoughtfully, making our last meal here so memorable. Especially after learning that he's the reason Cathal dumped Nina, something I'll never forgive him for, even if his reasoning makes sense. If Cathal went running just hearing of her mental health issues, what good would he be if she has an episode?

ISIAH

I swirl the ice in my tumbler as it clinks against the glass before taking a long sip of whiskey.

Across the table, Bella sips her own glass of whiskey. Silence falls between us, but it's oddly comfortable. It has been ever since the day after I admitted I have a vendetta against her father.

The week in the Maldives had seemed like a good idea. A perfect chance for me to force my wife into submission, and yet instead, I feel myself falling for her. At least, I think that's what's happening. It's sickening.

The servers from the restaurant dedicated to serving only us come out with the last course, dessert. However, all I really want to eat is Bella. It's our last night and I fear if I don't tell her the truth, everything will change once we're back in Washington.

"Chocolate souffle," he announces before

removing the silver lid off the platter from Bella's first and then mine. "Enjoy."

Bella licks her lips. "I love chocolate. I didn't think I could manage anything else but screw it!"

That word, love, makes me tense. Could I really ever love again?

I knew love, in a different capacity, with my brother Aiden. And yet, somehow, this beautiful vixen has started to deconstruct the walls of steel which were built around my heart the moment he died.

"Bella," I mutter her name.

She looks up at me, brows furrowing no doubt at the seriousness in my tone. "What is it?"

I shake my head. "I know we've had this push and pull between us since the day we met practically, but I want to put it all behind us."

"Behind us?" she questions.

I nod. "Yes, I feel we've made good progress here on the island."

She bites her bottom lip. "I'm not sure that you forcing me to bend over the bed so you can spank me raw, is progress."

I chuckle. "Then why did you moan my name the entire time?"

Her cheeks flush and it's detectable even in the dim candlelight. "Don't be so crude."

I arch a brow. "You're the one who mentioned me bending you over."

She shakes her head and sighs. "How can we put it behind us when you drive me insane?"

"Because the truth is, despite who you are, I think I'm falling for you." I grind my teeth the moment those words are out. "You make me feel like no one else ever has."

Her eyes become shuttered as she shakes her head. "Despite who I am? What the hell is that supposed to mean?"

I swallow hard as I wonder if slipping that in is going to end in disaster. "A Benedetto."

"So, you decide to tell me you're falling for me, despite my family who you hate? Is that correct?" She sits up straighter, the anger building in her eyes. "And why exactly do you hate them? You still haven't made it clear what my father did to you."

This is going worse than I expected, and despite wanting to be truthful with her, I can't. There's no way I can tell her who I really am. Joe Isaiah Dalton. It's just not an option.

"It doesn't matter why."

She slams her hand down on the table. "Of course it matters. Do you expect me to feel anything but contempt for a man who has shattered my sister's dreams?" She stands then, her rage building like lava simmering beneath a volcano ready to erupt. "Or who admits that he wants to destroy my family? I may not like them most of the time and what my father does is inexcusable, but they *are* my family. My flesh and blood. You have some nerve if you think I'd feel anything for you other than hatred."

"You don't hate me," I say, hating how much her words sting.

"I do. You can't expect me to feel anything other than disgust toward you."

I stand then, needing to salvage this somehow. "Then why are you always coming back for more, love?" I walk toward her, but she backs away.

"Stay the fuck away from me!" And then she turns and runs.

I sprint after her, effortlessly catching her as she tries to run in her dress, which almost trips her up. My arms wrap around her waist and I hoist her over my shoulder.

She slams her fists into my back, but I hardly feel them. Her words have cut me deeply, and now I'm going to take my pain out on her. "What are you doing?"

"You may not care for me the way I care for you, but you're still my wife. I'm taking you to bed."

I carry her to the villa and straight into the bedroom, her fists still pounding against my back. Her fighting only enrages me further. After so many years of being closed off to all feelings, the moment I let my guard down, she's battered my already bruised heart. And she's physically battering me too. After ensuring the door is firmly locked, I move to the bed, as I need to have her, whether she wants me or not.

The moment I place her on the bed, she springs away from me, fear and loathing written in her azure eyes. Her chest rises and falls as if having her last breaths on this earth and I know in this moment she despises me. The pain I feel at the revelation is like a ton of bricks falling on me from above, however that would be more acceptable as I wouldn't feel a thing if I were dead.

I step closer, and the air seems to crackle between us.

She steps backward until there's nowhere else for her to go, and there's barely an inch between us. "You aren't acting like a man who loves me," she says.

In one swift motion, I grab her chin, forcing her to look into my eyes. My hand slides around her throat in a possessive grip, feeling her pulse quicken beneath my palm.

I feel her breath flee her chest as her eyes become full of lust despite everything.

I tilt my head. "I've never loved a woman before, Bella. I won't accept that you feel nothing toward me." I gently squeeze her throat and her eyes flicker shut as her pulse quickens beneath my palm. "You may not feel it yet, but I won't rest until you do." Her lips press together in a thin line as she stares into my eyes, unwavering. "You are mine, despite who you are or what your family has done to me in the past."

"You're crazy if you think I can ever feel anything for you. A man who won't tell me why he hates my family so badly."

I press my lips against hers in an all-consuming kiss, my tongue claiming every inch of her mouth as a way to reiterate that she belongs to me. Against her will, she surrenders to the pull of my embrace. When I finally release her from the passionate kiss, a desperate yearning burns in her eyes. I want more than just possession of her body; I want her love and devotion, but I have no idea how to win it.

The air is heavy with desire, and my grip on her throat tightens as I kiss her again. Our tongues continue to dance in sync as I release her throat and hike the hem of her flowing cream dress up to her hips. I move to her neck with my lips and trail them to the sensitive skin at the nape of her neck, taking my time until I reach her collarbone. Sinking my teeth into her collarbone, she yelps in surprise.

"What the—"

"Quiet," I bark, tightening my grasp on her, as I force her around so that she's facing the wall, her back arched slightly. And then I spank her round, lace-clad ass hard with my hand, groaning when her skin turns pink instantly. "I want you to tell me how badly you want me."

"No," she says back, glaring at me over her shoulder.

"Are we back to this again?" I ask, tearing apart her knickers. The number of knickers I've destroyed on this honeymoon is amusing. I had to order her more pairs because she didn't bring enough. She may as well forget underwear altogether.

And then I kneel behind her, worshipping her cunt with my tongue. She's so damn delicious that I could spend every night feasting on her instead of food.

The moment my tongue touches her clit, it forces a moan out of her.

I can't help but get lost in her, forgetting the hurtful things she said as pure pleasure takes over. Her back arches as she pushes into me, demanding more, and so I give her what she wants, thrusting my fingers deep inside her.

The most exquisite gasp escapes her lips and I palm my cock with my free hand, needing to release it. Unzipping my trousers, I continue to lick and finger her while pulling my cock out and fisting it up and down. The desperate need to be inside her is clawing at me, tempting me to fuck her, but I won't enter her until she comes.

Instead, I continue to drive her higher and higher with each lick of her clit and thrust of my fingers into her tight, wet channel.

"Isiah," she breathes my name, her fingers scraping down the wall.

"Yes, love?"

Her back arches further. "I'm going to come!"

"Good," I say, returning my tongue to her clit. And then I spank her ass. The sting sends her over the edge as her body convulses in my hands, a flood of arousal spilling onto my tongue as I try to lap up every drop. My cock leaks precum onto the floor as I devour her, knowing that despite my need to bury myself inside her that I can't stop tasting her. She's heaven.

And when I'm sure she's finally recovered from her climax, I stand and turn her around, kissing her before she can say a word.

Her arms wrap around me and the embrace makes my black heart sing. My love for her may be flawed, but I never believed I'd love anyone, so it's better than nothing. All I know is she's my most prized possession and I won't let her go for all the money or power on this earth.

I drop my boxer briefs and trousers the rest of the way to the floor before lifting her in my arms. Forcefully, I push her back against the wall and rest my cock at her entrance, watching the expression on her face as her chest heaves up and down. Grabbing the top of her dress, I pull the strings open and reveal her beautiful breasts and hard nipples, sucking on each one in turn and making her moan.

"Isiah," she breathes my name.

"What?"

She bites her inner cheek nervously, which I notice she does a lot when she's unsure about what she's going to say. "Fuck me," she murmurs.

I groan in response, the temptation to take her here and now overwhelming me. I keep her against the wall as I lower her onto my rock-hard length, penetrating her inch by glorious inch until I'm fully seated inside her.

For a moment, I remain still, loving how deeply connected to her I am physically as well as emotionally. And then, once she looks ready to burst from frustration, I begin to thrust in and out slowly and deeply, feeling the tightness of her walls as they contract around me.

"You feel so fucking good wrapped around my cock," I growl into her ear as I fuck her against the wall, driving in at a slow yet forceful tempo.

She moans, throwing her head back as pleasure overrides all other senses. Her anger toward me melts away, but I know it won't last long, and I need to make the most of this moment.

My thrusts become more aggressive, and the intensity of my desire for her grows. She grips my shoulders tightly as I drive into her, our breathing becoming faster and more erratic as we inch closer to mutual climax. My movements become more urgent and desperate and I can feel her response through every nerve in my body when I hit the spot inside her that brings forth a wave of pleasure. Her moans become more frequent and I know she's close, so I slow down to give us both time to savor this moment, as I never want it to end.

I increase my thrusts, pushing her further and further until she's screaming my name. Her tightness around me only makes me harder and soon I find myself on the brink of orgasm, but I hold on as long as possible so that I can enjoy every second with her. Her grip on me tightens as she gasps for air, her beautiful face illuminated by the moonlight streaming through the window behind us.

"I want you to come for me, Bella," I breathe, pressing my lips against her collarbone as I continue to fuck her against the wall, my arms straining from holding her up.

She shudders as I push harder and faster, sinking my teeth into her skin as I force her over the edge. Her body jerks uncontrollably as she cries out my name, clamping her eyes shut.

Finally, when I can no longer take it, I explode inside her, filling her with my cum. Only once every drop is out do I pull my still semi-hard cock out of her. And then, I lower her to the floor as my arms are killing me and press my forehead against hers, trying to catch my breath.

"I'll never get enough of you, Bella," I breathe.

She doesn't speak but tries to move. I hold her there, breathing her in and knowing that I can't open my eyes and see that anger again.

When I feel her hands cupping my cheeks, I dare to open them. There's no anger in her eyes, only confusion as she kisses me softly. Despite her insistence that she feels nothing, my love for her hasn't diminished in the slightest—if anything, it's grown stronger and more passionate than before.

34

BELLA

The bell jingles as I open the door to the coffee shop, hit by the sweet smell of freshly brewed coffee and hints of roasted hazelnuts, almonds, and cinnamon. I scan the room, searching for the familiar face of my sister. There she is, her eyes glimmering with curiosity, as if she already knows what I'm about to tell her, which is ridiculous. She can't know.

I take a seat across from her. She drums her fingers restlessly on the wooden table as she watches me silently; her gaze is heavy with worry. "How was the honeymoon?" she asks cautiously.

My stomach twists and turns with guilt when I see her drawn face and dark circles beneath her eyes—she clearly hasn't been sleeping well. "It was...intense," I finally manage to say.

She tilts her head at me questioningly. "In what way?"

353

I swallow hard before replying. "Isiah wants vengeance against our father. He told me one night after we barely escaped a shark attack."

Her eyes widen in shock. "A shark attack?"

I roll my eyes. "How is that the part of the sentence you pick up on over the fact my husband wants to bring down our family?"

"Shark attack is pretty crazy."

"Right," I say, nodding. "But Isiah wants to destroy the Benedetto family."

"He told you that?"

"More or less."

She takes a sip of her latte, her expression heavy with thought. "Did he provide any reason why?"

I give a slight shake of my head. "No, but I intend to find out what his motive is."

Nina nods and a silence falls between us as she fidgets with a strand of hair. "Did he mention anything about Cathal? I believe they've become friends."

I swallow hard, as the conversation about what he did comes to the forefront of my mind. It would break me to tell her that Isiah was the one to break them apart, so I stay quiet. "Didn't mention him at all."

Her shoulders slump. "I really think I loved him, Bella."

I grab her hand and squeeze. "I know, but if he was worth it, he would still be seeing you."

Nina shakes her head, her expression grim. "I guess, but it was so out of the blue." She clears her throat. "One minute he can't keep his hands off of me, and the—"

"—Wait, are you saying you had sex with him?"

Rage floods through me because if that man fucked her and left her hanging, I'm going to murder him. She, too, was a virgin.

"Yes, I was too embarrassed to mention it when he ditched me just after."

"Motherfucker." I clench my fists, wanting nothing more than to annihilate Cathal for hurting my sister. "If I ever run into him again, I'll—"

"You'll do nothing," Nina snaps, glaring at me. "I'm a big girl. I can handle it if a man doesn't want me."

It takes all my inner strength not to mention that the only reason he doesn't want her is because my asshole of a husband scared him off.

"Fine," I say, trying to calm the anger rising within me. "What am I supposed to do about Isiah?"

Nina arches a brow. "You need to try and find out what exactly he plans to do. Do you think he'd try to kill us?"

I swallow hard, considering he basically confessed his love for me the night before last, it's unlikely he'd murder me, but I have no idea what goes on in that warped mind of his.

"I don't think so, but I couldn't be sure." I swallow hard. "But the hatred he has toward Dad..." I shake my head. "He might kill him."

Nina pales slightly. "I may not like the man, but I don't wish him dead. He's our dad."

"You might think differently if you knew what he's involved in."

"What is he involved in?"

My stomach churns with sickness at the thought of relaying the information I learned the night at Insignia. "He runs a pedophile ring, selling kids at an auction."

Nina's eyes go so wide they look like they're going to pop out of their sockets. "Are you serious?"

I nod. "Insignia is where he runs it from."

"That's vile." Her expression is one of pure disgust and shock, mirroring the way I felt when Isiah told me. She shakes her head. "I've always known he's a criminal, but that goes beyond the bounds of a mafia leader, right?"

I nod. "Yes, Isiah found out and someone who works for him started the fire."

She gasps. "He was behind the fire?"

"Yes."

"How long have you known this?"

I bite the inside of my cheek. "Isiah admitted it to me the night of the fire."

Nina looks hurt by that revelation. "Why didn't you tell me before?"

I know I didn't tell her because I wasn't sure how I felt about the whole situation. What Isiah did was reckless and dangerous, and yet I can't fault him for it, not if it saved innocent children from a terrible fate.

"I've been processing what it meant."

Nina nods. "I don't know how to process it. I always knew our dad wasn't a good man, but this?" She shakes her head. "It's hard to believe."

I take a sip of the latte Nina ordered me. "I know, and I'm certain Mom knows about it."

Nina frowns. "Really?"

"It's why she hasn't been to Insignia with Dad for so long, because she found out, I'm sure of it."

"How can she even stand the sight of him after finding that out?"

I shake my head. "I honestly have no idea, but back to the point at hand. Isiah clearly has it out for our dad, but possibly the entire family, too. He targeted me for a reason, one I'm yet to discover."

Nina swallows hard. "Do you think he wants to hurt us?"

I think back to the conversation we had over dinner, and I'm certain he wouldn't hurt me. The rest of my family, though? "I can't be sure. It's possible."

"There's only one thing to do, then," Nina says.

I sit forward in my seat, waiting to hear what kind of plan she has. "What?"

"You'll have to turn into a detective and follow him everywhere."

I arch a brow. "You know how terrible I am at being inconspicuous. He'll probably detect me right away."

She smiles, shaking her head. "You were always

the worst at playing hide and seek out of our siblings, but you can do this, I'm sure of it."

I'm glad she's confident, because I'm not. Isiah is sharp. Following him around Washington won't be an easy feat. "I'll try," I say.

She squeezes my hand from across the table. "How is everything else?" There's a pitying look in her eyes, and I know she means am I struggling with being intimate with a man I profess to hate?

"Oddly good," I admit, hating the way it feels to say that.

Her eyes widen. "Really?"

I nod. "We got along better than I'd ever imagined on the honeymoon." Except for when I found out he scared off Cathal from asking Nina to marry him. And even then, he managed to reason with me, since Cathal clearly isn't right for Nina if he just ditches her at the first mention of mental health issues.

"Going back to the shark attack... What the hell?"

I laugh. "I was pissed off at Isiah and went swimming a little too far out."

Her eyes widen. "You were alone?"

I swallow hard, as I know this story makes Isiah look like some kind of hero. "Yes, but Isiah noticed sharks swimming nearby and came out to get me."

"And they attacked you?"

"Isiah managed to punch the shark in the nose and it swam away, giving us a chance to escape."

Nina shudders. "That's so lucky he came to your rescue. Did you even see the sharks?"

I shake my head. "Enough about my trip. What've you been up to since I've been gone?" I ask.

Her lips purse together and I know the look in her eyes she's been regressing. "Not much."

I reach for her hand and squeeze, forcing her to look at me. "Nina, I can't let you go off the rails again. You look like you've not been sleeping."

She sighs heavily. "I'm not about to go off the rails. I just think what happened with Cathal put me in a down mood, that's all. And with you not there to cheer me up, the house is..."

"Empty?" I ask, as it's how I felt whenever I spent time there without her.

She nods. "Yeah."

I have no idea how to make it better, but I decide we have to have another night together before I'm stolen away from the city in a few weeks to live in England. "How about I come over tonight for a sleepover?"

Nina tilts her head. "Will your husband allow it?"

"Screw him," I say. Even as I say it, I know it's foolish to think that Isiah won't get angry at me disappearing for the night.

"It's your funeral," Nina says.

"I won't allow my husband to dictate what I can and can't do. I'll head back to the apartment as I've got a few errands to run, and then I'll get some belongings and meet you at the house at about four o'clock," I say.

Nina smiles. "I can't wait. Can we order in?"

I give her an incredulous look. "Of course we're ordering in. There's no way I'm coming back to have dinner with Mom and Dad." I finish the rest of my latte and place the cup down.

"See you in a few hours, then?"

Nina nods and stands as I do, pulling me into a tight hug. "I really did miss you, Bella."

I hug her tightly in return, tears threatening to build in my eyes as reality begins to sink in. Nina and I are going to be torn apart, and there's nothing I can do to stop it. My best friend in this world will no longer be by my side and that notion hurts more than anything, especially as I know she's alone. Forcing a brave face, I pull out of the embrace and give her a smile. "I'll text you when I'm on my way."

She gives me a bright smile that makes her whole face light up. "Great."

I turn away and head for the exit, the tears welling in my eyes finally spilling down my face as I'm already mourning what had been. Life with Isiah is going to be hard enough, but it will be so much harder without Nina by my side.

35

ISIAH

*B*ella isn't at our apartment when I return and I'm thankful.

Jane texted me that she's going to give me a call. Like clockwork, my mobile phone rings and I answer the call on speaker right away, pacing down the hall, my heart racing. Undoing my tie, I feel like I'm suffocating.

"Isiah?" Jane's voice sounds grim. "We need to talk. Did you get my message?"

"Yes," I say simply, sighing heavily. "You've got news about the auctions, right?"

"Unfortunately, yes." She sighs heavily. "Clearly, the fire wasn't enough to put them off. We need a different plan of action if we want to stop them for good."

I grind my teeth as I knew the fire wasn't enough to put a stop to the perverse auctions, but it did slow them down at least. "It will require a more permanent solution. If you gather each and every person who's involved, I'll tear the hearts out of their chests."

"An inviting proposition, but I think that may be a little too messy. After all, some of these people are politicians and well connected."

I rub a hand across the back of my neck, as I know that my plan to annihilate the Benedetto family as a whole has taken a back seat since my revelation over my feelings for Bella, but I can still focus on Gio.

According to my sources, he's the one that ordered the hit on my father that night. The one that sent the masked thugs into our home. Masked thugs who shot my brother as a way to send a message to my dad.

"Fine. Shall we meet to discuss our next plan of action?"

Jane clears her throat. "Sure, you want to come to me?"

I look around, knowing Bella could turn up at any moment and there's no way I'd want her to know what I'm up to. "Yes. I also have another very important job for you, but it's going to be tough."

Jane laughs. "There's no hacking job that's too tough for me."

"That's modest." I check my watch. "I'll be there in fifteen."

"Sure, no rush."

I end the call and stow my mobile phone in my pocket, turning around to leave the flat when I freeze. Bella's keys are on the hallway table, which means she is here and possibly heard my conversation with Jane. Her parking space was empty when I pulled up, so I have no idea where her car is.

Fuck.

I turn back around and head toward the bedroom, it's the only place she can be. The flat is not a big place with an open plan living and kitchen area and one bedroom with ensuite bathroom. The moment I open the door, she practically falls out of the bedroom with an overnight bag slung over her shoulder.

I narrow my eyes. "Were you eavesdropping?" I ask, glaring at her.

Her face turns red as she shakes her head. "No, I had a shower and when I got out, I heard voices. I didn't know it was you."

"Bullshit. Who else would it be?"

"A burglar," she suggests.

I sigh heavily, as she's not being serious. "What did you hear?"

"I heard nothing but droning voices."

I watch her face, trying to work out if she's lying or not. It's hard to tell. My eyes move from her face to the bag she's clutching onto over her shoulder. "Why have you got an overnight bag?" I ask.

Her lips purse together. "I'm going to spend the night at home with Nina. She needs me and if I'm going to be leaving for London soon, then I want to spend some time with her."

"And you hadn't intended to tell me?"

She stands straighter. "I don't have to tell you where I'm going."

"Do you really believe that, Bella? We're husband and wife. I deserve to know where you are, especially if you're spending the night somewhere other than our home."

Her eyes narrow. "Fine, I'll tell you now. I'm going to stay with Nina for the night."

I laugh as she's not getting out of this that easily. "You had every intention of skipping out of here without saying a word, which means I need to punish you," I say, stepping closer to her.

Her eyes narrow. "Don't start that shit again just because we're back in Washington."

"What shit?" I ask, tilting my head. "You know you love it when I punish you." I grab her hips and yank her against me, forcing her to drop the bag onto the floor.

My hands move up her body and I grab her wrists, pinning them above her head, as I lean forward, nipping her earlobe with my teeth. "You are being very naughty, Bella," I murmur.

She shudders before me and I can feel the electricity building in the air between us. If she won't be here tonight, I have to have her now and quickly because Jane is expecting me.

It's insane how Bella can derail me so easily, as it's vital that I put a plan into place with Jane as soon as possible to bring down her father and the other pedophiles running this ring.

"I'll be late to meet Nina," Bella says, her voice raspy as I continue to kiss her skin. I press my lips against the nape of her neck, trailing light kisses down to her collarbone.

"You know you need to be punished," I murmur, feeling her tremble beneath me.

My mobile phone rings and I pull it out of my pocket, groaning when I see it's Henry. "I need to take this." I release Bella's wrists and she moves away from me.

"Good, I've got to get going."

I narrow my eyes at her. "If you are spending the night away from me, then I need to get my fix now."

"Fix?" she asks.

I pick up the call. "I'll call you back in twenty." I end it before he can say a word and stow my phone in my pocket. "Yes, you are my addiction, Bella." I move toward her, watching the way her breathing labors the closer I get. "And I need to have you right now."

She swallows hard, shaking her head. "I told you I'm going to be late to meet Nina."

I stare at her and realize that if I ever want my wife to feel the same way about me as I feel about her, I need to back off. Nodding, I step back. "Fair enough. Go."

Her eyes flicker with confusion as she stays rooted to the spot. "What?"

"I said you can go. I'll see you tomorrow."

She arches her brow. "Is this a trick?"

I shake my head. "No, it's me respecting your

decision. If you decide you need to get going, then fine."

Bella bites her bottom lip in a way the drives me crazy, eyes filling with desire. "And if I say I want to stay?"

I can't help the smirk that graces my lips. "I thought you were going to be late?"

She frowns at me. "I am, but you've made me hot and bothered and it's not like I can see to it myself in front of my sister, is it?"

I tilt my head. "You shared a room with her for years. What did you do?"

She shrugs. "Used a guest room when the need called for it."

I laugh and yank her against me, enjoying the feel of her soft curves against my body. "I've got to get going too, unfortunately, love, so we'll have to take a rain check." The idea of her frustrated and dreaming of me tonight makes me harder than nails, and so, I think some delayed gratification would be a good thing for her.

She grunts in frustration. "Fine, let go of me." Pushing her hands against my chest, she tries to break free.

"Not so fast." I grab her chin and kiss her, slipping my tongue into her mouth and drawing a tantalizing moan from her as the need between her thighs no doubt deepens.

It's torture to ignore the basic need to have her here and now, but slowly, I force my lips away from hers and gaze into her eyes. "Have a good night," I murmur.

Her eyes flash with irritation and then she does something that shocks me. Dropping to her knees, she fumbles with the zipper of my trousers to pull my cock out, slipping it between her lips before my brain can catch up and stop her.

I groan, clamping my eyes shut at the amazing sensation as she works me in and out of her throat. "Fuck, Bella. You are such a naughty girl, taking me into your throat without being told to."

She takes me deeper and I almost come down her throat, struggling to control myself.

I grab a fistful of her hair and yank her back, leaning down and looking her dead in the eyes. "Tell me you're a dirty girl, love."

Her eyes dazzle with defiance.

"Now."

She purses her lips before opening her mouth. "I'm your dirty girl, Isiah."

"Fuck," I breathe, before smashing my lips to hers and kissing her. And then once I've made her breathless, I shove my cock back into her throat and make her gag. "You are so fucking filthy it drives me insane."

She moans around me, her eyes clamping shut as she relaxes her throat and allows me to fuck it. All control of my urges shattered as I lose myself in her, driving forward as she swallows me whole, moaning the entire time. I gaze down at her, noticing her hand is under her skirt as she plays with herself.

That's all it takes to send me over the edge as I shoot rope after rope of cum down her throat, making her choke and gag, as I didn't give her a warning. My climax came too fast.

Once every drop is drained, I yank her to her feet and hoist her over my shoulder, carrying her into the bedroom and placing her down on the bed. And then I devour her. My tongue probing at her soaking wet cunt as I taste her deeply, lapping her up as if she's the best meal I've ever had in my life. And she is. She is delicious and I know I'll never get enough of my wife. An eternity wouldn't be long enough.

With a growl, I pin her to the bed with my hand, crushing her against the soft sheets as her cries of pleasure fill the air. "Stay still, baby," I order, exploring every inch of her body with my tongue like a thirsty man to water.

My teeth graze over her sensitive nub, making her entire body quiver beneath me. I push three thick digits inside her in one rapid motion, sending shock waves of pleasure through her body at the sudden invasion.

"Isiah! Fuck!" A scream escapes from between her clenched teeth as she shatters at my touch.

I keep on licking and sucking, tasting her delicious arousal as she shatters for me. Her body shuddering violently as wave after wave of pleasure courses through her. In this moment, it is all too clear—this woman who lies before me is true femininity and perfection. In this moment, I know she'll always be mine, no matter the cost. Slowly, Bella is becoming more important to me than anything, even my desire for revenge.

BELLA

*D*espite claiming that I didn't hear his conversation, I heard every single word. And now, I'm going to be late meeting Nina because he insisted on fucking me and I have no choice but to follow him to wherever he's meeting that woman on the phone.

I need to know what his plan is and how he intends to harm my family. A part of me agrees with his intention to stop my father in his tracks, but what if he kills him? Our family will be in ruin and Cain would be forced to take over leadership, and there's no way in hell he's ready for that. He needs to grow up first.

Isiah Darcy is a man fueled by darkness and I don't know how far he'd go to get revenge for whatever wrongdoing my father did to him. I need to find that out.

He pulls up outside of an apartment block and gets out of his Porsche, smoothing down his navy-blue dress jacket. It's crazy how he dresses so well all the time. It makes it more difficult to concentrate. Quickly, I park my car opposite and watch him at a distance as he climbs the steps of the entrance and presses the intercom on the side. Within minutes, he's buzzed in and disappears inside.

"What are you up to?" I murmur to myself, narrowing my eyes.

I have no idea which apartment he's visiting, but I have to try to find him. Climbing out of my car, I lock it and then head across the street, which is relatively quiet.

A man is just about to head into the building and he sees me, smiling and holding open the door.

"I've not seen you here before, sweetheart."

I glare at him. "I'm not a sweetheart, and I'm married."

He notices the ring on my finger and shrugs. "Never stopped me before."

"Gross," I say, dodging around him and rushing up the stairs.

"Rude bitch!" he shouts after me.

I ignore him and climb the first set of steps and pull my cell phone out of my pocket, dialing Isiah's number and listening at the entrance to the corridor. The dial tone sounds, but I don't hear the phone ringing in any apartment, so I head up the next set of steps and listen again, thankful he hasn't cut me off. Again, nothing. The call goes to voicemail and I sigh heavily, moving to the next floor and calling him again. This time, I hear the distant jingle of his ring tone coming from the second apartment on the right, which I approach. Once I'm sure he's in there, I end the call.

"Fuck's sake," Isiah says, shaking his head. "Sorry, I'm not sure what my wife could want from me all of a sudden."

"Wife?" a woman's voice questions, sounding almost jealous. "I didn't know you were married."

"It's recent," he says. "If she calls again, I'll have to take it." There's some rummaging around in the apartment, and then I hear the woman speak.

"So, how are we going to stop this pedophile ring?"

"I don't see any other option but assassinating everyone involved. Do you?"

There are a few moments of silence. "No, but a few of the targets are in the fucking government. They're not the kind of people you kill and walk away from it unscathed."

Isiah laughs. "I thought you knew who I was?"

"I do, but that doesn't make you invincible."

I hear footsteps padding up and down the room. "It's our only option. I don't care what it takes. I'm taking this pedophile ring down even if I go down with it."

"That's admirable," the lady says. "But what

about your plan for revenge on the Benedetto family?"

I straighten then, my heart pounding harder than ever.

"It's part of my revenge. Killing Gio Benedetto is the top of that list."

"And what about the rest of the family? I thought you wanted to annihilate them, too."

Pain claws at my chest. If he said that, it means he intends to kill me too, a woman he professed to love merely two days ago.

"Let me worry about my plan. If I pull this off, God knows how many children we'll save from a terrible fate."

Tears prickle my eyes as I finally have the confirmation I need. Isiah intends to kill us all, not just my father, but my mother and siblings as well. His hatred for whatever my father did to him is so deeply embedded that there's no way he can ever truly love me. I wonder then if it was all a ploy to try to keep me blind to the truth, telling me he loves me.

Unable to listen any longer, I turn away and rush down the corridor, accidentally crashing into a cleaning cart and knocking it to the ground.

"What was that?" Isiah asks.

Shit.

I run for the exit. By the time I get to it, I can hear him fumbling with the apartment door. Rushing down the stairs, I try not to fall, knowing he might catch me.

A monster who wants me dead, along with the rest of my family.

"Bella!" He growls my name from behind me as I'm about to run down the steps of the apartment building. "Stop."

Tears are streaming down my face, and I don't want him to see me like this. I don't want him to know how much his lies have hurt me. For a moment, I thought I was falling for him, too.

I turn to face him, narrowing my eyes. "Why? So you can murder me here in the street?"

His jaw clenches and he shakes his head. "You don't know what you heard."

"I know very well what I heard. You intend to annihilate every member of my family." I cross my arms over my chest and wait for his response.

"Can we talk?"

"Talk?!" I shake my head. "There's nothing to talk about and now I really am late meeting Nina." I clench my fists by my sides. "Goodbye, Isiah." I turn away, but suddenly his palm is wrapped around the back of my neck as he forces me around to face him.

"You don't say goodbye to me like that, love."

My nostrils flare as I stare into those beautiful, bright blue eyes, knowing that they're a part of his mask. Everything about this man's appearance is a mask, hiding the truth beneath. He's a monster with no heart. "I won't play this game with you anymore. If you want to kill me, then kill me. Otherwise, leave me and my family the fuck alone." I stare into his eyes, challenging him to make a move.

"You don't understand," he mutters.

"I don't need to understand." I turn to leave, but he grabs my wrist.

"Please, Bella." There's desperation in his tone. "Just let me explain."

"Fine, explain," I say, placing my hands on my hips.

He glances at a homeless man who has been lingering nearby, watching us. "Not here."

"Here is as good a place as any."

He starts forward and grabs my wrist forcefully. "No." He shakes his head. "I said not here." There's a firmness in his tone as he drags me down the steps toward his car.

"Where are you taking me?"

"There's only one place I can explain everything to you." His expression is haunted as he unlocks the Porsche. "Get in."

I hesitate for a moment, my heart pounding in my chest as I take in Isiah's serious expression. The feeling of his fingers on my wrist and the intensity of his gaze makes me feel uneasy, but eventually I nod and reluctantly get into the car.

Silence fills the air between us as Isiah drives to an undisclosed location. If he's finally going to explain everything, I sense there's no use pushing him to tell me where we're going.

My stomach twists in knots as he keeps stealing

glances toward me out of the corner of his eye, but he doesn't say a word. Only the deep hum of the engine falls between us as we drive through town. I can't help but feel a deep sense of dread about what he's going to do to me considering what I heard.

What is his plan? To take me somewhere and kill me before he takes care of the rest of my family?

I'm shaking in fear, regretting getting into the car with him, as maybe now I'm a liability since I know his intention is to kill my family. Grabbing my cell phone carefully, I type a text to Nina, but he sees.

"What are you doing?" he asks, eyes narrowed.

I swallow hard. "Just replying to a text."

"Hand me the phone, Bella. I'm not going to hurt you."

I swallow hard and place the phone in his outstretched hand. "Are you sure about that?"

His jaw clenches. "There's no chance in hell that I'd ever hurt you, love." The sincerity in his tone reassures me a little, as my mind and heart are at war with one another.

After a fifteen-minute drive, he parks outside of the entrance of Dumbarton Oaks Park and kills the engine.

"Why are we here?" I ask, looking at him.

All of a sudden, the normally arrogant and cold man looks ready to break. He's withdrawn, and the expression on his face is one of pure anguish. "I'm going to tell you everything inside that park," he murmurs quietly, getting out and waiting for me to follow.

I do silently, staying a few steps behind him as he leads me into the park. After a tense fifteen-minute walk, he comes to a stop at the foot of a large oak tree. He looks so small as he stands there, staring at the ground.

"Fifteen years ago, almost to the day, I lost the one person that meant the world to me."

I swallow hard and move to stand next to him, taking his hand in mine as it feels right in this moment.

He takes a deep breath. "My brother," he starts, his voice breaking as if from the emotion. It's so strange seeing him like this. "My twin brother, Aiden —he was killed on your father's orders."

It feels like all the blood leaves my body at that moment. "What?" I whisper.

"You heard me, Bella. Don't make me say it again."

I clench my jaw, instantly feeling bad. "I'm sorry. Why would my father kill your twin?"

"A warning," he says.

My brow furrows, none of this makes any sense. "I don't understand."

He closes his eyes. "This is the first time I've ever told anyone this story." The look of pure anguish on his face makes my heart ache for him, and he hasn't even told me the story yet. "We were fourteen years old and playing video games at home alone one night.

Our father was out working somewhere." I notice the visible shudder that moves through him. "It was getting late, about eleven o'clock, when we both heard a bang and four masked men broke into our home. They demanded to speak with our father, but he wasn't there." He clenches his jaw, as if it's hard for him to continue.

"You don't have to tell me anymore," I say softly, as I've already heard enough. My father is the reason his twin is dead. It all makes sense now why he harbors such hatred toward him and my family.

"I want to," he says softly.

I nod in response, unable to refuse considering how haunted he looks. It's clear he needs to tell me his story, even if it only makes my hatred for my father deepen.

"After they checked the entire place over to ensure we weren't lying, one of the men approached us and aimed his gun at Aiden." He draws in a deep breath as if he's struggling for air, his mouth opens a couple of times, but no words come out.

I squeeze his hand in encouragement, realizing how hard it must be for him to tell me this story if he's told no one in fifteen years.

Isiah looks me in the eyes then and the pain in his own is palpable. "He shot him in the head without a moment's hesitation, and then he said to me, tell your father that Gio Benedetto sends his regards and if he doesn't get the fuck out of town tonight, he'll be as dead as his son."

I feel his pain and sickness claw at my insides as I wonder how my father could be so heartless to send men like that into the home of two children, but one thing doesn't make sense. "Who was your father?"

"Samuel Dalton. My real name is Joe Isaiah Dalton."

Dalton. I remember James Wick mentioning that name the night of the party. "James knows who you are, doesn't he?"

He bares his teeth at the mention of him. "Don't speak his name. He's part of the reason my brother is dead."

I straighten. "How?"

"I don't know exactly. All I know is that my father treated him like a son. He lived with us but was a little older, so he was supposed to be with my dad when Aiden died. There was a fire at one of my father's warehouses and we assumed he'd died in that." Isiah clenches his fists by his side. "He clearly had something to do with it, as the snake is alive and well. Only men who defaulted to your father's side lived."

I nod in response. "So, your father and mine were rivals?"

"My father ran the Irish territory, but he was greedy and overstepped into your father's territory. I blame him too, but I'll never be able to forgive the man who ordered the hit that led to my brother's death."

It all makes perfect sense now. For fifteen years, this man has been thinking about nothing but getting revenge for the death of his brother—his twin. I can't imagine what I'd want to do to anyone who took Nina from me, and we're not twins.

"I'm so sorry, Isiah... Or is it Joe?"

He shakes his head. "No, I've gone by Isiah for the last fifteen years. It's my name now." His brow furrows. "You're not the one who should be sorry. I targeted you, Bella." There's a haunted look in his eyes. "I intended to kill you and your family."

The confession doesn't surprise me. I'd felt it. Something was off with his motive to marry me from the start, but I can't help but feel mixed emotions at him admitting he wanted to kill me. "And now?" I ask.

His eyes shoot from the ground to me. "And now there's nothing in this world that could force me to hurt you. I'd kill to keep you safe, Bella."

My stomach twists as he grabs my hand and yanks me against his side, kissing me softly. "I had to tell you here, because this is where my brother is buried."

I pull back to look in his eyes. "I didn't know there was a grave in Dumbarton Oaks Park."

He shakes his head. "There isn't." A silence falls between us as he stares at the ground, transfixed to one spot. "That night, my father forced me to single-handedly dig Aiden's grave and bury him right here under this oak tree."

Pain claws at my chest as I wonder how his father could be that cruel. "That's disgusting. Not that he's buried here, but what your father made you do."

He nods in response. "I wished every day that it had been him instead of Aiden." His Adam's apple bobs as he swallows, and I'm surprised that he hasn't shed a single tear telling me this story.

A flood of dread sweeps through me as I wonder if he still intends to hurt the rest of my family. I may be in the clear, but what about Mom, Luciana, Maria, Cain and Nina?

"What about my family?"

He looks me dead in the eye. "I'll spare them all, except your father."

I have no real love for my father, especially not after the way he handled things with Isiah, practically encouraging him to take advantage of me, however standing by while he's murdered feels a little wrong. But then I think about the children he's harmed.

"If it helps at all to come to peace with the idea, perhaps I can show you some of the evidence I have on him in relation to this pedophile ring." His jaw works. "Turns out your father isn't just a ringleader."

My nostrils flare. "What do you mean?"

He shakes his head. "It's probably best you don't know."

I grab his arm and squeeze. "I need to know."

"The ring that he runs requires all members to partake."

My stomach dips because I was worried he was going to say something like that. I feel numb as I stare at him. "Are you saying my dad is a pedophile?"

He nods. "We have evidence that he's done terrible things to children, yes."

"I think I'm going to throw up," I say, clinging onto his arm as my head swims a little. My dad is a bad person that I've always known, but what Isiah is saying is beyond anything I've imagined. And it makes me wonder if my mom knows everything since she never goes to Insignia anymore.

"Do you understand why I can't leave your father alone?" he asks.

I nod in response, certain that whatever happens to him, he deserves it ten times over. "Yes."

The relief on his face speaks volumes. "Good, because I don't know what would have happened if not." His jaw works as he stares at the spot where I assume his brother is buried.

"What was he like?" I ask.

Isiah turns to me, the deepest sorrow I've ever seen burning in his eyes as he shakes his head. "He was my best friend and a far better person than I ever was, even before he died. Kind and loving and just everything I'm not."

I grab his hand and squeeze. "Are you sure about that? As you say that you are falling for me, is that not true?"

"Falling?" He shakes his head. "I've well and truly fallen, love." He yanks my hand and pulls me into his chest and kisses me gently, as if trying to prove just how deeply he feels.

And in this moment, I allow myself to admit that

I've been falling for him to, despite the way he's treated me at times. I think I'm going to have to take a rain check on Nina entirely tonight, as things just got more complicated than before. I misread Isiah entirely, and the truth is far worse than I could have imagined. All along, it turns out my father has been the monster, not Isiah.

37

ISIAH

The storm clouds above the car seem to match the dark and heavy burden that weighs on my conscience. However, since spilling all my secrets to Bella, a sense of relief courses through me. It's as if I have unburdened myself from carrying this pain in silence and alone. Although I'm relieved, that feeling was quickly replaced by the dread of facing the implications.

I have treated her with such cruelty and contempt; initially, because I wanted to cause misery to all members of her family, but as time passed and my feelings for her developed, I took pleasure from how easily I could rile her up—usually resulting in the hottest sex I've ever had in my life.

Everything has changed now. Finally, she knows about me and everything I have done, yet here she sits beside me with a look of understanding in her eyes— not the anger or disgust I had expected.

She squeezes my hand softly as it holds the gear stick, jarring me out of my thoughts. "What are you thinking?" she asks quietly, tenderness taking over where irritation usually resides.

I shake my head; unable to articulate how much she means to me in words. "I'm thinking that I don't deserve you."

The surprise in her gaze shows she didn't expect such an open display of emotions from me. "What?" she breathes.

"You heard me. I don't deserve you, Bella."

Her lips straighten into a line. "You deserve to be happy, Isiah, especially after everything you've been through."

I swallow hard as it's difficult to believe that I deserve happiness since my life has consisted of misery for fifteen years.

"Do you think you can be happy?" Bella asks, as if reading my mind.

"I honestly don't know." I squeeze her hand back. "I hope so."

She gives me a wistful smile as I roll along in the slow traffic, wishing we were almost home. "I hope you can be. Now that you've been honest with me, I think everything will be different."

"How can you be so understanding after I told you I wanted to kill your family and you?"

She looks thoughtful and to my dismay, the traffic starts to move again at that point, forcing me to take my eyes off of her. After a few moments of silence, she speaks. "Because, despite how terrible you've been to me, I felt so connected to you for some stupid reason. And now I know the truth..."

I glance at her and she shrugs. "I don't know. It just makes so much sense why you acted the way you did. If Nina had been murdered, I'd want revenge on anyone involved, too."

Hope flares to life in my chest, noticing the admiration in her eyes as she looks at me.

Could she feel the same about me as I feel about her?

It seems impossible, but I can't help but hope. However, hope is a dangerous thing to have as it can be crushed as quickly as it blooms.

Finally, we make it back to our flat and I park in my spot, shutting off the engine. For the first time since it happened, I have someone to talk to about Aiden and his death, and yet I can't find any words.

"Let's go upstairs and I'll cook dinner," Bella says, squeezing my hand.

I nod in response and get out of the Porsche, locking it. I hate how vulnerable I feel, because I was always taught to hide all vulnerabilities from such a young age. It feels wrong that Bella knows my weaknesses. We get into the elevator in silence and ride up to the tenth floor where our little flat is. It's luxurious but far smaller than I'm used to, but it's all I could find on short notice and for only a short term let.

Bella leads the way and unlocks the door, walking inside and immediately heading for the kitchen to prepare dinner, but I'm not hungry, not for food anyway.

As I watch her move, all I can think about is having her right then and there. It's the only thing that can ease the pain and make me feel right again.

I move closer to Bella in the kitchen and snatch her wrist, forcing her to drop the gleaming kitchen knife.

She stares at me with a perplexing blend of surprise and interest dancing in her eyes. "Isiah?"

She seems almost terrified as I pull her closer, my heart thudding deafeningly as I lock gazes with her stunning sapphire eyes.

"What are you doing?" she whispers softly.

A feral growl tears from my throat as I yank her against me, gripping her other hand tightly. Our mouths crash together and my worries are forgotten in a raging fire of desire. Every thought, every impulse coalesced into one single urge—to be closer to her in body and soul.

The heat between us rises higher as I lift her in my arms, carrying her over to the kitchen island and placing her on the edge. "I need you," I murmur against her lips.

She gasps softly as I move the hem of her skirt up to her hips and look down at her perfect cunt, entirely bare for me.

"No knickers?" I ask.

She shrugs. "You destroy so many pairs. Why bother wearing them?"

A small smile curves my lips at the thought that she's constantly anticipating our next encounter when she dresses herself for the day.

Softly, I kiss her lips, exploring them leisurely. Her warm mouth returns my kiss with a passion that hasn't been there before—as if now she truly understands me. We are like two pieces of a puzzle that finally fit together.

Ripping agony twists in my chest as I helplessly struggle to find words that can adequately communicate the tumult of emotions raging within me. Our lips touch, and I'm overwhelmed by a feverish desire, pushing my shattered pieces forward into her welcoming embrace. In this moment, I'm sure she's the only one who can mend my broken heart and quell the fire of rage burning in my soul. I've been endlessly careening down an abyss of self loathing for too long—but now I have someone to grab me and haul me from the darkness.

I begin to undress Bella, not wanting any fabric between us. Bella tears off my tie and chucks it aside, unbuttoning my shirt and pulling it apart. Then her hands move over every inch of my chest, skating over the two tattoos. Her brow furrows as she traces the oak tree on my left pectoral. "This is the tree, isn't it? Where Aiden is buried?"

I swallow hard. I wanted a tattoo to remember him by, but I couldn't have anything obvious. Nodding, I capture her lips, not wanting to talk anymore. All I want to do is drown in my love for her and never face reality again. She makes me feel alive, a sensation I haven't felt for fifteen years.

And then I drop my trousers and briefs to the floor, positioning myself between her thighs and gazing at her soaking wet pussy, glistening with her arousal. She moans as I slide the head of my hard cock through her soaking wet entrance, eyes alight with a desire that almost undoes me entirely. "Fuck me, Isiah," she murmurs.

Hearing her say those words is like throwing petrol on a fire as I thrust forward, burying myself to the hilt in her and fulfilling her wish.

Bella's back arches as the most spine-tingling moan escapes her and she grips onto my shoulders, drawing me desperately closer to her. Every touch sends a spark of pleasure radiating throughout my entire body like a burning flame. Grabbing her hips, I impale her over and over, slamming my hips forward in desperation to get deeper than ever inside her. The need to make her understand just how much I love her drives me as I capture her lips again, swallowing her moans of pleasure.

My teeth graze against the juncture between her neck and shoulder as I kiss my way slowly up to her mouth, holding my cock deep inside her.

"Please, Isiah," she breathes, her blue eyes piercing mine. "I need you to fuck me."

I cup her breasts in my hands, gently playing with her nipples and watching the way her lips part sensually. "Is that right, love?" I ask, continuing to tease her with my teeth, lips, and fingers.

"Please," she gasps.

I kiss her then, moving my hips slowly, making her feel every inch as I slide in and out at a torturous pace.

"Isiah," she breathes my name in a plea, wanting more.

I stop and raise my brow, looking into her eyes. "What?"

"Stop messing around and fuck me."

I smirk. "You have such a filthy mouth lately. Tell me exactly how you want me to fuck you."

Her cheeks turn a deep red as she swallows hard. "I want you to fuck me hard."

I groan, thrusting hard and deep, her tight pussy gripping me hard. Leaning forward, I continue to fuck her and whisper in her ear, "I can't deny you anything." I move back and gaze down at where our bodies connect. "Watch my cock disappearing inside you," I order.

She does as she's told, eyes dipping to look between us as I thrust into her, her lips pursing together as the heat in her eyes blaze brighter.

"Doesn't it look so fucking good?" I ask.

She nods, eyes finding mine. "It looks good and feels good. I want you to fuck me like this forever."

I growl then, overcome by the emotions and desire raging in my veins as I lift her off the counter and spin her around, molding my chest to her naked back.

Her firm buttocks pressed against my raging erection. "Careful, love, the way you're talking is making me want to fuck that pretty little ass of yours and see how fast you come. As I know how much of an anal slut you are." I grab a fistful of her hair, forcing her back to arch more. "My anal slut."

"Do it," she breathes.

I smirk against her ear, dragging the tip of my teeth against the lobe. "Are you asking me to fuck your ass?"

She nods.

I spank her ass cheeks. "Let me hear you say it."

"Fuck my ass, please, Isiah."

That's all it takes as I bend her over the counter, my cock throbbing to be buried inside her tight channel. Grabbing a bottle of olive oil off the counter, I pour some onto her asshole and my cock, lubing it up. Lining my cock up with her tight ring of muscles, I push forward, groaning at the way her channel squeezes my dick, taking it like a fucking pro.

"I'll never get tired of watching your ass swallow my dick, love." I spank her round ass cheeks, my balls aching for release as I begin to move in and out of her, knowing that nothing in this world feels as good as being inside my wife. I grab the back of Bella's neck, forcing her to lift up and arch her back. "You are taking my cock so fucking well, baby," I breathe, knowing that I'm consumed now with pure, unadulterated lust.

"Fuck me harder," she whines.

As if I'm a slave to her desires, I do as she says, my muscles straining as I slam into her like an animal. I lose myself in pleasure, every wave and ripple of pleasure sending shockwaves through my body as we move together like one entity. There is no denying the need radiating between us as our souls intertwine, creating a fire like no other.

"Fuck, Isiah," she cries out, her entire body shaking as she teeters on the edge of no return.

I slide my arm around her throat and pull her further back, partially blocking her airway as I bring my lips to her ear. "I want you to come so fucking hard on my cock that you almost pass out. Every fucking muscle gripping onto me as if you never want our bodies to be disconnected again. Do you understand?"

She nods, unable to speak as I block her airway.

Keeping my arm around her throat and I rut into her harder and faster than before, every muscle in my body screaming in pain at the force. And then, reaching around with my other hand, I pinch her clit.

Bella screams her pleasure, the sound making my balls draw up ready to explode too. Her muscles spasm around my cock, gripping it in a way that sends me careening over the edge. My cock swells and pulsates as my cum explodes inside her, filling her tight ass to the brim. I pump through it, fucking both of us through our orgasms as I unload every drop.

"Good girl, take every fucking drop," I growl.

Bella moans, her body limp in my arms as I

release my hold on her throat, allowing her to take a full breath of oxygen into her lungs. She collapses on the kitchen island, her breathing ragged as her back rises and falls.

Grabbing her shoulders, I force her upright and groan when I see my cum spill out of her asshole. "Push it all out for me," I order.

She glances over her shoulder, brow furrowed. "What?"

"I want to see how much cum is in your ass. Push that cum out of your ass, baby."

Bella does as she's told and I fist myself as I see it dripping out of her ass and down onto her pussy.

"So fucking pretty." I gather some of it up and shove it back in her ass. "By the time I'm through with you, it's going to be leaking out of every hole," I murmur.

Bella stiffens slightly. "What about dinner?"

"Fuck dinner. You are all I need." And it's the truth. As I spin her around and kiss her deeply, I know that Bella is my salvation. The only good thing in my life and the only thing in this world worth living for.

38

BELLA

The mall is busy, and I hate being in crowded places, but Nina dragged me shopping. Apparently, I needed to make it up to her for ditching on our girls' night three nights ago.

Despite feeling some relief that Isiah has come clean, I need to get away from him. Everything he told me that day is still difficult to get my head around, although it finally makes sense why he has been such an asshole to me. It appears all was not as it first appeared when it came to Isiah Darcy. And despite knowing the truth for three days, I haven't been able to tell Nina. I just don't know how to tell her that this man intended to murder us all, but now I'm alright with that because of what our father did to his brother.

It's all too complicated.

"Bella and Nina! It's so good to see you," a voice says.

I spin around on my heel to face who spoke. My eyes fall upon a familiar, friendly face, but then I remember what Isiah said. James was instrumental to Aiden's death and my stomach churns.

"James," I say his name in a tone that is less than thrilled.

Nina, on the other hand, beams at him. "It's so good to see you." Even as she tries to remain calm, I can see the turmoil in her eyes as this man works for Cathal.

Isiah mentioned that both James and Cathal know who he is. Apparently, Cathal used to be his best friend before my father chased his family out of the city. And I remember him mentioning Isiah's original name, Dalton, when we met together one time, clearly a taunt.

His eyes land on me. "I hear congratulations are in order, Mrs. Darcy." There's something in his expression that I can't quite place, but suddenly I wonder how I ever liked this guy. "How have you been?" he asks.

"I've been fine, thanks. You?" I ask, unable to keep the coldness out of my tone.

His jaw clenches. "Well, thanks. Is there something wrong?" he asks.

Nina squeezes my arm, alerting me to the fact that Cathal is heading in this direction. "I'm going to the bathroom. Come get me when he's gone." And then she scurries off, leaving me alone with James.

"Why would something be wrong?" I ask.

The corner of his lip curls upward. "You just seem off." His eyes narrow. "What has Isiah told you about me?"

I shift uncomfortably as Cathal joins us. "There you are. I wondered where you'd gone to." He smiles at me. "It's lovely to see you, Bella. How is married life?"

I shoot James a look as I say, "Better than expected, honestly."

James' expression changes. "I think he's told Bella the truth."

I give him a glare. "I don't know what you're talking about."

His expression goes from angry to concerned. "Cathal, can you give us a moment?"

"He's not going to leave your family alone, Bella." His jaw clenches. "Isiah is the reason I'm second in command to Cathal."

"What do you mean?" I ask.

"He told you about his brother, no doubt?"

I hesitate to confirm anything, but in the end I nod in reply.

"However, he didn't tell you what he did to me. His father loved me like a third son, but Joe hated it. He was jealous of me, that his father loved me more than him and his twin." He sighs heavily. "The night Aiden died, I should have gone with them, but Joe made sure I got left behind."

"That's not what he told me," I say, as it seems

like the last thing Isiah would have been thinking of after losing his twin.

His eyes narrow. "All I'm saying is watch your back and your family's back. If he believes your family had a hand in his twin's death, he'll kill all of you."

"I highly doubt that's his intention," I say, despite knowing it was.

James straightens, clearly realizing that I trust Isiah's word over his. "He's a liar, Bella. I'm telling you to be careful around him."

I sigh heavily. "And I'm telling you, I don't need to be. I think it's you I need to be careful around."

His jaw clenches and I see the anger simmering in his eyes. "Whatever he's told you about me, it's not true."

"I don't wish to discuss the matter further," I say simply, wanting to leave it at that.

James' expression turns furious as he clenches his fists, angry that I'm not listening to what he has to say. "I'd watch how you talk to me, Bella," he says, his voice dangerously low.

A shudder races down my spine as I step away from him because he's finally showing his true colors.

Cathal returns, brow furrowed, as he can sense the conversation is getting heated. "What's going on with you two?"

I'm about to open my mouth and tell Cathal the truth when James shakes his head. "Nothing. We better get going." He nods toward the exit. "Haven't we got a meeting to get to?"

Cathal looks at his watch and nods. "Yes, unfortunately. It was good to see you, Bella."

I narrow my eyes at him. "Can't say the same. You're lucky I'm not murdering you on sight."

His Adam's apple bobs as he swallows, and he shakes his head. "I never meant to hurt her, it's just…"

"It's just you can't handle the idea that she has struggled with mental health in the past?" I glare at him because my rage is building at being confronted with this asshole. "Clearly, you didn't deserve her, anyway."

His jaw clenches. "How is she?"

I shake my head. "You don't have the right to ask."

There's sadness in his expression, but he doesn't contest that fact. Instead, he nods. "No, I guess I don't." He turns to James. "Yes, let's leave."

James gives me a smirk as he turns away and leads Cathal from the truth, but I've got to admit I think they both deserve each other.

I turn away from the two men and head toward the bathroom. As I approach the door, I can hear muffled sobbing coming from behind it. When I open it, my eyes fall on Nina, who is standing in front of the mirror, crying uncontrollably. She turns to me and her expression crumbles further.

Fuck.

Cathal really did a number on her. I quickly close the door and rush to her side, wrapping my arms around her in a tight embrace. "I'm sorry, Nina."

She takes a deep breath before pulling away from me slightly and wiping away her tears. "It's not your fault. Just seeing him was hard, you know?"

I nod in response, imagining it would be difficult to see him, especially since she loved him and he broke her heart. "I know, but he doesn't deserve you. I thought we established that?"

Her lips purse together. "Who am I kidding, Bella? It's me that doesn't deserve him. I'm too broken."

Rage flares within me because that's what she believes. "That's bullshit. He's the one who is broken for walking away from you like that."

I can tell by the look in her eyes she doesn't believe me.

"How was he?"

I shake my head. "I didn't ask, and I didn't want to know. I told him he was an asshole."

Nina's mouth drops open. "You didn't, did you?"

"Of course I did. That man was an asshole to you." I glare at her. "I should have threatened to kill him for what he did."

She tilts her head. "You realize he's the leader of the Irish mafia? He'd probably have to murder you if you threatened him like that in front of his second in command."

I'm well aware of that, and it's the main reason I

didn't give him a harder time. "Yes, but if it weren't..." I shake my head. "He wouldn't have left here alive."

Nina laughs, wiping the tears from her face. "You don't have it in you to kill someone."

She's right. Even so, it doesn't stop me wanting to hurt the man who hurt my sister so deeply.

"What did he say?"

I purse my lips. "He asked how you were, and I told him he didn't have the right to ask."

"So, he mentioned me?" she asks, an irritating amount of hope in her voice, as despite all he's done, I can tell she still hopes that he'll come back and beg for her forgiveness.

"Yes, but that's not—"

"Bella, just let me enjoy knowing that for a moment before you tell me how it makes no difference to what he did."

I purse my lips together, as I know that Isiah was instrumental in breaking them apart. Perhaps Cathal was easily swayed to ditch her by his long-lost best friend and he really does still care for her.

"Fair enough. Have we done enough shopping for the day?" I ask.

Nina purses her lips. "I guess so, but we have to get some food." Her stomach rumbles then. "I'm so hungry."

"What are you craving?" I ask.

"How about a burger at Jamie's?" she suggests.

I narrow my eyes. As it's a well-known fact that

Jamie's is a popular hangout for the Irish, and since we just ran into Cathal and James, the likelihood is they'll be there. "Nina, is that a good idea?"

She gives me an innocent look. "What? I want a burger, and apparently, they've got the best in the city."

I sigh heavily, seeing through her easily. "Fine, let's go."

She gives me a forced smile. "One moment, I'll just sort this mess out." She signals to her face, which isn't a mess. Nina is always so damn beautiful.

I watch her as she dries her face and then applies a little makeup to hide the redness around her eyes. Once she's ready, we walk the short distance to Jamie's. Instantly, I spot Cathal near the back with James, and wish to God Nina hadn't been so desperate to come here. James is clearly as ghastly as Isiah made him out to be after the conversation we just had.

"Are you sure about this?" I ask, noticing that Nina's eyes find Cathal as quickly as I did.

She nods. "I won't shy away from him, Bella. Wouldn't that be weak?"

I arch a brow. "Then why did you run to the bathroom in the mall?"

Her lips purse. "I was scared, but now I want to face him. I think I have to."

I get that she wants some closure, but whether this is the right place to get it, I'm not so sure. However, I know better than to stop Nina from doing what she wants.

Nina walks right up to the bar, mere feet from Cathal. The bartender smiles at her and leans over, clearly flirting. "What can I get for you, sweetheart?"

Her cheeks flush pink, and she swallows hard. "We'd like a table and two glasses of pinot noir, please."

Cathal hears Nina's voice and his eyes snap toward her, and then he notices the guy behind the bar making eyes at her. That's when I see a change in him. His whole body stiffens, and he looks like a lion ready to chase off another male invading his territory.

"Darragh, focus on the work and not the women," he snaps, walking closer to Nina.

"Bella." He nods at me and then turns his attention back to Nina. "Nina," he says her name in a breathless tone. "It's good to see you."

Nina holds her head up high and looks him in the eye. "Can't say the same, and if I want to flirt with the bartender, then I will."

Although I'm proud of her for speaking to him like that, his expression turns furious. I've seen a similar look in Isiah's eyes when I flirt, and I know how dangerous it can be. Nina doesn't know the kind of man she's messing with.

I tug at the sleeve of her shirt. "We should find a seat."

Cathal shakes his head. "You will sit with me."

"No thank you," I say, glaring at him. "I don't particularly like your man, so there's no way I'm sitting with him."

"James?" he confirms.

I nod in response.

"You and he were good friends. What happened?"

"Isiah told me the truth."

Nina straightens. "What truth?"

I swallow hard as I realize that if I tell her now, she'll know I was withholding information. "It's not important what the truth is."

"If I need to know something about my second in command, then I need to know." Cathal's dark eyes are intensely fixed on me now.

I shake my head. "Ask Isiah."

His jaw clenches. "We will sit at another table then." He nods toward an empty table and chairs away from James and the rest of his men.

Nina and I exchange uncertain glances, but in the end, she relents and follows him to the table. James' eyes remain on me the entire time, watching me like a hawk. He's no doubt worried about what I might reveal to his boss about him, but it's not my place. Cathal will have to confront Isiah about that.

Cathal holds out a chair for Nina, acting like a gentleman, when we all know he's nothing but a scoundrel. And then he sits next to her, too close for my liking.

"Look, let's cut the crap," I say, making Nina's

eyes go wide. "Why are you forcing us to sit here with you when you were a complete and utter ass to Nina?"

He runs a hand across the back of his neck. "Because I regret the way I handled things." His eyes move to Nina. "I'm sorry, Nina. I was an idiot for ending things the way I did."

Nina doesn't crack as she stares at him with hardly any emotion in her expression, despite the fact she was crying in the bathroom in the mall only twenty minutes ago. "Yes, you were an idiot."

"I've regretted it every day since."

Nina shuffles, a part of her resolve cracking. "You have?"

He nods in response. "Let's just say I'm used to being alone, and the idea of someone relying on me made me bolt."

I glare at him. "Because you're a coward."

A flash of rage enters his dark eyes and his fists clench. "You are lucky, Bella, that we aren't sitting with my men, as I don't allow people to talk to me like that."

Nina clears her throat. "Talk to you like what? She's merely stating the truth."

Cathal's lips purse into a thin line as a waitress comes over to take our order.

"Hey, Cathal. You guys eating?"

Nina nods in response. "I'll take one of the famous burgers I've heard so much about."

She smiles at her. "Of course."

"Make that two," I reply.

Cathal shakes his head. "Nothing for me, as I've already eaten."

"Okay, two burgers coming up."

An awkward silence falls between us as the waitress leaves, and none of us speaks.

Cathal runs a hand across the back of his neck. "Can we talk about this?" he asks, looking at Nina.

"Talk about what?" she asks.

"You and me."

I shake my head. "You've got to be—"

Nina grabs my hand and forces me to look at her. "Bella, can you give us a few minutes alone?"

"Are you sure?" I ask.

She nods. "Just a few minutes. Please."

I swallow hard, glancing at Cathal, who I don't trust in the slightest. "Fine." I stand and walk toward the bar to give them their time alone, sensing it's a bad idea. All the while, I keep my eyes on Cathal and Nina, wanting nothing more than to protect my sister from any more hurt. She's come a long way since her low when she almost killed herself, and the last thing I want is that son of a bitch sending her spiraling back into a blackhole without me there to pull her out.

ISIAH

*J*ane sits opposite me with three of the men she recruited the last time to get the children out. Bella is spending the day with Nina, so it made sense for us to meet today to work out how we're going to stop Gio's perverse dealings in children once and for all.

"Anyone have any smart ideas, or are we going to need to use brute force?" I ask.

This club we're meeting at is owned by the eldest of the three men, and according to Jane, it's the safest place to have this meeting. Even so, I'm on edge. Other than my own men in London, I trust no one, and even they, at times, don't earn my trust. After all, I had to deal with traitors the last time I went back. The thought puts me on edge as I eye the three men I know nothing about. All I know is they're all desperate to stop this pedophile ring, no matter the cost.

"We kill them all," the gray-haired man says, cracking his neck. "And then we save the children."

The two other men nod. "It's the only option. Once they're dead, then it ends."

Jane swallows hard. "A few of them are politicians. It's not like they can just up and disappear without powerful people searching for them."

The youngest of the three clears his throat. "We make it look like an accident, a gas leak and blow the place up."

"I assume it's not being held at Insignia this time?"

Jane shakes her head. "No, they're going out of town to some country club. It's secluded and very secure." Her lips purse. "Which means it's going to be even harder to infiltrate, especially after last time."

I have never been one to back down from a challenge, but it means we'll need more men. And more men, means more people I don't know and therefore can't trust. "How many bodies would we need?"

"A shit ton," the one guy who hasn't yet spoken says, eyes narrowing. "It's going to be an all out fucking war."

I shake my head, the last thing I need is to start a war in Washington, and yet, I fear there's no avoiding it if I want to stop these assholes once and for all. "Then we do what we've got to do."

The older guy nods, a slight smirk on his face. "Damn right we do."

A sense of dread coils in my stomach as I wonder

if I can trust this guy, or any of them for that matter. Jane fidgets slightly in her seat, and I notice she's surprisingly quiet around these guys. "Once you get the children out, how do you return them to their families?" I ask.

The gray-haired guy nods at the youngest of them. "Harley deals with it. Contacts the families and gets them reunited. He's almost as good a hacker as Jane."

"What's your name?" I ask.

He sits up straighter and looks me dead in the eye. "Ethan, and this here is Ian." He signals to the guy on his right.

"Okay, glad we are all acquainted. Do you have enough guys to pull this off?"

He nods in response. "Of course."

"Then we do it. Whatever it takes. If we have to slaughter every fucker in that building, then that's what we'll do."

Ethan laughs, nodding. "I like this guy. Where did you find him, Jane?"

Her lips purse together. "I didn't find him, he found me," she says in a soft voice. And then she shakes her head. "We have one week exactly to plan this and go in as prepared as possible."

"If I show up without an invitation, Gio will be suspicious," I say.

Ian shrugs. "Then get a fucking invite."

"It might not be that easy. If I can't get one, I'll come along with you in disguise."

Ethan and Ian exchange odd glances, but they don't refuse.

Harley fidgets a little. "As long as you don't get in our way."

I clench my jaw. "Do you know who the fuck I am?" The kid is disrespecting me, and I won't stand by and let him do it, especially not when I'm bank rolling this entire fucking thing.

The kid, who can't be older than twenty-one, shrugs.

Ethan holds his hand up. "You'll have to forgive Harley. He's in his own world at times."

Ian gives him a nudge. "Have some respect, kid."

I don't sense there's much sincerity in that, but the fact is, if it weren't for me, none of this would be going ahead. Taking a deep breath, I calm my nerves and nod. "How many men do we need? I want a rough number."

Ethan rubs a hand across his messy, graying beard. "Honestly? I'd say we need at least ten of our guys to pull this off, in addition to us three." He glances at Harley. "Obviously, Harley will be in the van stationed nearby with Jane."

Jane nods in response, but I still find it weird how quiet she has been this entire meeting. It's as if these guys are running things, not her, and that makes me even more uneasy.

"Fine, I'll leave it to you to arrange everything?"

Ethan nods. "Yeah, we'll get you the details as soon as they are finalized."

"Thanks," I say, standing and offering him my hand.

He eyes it warily, as if I'm the one he needs to be wary about, which is ridiculous. I'm paying him for his services. Finally, he takes it and shakes it firmly.

"Until next week," he says.

I hold his gaze, still unsure about trusting guys I've only just met. And yet I know I don't have a choice. My men are thousands of miles away, and I don't have anyone else I can trust.

Cathal did come to my mind, and I know he would possibly be able to help me out, but I know he wouldn't want to be involved in a direct attack against his rival, Gio. It would cause war and that's something any sane leader would want to avoid, especially while he's facing a rocky takeover since his brother's death.

"See you then," I reply, letting go of his hand and glancing briefly at Jane, who meets my gaze but has an unreadable expression in her eyes.

I don't say a word and walk out of the club, feeling a little on edge. There's something about those guys I don't like. Granted, they're scumbags who are helping out just for the money, although Jane insists they're mercenaries that want to save kids, I'm not sure I buy it.

For now, they're all I've got.

A buzz catches my attention and it's a text from Cathal, asking me to meet his ASAP at Jamie's. I'm only a five minute walk away, so I leave the club and head in that direction.

Cathal is sitting at the bar when I arrive and instantly he notices me, waving me over. "Isiah, that was fucking quick." His eyes are wide.

I shrug. "I was in the neighbourhood."

He nods. "It's been a while. How's married life?"

"Cut the crap, Cathal. Tell me why you wanted to meet."

He draws in a deep breath. 'I'm sure you've heard from Bella, about our run in earlier," he began very slowly. "She was here at this very bar, and she told me something strange. She said you knew the truth about James." He pauses, running a hand through his dark hair. "She wouldn't tell me what it was, but said if I wanted to know, then I should ask you."

My heart sinks as I realize what she had done—alluding to the fact that James betrayed my family without saying it outright and directing Cathal to me. My jaw clenches in anger.

"You remember James was like a brother to us," I murmur more to myself than to him.

He nods. "Of course."

I rub the back of my neck before continuing, "I assumed he'd died when we fled the States, because no one survived other than the traitors. And that's exactly what James turned out to be—the only one who knew my dad's inside secrets, which eventually brought our family down..." My voice trails off as I consider the full implications of his betrayal. My revenge plan should include him, but the fact he's Cathal's second in command makes it impossible. "It all made perfect sense when I saw him alive and well by your side at the party Gio threw."

"Are you certain?" he asks, narrowing his eyes further.

I nod in response. "Yes, he's a snake, Cathal. He always has been."

Cathal exhales heavily as he processes my words. "I wanted someone I could trust," he mutters regretfully, "but if what you're saying is true, then clearly I can't trust James."

I shake my head. "I don't think you can." My eyes narrow. "Sorry to be the bearer of bad news."

Cathal shrugs. "I'd rather know who I have by my side. How is your plan going, anyway? I noticed Gio's still alive and well."

It feels strange talking to him about this, especially since within the week, Gio Benedetto will cease to exist, but I nod. "Not for long. All is in place to take him down."

"Do you need any assistance?"

I look my former best friend in the eye and wonder if he would have been a better ally than the men Jane has lined up. Even so, I'm certain there's no getting out of it now, so I shake my head. "No, I've got it covered."

His brow furrows. "Fair enough." He hands over a card. "Have my number just in case you need help out of a bind."

I take the card, despite feeling certain I won't need

to use it. "Thanks," I say, slipping it into the inside pocket of my jacket.

"You didn't answer me. How's married life?" He arches a brow. "Do you still intend to include your wife and the rest of her family in your plan?"

I shake my head. "No, just Gio."

Cathal smiles. "Glad to hear it. Especially since I hope to marry Nina one day."

"I thought you were going to steer clear of her?"

Cathal swirls the contents of his glass around and then takes a sip. "I tried." He shakes his head. "Believe me, I tried, but she's just too…" He trails off. "Addictive."

I laugh. "I know the feeling."

"So you're falling for your wife?" he asks.

I nod in response, as it's the truth and I have no reason to lie to him.

"That's a huge turn around, considering I got the sense you had intended to kill her."

Shame coils through me as it was my intention to kill innocent people who weren't directly involved in Aiden's death. And yet, if I hadn't walked this path, then I'd never have met her.

"All things happen for a reason," I say simply.

"I'll drink to that. What do you want?"

"A scotch on the rocks."

Cathal calls over the bartender and orders my drink, who pours it. "To finding love in the most unlikely of places," he says, lifting his glass up.

I clink mine against his. "Cheers."

We both drink and silence settles between us, and it feels like nothing has changed between us. In a way, I wish that were true. How simple my life would have been if Gio Benedetto hadn't struck down Aiden. The question is, would I have found Bella?

Something deep down tells me that no matter what, we would have found each other.

———

I sit at the kitchen island, gripping a full glass of ice-cold scotch in my hands. The surrounding air seems to crackle with tension as Bella walks into the kitchen. Her eyes flicker to mine before settling on the amber liquid in my hand.

"You started early, huh?"

I clench my teeth together, willing myself to remain calm. "Needed something after my meeting this afternoon."

The corner of her mouth twitches, and I know that she's intrigued. "What kind of meeting was it?"

I pat the stool next to me, silently asking her to join me. She hesitates for a moment before taking a seat, her gaze never leaving my face. I take in a deep breath and finally let out what I've been avoiding addressing with her lately. "Jane and I met with some men who are going to help shut down the pedophile ring."

Bella's throat bobs as she gulps, her fear apparent. "When? When do you plan on making a move?"

My grip tightens around the glass in my hand, though my voice remains surprisingly steady when I answer. "We are striking next week—but you need to understand that there won't be any mercy shown to him; not after everything he has done."

Her features harden into determination and she looks me straight in the eye. "He deserves no mercy. I want him gone, but you must promise not to harm anyone else in my family."

My lips curve up slowly into a smile and I press my free hand over hers. "Agreed."

A ghost of a smile passes over Bella's face and she stands abruptly, moving toward the cupboards. "Let me make you something to eat then; it's the least I can do after the day you've had."

A laugh slips from my lips and I stand up, wrapping an arm around her shoulders. "No need. I already ordered us dinner."

Her brow furrows. "What have you ordered?"

"Indian food. I want you to try it."

Her lips purse together. "I don't like anything too hot."

I shake my head. "I know, don't worry. I've ordered a selection and you're sure to like something."

She tilts her head. "How can you be so sure?"

"Because I ordered chips just in case." I wink.

"Seriously? You ordered chips from an Indian takeout?"

A knock on the door interrupts our conversation,

and I go to answer it, finding the delivery driver with several large brown bags of food. He gives me a cheery smile as he hands them over.

"Enjoy your meal!"

"Thanks, mate." I shut the door and return to the kitchen where Bella is waiting expectantly with the plates and cutlery already on the kitchen island. Placing the food on the counter, I unwrap each dish revealing an array of different curries, naan breads and rice dishes.

"I'm starving," she says, picking up one of the dishes and pulling the lid off. "Wow, that actually smells delicious. What is it?"

"A chicken *balti*."

Her lips purse together. "Is it hot?"

I shake my head.

She grabs a spoon and digs in, placing a helping on her plate, followed by some rice to the side. "Let's see what all the fuss is about, then."

I watch her as she takes a hesitant mouthful of curry and rice from the spoon, her eyes widening almost instantly as she swallows. "That's delicious."

"I'm glad I'm the one who got to introduce you to a whole new a new type of cuisine."

She nods. "Me too." Bella grabs some of the naan bread and more curry, pilling up her plate with food.

I can't help but smile as I watch her, knowing that somehow, out of all the heartache and pain of losing my twin brother, I found the other half to my whole. Aiden was my world back then, and although he'll never be gone in my heart, finding Bella feels like I can start to heal the hole that he left gaping and raw.

"Why are you looking at me like that?" she asks, her cheeks flushed a little.

"Like what?"

She shrugs. "Just very intensely."

I grab her hand, which rests on the island between us. "Because it's how I feel about you. Intensely in love."

Her throat bobs as she swallows, as she's yet to tell me she feels the same. "I...I don't know what to say."

"Don't say anything." The last thing I want is for her to feel she has to say it out of obligation rather than feeling it.

She nods in response, and while I tell myself I'm glad she isn't feeling pressured into saying it, a part of me aches for reciprocation. But, I know that I was terrible to her to start with. A royal asshole, as that's how her father expects a strong leader to be, plus it was fun winding her up at times, but I fear it may mean she'll never be able to love me the way I love her.

"Have you painted anything lately?" I ask, as I set up the spare bedroom with all the painting equipment.

"No," she says firmly, her gaze unwavering. "I can't bring myself to paint right now."

"Why not?" I ask, studying her for any sign of unease.

"Because I feel like a fool," she replied. "To think

that I never knew my own father all these years. It's like I've been living a lie."

"You couldn't have known what he was up to all this time. All of your family is blind to it."

Bella snorts. "I don't think my mother was blind to it."

I pause, considering her words carefully. I highly doubt Viola could have possibly known the full extent of Gio's atrocities. She would have never stayed with him if she did.

"I wouldn't be so quick to judge your mother," I say softly. "She obviously has no idea the monster he is or else she would have never been in his life at all."

Bella presses her lips together and stares down at her plate as if it will provide an answer. After a few moments of silence, she looks up and sighs deeply.

"Painting seems pointless right now, anyway."

"Fair enough," I reply, knowing when to quit.

The two of us consumed our meal in silence, dark thoughts moving back and forth in my mind like a chess game. Could Bella really come to terms with the fact that I will kill her own father? And take my sweet time doing it? His death deserves to be slow and excruciatingly painful, yet at the same time, I don't wish for him to become another wedge between us. All I can do is pray that one day soon she will grow to love me as much as I love her.

BELLA

"There's no way I can stomach this," I say, eyes trained on Isiah as he tightens his tie.

He tosses a hand through his luscious brown hair and turns to me, his lips curling into an angelic smile that sends electricity through my veins. "What choice do we have? We've been invited to dinner by your parents. We can't exactly refuse."

"Faking the flu is always an option," I suggest.

A booming laugh escapes his throat, and he comes closer, brushing his lips against my neck ever so gently, sending an unyielding fire coursing through my veins. It's maddening how one touch from him has the power to make my heart thunder and render me completely speechless.

Why does he have such power over me?

"I'm sure you can handle one dinner, love. How do you think I managed to sit with your father evening after evening before we married?"

I turn to face him, shaking my head. "I don't know." It's something that has been on my mind, especially as I understand now the depth of hatred that he harbors toward my dad. "How did you manage not to show it? How did you control your emotions?"

He shrugs. "I've been forced from a very young age to conceal my emotions, so I guess it comes as second nature to me."

I swallow hard. "It kind of scares me, though."

"Scares you, why?" he asks, brow furrowed.

"You're such a good actor. How do I know if anything you say to me is true?"

His expression turns serious. "There's no need for me to act when it comes to you, love." He kisses me then, stealing the breath from my lungs and eradicating any worries I have about the way he feels for me. "Convinced?" he asks, as he breaks away to search my eyes.

I nod in response. "For now."

He laughs, and it's the most beautiful sound I've ever heard. Lately, he's laughing a lot more around me and I must admit every time I hear it, it makes my heart flutter like an excited schoolgirl having her first crush.

I groan. "This is going to be awful. I haven't had to face my dad since I found out the truth." I shudder, as I'm not sure how I can face him, knowing how sick and twisted he really is.

"You'll be fine, trust me." He squeezes my hips.

"I'll be there to help you through it. And this time next week, he'll be..." Isiah trails off, obviously thinking better of mentioning the fact that he'll be dead, since Isiah intends to murder him.

"Dead," I finish.

His lips purse together. "Is that why you are worried?"

I shake my head. "No, I told you he deserves to die, but I don't like the idea of having to pretend everything is okay, considering what I know."

"Focus on the rest of your family, not him."

I nod in response, knowing he's right. We can't back out last minute, no matter how badly I want to. "Okay, let's do this." I take a step back from him. "How do I look?"

His gaze darkens, and he closes the gap between us again. "Dangerous question to ask me, love. You look like you're ready to be devoured."

I shake my head, placing my palms firmly on his chest to push him away. "We don't have time."

"Well, to answer your question. You look delicious."

I roll my eyes heavenward. "You can never be serious, can you?"

He laughs. "I'm being deadly serious."

I lace my fingers with his and move past, pulling him toward the door of the bedroom. "Come on, we're already running late."

Isiah stops me at the door of the apartment, tugging me sharply into his embrace. His lips meet mine in an intensely passionate kiss that leaves me breathless. He whispers softly against my lips, a soothing assurance. "Everything will be alright tonight."

I smile, as it's almost impossible to liken the man who stands before me with the man I met almost three months ago at that party Dad threw. He's no longer out to make my life miserable. Instead, it's as if his sole mission is to make me happy and I can't believe the way I feel about him. A man I believed to be arrogant and cold. He's far more complicated than that—special even.

We get into the town car waiting on the street for us and Isiah keeps his hand laced with mine, squeezing gently.

It's amazing that in such a short space of time, I've come to almost depend on this man. His strength is inspiring and as I gaze at his beautiful face, I know that I'm the luckiest woman on this planet to have won the love of a man so damaged.

"Stop staring, love. It's rude." He looks at me then, a wry smile on his lips.

I roll my eyes. "I apologize, you're just so darn handsome."

He arches a brow. "And don't I know it."

I punch him in the shoulder playfully and he laughs. "There's no need for violence."

"You know, Cathal is going to be there tonight."

Isiah's brow furrows. "Why?"

"Because Nina is giving him a second chance. I

really don't know how to feel about it, as he might hurt her again."

"He might." Isiah nods. "But I think if he was the one who came crawling back to her, it's highly unlikely."

"Why do you say that?"

Isiah squeezes my hand. "Because clearly he loves her enough to admit he was wrong. I knew Cathal when we were younger, and he never admitted when he was wrong."

"Is that supposed to be reassuring?" I ask, as it just makes me dislike him more, knowing he's the kind of man who can't admit when he is wrong.

He laughs. "I'm not sure. I'm just saying that Cathal isn't a bad guy."

"I heard he killed his own brother."

"I heard the same," Isiah admits.

"And you believe that's true?" I ask.

"Possibly." He tilts his head in thought. "Most probably. His brother was an asshole."

My eyes widen. "So is mine, but I wouldn't murder Cain for being an asshole."

"No, I must admit it must take a kind of person," Isiah says, as the town car comes to a stop.

"The kind of person I don't want near my sister."

"He might be good for her."

I clench my jaw as I don't know how a man guilty of fratricide could be any good for my mentally fragile sister. "We'll have to agree to disagree on that matter."

The driver opens the door and I slip out, closely followed by Isiah.

"And yet, you are with a man who intended to murder your whole family," he mutters into my ear.

"Intent is a little different that actually carrying out the act."

He kisses my neck softly. "Very true, love. Come on, let's put on an act."

Isiah leads me into my former home, and it's never felt less like home before. The cold stone and gilt entryway gives off an air of unwelcoming grandeur, as if the house is telling us it doesn't want us there. Beneath my feet, the marble floor feels icy cold through the soles of my shoes, adding to the sense of foreboding, and yet I'd never noticed any of this when I lived here.

"Has this place always been so..." I trail off.

"Hostile?" Isiah finishes for me.

I nod in response.

"Yes, it was the first thing I noticed when I stepped foot in here the night after the party."

I wrinkle my nose. "I can hardly believe I lived here most of my life. It feels so foreign to me now, which makes no sense. It's only been a few weeks since the wedding."

Isiah kisses the back of my neck. "Don't worry, you'll never have to live somewhere like this ever again."

I smile at him, and that's when the maid comes to

greet us. "Everyone is gathered already in the dining room. If you'd like to follow me."

I swallow hard and Isiah gives me a gentle nudge, forcing me to follow her. My stomach flutters with butterflies as I dread the idea of seeing my dad. The maid, as usual, announces us as guests, and it feels utterly odd being on the other end of the announcement.

"Mr. and Mrs. Darcy," she announces.

Dad gets to his feet almost instantly, walking around to welcome Isiah. If only he knew the truth, he wouldn't be so quick to welcome a viper into his home. And yet, the true villain here is my dad.

"It's so good to see you, Isiah." He glances at me. "Bella."

I glare back at him, about to say something when Isiah cuts in.

"It's good to see you, too. We apologize for not coming by sooner, but you know how it is when you are newlywed."

Dad's eyes flash and he smirks. "Indeed."

I should have known his depravity ran far deeper than I ever believed when he belittled me for being taken against my will. The man is a disgrace.

"Well, please take a seat and join us. Cathal is here tonight as well."

Isiah and Cathal shake hands, but then I notice James Wick is here. "Good to see you," Isiah says.

Cathal nods. "And you."

"Come, have a seat," Dad says, placing his hand on Isiah's shoulder.

I struggle to believe that he can contain his rage when that man touches him. James Wick, being here, only adds insult to injury. We take our seats at the dining table, my siblings bickering already amongst themselves. I can't help but notice that James is sitting beside Luciana.

As I sit down, Luciana looks at me from across the table. "How's it not being a virgin now, Bella?"

"Luciana!" Mom scolds.

She laughs and shrugs. "What? It's just the truth."

"When are you going to grow up, Luciana?" I ask.

Cain chuckles. "See, you're still a prude, Bella."

Isiah growls softly. "Watch how you talk to my wife."

Everyone straightens, the look of surprise on their faces is hilarious and I feel my admiration for the man next to me deepen. It's rare that I see Cain rendered speechless by anyone, and he looks like a fish out of water right now.

Isiah squeezes my hand beneath the table and I squeeze back, unable to believe the way this man is making me feel, considering a few months ago I despised him.

"I'm glad to see you two are getting on so well," Dad says, but he doesn't sound genuine at all. His eyes fixed on Isiah in a way that suggests he doesn't respect the way he came in to my defense against Cain.

Nina elbows me in the ribs. "Hey, stranger."

I manage to conjure a weak smile in response. "Hey, how is everything?"

Her lips thin with anger. "I've tried ringing you three times and you haven't returned my call. What gives?"

My throat tightens, cutting off any excuse I can muster. "Nothing, I've just been busy."

Fury flashes in her gaze. She knows I'm lying, that much is clear. But I'm not ready to tell her why I can't stand the thought of her with Cathal, as he hurt her before and I don't trust he won't do it again. "Bella, what is it?"

I shake my head. "I can't believe you're giving Cathal a second chance."

The green depths of her eyes ignite with rage and hurt. "How does it concern you?"

"I don't want to see you get hurt," I say softly, my chest tightening with guilt. "I'm—"

"No!" she cut me off and all the conversation around us immediately ceases in shock, every pair of eyes now on us. "I'm not some weak-willed creature that needs protection from everything that could ever go wrong in life," she continues fiercely. "I am strong enough to handle whatever comes my way—and that includes Cathal."

Cathal clears his throat. "I don't want to get in the

middle of this, but I promise you, Bella, I won't hurt her."

I turn my attention to the Irish mafia leader, searching his dark eyes for the truth. He believes that's the case, but he hurt her once. It means he can do it again. However, Nina is right. I'm going to be thousands of miles away and I can't protect her for the rest of her life. Perhaps that's not what she wants, anyway.

"How long have you felt this way?" I ask.

"I just don't want to be treated like I could crack easily because of one mistake I made in my life."

I nod in response and grab her hand, squeezing. "I'm sorry."

She smiles at me. "I can't stay mad at you, you know that."

The rest of the family stop staring and start to talk amongst themselves. Of all the things I expected to happen tonight, Nina confronting me wasn't on the list. And that's when my attention moves to Dad, who is busy focusing on his food rather than his family.

How could we all have been so blind to the truth?

"Bella, how is married life treating you?" Mom asks, drawing my attention away from Dad.

I shrug. "It's not as bad as I expected."

Maria giggles. "In other words, she's getting fucked a lot."

"Maria! I will not warn you two girls again. Another crass word from your mouths and you are both leaving and going to bed hungry."

Maria shuts her mouth, but Luciana is still laughing. The two of them are a total nightmare, but I hope as they get older, they won't be so stupid.

Cain clears his throat. "I've got to admit, Darcy, I'm impressed with your work. If you wouldn't mind some time, I'd love to grab a drink and discuss your success. After all." He glances at Dad. "Our father won't be here forever and I'm in line to take over."

Dad nods. "Indeed, it's a good idea. Cain has a lot to learn."

Cain's jaw clenches. I know that Dad has always treated him like nothing more than a baby. It may be one of the reasons why he always acts so immature.

Isiah clears his throat. "Sure, I'll be in touch to arrange it."

Cain smiles, looking thankful that Isiah agreed, as it's not like him to ask for help from anyone.

And I know he's going to need a lot of help after Isiah kills our father. Cain isn't ready to lead, but I can't think about that right now.

Dad clears his throat. "We're up against some kind of threat, as always. Four of my long-standing men have been murdered in the last week."

I glance at Isiah as he tenses a little before quickly recomposing himself. "Do you have any suspects?" he asks.

Isiah had revealed that he'd identified the four men responsible for breaking into his house fifteen years ago in masks. The men who had murdered his brother, Aiden. And he'd made it clear that he intended to murder them—it feels almost surreal, knowing that I've accepted it as if it were common-place and inevitable. Clearly, he went through with his plan.

As I glance around the table at my family, I think ahead of the days following my father's impending death. Life will never be the same again; I only hope I have the strength to keep this truth concealed from all those who love me, or I might lose them all.

The rest of the evening goes smoothly, and my dad unfortunately invites Isiah and Cathal to have a drink with him in his study. However, it gives me a chance to apologize to Nina.

"Hey," I say as I walk over to her.

Her expression is irritated. "Hi."

"I'm sorry for not trusting that you know your own mind."

She sighs heavily. "I know you are just looking out for me, but you can't do that for the rest of my life." She pats the space next to her on the sofa. "Sorry for snapping like that."

I shake my head and take her hand as I sit. "You're right, and you have nothing to apologize for."

Maria approaches us, an odd look on her face. "I'm not sure what the hell she's thinking."

"Who?" I ask.

Her lips purse together. "Luciana has run off with James. They went almost an hour ago now." She passes me a letter, which is in Luciana's handwriting.

"I've known for a while they were sleeping together, but—"

"What?!" I ask, jumping to my feet. "He's a forty-year-old man and Luciana is only fifteen."

Nina looks gobsmacked. "Why didn't you tell anyone?"

Maria looks down at her feet. "I-I... I don't know."

"Fuck's sake. We better tell Dad, Isiah and Cathal. They should be able to find them and bring them back," I say.

Immediately, I wonder if I've always been such a terrible judge of character. My initial opinion of Isiah was that he was a complete and utter asshole, stuck-up and womanizing. And I believed James was a gentleman, down to earth and kind. How wrong I was.

I rush to my dad's study and open the door, not bothering to knock.

"Bella! What is the—"

"Shut it," I say, shaking my head. "We've got a crisis. Luciana has run away with James Wick. Apparently, she's been sleeping with him for a while."

My dad's expression turns furious as he glares at Cathal. "Your man has run away with my fifteen year old daughter. What is the meaning of this?"

Cathal holds his hands up. "I honestly had no idea." He glances at Isiah. "Are you thinking what I'm thinking?"

Isiah nods. "It's time to go on a hunt."

Nina steps inside. "You are going to find them?"

Cathal nods, his eyes blazing with determination. "Yes, we're going to find that bastard and ensure he pays for taking advantage of a fifteen-year-old girl."

"Good," my dad says, as if he can say anything on the matter considering what he does to children.

Isiah stands and moves toward me, gently encasing my hands in his. It's impossible to ignore the way my stomach twists in worry, as this man has become so important to me. "Be careful," I say.

He grins at me. "I'm always careful, love." He leans toward me and captures my lips, making me melt into him.

Once we break apart, I shake my head. "I mean it. I don't want anything happening to you."

He leans toward me and whispers, "It's not me you should be worried about, love. It's the other guy. Trust me."

"Give him everything he deserves for this." I watch him as he and Cathal leave.

At least Isiah is getting the chance to get revenge on James Wick and bring a groomer to justice. I hope he makes him die a slow and painful death for taking advantage of a fifteen-year-old girl. It's ironic how the tables have turned since the day we first met.

ISIAH

*C*athal sits in silence by my side as we travel toward the motel that Jane tracked his phone to.

The idiot hasn't even fled Washington yet, which is ridiculous.

Cathal sighs heavily. "I should have dealt with James sooner." Cathal's brow furrows. "I thought it odd I couldn't get in touch with him earlier. Perhaps he knew what was coming."

"Perhaps," I say, thankful that James fucked up so badly. Once James is dead, then my revenge is well and truly complete. "I'm not going to lie. I'll be happy to see him dead."

Cathal swallows hard. "He betrayed your family. In a way, he's the reason Aiden is dead, so I get why you'd want him dead."

I nod in response, as I knew he was untouchable

the moment I found out he was Cathal's second in command. There was no way I could kill him behind Cathal's back, as it would cause too much unrest in the city. It's the perfect end to my vengeance, as James deserves to pay the ultimate price for selling our family out and betraying the one person who valued him in this world.

"How are we going to play this?" I ask.

His lips purse together. "Motel rooms are pretty tough to break out of, there's normally one entrance and exit, but we'll scope it out before we strike."

I nod. "Sounds good. We're five minutes out."

"How could I have been so blind to who I had so close to me in my organization?"

I glance at him and notice the turmoil swirling in his dark eyes, knowing it's not just because James has run off with Luciana, it's because he's one of the reasons Aiden is dead. "You didn't know," I say simply.

He looks at me then. "I should have."

I clench my jaw and focus on the road, knowing that James was always the master of deception. Someone who easily fooled my father for many years. "It's what he does, betray people," I say.

Turning left off the road, I pull into the motel car park and park out of sight of the rooms, to ensure James doesn't notice us. "This is it. Do you want to scope it out while I find out which room they're in?" I ask.

Cathal nods. "Yeah, see you back here?"

I get out of the car and walk into the office of the motel where a small, mousy woman sits behind the desk. "I need to know which room someone is in."

Her eyes narrow.

I pull out a hundred-dollar bill. "Is this enough?"

She grabs it from my grasp. "Yeah, who the fuck are you looking for?"

"Paddy Kendall, he's staying here with a young girl." My lips purse together as we discovered James has a fake identity. "An underage girl."

"Shit, I thought it was his daughter." She nods. "It's room seven. Do you want a copy of the key?"

I arch a brow. "What's it going to cost me?"

"Nothing." She grabs the key from behind her. "I hate pedophiles."

"You and me both," I say, taking the key from her. "Thanks."

Cathal is back at the car when I return. "There are windows at the back, but they won't open enough for anyone to get out."

"Room seven." I hold the key up. "Even snagged the key."

He smirks. "Let's get this son of a bitch."

We march toward room seven and Cathal pulls out his gun as I slide the key into the lock slowly. And then once it clicks open, I force the door open quickly to find James and Luciana lying on the bed, kissing. Thankfully, both of them are still clothed.

"Move away from the girl, you dirty son of a bitch!" Cathal shouts.

"Oh my God," Luciana says, her cheeks flushing instantly.

James' eyes go wide as he jumps to his feet, holding his hands up. "Boss, I—"

"Don't!" he snaps, rage simmering in his dark eyes. "You were intending to run off with Luciana, weren't you?"

He draws in a deep breath. "No, I was just..."

"What money were you going to live off of?"

James looks scared now as he moves backward toward the wall, but there's nowhere for him to go. "My own savings."

"Bullshit. This is where the money has been going, isn't it?"

Turns out Cathal has been dealing with someone skimming off the top since his brother died, and Jane managed to trace the money to an account in James' fake identity, Paddy Kendall.

James' Adam's apple bobs. "I knew that Joe wasn't going away," he admits, shaking his head and staring right at me. "And I knew he'd spin some lies about me, so I made arrangements—"

"You fucking stole from me, and you know what happens to people who lie to me."

James turns pale. "Surely we can talk about that."

"No chance in hell." Cathal looks at Luciana. "Luciana, go outside and wait for us."

"But, I—"

"Now," I say, fixing her with my most intense gaze.

She shudders before racing out past me.

"Now, you and I are going to have a proper conversation back at the warehouse. Get up." Cathal keeps the gun trained on him as he walks toward me.

Once he's within reach, I grab his hands and slap handcuffs onto his wrists. "You should be very afraid, as I'm finally getting justice for Aiden," I say.

James doesn't say a word as I march him out of the motel room and push him into the backseat. Luciana sits up from next to Cathal, and I sit in the back with James, my gun trained on him. Getting revenge on James will help complete my revenge plan, as he had a hand in Aiden's death, but once he's dead it leaves Gio for the finale.

THE DAY I've waited fifteen years for has arrived. Tonight, I will destroy Gio's pedophile ring and bring it down, along with him. The darkness within me sings at the thought of tearing him apart slowly and painfully.

Bella is already up and cooking breakfast when I wake, prancing around the kitchen in nothing but my shirt and an apron. And as I watch her, I wonder if somehow Aiden sent this angel to me. After all, his death was the reason I was so driven to take down the

Benedetto family, and that led me to Bella Benedetto, the love and light of my life.

The clatter of silverware jolts me back to the present. "Holy shit, don't sneak up on me like that!"

I smirk as she clutches her chest. "I didn't sneak up on you. I simply left the bedroom. It's not my fault you're deaf."

She narrows her eyes. "I'm cooking you breakfast, and you're just standing there gawking at me."

I arch a brow. "Can you blame me?"

She draws in a deep breath and behind the smile that graces her lips, I see the unease etched into her features.

"You are worried," I say softly, taking a step closer to her.

She swallows hard and shakes her head. "I don't know what you're talking about."

In one swift movement, I close the distance between us, trapping her slender frame between my arms and the kitchen counter. She stiffens momentarily before relaxing under my touch.

"It's natural to be worried," I whisper against her ear, caressing her skin lightly with my lips. "What I'm going to do tonight is dangerous and your father..." I trail off, unsure how to show my understanding about how hard my plan to murder her father must be for her to come to terms with. Especially since I never had a close relationship with my own father. If it hadn't been for the bratva murdering him, I would have gladly done it myself. However, Bella's hatred toward her own father is new and fresh.

"It has nothing to do with my father." Her voice trembles slightly as she speaks, and I can sense the anxiety simmering beneath her words. "I never had a great relationship with him before I found out the truth, and now ... " she trails off, her blue eyes darkening with emotion. "I want him dead so badly, I just..."

"You just what?" I demand, my fingers tightening around her waist.

Her blue eyes bore into mine, as if looking right into my soul. "I don't want you to get hurt," she admits softly, her voice barely above a whisper.

Those words make my heart sing, as it means she cares what happens to me. Her anxiety doesn't stem from what I plan on doing to her father, but about what might happen to me if things take a turn for the worse.

"Why do you look so happy about that?" she asks, punching me softly in the shoulder.

"Because it means you care about me, love."

She rolls her eyes. "Don't let it go to your head."

I kiss her again. "I wouldn't dream of it. Now, what are you cooking? It smells delicious."

"A breakfast frittata with bacon, egg, and cheese."

I lick my lips. "Sounds amazing." I draw her body even closer to me. "Although not as amazing as devouring your sweet little pussy first."

She shakes her head. "Isiah. It'll be ready in five minutes."

I arch a brow. "Are you suggesting I don't have the skill to make you come in five minutes?"

"I'm suggesting you stop messing around and let's eat," she says.

I smirk and trail my hand slowly down her back to cup her ass. "Oh, I'm more than capable of making you come in less than five minutes," I murmur against her lips before kissing her hungrily. My kiss leaves her breathless, and a flush creeps up over her skin as she melts into me.

And then I drag her to the kitchen table and lift her onto it, forcing her to lie down. I pull my shirt up to reveal her beautiful cunt, glistening with her arousal already.

"Delicious," I breathe, before greedily lapping at her cunt, wanting to devour every part of her.

My cock twitches in anticipation, even though I won't have time to fuck her.

I circle her clit with my tongue, teasing her until she is writhing beneath me, her moans becoming more urgent.

My fingers slide inside her and start to thrust in rhythm against my tongue. Breaking away for a moment, my fingers still plunging in and out of her, I look into her eyes. "You taste so fucking good."

Her lips part as she caresses her own nipples gently.

"Good girl, play with your breasts for me," I

demand, before returning between her thighs and sucking her clit forcefully.

"Fuck, Isiah!" she cries out, as she gets close. I increase the tempo of both my tongue and fingers, chasing her release. She screams out as she comes apart for me, a flood of arousal pooling at her entrance as I lap it up with abandon, desperate to consume her.

I pull away from her and smirk. "I made you come with at least a minute to spare," I say, since her timer hasn't gone off yet to signal the food is ready.

She looks up at me in awe, a mixture of pleasure and admiration in her eyes. "You weren't lying," she says breathlessly as I help her stand back up straight again.

"Of course not," I say smugly as I take a seat on one of the chairs at the kitchen table, pulling Bella into my lap so that she is straddling me. "Now let's eat." I kiss her softly.

She tries to break away from me. "You'll have to let go of me then, as the food is in the oven."

"Hmm, I'm not sure I want to let go."

"Isiah," she says my name in irritation. "The food will burn."

"Fine," I say, releasing her hips and allowing her to jump off my lap and fetch her frittata out of the oven. It smells delicious and as I watch her place it on the counter, her cheeks flushed pink still from the climax I forced from her, I know that my life is so much better with her in it.

She dishes up two portions onto plates and passes me one. "*Buon Appetito!*"

"*Grazie,*" I say in response, earning me a smile that could light up the entire world. That's what she does for me—she banishes away the darkness. I only wish that she could learn to love me despite the shadows in my soul.

BELLA

I take a deep, shuddering breath and force myself into the elevator from the parking lot. My heart feels like a caged animal, pounding against its prison walls as I press the button for the tenth floor, where our apartment is. I'm on edge and have been all day, as the elevator rises.

The ding signals my arrival and I step out into the corridor. The tension in the air is palpable, seeping through the walls like a storm. Although, I knew it had nothing to do with the apartment block and everything to do with me.

Isiah will be carrying out his plan tonight—the one I agreed to without hesitation. He will take my father's life, along with the lives of his monstrous accomplices, those who prey upon innocent children. He's turning out to be a hero, saving Luciana from that predator of a man, James Wick. I know he killed him, as Luciana was inconsolable about it, saying she loved him.

How do you explain to a fifteen-year-old girl that what James Wick did was wrong? That it wasn't love but manipulation and control. In time, she will get over it and one day she'll find out what true love really feels like.

A part of me felt dead inside when I agreed to my dad's murder—a part of me that still believes that all life is precious and valuable, even that of an abusive criminal like my father. But what Isiah uncovered was enough to make anyone want him gone and forgotten forever. His wickedness makes me sick—though my mother isn't much better for allowing it to go on. But Isiah promises the rest of my family will be safe from harm. He'll get his revenge tonight for Aiden's death, and he'll stop a monster in the process.

I push these thoughts aside and turn the corner to our apartment, coming face-to-face with the door. It has become a sight that usually fills me with excitement at seeing my husband, yet today everything feels different.

My heart beats faster as I approach it, unable to shake this sense of foreboding. I don't know why, but something doesn't feel right. I reach for the key in my pocket and place it in the door to find the door is already unlocked. My brow furrows, as it's unlike Isiah to leave it unlocked, but perhaps his mind was elsewhere.

I push it open and step inside, placing my keys

down on the console table. And that's when I hear the click of a gun cocking, making me freeze in place as I glance toward the living room.

Three men are sitting on my couch, wearing masks, and each one has a gun pointed at me.

Perhaps I wasn't being paranoid.

"What do you want?" I ask, my voice shaking.

The man in the middle signals for me to move forward. "Come here."

I swallow hard, unsure whether I can actually bring myself to move forward. I've never been in this kind of situation before, despite being the daughter of a mob boss, but I manage to force my feet forward.

"Take a seat on the stool." He points to the stool at the kitchen island.

I swallow hard and sit down. "Who are you?"

"It doesn't matter," one of the men snaps. "You are coming with us, sweetheart."

The largest of the men moves forward and grabs my wrists, tying them together with a cable tie before I can fight.

I squirm, attempting to get to my feet, but he lifts me off of them as if I weigh nothing.

"You can thank your husband for this. We need collateral to ensure he doesn't get in our way."

I shake my head. "I don't understand."

"You don't need to understand. Frank, carry her out to the van."

I kick out and manage to land my foot in his crotch, making him double over and drop me. It's almost impossible to keep my balance as I try to run toward the door, unsure how exactly I'm going to open it, when one of the other men grabs me and yanks me back against him.

I shudder at the proximity of him as he molds his chest to my back. "Be careful, sweetheart. Frank gets turned on when a woman fights." He nips the lobe of my ear with his teeth, making my stomach roll with sickness. "In fact, we all do." That's when I feel the hardness of his erection against my ass and my whole body turns stiff. "Please, don't—"

"Silence," he growls. "Now this is going to go one of two ways. Either you stop fighting and come with us and you won't get hurt...at least not yet. Or you fight and see what it's like to be taken by three men at once."

I purse my lips closed in pure terror at the prospect and give him one nod. "I'll come with you."

"I thought you might." He sighs heavily. "Shame, I would have loved to fuck you."

The other two men laugh, but all I feel is queasy as he pushes me out of the door and toward the elevator. We ride it all the way down to the lowest parking level and he pushes me out, guiding me toward a black van.

There's a man inside the van who opens the back and the man behind me pushes me inside, slamming me into the metal floor so hard that I'm surprised my nose doesn't break.

I shuffle as best I can to one side but can't sit up.

"Stay down and don't move." Suddenly, every-thing goes black as they stick a hood over my head. It only heightens the terror spiking through my veins as I remain as stiff as a board, wondering how I'm going to get out of this.

My mind is racing with questions, none of which I can ask unless I want to be violated by these men. A shiver courses down my spine as I remember how my skin crawled just being touched by one of them.

Does this have something to do with the pedophile ring Isiah is trying to bring down? And if so, does that mean my father is behind my kidnapping?

I can't recognize any of the voices as my father's men, but you never know. He has hundreds of men on the payroll who I've never met.

"What time are we meeting them at Red Cove Country Club?" one of them asks.

I freeze, as Isiah mentioned, that is the club where he was headed tonight for the auction to bring those motherfuckers down once and for all.

"Nine o'clock. It gives them enough time to finish off the leaders and then we come in with the leverage."

A man laughs a deep laugh. "That British son of a bitch will either do as he's told or watch while fifty men fuck his wife."

The blood in my veins runs cold as I realize they're talking about Isiah. He had mentioned he hated trusting people he didn't know to help him with this, and that he was unsure about the guys Jane had brought in. And it turns out, his intuitions was right.

"I'm hoping it's the latter. The bait is hot as fuck. I'd stick my cock in her ass and see how well she takes it."

Rage simmers to life in my veins, these men are fucking disgusting. And as I lie on the dirty, cold floor of the van, I can't help but wonder what is more important to Isiah. I've seen his reaction to men flirting with me and it's damn right animalistic, but what happens if I come between him getting his revenge on my father? What is more important to him?

The van suddenly takes a sharp turn, slamming me into something hard on my right. I try to move, but it's impossible with my hands bound behind my back.

"We're here, boys."

The engine turns off and I can feel the blood draining from my body at the thought of being used by these men. As I am dragged out of the van, all I can think about is Isiah.

Suddenly, I feel two hands grab my jacket and yank me out of the back of the van, forcing me to my feet. "Move. Now," a man barks.

I move my feet as I'm dragged along by these men, unable to see where I'm going. And then they stop and I hear the fumble of keys.

"Hurry up, Corbin!"

The one who must be Corbin growls. "You fucking do it if you'd be quicker, Chris."

"Out of my way," he growls, and then I hear a door creak open. "Was it that hard?"

I'm shoved forward, almost losing my footing but being yanked back upright before I hit the floor. "Watch where you are walking."

"I would if I could see," I spit back.

That results in a sharp whack to the back of my head. "Keep your mouth shut, bitch. Unless you are sucking my cock."

I grind my teeth as this guy is getting on my nerves. "Put it near my mouth and see if I don't bite it off."

He hits me again.

"Corbin! Don't hit the leverage, you stupid son of a bitch," someone shouts.

At least someone said it, as he is a stupid son of a bitch. I'm dragged a little further and then suddenly I'm forced into a chair. I feel hands grab my ankles and tie something tightly around them, binding me to the chair and making dread sink deeper in my stomach.

"Please, what are you doing—"

Someone smacks me in the face. "I said shut it!"

I swallow hard and shut my mouth, knowing that these kinds of men aren't going to listen to reason or even tell me what is going on. And so I resign myself to the fact that I'm going to have to sit and await my fate, whatever it might be.

"How far along are they with the plan?" I hear a man ask.

"Fuck if I know. Ethan said to wait until he called."

There's a deep sigh from the other man. "Let's wait outside. It's stuffy in here."

I hear the men's footsteps as they move away and then the slam of a door, and then the unmistakable click of a lock turning.

I'm alone, in a chair, blindfolded and bound with no hope of escape. Even if I did manage to free myself, I'd still be trapped in this godforsaken place with no idea of where Isiah is. The air is heavy, but I feel my heart start to thump harder in my chest as fear sets in.

The thought that he might already be dead sends a chill down my spine and makes my chest clench, and I have to push the thought out of my head as it's too painful to think about.

Instead, I contemplate what might happen to me. Are these men going to let me go? Or will they kill me? It's impossible for me to know and all I can do is wait and hope that somehow everything works out for the best. I take a deep breath and push these thoughts away from my mind for now. The only thing keeping me calm is that Isiah is so strong I know he won't be easily defeated, and if he survives, I know he'll come for me. All I can do is sit completely helpless in complete darkness, surrounded by an eerie silence.

43

ISIAH

The party is in full swing as classical music travels from the building out into the surrounding woodland. Anyone would think that a cultured and civil party was taking place, but we all know the truth. Those fuckers are dressing up and attending this thing to buy young children to violate. Red Cove country club is the ideal location to sneak up on unsuspecting pedophiles and end them once and for all. It's secluded and miles from any help.

The only problem is the guards. There are more security guards than Ethan anticipated, which means we're outnumbered two to one.

"Any smart ideas?" I ask Ethan.

He shakes his head. "Surprise will be our friend. If we can sneak up on as many guards as possible and take them out silently, then we have half a chance."

I don't like leaving things to chance. I'm so used to being in control and right now, nothing is in my control. These men are running this operation and I feel out of the driver's seat.

"Fine, we have no choice. Give the order."

Ethan's eyes flash, as if he's not used to being told what to do, but he does give the order.

"Let's move forward then," he says, nodding toward the left side entrance which we are taking. Silently, we move as a unit in the shadows toward the building, knowing that one wrong move could spell disaster for all of us.

Ethan takes the lead and wraps his arm around the first guard, snapping his neck with little effort. The man falls to the floor as I sneak up behind the second and do the same. When I turn around, I notice the spark of admiration in Ethan's eyes, no doubt impressed I could kill as easily as he could. My well dressed and manicured appearance throws people off at times, but I always have been and always will be a ruthless killing machine. It's what my dad brought me up to be.

As we move toward the entrance, I'm thankful that at the moment, everything is going to plan. Even so, I can't shake this sense of foreboding, as if something terrible awaits around the next corner.

We make our way through the side entrance and into the main entryway, where we find more guards. This time, we're spotted and the guards start to shout, pointing their guns at us.

"Fuck!" Ethan exclaims.

I duck down behind a pillar and pull my gun from my pocket. "Cover me."

He nods in response and I move out of cover to shoot, taking down two men before anyone shoots a round. Clearly, they've got the guards in numbers, but they aren't very skilled. The bodies pile up quickly, as Ethan grabs the opportunity and also breaks cover, taking down the three more guards in quick succession.

Grabbing the radio from his belt, he speaks into it. "We're made. Go in guns blazing, boys."

I'm certain that everyone inside must have heard the commotion, and it means Gio might be more difficult to get to.

The man is a coward in my eyes and he'll run at the first sign of trouble, which means time is limited.

"Ethan, you go get the kids and secure the place. I've got someone I need to find."

He nods. "See you when it's over."

I rush through the hall and toward the main events room, where the partygoers are congregated. When I get to the room, it's utter carnage. Bodies of the pedophiles are piling up and there's blood everywhere.

If any of those fuckers have killed Gio, I'll murder them. They know he's got to be saved for me. As I search the room, I see no sign of him.

"Fuck," I mutter, holding the gun to my forehead as I try to work out where he would have gone.

One of Ethan's guys rushes past. "Hey, you."

"Yeah?"

"Have you seen Gio Benedetto?"

He shakes his head. "Nah, sorry man."

I sigh heavily, glancing around the room. If he's not here where all the other guests are, where is he?

"Isiah," one of the men says, drawing my attention.

"Ethan has found the kids and the guy you're after."

I tense hearing he's found Gio, realizing that I'm on the precipice of getting the revenge I've craved for fifteen years. It feels surreal.

"Where?"

The guy nods back the way I'd come. "In the bar. It's the first door on the right of the entrance."

My heart beats harder and faster, making me feel a little sick as I have waited too long for this moment, and now that it's here, I don't know how I feel. The entryway was eerily silent as I follow the guy's instructions and enter the bar, only to come to a jarring halt when I see Ethan and most of his men standing there, guns pointed at me.

"What the fuck is going on?"

I glance around the room and see Jane to one side, glancing down at her feet.

"What is going on is that you've been played, Darcy," Ethan says, pointing a gun at my chest.

I run a hand across the back of my neck. "And why exactly are you double-crossing me?"

He nods to one of his men. "Apprehend him."

It's hard to believe that this was all a ploy. For what end? I don't know. Since there's no sign of Gio, I'm starting to wonder if that son of a bitch managed to get one up on me.

Could he be behind all this?

If Gio is behind it all, then I seriously underestimated him and his intelligence. One guy grabs my arm and tries to pull it behind my back. I slip free and slam my fist into his nose, enjoying the audible crack that echoes through the vast room.

Another comes at me, trying to tackle me to the ground, but I step to the side and slam my foot into his crotch, making him screech like a little girl. I know fighting is futile in the long run, considering I'm outnumbered, but I won't just stand there while these fuckers walk all over me.

"Are you sure you want to do this, Ethan?" I ask.

His jaw works. "Certain."

He's going to regret crossing me, that I'm sure of.

"Get him, boys," Ethan instructs.

Men come at me from all angles, and I manage to ward a few of them off before they overwhelm me, tackling me to the ground.

"Motherfuckers," I say, as they haul me to my feet and tie my hands together. "Why the fuck are you doing this?!"

"All will be revealed soon. I have something that is precious to you, I believe." He tilts his head, a smirk on his lips. "Well, someone."

All the blood drains from my body, as the only person on this earth that is precious to me is Bella.

"Who?" I ask.

"That very fuckable wife of yours."

I start forward, insurmountable rage flooding my veins at breakneck speed as I try to get at him, growling like a rabid dog. "You keep your fucking hands off of her."

"That, Isiah, is up to you."

I bite the inside of my cheek, trying to find a way to bottle up the rage, trying to take control of my body. "What do you want?" I spit.

"It's simple, really. You walk away with your girl and the man you want to get revenge on."

My brow furrows. "Walk away from what?"

"The pedophile ring. We are taking it over."

Sickness twists my gut as I realize what he's saying. This son of a bitch and his men didn't want to save kids. They saw dollar signs and want to keep running this sick and twisted ring.

"You've got to be kidding me."

"Jane alerted us to a competing operation, so we wanted to add it to our portfolio."

"You are children traffickers?" I confirm, angry with myself, that I didn't follow my instincts and do more digging on these guys, trusting Jane completely.

Ethan nods. "Amongst other things."

I glance at Jane, who is standing to one side, eyes at her feet. "I can't believe you are in on this, Jane."

Her eyes shoot up and they're glistening with

tears, as if she didn't really want this to happen. Her throat bobs as she swallows, and she glances nervously at Ethan.

"Jane has been with us since she was seven years old, haven't you, sweetheart?" The man winks at her. "Of course she was going to tell us about a competing operation because she's a good girl."

Fuck.

I was right about Jane all along. The only thing is, she's still under the thumb of her abusers. My heart clenches at the thought that this woman I trusted has been so badly abused she does whatever these men say. Once I get out of here, she won't be included in the executions. Instead, I'll free her from the chains these men have kept her in.

"So you just want me to walk away, that's it?"

He nods. "Yes. Or we will gang rape your little wife in front of your eyes before killing both of you."

My fists clench by my sides. He's going too fucking far. If he lays a hand on her, I'll cut his fucking dick off. Hell, I still intend to cut it off by the time I'm through with him just for thinking about it.

"Fine, let me see her first. I want to see that you have kept her unharmed."

Ethan nods. "Go fetch the leverage."

Leverage.

This man will wish he hadn't been born soon enough. There's absolutely no chance that I'm leaving this place and these men to sell off these kids, or any kids in the future.

Any operation that existed before this day will be obliterated from the face of the earth. Clearly, Ethan doesn't realize the kind of man he's messing with.

My body hums with tension as a plan rapidly takes shape in my mind; thankfully, I had taken the necessary precautions for a situation like this. Cathal will be here if he doesn't get word from me within an hour. It's been two hours and I know that he'll be on his way—perhaps even already here.

My rage bubbles like lava under my skin as Ethan's goons drag my wife into the room. She is bound and gagged with a hood over her head, and I see she's struggling against the ropes desperately. The knowledge of what they did to bring her here sets my soul ablaze, my determination surging like a firestorm within me. These men will pay dearly for their actions.

Without a word, the thugs loosen Bella from her restraints and pull off the hood, shielding her face. Her eyes are brimming with desperation and terror, tears streaming down her cheeks as she looks around the room. Finally, she spots me and the relief in her beautiful blue depths is enough to undo me. I've longed to see her look at me like that, but not under these circumstances.

An onslaught of emotion overwhelms me, so powerful it feels like my heart is being ripped apart. Until now, she believed that she was alone in this fight, but now she can see that I'm here; ready to do whatever it takes to get her out safely.

44

BELLA

The click of the door alerts me to someone entering, but since these assholes insist on keeping this hood over my head, I can't see who it is.

I don't know how long they've had me. It's felt like a lifetime, but it's probably no longer than a few hours. They'd mentioned to one another that they'd stash me somewhere safe in the grounds of the country club, and then they'd left me here.

"Come on, sweetheart. We've got someone who wants to see you." The guy roughly undoes my binding and yanks me to my feet, dragging me God knows where.

I hate that I'm so overcome with fear, desperate to find an escape, but feeling hopelessly trapped. It feels like I'm marching to my demise. The creak of a door opening sets my already fried nerves on edge.

"Here she is," the gruff voice says, as I'm pushed forward and lose my balance, falling onto the floor.

A soft growl is audible nearby as I put my sore hands out to sit up, feeling my entire body aching from being held in one position for however long.

Suddenly, the hood is ripped from my head and a blinding light forces me to shut my eyes. I open them a little, waiting for them to adjust. Finally, they adjust and I manage to take in my surroundings.

We're in some kind of large events hall, which is lavishly decorated with glistening chandeliers and ornate gold-framed paintings. The walls are a deep shade of red that perfectly complements the light oak floor.

At the far end of the room, in an area covered by a golden rug, I can just make out a grand piano with intricate designs carved into its surface. Its keys are polished to perfection, and it looks like it has never been used before. And my veins run cold when I see a group of seven children in chains in the corner, all of them looking beyond terrified. The youngest can't be much older than six years old, and the hatred toward my dad hits me with renewed vigor.

How could he?

I force my eyes from them, otherwise I'll drown in a sea of guilt that I may not be able to do anything to stop their abuse. And that's when my eyes snag on the man standing near the back of the room.

Isiah.

His eyes blaze with fury when he sees my face and I see his jaw clench. I can't work out whether the rage is aimed at me or the men surrounding me.

"So, Darcy, what will it be? Are you going to let us violate your wife? Or are you going to walk away and hand the keys to this operation over to us?" an older man asks with graying hair.

At that moment, I realize that they don't intend to stop Isiah from killing my father. They want to run the pedophile ring, not bring an end to it. They don't work for my father. As I gaze around the room, I see no sign of him.

Is it possible my dad is already dead?

The turmoil in Isiah's eyes hits me, and I can completely understand it. How can he leave innocent children to be violated by men like this?

"You really are a piece of shit, Ethan," Isiah says, scowling at him. "I paid you to help put an end to this, not continue it. I assume there isn't a sum you would take in order to walk away."

Ethan smirks. "Too much money to be made and you ain't paying enough." He tilts his head. "Hell, you don't have enough to pay us. Do you know how much one of those kids brings in?"

My stomach twists with sickness as it doesn't matter if they bring in a billion fucking dollars. It's damn right demonic to profit off of their abuse.

Isiah's expression remains unreadable. He's an unwavering wall of stone, even in such a precarious situation.

"As I said. If you let her go, I'll leave you alone," Isiah says, his voice firm.

Ethan smirks. "How can we be sure you won't try to get revenge?"

Isiah squares up to the brawny, graying man and looks him dead in the eye. "Revenge for what? I wanted to bring down Gio and murder him. That was my main aim. Sure, I wanted to help the kids in doing so, but it's not my concern. You give me Gio and you give me my wife, and you'll never see me again."

The man, Ethan, appears to be convinced as he nods his head. "Fair enough." He glances at the man holding me. "Corbin, release her."

"Fuck," he mutters. "Another case of blue balls."

A shiver starts at the top of my spine and finishes at the base, hearing him talk like that. This disgusting son of a bitch hoped that Isiah wouldn't agree and that he'd have to watch me get gang raped by him and a load of other men.

And yet, as I look into Isiah's brilliant blue eyes, somehow I know this isn't over. He won't allow those children to be abused, so I go along with his plan. If it were me or the children, I'd pick the children ten times over.

"Go to your master, little girl," Corbin says, pushing me forward.

I walk toward Isiah, my heart pounding unevenly in my chest. When I get to him, he doesn't embrace me, merely grabs my wrist and yanks me toward him. "Don't say a word, love," he whispers into my ear.

"Now, you leave us to get on with our business," Ethan says, glaring at him with a pointed look.

Isiah nods in response, his expression unreadable as he leads me out of what looks like a dining hall and into the main entryway. I'm tense as we move away from them, wanting to demand why he'd pick me over those poor, defenseless children.

He doesn't say a word, marching me down an empty corridor to God knows where. "Isiah," I say his name softly, but it's as if he doesn't hear me, lost in his own thoughts. "Isiah!" I say louder, yanking his hand to force him to a stop.

He shakes his head. "There's no time to talk, love," he says, trying to carry on.

I fight him and stand my ground. "You can't leave those children in the hands of those men." There's no world in which I allow him to drag me out of here and leave those children to the abuse that might befall them. I'd rather die trying to save them.

His jaw clenches. "Do you really think I'd leave them?"

"Then why are we leaving?"

He shakes his head and a small smile plays at the corner of his lips. "I'm not, you are." He tries to pull me further down the corridor, but I yank him again.

I know why he's smiling, because he knows I'm not going to accept that. "No fucking chance. I'm not running away while you stay to fight those men."

He shakes his head. "Cathal is on his way."

Of all the things I thought would come out of his mouth next, that was not it. "Cathal?" I confirm.

Isiah nods quickly, glancing back the way we

came. "He gave me his card, and I had a bad feeling on the way here, so I gave him a call, told him to come if he hadn't heard from me within an hour." The sound of motorcycle engines and cars grow louder outside, as if on cue. "And it sounds like he's here."

It just doesn't sit well with me not knowing what happens to those poor, defenseless children. "So we just walk away and leave Cathal to deal with it?"

"Of course not." He grabs my shoulders and looks me dead in the eye. "You walk away and I go back and make sure everything goes as planned."

I shake my head as I won't accept him leaving me out of this. We're husband and wife, a team. "No. I won't let you treat me like a second-class citizen who can't fend for herself. I'm a woman, not a cripple."

Isiah smirks, shaking his head. "I'm not treating you like a cripple. It's just dangerous."

"Life is dangerous, especially with a man like you. Do you intend to wrap me in cotton wool?"

He sighs heavily, as he no doubt realizes that there's no chance he's leaving me behind. "I'll tell you the truth."

I look at him expectantly then. "Go on then."

His Adam's apple bobs as he swallows. "It has nothing to do with your sex, Bella. It's because losing you would ruin me, love, and I won't risk it. Not when I finally feel like life is worth living again."

"Isiah," I breathe, pain clawing at my chest at the declaration.

"You are the light of my life, and I won't have it extinguished by these men. Do you understand? I've lost too much."

I reach up and cup his chin in my hands, knowing without a doubt that I love this man completely. The way I feel for him utterly reversed from the day we first met, since I professed to despise him, and now... Now I don't even know how to put into words the way I feel about him. "And what if I lose you?"

His jaw tightens. "I'm sure you will recover, love."

I shake my head. "No, because I love you, Isiah."

His expression turns serious and there's a glimmer of tears building in his electric blue eyes. "You can't. I'm not lovable."

My eyes fill with tears at that and I open my mouth to speak, feeling such heartache that my father made this man feel so worthless by simply taking his brother's life, when the click of a gun cocking behind us forces both of us to freeze.

"Don't move, you slimy son of a bitch."

All the blood drains from my face at the sound of that voice. I'd assumed Isiah had already taken care of him, but it looks like the tables have turned.

Are we about to be ended by my father?

ISIAH

*a*s Gio levels the gun at me, I know this night has gone from bad to worse faster than I could've ever imagined. All of my meticulous planning, all for naught.

Thankfully, something in my gut told me to call Cathal before coming. Otherwise, there would be no hope for Bella and I. Despite facing off against a mob boss who is hell-bent on taking me out after what I just did to his operation, I know somehow that everything is going to work out.

I wouldn't let those deadbeat criminals get away with this, and I won't allow Gio to get away either.

"Put the gun down, Dad!" Bella shouts.

Gio's head snaps up, his face twisted with anger as he stares at her. "You don't know the things he's done, Bella."

"What about the things you have done? The sick and depraved things!" Her voice is full of disbelief.

Gio clenches his fists as his eyes fix on me, dark and menacing. "What lies have you told my daughter?"

"No lies. I have the proof of how sick you really are. Young boys and girls, aren't I right, Gio?"

Rage contorts his features as he realizes what I am implying. "Asshole. I invited you into my home and—"

I cut him off with a wave of my hand. "Yes, the biggest mistake you ever made."

"Why is that?" Gio demands through gritted teeth.

The satisfaction I feel at knowing how clueless he is makes me almost giddy as I finally let out what I have been holding back for so long. "Do you remember Joshua Dalton?"

Gio's eyes narrow. "Yes, he was a whiny son of a bitch who I chased out of town. What of it?"

"I'm his son," I state simply, watching the shock on his face with malicious pleasure.

He stumbles over himself to reply, "Impossible! Are you telling me Joshua Dalton fled to London and became the king in less than fifteen years?!"

I give a slow nod of confirmation and continue on pointedly, "And do you know what happened the night you sent us packing?"

He stays silent, knowing exactly what I'm referring to—yet words fail him now that he knows exactly who he has been dealing with.

"Do you know?" I repeat.

His jaw clenches as he nods slowly. "Your brother's death was never the intention."

"I don't care if it was the intention or not. You ripped my twin from me." I clench my fists. The rage building within me is almost impossible to temper. "He's buried in an unmarked grave because of you."

"I hardly feel I can take all the blame." He stops, then his mouth drops open. "You're the one that murdered my four men?" His eyes flash with rage. "You chopped them into pieces and sent them to me in boxes." Gio's eyes shift to Bella. "Surely you can't stand by this man's side when he's such a psychopathic liar and killer?"

Bella tilts her head. "And what are you then, Dad?" She clenches her fists, also looking as furious as I feel. "A psychopathic liar, killer and also a pedophile!"

"It's merely business. If I don't partake, I can't be the one to run the ring."

"Oh my God, how can you stand there and say that?" Bella looks about ready to rush over to him and strangle the life from him. "You're talking about innocent children, you sick son of a bitch!"

"How dare you talk to me like that!"

In Gio's state of distraction, he hasn't realized that I've pulled my gun on him and now have it aimed at his head. "I wonder who's the best shot, Gio."

His eyes move back to me. "If you shoot, Bella dies. You may well be able to shoot me, but I will have time to shoot her, too."

"And what makes you think I care about what happens to your daughter?" I have to act cool, otherwise this could escalate fast.

"I heard you talking to her, telling her you can't lose her, you sad son of a bitch," he snarls.

"And you would kill your own daughter?" I confirm.

He turns his nose up. "She would stand by while you kill me. What's the difference?"

"The difference!" Bella shouts, starting forward a step. "You are a pedophile, that's the difference. And I've done nothing wrong."

I grab her wrist to stop her advancing any further.

"I'm not a pedophile. I merely do what has to be done for the sake of the family."

Unbelievably, I think he actually believes that ridiculous notion. As if the pedophile ring was an endeavor necessary for the multi-million criminal organization he already possesses.

"That's bullshit and you know it," Bella says, shaking her head. "The family and the business do fine without that disgusting part of it, which you keep a secret. You make me sick." Her eyes narrow. "Does mom know what you do?"

He clears his throat. "Your mother knows parts."

Bella shakes her head. "So what now? You are going to shoot me dead while Isiah shoots you?"

His eyes narrow. "How about we all walk away?"

"There's no way I'm allowing you to walk out of

this place alive, Gio."

For the first time in this conversation, I see fear in his eyes as he realizes he's coming up against a man who won't quit. I'll die before I let him walk out of here unscathed.

"Then it appears we're at an impasse," he says.

I nod. "It appears so."

My heart beats loudly in my ears as I try to think of a way around this that doesn't lead to Bella getting hurt. Cathal is here, and at the moment, my only hope is I can stall long enough for him to find us.

"You let us go and I let you go, and then what happens?" I ask.

Gio's eyes narrow. "Fuck off back to Britain or I'll kill you like your weak and pathetic brother."

I clench my fists then, the rage threatening to turn into a dark and all-consuming storm. "He was fourteen years old." I try to tell myself that this idiot is trying to get a rise out of me, but it's a low blow. Talking of Aiden like that is a surefire way to make me lose my shit.

"Don't move, any of you," Cathal's voice echoes through the corridor and I can't help but smile as I lock eyes with him.

"Guns down," he barks.

"Oh thank God you are here, Cathal," Gio says, shaking his head. "Isiah isn't the man we thought he was."

Cathal approaches. "Both of you, put your guns on the floor."

Gio reluctantly does as he's told and so do I, knowing that he isn't going to betray me.

"Gio, hands on the wall." He points his gun toward the wall.

Gio's brow furrows. "What the fuck for? Go and apprehend that son of a bitch. He's been lying about who he is."

"Isiah called me to come and help him out with this pedophile ring." Cathal grabs Gio's wrists and puts a pair of handcuffs on him roughly. "And there's one thing in this world that I despise with a passion. It's someone who abuses children." He pushes him hard against the wall.

"He's mine," I warn.

Cathal smirks. "I know. Don't get your panties in a twist." He looks at me then, dark eyes blazing with fiery rage. "As long as I get to be there when you kill him. I want to see this piece of shit brought to justice for what he did to Aiden."

"You knew?" Gio asks, sounding in shock.

"Yes, since the day I saw Isiah at Bella's party. Joe and Aiden were my closest friends before they disappeared."

Gio opens his mouth and then closes it, before looking to his daughter. "Bella, you can't seriously stand by why these two murder me. I'm your father!"

"Great father you are," she spits, glaring at him. "What is it you said when I told you that Isiah had taken advantage of me, touching me without my consent?"

"Let's be honest here, love. You know you wanted me to touch you, really."

She glares at me then. "Shut up." Her attention moves back to her dad. "You said it's pretty standard practice." Tilting her head, she laughs. "Well, as far as I'm aware, killing family members of other mafia leaders often leads to an eye for an eye." She pauses a moment. "It's pretty standard practice."

I can't help but feel so much pride as I watch my wife, knowing without a doubt that I love her more each day that passes.

"There's a basement in this place," I say, looking at Cathal. "Can you take him down there while I get Bella somewhere safe?"

"No," Bella says, shaking her head. "I want to come with you."

I grab Bella's shoulders, as I expected this might happen, and look her dead in the eye. "There is no way that I'm allowing you to see that side of me. Not to mention, witness your own father's death. You may be angry with him and even know that you'll never be able to forgive what he did or what he was, but you can't darken your soul like that."

She draws in a deep breath and I'm ready for her to argue, but instead she nods. "You're right."

I arch a brow. "I am?"

"Yes, I don't want to witness it." Her shoulders slump a little as she glances at Cathal. "Where can I go that is safe?"

"The events room. All my guys have apprehended

those idiots and they're looking after the kids." His jaw clenches. "Join them there."

She nods. "You don't need to come with me." Her eyes move to her dad, who looks terrified. "Goodbye, Dad."

"Bella, don't just leave me to these animals... Please."

There's a mix of emotions swirling in her eyes as they fill with tears. "I can't save you. No one can." With that, she turns around and strides back the way we came.

I lead the way to the basement, Cathal dragging Gio along with him. The door creaks loudly as I push it open and we descend into the darkness, as the scent of dampness and mildew fills my nostrils. It's the perfect place to exact my revenge. Somewhere no one will hear this piece of shit scream.

As I glance at Cathal, I wonder what he'll think about my intention to torture Gio long and slow, as when I knew him before we were just kids.

"Please, you can't kill me. What about—"

Cathal slaps him to silence him. "Shut it, old man."

I guess he's just as brutal as I am. After all, he's a leader here in Washington.

"Chain him to the wall," I say, nodding at the wall where there are two chains hanging from it. Clearly, this place was used for the same intent I have in the past, as there're knives and tools on a table, all of which look a little rusty. "This is

476

perfect," I say, running my finger over the hilt of a rusty knife.

Once Cathal has finished chaining Gio, I turn around with the knife in my hands.

"Have at him, Joe." His jaw clenches. "Can I call you that?"

"Not in public, but now it makes sense." I nod.

He smiles at me. "Don't hold back. Make him bleed."

"Come on, both of you. I agreed to you marrying my daughters, and this is how you repay me?"

I arch a brow and glance at Cathal. "Marriage."

He nods. "Yeah, but doesn't look like I need his permission anymore, anyway."

Turning my attention back to the man I've longed to torture for fifteen long years, I close the distance between us.

"I'm going to enjoy this as it's been a long time coming," I say, as I press the blade of the knife against his throat.

His eyes widen with fear and he begins to struggle against the chains, trying desperately to free himself. The sight of him so powerless gives me a sick kind of satisfaction, knowing that revenge is finally in my grasp.

Taking my time, I cut away his clothing, savoring each tremble of fear as I gently nick his skin in the process. His skin is pale and slick with sweat from his terror, and I revel in it.

"You tore my entire world apart that night, and

now I'm going to tear you apart," I muse, running the rusty edge of the blade along his sternum, only grazing the surface of his skin.

"Any last words before I make you scream in agony?"

Gio's mouth opens and closes like a fish out of water. "Please——"

I press harder beginning to cut into his skin, cutting off his ridiculous plea for mercy. His men didn't show my brother any mercy and I won't show him any.

The rustiness of the blade only increases the amount of pain he must feel as I carve intricate patterns on his skin, taking my time to make sure he feels every slash of pain and agony that goes through his body.

His scream of pain is like music to my ears, and yet even as I get my revenge, I know nothing will be enough to appease the agony that this man inflicted on me, sending those men into our home. Aiden is never coming back.

A terrible fact that I've spent too long avoiding thinking about, fixated on this notion of revenge. Blood trickles down his skin in a beautiful display of carnage as I carve him, losing myself in the pain and hatred that has lived inside me for more than half of my life.

As I slam my knife into his left leg, tears prickle in my eyes. Tears that I've not felt since that night fifteen years ago in Dumbarton Oaks Park. I was sure I would never cry again, but being here, torturing the man who tore my world apart all those years ago, is giving me some kind of closure. No matter how sick it may be. No matter how tortured and twisted I've become, this is what I needed.

Something takes over as I begin to go to town on him, reveling in the screams of pain that tear from his throat. And the way the blood spurts from his body with each slash of my knife. It isn't until Cathal's hand lands on my shoulder, God knows how long later, that I'm pulled from the chaos of my mind.

"Isiah, I think that's enough. Don't you?" he asks, his voice a little shaky.

I shake my head, trying to shake off the blood lust haze that has filled my mind, and the scene in front of me is one of pure carnage. Gio's rasping breaths prove that he's barely hanging on to life and my stomach churns with sickness.

I got my revenge, and it's bittersweet. This man deserved to die more than I ever knew before I returned to Washington, but somehow I need to move on and heal the wounds that have been so deep since the day Aiden died.

As I plunge the knife deep into Gio's heart, ending his agony, I am finally able to let go of all the hurt and anger that has been bottled up inside me. As I step back from Gio's battered body, all I can do is feel thankful for the closure that this experience has brought for me and look to a bright future with the woman I love.

46

BELLA

The air is heavy with the scent of blood and my heart thumps wildly in my chest as I survey the aftermath. Men scurry around the room, dragging lifeless bodies away and cleaning up the splattered blood on the walls while a wave of dread fills me as I recall how quickly Isiah's feud with my father spiraled out of control.

After being taken away by Isiah and Cathal an hour ago, I can only imagine what kind of torture they were inflicting on him.

Fear worms its way into my chest, making me shiver as I consider how far Isiah will go to avenge his brother's death.

My father is a villain, and I have come to accept that. But with every wicked deed Isiah undertakes, I fear his soul is darkening further. He didn't want me to witness what he'd do to my dad, because he knows I'd see him differently.

My thoughts are interrupted when I spot a woman lingering nearby, her eyes glistening with tears.

I approach her cautiously. "Are you okay?"

She swallows hard before replying softly, "I think Isiah is going to kill me, she mutters hoarsely, her voice familiar yet elusive in my memory.

"Why?"

She swallows hard. "I betrayed him," she admits, averting her gaze. Despite the fear coursing through my veins, I want to know more, but a sudden shout cuts off my question before it made its way out of my throat. One of the men shouting at Cathal, who has just walked into the events hall.

Isiah follows closely behind and is splattered with blood, which I assume is my father's, making bile rise up in my throat.

The woman notices him also, shuddering with fear. "Oh, shit."

Isiah walks straight toward me, locking eyes with me. His gaze is intense, unreadable, and mysterious all at once.

He pulls me against him and kisses me hard before speaking against my lips: "I'm so glad you're okay."

There are marks across his cheeks where it looks like he's been crying and I trace them with my fingers. "Are you okay?"

His jaw clenches as tears fill his eyes, but don't fall. "I've never been better, love."

I swallow hard, and as I look into his eyes, I'm sure he's telling the truth. Isiah needed revenge, although many say it is a useless thing to cling onto. I believe he did need it. It was the only way he could move on from his brother's death.

"Isiah, I—" the woman starts.

"Jane, don't say a word," he says, turning to look at her.

She trembles in fear, gazing down at the floor.

"I don't blame you for any of it."

Her eyes snap up. "I set you up."

"You set me up because despite me believing that you were free of your abusers, you weren't. I understand why you did what you did, and I forgive you."

She weeps then, tears freely flowing down her face.

"I think you will need some therapy, though," Isiah says, placing a hand on her shoulder. "I'll pay for it."

Her throat bobs as she shakes her head. "Why?"

"Because I hate pedophiles and I hate that it took so long for someone to save you from them."

Her lips wobble and then she cries some more.

Isiah pulls her into a hug, holding her close.

I feel my chest ache as I realize how much I misjudged him when we first met. His heart is pure and even if his past has twisted him into a man filled with darkness, that remains the case. He can show this woman he barely knows compassion, and despite being a mob boss and criminal like my father, he's a hundred times better man than he ever was.

Jane is a mess when he finally releases her from the hug, and he calls Cathal over, speaking to him in hushed tones.

Cathal nods once he's finished speaking and ushers Jane to him. "Come on, we're going to get you help," he says.

Isiah turns to me then, eyes brighter than I've ever seen before. "It's over, love."

I feel those words deep as he's right. His feud is over, but our life together is only just beginning. "I meant what I said earlier."

His jaw clenches. "I'm not sure how you feel that way about me."

I laugh. "Honestly, neither am I after all the shit you've done."

He chuckles and then takes my hand, looking into my eyes. "Come on, love, let's find somewhere private so I can show you just how much you mean to me," he murmurs.

I swallow hard, wondering if there's something wrong with me for wanting to agree, knowing what Isiah just did to my dad. And yet, I can't find it in me to refuse, instead I nod.

He leads me up the stairs of the country club as we search for a bedroom, my heart thumping wildly in anticipation.

Once we get to a room, he nods to the bed. "Wait for me there. I need to get cleaned up."

I shake my head. "No, I'll help you," I say simply.

His throat bobs as he swallows, but he doesn't refuse as we both enter the bathroom. He takes off his shirt then and I grab a flannel off the shelf and douse it with water.

"Are you sure about this?"

I can see the turmoil in his eyes as he thinks it's hard for me to help him clean my own father's blood from his skin, but the fact is, I'm glad he's dead. And, I want to help him heal from this, as I know getting his revenge was just the start. He's harbored so much hate and anger, I sense he's never really stopped and grieved the death of his brother.

Slowly, I start to wipe away the blood from his arm with a damp rag. My hands run across every line of definition in his body as if I'm trying to memorize them by touch alone—each scar, every muscle.

I take my time, exploring him and teasing him as I notice his jaw clench as if he's holding himself back from devouring me. It makes me feel more powerful than I've ever felt. Lastly, I clean his face and then dump the bloodied flannel into the sink, moving around him to wash my hands.

Isiah grabs me suddenly, yanking me against his powerful body. "I love you, Bella," he breathes, the raspy quality of his voice sends shivers down my spine.

"I love you, too," I murmur. My heart races, my breath hitching as I gaze into the depths of his brilliant blue eyes. He leans in, his hot breath skating across my lips for a moment before he brings them against mine. Heat explodes through my body the moment he kisses me. His fingers lace through my hair, pulling me closer with each passing moment.

"I need you," he says raggedly against my mouth, his grip on me tightening.

A thrill runs through me at his words. "What are you waiting for? Fuck me, Isiah."

He growls, the beast that I have grown to crave surfaces as he effortlessly lifts me onto the bathroom countertop.

His gaze never leaves mine as he pulls off my shirt. "You are so fucking beautiful, Bella," he says, eyes moving now from my face and down to my breasts. Before I can say a word, he moves forward and his lips descend on my neck as he kisses me softly, moving lower with each kiss. The sensation of his touch ignites fire inside me as he explores my body with his hands and tongue. His fingertips softly dance around my sensitive nipples, drawing out a moan from deep within me. Everywhere he touches ignites a fire spreading throughout my veins.

"That's right, Bella, moan for me," he purrs.

I shudder as he kisses lower, his tongue and lips moving down my stomach. Once he gets to the belt of my skirt, he hikes the hem up and meets my gaze, a hungry glint in his eyes.

"Tell me what you want."

My mouth goes dry. "I want you," I say.

He smirks. "Do you want me to eat your dripping wet cunt?"

I swallow hard and nod.

"Let me hear you say it," he demands.

My heart pounds in my ears. "Please, Isiah."

"I want specifics," he says.

I feel like I'm burning up at the thought of voicing my desires, but the need to feel him between my legs wins out. "Please lick my pussy."

He groans and then delves between my thighs, sucking my clit into his mouth forcefully and making me moan.

"Oh God," I breathe, clutching the countertop as he licks and sucks at my clit frantically, driving me higher and higher with each movement. Throwing my head back, I know if he's not careful, I'll come apart in record time.

Suddenly, he stops licking me. "Look at me," he demands.

I open my eyes and find him gazing up at me with a hunger deeper than I've seen before.

His hand moves up my body, his fingers lightly tracing the outline of my nipples as his mouth works at my center, inching me closer to the edge with every passing second.

"Come for me, love," he says gruffly, eyes fixed on my face.

A gasp escapes my lips as he moves his other hand between my thighs and slides a finger deep inside me. And that's all it takes. He sends me over the edge into oblivion. His tongue swirls around and around, driving me insane, until finally I'm screaming out his name in ecstasy as wave after wave of pleasure flows through me. He licks every drop of my arousal from me as if he's drinking me in like a man who's been in the desert without water for days.

"Fuck, you come so damn well," he murmurs, standing and kissing me harshly, his tongue thrusting through my lips as I taste my own arousal on him. It renews my desire with even more intensity as I lace my fingers through his hair and try to draw him closer.

"Fuck me, Isiah," I murmur into his ear as he kisses my neck again.

"Ask nicely," he murmurs.

My skin prickles with anticipation as I reluctantly comply. "Fuck me hard with your big cock and make me come, please," I whisper, finding my inhibitions obliterated by this point.

"Fuck," he breathes, the zip of his pants audible as he frees his cock from the confines of his briefs. "You asked for it," he growls into my ear. His hands find their way to my hips, gripping them tightly and in one swift motion, he embeds himself deep within me.

Isiah buries his face into my neck as he moves in and out at an unrelenting pace, his soft, brown hair tickling my sensitive skin with each thrust. His hands grip my hips possessively and increases the pleasure limitlessly as he becomes the dominant animalistic man I've grown to love. Isiah entwines his hands in my hair and pulls back until his gaze meets mine. He nibbles on my lower lip before bending down to take each of my nipples between his teeth.

My body responds to the dual sensation and I can feel the orgasm slowly building up inside me.

"Harder," I plead, wrapping my arms around him.

He bites my nipple then, the pain sends a thrill right to my center. "Careful what you wish for, Bella."

"Fuck me harder," I goad.

He looks into my eyes then. "I'll show you hard, love."

A shudder of trepidation courses through me as he looks more determined than I've ever seen.

He slams inside me without warning, his ferocity pushing me beyond my limits, and I can feel my orgasm building within me. His touch is electrifying, as if he's coiling something inside me that's ready to explode.

"Come for me!" he growls into my ear as his fingertips press into my hips so hard they're sure to leave bruises. A scream of pleasure escapes my throat as I reach the ultimate peak of pleasure and I can feel the warmth pulsing through me. My orgasm crashes over me like a wave, intensifying until all that remains is pure bliss. His lips meld with mine as he swallows my screams of pleasure.

"Isiah," I gasp, as he doesn't slow down, not giving me a moment to recover from the intensity of my orgasm. "What are you—"

Without warning, he yanks himself from me, spinning me around and forcing me to bend over the countertop. His hand crashes down on my ass, searing heat radiating through me and intensifying the need between my legs. "No questions. I'm not ready to stop," he growls, slipping back inside me with an urgency that threatens to bring me to another climax before I have time to catch my breath. My head spins as I struggle to comprehend what he's doing to me.

"Isiah," I gasp, feeling the explosion about to rip through me at any moment.

"You're going to kill—"

Before I can finish, he spanks me again and suddenly I'm soaring, enveloped in a wave of pure pleasure that brings tears to my eyes. And then I'm coming apart again in record time, my entire body spasming with pleasure as he continues to fuck me through it, driving me to heights like none I've experienced before.

"Please," I beg, knowing I can't take anymore. "I can't—"

"You can and you will," he breathes into my ear, his muscular body pressed against my back. "I need your ass wrapped around my cock before I come," he growls.

Tears prickle at my eyes because I'm sure I can't take it. "No, I can't—"

Before I can protest, he's lubing up my ass with something, his cock still plowing in and out of my pussy hard and deep. "I own you, Bella, which means if I tell you I need your ass, you'll take it."

I whimper as the thought of taking him in my ass and being forced to orgasm again is overwhelming. Suddenly, he's stretching my back passage with his fingers, pushing them in deep and making me so full as his cock still fills my pussy.

"Oh God," I breathe.

"That's right, worship your God, baby." He slams his fingers in and out of my ass. "As I'm your God and always will be. Isn't that right?"

I clamp my eyes shut, unable to even think past the tantalizing pleasure he's forcing from me.

He spanks my ass when I don't reply. "Answer me, Bella."

"Yes," I pant. "You are my God," I breathe, hardly able to speak. "You are my everything."

He growls then and pulls his cock from my soaking wet cunt, lining it up with my stretched asshole. "Always and fucking forever," he says, before pushing into the tight channel.

"Oh fuck," I cry, unable to believe how good he's making me feel.

"That's it," he breathes, pushing in and out of me harder and faster. "I love watching that greedy ass swallow every fucking inch of me." He spanks me then, making the pleasure heighten to new levels. "Your muscles are clenching round me, holding me tight like you never want me to fucking leave."

"I never want you to leave," I admit, arching my

back and meeting his thrusts, his legs slap against mine with each powerful thrust, the sound of skin against skin echoing through the room as he becomes feral, taking what he wants like a wild animal.

"I could die happy with my cock in your ass, love." I feel him swelling inside me, warning me that he's getting close to exploding. His hands grip my hips even tighter now, like a vice as he slams into me over and over again until we're both moaning each other's names, my body shaking with pleasure.

"Isiah," I gasp his name, trying to find the words. "I'm going to—"

He grabs the back of my neck and yanks me upright, his lips hot against my ear. "That's right, love, come for me. I want to feel those muscles clamp down on my cock as they milk my balls. Your tight little ass is going to be so full of cum."

His dirty talk makes the pleasure unbearable with his cock deep inside my ass, and I come apart, unable to hold on any longer.

"Isiah!" I scream his name as I feel his cock get impossibly hard.

He growls forcefully against my ear, pounding twice more before exploding inside me. His cock pulsing deep in my ass as he spills every drop of cum. He keeps rocking back and forth for a long time after we've both climaxed, making sure every drop is spilled within me.

"Goddamn, Bella," he gasps, his voice so deep and raspy. "You're the most amazing woman on this fucking planet." He finally pulls his semi-hard cock from my abused ass and spins me around, kissing my lips passionately. "I'll never tire of being inside you." He pauses a moment, his lips brushing against mine. "Making love to you," he breathes quietly.

My eyes prickle with tears as the way I feel about this man is so utterly confusing and yet nothing has ever felt so right before, either.

I kiss him back then, letting my tongue dance leisurely around his mouth before breaking away and pulling his forehead against my own. "I love you so fucking much, Isiah," I say.

His body tenses against mine as I know he doesn't believe he deserves love, but he replies without hesitation. "I love you too damn much, Bella, and I don't fucking deserve you."

I know that he's got some progress to make, but he deserves as much happiness and love as anyone else. And I intend to make him see that, as we have all the time in the world.

47

ISIAH

*B*ella clings to me as if I'm a crutch as we stand outside of the country club, and I don't understand it.

Why does she believe I'm her knight in shining armor after all the shit I put her through?

Cathal and his men are finishing the preparations to torch the place, ensuring the bodies are all in believable places and that any gun casings are cleaned up.

"Are you sure about this?" she asks, her lip wobbling slightly.

I squeeze her tightly. "There's no other choice. If anyone found out it was us that brought the pedophile ring down, we'll be dead." I watch Cathal and his men emerge from the building. "It needs to look like a terrible accident."

Her throat bobs as she swallows. "Do you think it will work?"

"It has to," I say simply.

Cathal approaches me and places a hand on my shoulder. "Do you want to do the honors?" He's holding two petrol bombs they've conjured together from wine bottles from the party.

"Together?" I suggest.

He smiles then and nods, handing me just one of the bottles. "Together, for Aiden."

Bella reluctantly releases me as I walk toward the building where the window to the events hall, where the party was gathered, is open for us to throw the bombs in.

Cathal pulls a lighter out of his jacket and flicks it alight, placing it against the rag sticking out of my bottle first. And then he quickly lights his own.

"On three," he says, and then he counts us down. We both release the bottles through the window together, and it goes up like a fucking tinder box.

Cathal bolts away, but I stand there for a moment, watching as the place sets alight. It's a poignant moment as it marks the end of an era for me. Finally, I have got justice for Aiden and it makes me feel lighter than I've felt in too long.

"Isiah!" Cathal calls my name with a sense of urgency as I fail to move away from the inferno.

Despite his warning, I'm rooted to the spot as I savor this moment. Finally, after so long, justice has been done.

After a few more moments, I hear Bella's panicked voice calling my name, "Isiah!" It's as if she believes that I won't get out of the way in time, but I know what I'm doing. She has to understand how long I've waited for this moment; fifteen long and torturous years.

With a deep breath, I turn away from the crackling fire and stride toward Bella, who rushes into my arms before I can even reach her.

"Don't ever do that again," she warns.

"What?" I ask, pulling back to look at her.

"Set a building ablaze and stand there as if you intend to go up in flames with it."

I can't help but feel shocked that she even cares whether I go up in flames or not, and then I remember her declaration tonight, more than once, of love. "I wasn't intending to go up in flames, I just needed to see the place burn as closure." I take her hand and look into her brilliant blue eyes. "However, it's hard to believe that anyone cares what happens to me."

There's a pitiful look in her eyes as she shakes her head. "Of course I care what happens to you." She takes my chin in her hands. "I told you, I love you."

"I'm not sure why," I murmur, honestly unsure why she'd love someone as broken as me.

She kisses me then, her soft lips gentle against my own. "Because you're the most amazing man I've ever met, even if I hated you at first."

I press my forehead against hers, knowing that she's the most amazing human I've ever met. Somehow, she's managed to bring me back from the brink of oblivion. For too long I've been drowning in my own hatred as it festered within me, revenge being my only purpose on earth. Bella is my new purpose.

"We had best get the fuck out of here before the police turn up," Cathal says.

"Okay, we'll be heading back to our place," I say, knowing it wouldn't be a good idea to go anywhere near Bella's home until they learn the news.

Bella swallows hard. "And wait?"

I nod in response.

Cathal clears his throat. "Okay, I'll be in touch soon."

"Come on," I say, grabbing Bella's hand and pulling her toward my car.

We both get in as Cathal and his men also rush away, many of them jumping onto motorcycles and into vans as the engines rev.

As I slide the key into the ignition, I glance in the rearview mirror at the carnage behind me. It's insane to believe that it's finally over, but as I stare at the burning country club, I can't deny that it looks beautiful in its destruction. The flames reach high into the sky, their bright oranges and yellows reflecting off of the black smoke that twists and turns from the chaos below. It's a sight to behold, a sight that will never be forgotten.

I quickly turn my attention away from the fire and start the car, driving off into the night, Bella's hand firmly intertwined with mine. And in this moment, I am certain that everything will be okay. It's as if I've been reborn, finally shedding a weight that has been so heavy to bear. With Gio and the men involved dead, and Bella by my side, I feel as free as a bird.

The far-off sirens in the distance give us a warning that we need to get off the property.

Bella looks worried as she squeezes my hand. "We're going to get caught."

I shake my head. "No, those sirens are further than you think."

I get to the end of the long drive and turn left, despite the city being the other way, as I don't want to risk passing the police.

"You're going the wrong way," Bella points out.

"I'm well aware, but we don't want the police spotting us at all. Especially not when I'm the son-in-law of one of the men who just died."

She nods. "Good thinking."

Speeding away, once we get to the next turn, I take a right and then circle back on myself so we end up on the main road back to Washington. There's a somber silence between us as we make the rest of the drive, anticipation of what's coming looming over us both like a dark cloud.

When we get back to the flat, we're walking through the front door when Bella's cell phone rings on the hallway table.

"Oh shit," she says, meeting my gaze. After a moment's hesitation, she rushes over to it and picks it up, looking at me with fearful eyes. "It's Nina. Do you think they know already?"

I shrug. "Only one way to find out."

She picks up the phone on speaker. "Hey."

"You need to get over here right now. There's been an accident."

I swallow hard. "What kind of accident?"

"There's no time to explain. Just get over here as fast as you can." She ends the call and I can see her hands are shaking.

"The news must be in," I say simply.

"How am I going to face them?"

I walk over to her and grab her shoulders, looking her in the eyes. "You will face them because you have no choice."

"Okay, you will be there by my side, right?"

I'll never get used to her looking at me the way she's looking at me now. All signs of contempt she felt for me when we first met are entirely eradicated.

"Always."

"Okay, let's go." She turns and marches out of the door, and I follow her.

Apprehension plagues me as I wonder how it's going to feel walking into that home after murdering Gio. It's a miracle I agreed to only kill him, and not the rest of her family, but as soon as my feelings toward her changed, I knew I couldn't hurt the people she loves.

I drive us over to the house and once we get inside, there's a solemn mood, even from the staff. The maid ushers us into the living room where her family is gathered, although there's no sign of Viola.

"What's going on?" Bella asks.

"Dad's dead. There was a fire at the party he was at," Nina says, tears streaking down her face as she holds out a hand to Bella.

Bella swallows hard and takes it, hugging her sister. "What caused the fire?"

"We don't have any details at the moment," Maria adds.

Her brow furrows. "Where's Mom?"

"She won't come out of her room. The moment she found out, she locked herself inside," Cain says.

At that moment, Cathal arrives. "Nina, I got here as fast as I could."

She rushes into his arms instantly, tears coming faster now. "Thank you. Oh, it's all a disaster!"

He holds her as she sobs, and I wonder how he or Bella will keep the secret from her, that we killed her father.

Cain remains silent, still clutching his half-drunk tumbler of whiskey.

Bella leans toward me. "Can you talk to Cain?"

I'm a little surprised she asks me, since I've never been much of a mentor, but a weight has fallen on his shoulders tonight. "Sure." Her brother isn't a bad guy, but he has the potential to end up as bad as Gio or a much better leader.

Bella follows me over to speak with him too.

"If you need any pointers, I can help," Isiah says.

Bella places her hand on Cain's shoulder. "You are going to be okay," she says.

501

Cain sighs heavily. "I'm not cut out for this shit."

She gives me pleading look.

"You can shadow me in London for a few weeks when we return, help you learn the ropes."

Cain's eyes widen. "Really?"

I nods. "Yes, but I won't take any shit. You'll do as you're told and take it seriously."

Cain straightens, a glimmer of hope in his eyes. "Okay, that would be great. Thanks, man."

I stiffen. "First rule, don't call me man."

"Shit, okay, sorry."

"We won't be staying too much longer, just until after the funeral, so you'll accompany us to London when we leave," I say.

"Thank you," Cain says, sitting up straighter and taking a sip of his drink. "I need all the help I can get."

He does need all the help he can get.

"No problem. We'll stay here tonight, I guess, in a spare room?" I look at Bella, knowing it would be what's expected.

She nods. "Yes, of course. I'm pretty tired."

Cain sighs. "I think we all are. Doubt I'll get much sleep, but I'm going to retire." He stands and gives us both a nod and then disappears off.

"I could do with lying down," Bella says.

"Me too, love."

"I'll just say goodnight to my sisters." She breaks away from me and goes to hug all three of them, before returning to take my hand.

I lead her out of the living room.

"Where are we going to sleep?" I ask.

She grabs my hand. "The best guest room. It's on the top floor."

"The attic?"

She nods and leads me up the main flight of stairs and then to the next flight that leads to the attic space.

She opens the door to a beautiful, characterful room with exposed beams and a large bay window at the front.

"This is a lovely room," I say.

She purses her lips together. "I used to come up here when it was unconverted and paint until my father banned me."

"How are you feeling?" I ask, wondering if she regrets allowing me to kill my dad.

"Guilty but thankful that he's gone, if that makes any sense."

I nod, sitting down on the edge of the bed and loosening my tie. "I'm exhausted."

Bella ditches her clothes and climbs into bed. "Me too. Let's try to get some sleep."

I sigh, feeling a little lost as it's all over. I'm not sure it's sunk in yet. Getting undressed, I climb under the sheets with her.

"What's on your mind?" She asks.

I run a hand through my hair. "It feels so surreal that it's finally all over."

"Your revenge plan?"

"Yes, it's all I've thought about for fifteen years."

"That must feel strange," she agrees.

I pull her close so her head rests on my chest, my arm around her. "It feels good, though. It makes me feel lighter."

A contemplative silence falls between us as we lie together.

Bella glances up at me. "I know it's crazy, but I really disliked you when we met."

I laugh. "You made that very clear, love."

"And somehow now I can't imagine living without you."

"Well, I do recall warning you."

"Warning me of what?" she asks.

"I told you once we got married that you wouldn't be able to help but fall for me."

She laughs. "I bet at the time you didn't believe it would have worked the other way around. That you would've fallen for me first."

I rub a hand across my chin because she has a point. "But did I really, or did you just fight it longer?"

"Who knows? And who cares? All that matters is that we're together now, properly. Not just because we were forced to marry."

"Agreed." I kiss the top of her head. "Sleep now," I breath, shutting my eyes and holding her tightly against me. I fall asleep fast, comforted by the notion that it's all over and I've found my soulmate in the process, even if it wasn't always smooth sailing.

CATHAL STANDS by my side in Dumbarton Oaks Park. He wanted to visit Aiden's resting place, and I obliged. We've been standing here for a few minutes and ever since I killed Gio, it's like the floodgates have opened. Tears streak down my face as, even fifteen years later, I find it hard to believe he's gone.

"This isn't what he deserved, but I got something to commemorate his resting place," Cathal says, pulling out a small brass plaque with Aiden's birth date and date of death on and his full name, Aiden Isaiah Dalton. "I've got permission from the guy who runs the park to attach it to the tree. No one will remove it."

It's hard to find the words to thank him, so I just nod in reply.

He steps forward and pulls out a screwdriver, working to affix the plaque to the outside of the tree. Once he's done, he steps back. "Sorry, Aiden. You should have had something like this a long time ago." Cathal glances at me. "If you had reached out, I could have—"

"My father insisted we could have no ties with Washington or our past life."

His jaw clenches. "I never liked your father."

"That makes two of us."

His eyes narrow. "Did you kill him?"

I shake my head. "No, thankfully an idiot son of a bratva boss decided to kill him, and I had to kill him in return." I meet Cathal's gaze. "I'm not going to lie. I wanted to congratulate him, really."

Cathal nods and gazes at the ground where Aiden is put to rest. "What happened that night?" he asks.

I swallow hard, knowing that I can speak of it now, no matter how hard it is. "We were home playing video games. You know how much Aiden loved playing video games."

Cathal laughs. "Yeah, he would have been playing them twenty-four seven if he could have."

I nod. "Well, four masked men broke into the house and Dad wasn't there." It feels like I'm being transported back as I remember the horror I'd felt looking down the barrel of a gun. "They wanted my dad, but since he wasn't there, they shot Aiden and told me to give him a message." My throat closes up a little. "I remember holding him for a long time, begging him to wake up, but he was already dead. They shot him between the eyes."

Cathal places a hand on my shoulder and squeezes. "I can't imagine what it was like."

I purse my lips together. "The worst part of that night was my father dragging me out here to dig Aiden's grave."

"He did what?!"

"He didn't even help, just stood and watched me dig. I was numb by the time we buried him, but father insisted we had to hide all evidence of what happened that night, including Aiden's body."

"That son of a bitch," he half growls, eyes flashing with rage. "I would kill him myself if he weren't already dead."

I smile sadly, as Cathal's friendship is something I've missed in London. I have many loyal men, but they're below me, whereas Cathal is my equal and our bond goes deeper than any bond I have with any other man on this planet.

"I've missed you," I admit.

He laughs then, arching a brow. "Careful, you don't want anyone to think the king of the London underworld has gone soft."

I clap him on the shoulder. "Tell anyone I said that, and I'll cut your tongue from your mouth," I say, half joking.

"That's more like it," he says.

"You and Nina will have to visit us in Letchworth." I swallow hard. "I know Bella is hesitant about leaving her. You better look after her and no breaking her heart this time."

Cathal glares at me. "You had a hand in that, if you don't remember."

I sigh heavily. "I know, and I was wrong, but I had no idea how you truly felt about her."

"It was my fault for not trusting my own feelings, but thankfully, she's giving me a second chance."

I clap him on the shoulder. "I'm happy for you."

He smiles. "So, what's next for the king of London?"

"Honestly, I need to get back as soon as possible. These couple of months away have been long enough."

"Well, don't be a stranger. You'll have to visit

Washington regularly."

I laugh. "I doubt I'd be able to keep Bella away considering how close her and Nina are." I glance at my brother's grave, now commemorated with a plaque on the tree. "And I want to visit Aiden more often."

"It must have been hard not being able to return for fifteen years."

It was one of the hardest and cruelest aspects of being forced away from Washington and banned from returning by my father out of fear that I'd be recognized. "It was."

A solemn silence falls over us and only the birds tweeting in the trees punctuate it. We stand there for a long while, neither one of us speaking, until the silence is finally interrupted by Bella.

"I'm sorry, I just wanted to check everything was okay."

I can't help but smile at the sound of her voice. It's like every aspect of her is a drug to me. "Don't apologize, come here." I hold my hand out for her to take and drag her against my side.

"I thought you wanted privacy, but you've been gone so—"

"Quiet," I murmur, pressing my lips to hers. "Cathal wanted a little time alone to see where Aiden is buried. You're fine now."

She kisses me quickly and then buries her head against my side, gazing at the tree. "That plaque is beautiful."

Cathal smiles. "It does look nice, doesn't it?"

"Could you both give me a moment?" I ask, squeezing Bella gently.

"Of course," Cathal says. "We'll stroll back and wait for you in the car."

Cathal offers Bella his arm, which she takes. Had it been anyone else, I'd probably lose my shit, but I trust Cathal more than any other man on this planet. Bella gives me a soft smile before walking away.

Kneeling down, I place my hand on the spot where my twin lies beneath, resting in peace, even if he never did get the proper send off he deserved. "It's done, Aiden. I made them all pay for you," I murmur, feeling the tears filling my eyes the moment I say his name. Tears that have eluded me for so long. "And in the process, I found my soulmate. I think you would have liked her." I laugh then, tears streaming from my eyes. "Hell, I bet we would have had to fight over her, as we always liked the same girls."

I draw in a deep breath, shaking my head. "I'll never forget you. I've carried a piece of you with me in my heart since you died, and I always will. I hope you know that."

A gust of wind rustles the trees, and for once, I allow myself to believe that it is him giving me a sign from beyond the grave. "I love you, brother. Forever and always." I let my tears land on the ground, knowing that I can finally move on now that his killers are dead.

EPILOGUE

BELLA

I'm a bundle of nerves as the town car snakes through the winding country roads. Today I'm visiting my new forever home; Isiah's country retreat in Letchworth. The slight nauseous feeling is either the fact that I'm nervous or that I'm three months pregnant with our first child. A fact I only found out about two days before we departed Washington, and I've yet to tell Isiah.

"You look like you're nervous," Isiah says, studying me closely with those intense blue eyes.

I swallow hard. "How did you know?"

He smiles softly. "You have this thing where your nose wrinkles when you're thinking about something that bothers you."

"No, I don't."

Isiah smirks. "Are you sure about that, love?"

There is no certainty of anything at this point—if Isiah says my nose wrinkles, then maybe it does.

Squaring my shoulders, I reply, "I'm just anxious to see our new home."

"It's new to you, but not to me." He rubs a hand across the back of his neck. "I meant what I said. If it's not what you want, we can sell it and find somewhere else together."

"I might love it," I point out.

"Perhaps." His eyes narrow. "But I'm not sure if you will think it's too pretentious or not."

I laugh as he knows after living at my parents' home for so many years, pomp is the last thing I want.

"Do you find it pretentious?" I ask.

He shakes his head. "Not at all. Otherwise I wouldn't have bought it."

"Well then, I'm sure I'll love it."

His smile makes my heart flutter and my chest clench painfully all at the same time, as it still amazes me how different life has become with him since everything changed between us. I had despised this man with a vengeance and now all I wanted was to make him happy.

"Honestly, your facial expressions today are gold."

I narrow my eyes at him. "Don't be an ass. I'm merely contemplating how somehow I feel completely the opposite about you today than I felt the day we first met."

He smirks then. "Thankfully, but I don't think you really hated me as much as you insisted you did."

I sigh heavily, as he's probably right. Even when

he made me mad with anger, there was this electric connection between us neither of us could deny.

"How far away are we?" I ask.

He chuckles. "It's like being in the car with a kid. You asked that twenty minutes ago."

I sigh. "Yes, and you just said not far. I'd prefer specifics."

"How about two minutes?" he asks, as the car slows and turns down a long winding road just before the sign for a small village.

"Really?" I ask, the nerves returning in full force.

He nods and grabs my hand, squeezing.

"Why am I so nervous?" I ask.

He laughs. "I honestly have no idea. It's only a house."

The winding country lane seems to go on forever until the trees clear to reveal a large and expansive estate. The sprawling brick manor house stands proudly atop a sloped lawn, surrounded by tall trees and a formal garden. The bright blue sky is reflected in the many windows dotting the façade of the building.

As we drive down the driveway, I'm struck by how beautiful it looks. It's undeniably elegant, yet homely, and welcoming at the same time. The property appears to be perfectly maintained, with manicured lawns, ivy climbing up the walls of the manor, and rose bushes lining both sides of the driveway leading up to it. We pass a small pond with ducks swimming lazily on top before coming to a stop in front of a large portico entrance where we can finally get out of the car.

"First impressions?" Isiah asks.

"It's stunning," I say simply, shaking my head. "They know how to make grand houses here in Britain, don't they?"

He smirks. "Of course. Would you like a tour?"

"Is the pope Catholic?"

He grabs my hand and yanks me toward the large front door and opens it to reveal an entrance hall with dark wooden floorboards and a tall ceiling with intricate plasterwork. It's classical and tasteful, unlike my childhood home, which is indulgent. A huge chandelier hangs from the ceiling, glittering in the sunlight that streams in through tall windows. A grand staircase curves up to the floors above, while several corridors lead off in different directions.

Isiah takes me down one of these corridors to the left and into a large room filled with canvases, brushes, and paints. I look around in awe as I take it all in.

"What is this?" I ask.

He smiles at me widely. "Your art studio. I had it commissioned for you."

"And what if I'd hated the house?"

"Then it would have appealed to the next owner, no doubt."

I look around the room. It's painted in a light blue-gray color, which is calming and peaceful.

Sunlight streams through the windows from three sides of the room, giving plenty of natural light.

"Take a look around," Isiah encourages.

I move further into the room and over to an easel which is set up with a large canvas in front of an arched window at the furthest end of the room. My eyes widen as the view of the garden from here is incredible, and instantly I want to sit down and paint it.

"Are you feeling inspired?" he asks.

I glance back at him to see he's following me, closing the gap between us. Ever since the night at the country club, I haven't been able to paint. A mental block has been stopping me from picking up a paint-brush, but as I stand in our home, my new home, I'm filled with hope for the future.

"I made sure you've got every possible supply you'll need to paint, love," he murmurs, wrapping his arms around my waist and pressing his lips against my neck. "Maybe you can paint me."

I shudder as he drags his lips gently across my skin. "Maybe I will."

"How about now?" he asks, pushing the strap of my dress down my arm.

"I don't think I need to be undressed to paint you."

He smiles. "You don't need to be, but there's no reason why you shouldn't be."

"I can think of a good reason. The moment I'm naked, there's no painting getting done."

He chuckles, and the deep and rich sound echoes through the room. "Good," he says, unzipping the back of my dress and forcing it down to the floor. And then he spins me around to face him.

"Now that's all the art I need to see." His eyes drop slowly down the length of my body and then back up again, drinking me in and turning me into lava with nothing more than a look.

"How about we make art in the process?"

His brow arches, and I know his interest is piqued. "I'm listening."

Stepping out of my dress, I strut over to the long rustic workbench, which has shelves above it with hundreds of paints. I grab a load of water-based paints off the shelves and open a duck egg blue, a silver, burgundy and an emerald green. And then get a load of sheets of drawing paper and place them over the workbench, pouring the paint thickly onto them and spreading it.

"What are you doing other than wasting good paint and making a mess?"

I stop and give him a sultry look. "We're going to fuck on it. Body art."

His gaze turns dark as he stalks toward me. "Are we now? And since when do you call the shots, Mrs. Darcy?"

I lick my bottom lip. "Are you saying you have a problem with my suggestion?"

He tilts his head, eyes narrowing. "My only problem with your suggestion is that I didn't suggest it first." He grabs my hips and yanks me against him. "I'm going to devour you and make art at the same time." He hoists me onto the sketching paper I'd put down. "Starting with a perfect print of those firm ass cheeks of yours."

I smile and shake my head. "I'm sure you won't be able to work out what is what by the time we're through."

He kisses me then, tongue slipping past my lips as he searches my mouth with desperation. "I need to be inside you," he breathes.

I swallow hard as he forces my legs apart and then drops between them, finding I'm not wearing any panties beneath the hem of my dress.

"You are such a good girl," he purrs, looking at me with adoration in his eyes. "Always bare, wet and ready for me." And then he sucks my clit into his mouth, circling it with his tongue so that every vein in my body blazes with heat.

I clutch hold of the edge of the workbench as he drives me wild, licking and sucking at me as if he's trying to devour me.

"I could feast on you forever, love," he growls, staring up at me before disappearing between my thighs again.

He continues to lick and suck at me, driving me wild until I'm completely lost to his touch, feeling as if I'm on the edge of breaking apart. He knows exactly how to move his tongue so that it feels like he's eating every inch of my flesh. His hands travel up my thighs, teasing me as he moves closer to where I most want him. When his fingers finally press against my entrance, a wave of pleasure rolls through my body and I moan loud enough for the whole world to hear.

"You are delicious," he breathes, teasing and taunting me with those talented digits.

"Please, Isiah," I beg.

His brow arches. "Please, what?"

"I need to come," I gasp.

He slides a finger deep inside me. His thumb circles my clit in alternating slow and fast motions while his fingers continue their exploration, pushing deeper and deeper each time. Every inch of me trembles with pleasure now as he increases both pressure and tempo, sending shockwaves of pleasure through my entire body.

"Is that right?" he teases.

"Please," I beg again.

He smirks and then pushes even deeper, hitting a spot that forces me to come apart.

"Fuck, yes!" I scream, my body trembling with pleasure. He licks up every drop of my arousal, drinking me in like a man starving for more.

And then he stops and strips his clothes from his magnificent body. I watch him, knowing that I've never seen anything so beautiful as him. He fists his cock hard in his hands, eyes dark as he watches me.

"Tell me what you want, love."

"I want you inside me right fucking now."

He arches a brow. "Ask nicely."

I glare at him. "Fuck me, please," I say sarcastically.

"You know I can't deny you, even if you are being sarcastic." He grabs me by the throat and lowers me down over the sketching paper and paint, all of it squelching under my back. "I'm going to fuck you so hard they'll hear you scream in London, love." He plows into me then with a deep, vicious thrust that takes my breath away. "Scream for me," he orders.

And then he starts to fuck me, rutting into me like a crazed animal and I do scream. I scream his name over and over, knowing that no matter how many times this man has me, it will never be enough.

I claw at his shoulders, wrapping my legs around his waist to draw him closer.

The move pushes him even deeper, and he growls softly, nipping my earlobe. "Such a greedy girl. It's never enough for you, is it?"

"I want it harder," I breathe.

He shakes his head in disbelief as he grips my hips so hard I know he'll leave bruises and then thrusts even harder, slamming into me with all his power.

And then, when I'm sure I'm about to shatter again, he stops.

"No!" I exclaim, eyes wide. "I was about to—"

He cuts my words off with a hand to my throat. "Not yet. I want you to come riding my dick, love."

My heart pounds erratically and an eagerness to be in the driving seat consumes me. It's rare that he allows me to be on top, although often when he does, it doesn't take long for him to overpower me anyway and seize control.

He maneuvers me as if I'm nothing more than a doll, climbing on to the workbench and lying down, so I'm straddling his muscular thighs.

"Fuck yourself on my cock," he orders, staring up at me with those intense blue eyes. "Now."

I swallow hard and lower myself onto his huge length, groaning as in this position he feels impossibly large. "Fuck, that feels so damn good," I moan.

He grabs my breasts and plays with them, making the pleasure heighten.

I move my hips slowly at first, teasing him the way he so often teases me.

His eyes narrow as he knows what I'm doing, but he doesn't scold me as I rise and fall slowly, moving my hips sensually. Every rise and fall makes his jaw clench harder, proving that he's struggling to maintain control.

Before long, he snaps and grabs my hips hard, taking control as he thrusts up into me with force.

"What happened to you wanting me to fuck myself?" I ask.

He sits up so that his lips are at the level of my breasts, sucking one nipple into his mouth. "You know I can't help myself," he murmurs, before sucking on the other one.

His hands move higher to my throat and he squeezes, as he knows that blocking my airway sends me over the edge.

"Isiah," I breathe his name.

"Yes, love?"

"I'm so close."

His eyes darken as he squeezes harder, his hips thrusting to meet my movements. "Good, I want you to come for me on my command."

The way he says that alone almost undoes me, but I hold on, wanting to please him. "Fuck, it's so damn hard to hold on."

He increases his speed, as if testing my resolve. And then, when I'm sure I can't take another thrust, he says, "Come on my cock like a good girl."

That's all it takes. My orgasm rockets through me like a bomb and my body explodes in pleasure. Wave after wave of bliss swirls through me, turning my insides to jelly. I scream out his name as he slams into me, pushing us both over the edge. His cock explodes deep inside me, filling me with his cum.

I collapse onto him, breathing hard. We're both struggling for air as the sound of our heavy breathing echoes off the walls.

Isiah wraps his arms around me and maneuvers both of us off the bench, sliding out of me, pulling my naked body against his as he turns us around to gaze upon the sketching paper coated in a mixture of paints. It's a beautiful piece of art work that we made together.

"Not bad," he muses.

I place my hand on his chest, knowing that there's

no use putting it off anymore. "I have some news," I say.

"Good news, I hope."

"It depends on your opinion on the subject."

He lifts up onto his elbow and looks me in the eye. "Why are you being so cryptic? What is it?"

I know I have to tell him, but I can't believe how nervous I feel. "I'm pregnant," I say, my voice quiet.

Isiah freezes for a moment, eyes widening a little. "What?"

"Three months, to be exact."

"When did you find out?" he asks, still not giving anything away.

"Only two days ago. I had been feeling sick for a while and realized I hadn't had my period in a while." I bite my lip. "So, I took a pregnancy test."

"And it's positive?" Isiah confirms.

"Yes, how are you feeling about it?" I ask, unable to read what he's thinking.

A smile cracks onto his lips. "Thrilled. I've been thinking about you growing big and round with my baby for far too long." He kisses me then. "I thought it was never going to happen."

Relief floods me, I'm so thankful to hear that he is glad. "Really?"

He squeezes me tightly. "Yes, really."

I kiss him then, feeling like I'm going to burst from happiness. When I break away from him, I whisper, "I love you."

He smiles, looking down at me with those stunning blue eyes I've come to know so well. "I love you too," he says, his voice soft and gentle.

We stand there for a moment, gazing at each other and I can't help but marvel at how far we've come since we met. I loathed this man at first, believing he was arrogant and cold. "I was so wrong about you when we met. It's insane."

He tilts his head. "You were too quick to judge."

I arch a brow. "Let's be honest, you didn't exactly show me the true you."

He nods. "No, I was purposely standoffish, as it's what was expected. But soon enough you melted my heart of ice, love. I fell for you so damn fast, despite trying to resist."

I wrap my arms around his stomach and pull him close, my heart swelling with love. "I can't wait to start a family with you," I murmur, burying my face against his muscular chest. For the first time in my life, I'm excited about what the future will hold. The one thing I dreaded for so long was being forced to marry a man like my father, and somehow my arranged marriage is the reason I found my soulmate.

THANK you so much for reading Pride, the first book in the Once Upon a Villain Series. I hope you enjoyed following Bella and Isiah on their journey.

If you enjoyed this book, you will probably like

the next one, Hook. It's on pre order with a current release date of July 31st.

It's a dark forced marriage romance, and here is the cover and blurb.

Hook: A Dark Forced Marriage Mafia Romance

He has stolen me from my fiancé and claims I belong to him now.

Piero Panarello was going to be my husband. Handsome. Charming. Rich. I'd started to fall for him until out of nowhere I'm stolen by his enemy.

Cillian Hook. Equally handsome, but not so charming. He vows to take everything from Piero, starting with me.

Cillian is ruthless and cold. He forces me down

the aisle and takes me as his wife against my will. All I can do is hope Piero comes to save me.

And yet, the longer I spend in this villain's clutches, the more my grip on reality shifts. Slowly, his darkness penetrates my soul and I finally realize that all is not as it first seemed.

There are two villains in this story. The question is which one will capture my heart?

ALSO BY BIANCA COLE

Empire of Carnage: A Dark Captive Mafia Romance

Cruel Daddy: A Dark Mafia Arranged Marriage Romance

Savage Daddy: A Dark Captive Mafia Roamnce

Ruthless Daddy: A Dark Forbidden Mafia Romance

Vicious Daddy: A Dark Brother's Best Friend Mafia Romance

Wicked Daddy: A Dark Captive Mafia Romance

New York Mafia Doms Series

Her Irish Daddy: A Dark Mafia Romance

Her Russian Daddy: A Dark Mafia Romance

Her Italian Daddy: A Dark Mafia Romance

Her Cartel Daddy: A Dark Mafia Romance

Romano Mafia Brother's Series

Her Mafia Daddy: A Dark Daddy Romance

Her Mafia Boss: A Dark Romance

Her Mafia King: A Dark Romance

Bratva Brotherhood Series

Bought by the Bratva: A Dark Mafia Romance

Captured by the Bratva: A Dark Mafia Romance

Claimed by the Bratva: A Dark Mafia Romance

Bound by the Bratva: A Dark Mafia Romance

Taken by the Bratva: A Dark Mafia Romance

Forbidden Series

Filthy Boss: A Forbidden Office Romance

Filthy Professor: A First Time Professor And Student Romance

Filthy Lawyer: A Forbidden Hate to Love Romance

Filthy Doctor: A Fordbidden Romance

Royally Mated Series

Her Faerie King: A Faerie Royalty Paranormal Romance

Her Alpha King: A Royal Wolf Shifter Paranormal Romance

Her Dragon King: A Dragon Shifter Paranormal Romance

Her Vampire King: A Dark Vampire Romance

ABOUT THE AUTHOR

I love to write stories about over the top alpha bad boys who have heart beneath it all, fiery heroines, and happily-ever-after endings with heart and heat. My stories have twists and turns that will keep you flipping the pages and heat to set your kindle on fire.

For as long as I can remember, I've been a sucker for a good romance story. I've always loved to read. Suddenly, I realized why not combine my love of two things, books and romance?

My love of writing has grown over the past four years and I now publish on Amazon exclusively, weaving stories about dirty mafia bad boys and the women they fall head over heels in love with.

If you enjoyed this book please follow me on Amazon, Bookbub or any of the below social media platforms for alerts when more books are released.

Made in the USA
Middletown, DE
08 June 2023

32266128R00321